USHABA

AN ORIGINAL BY THREE CONTINENTS PRESS
Washington, D.C.

OTHER THREE CONTINENTS TITLES:

ZIMBABWE: Prose and Poetry   *Solomon M. Mutswairo's Feso,*
the first Shona-language novel ever published, now translated
into English, PLUS 20 poems by Mutswairo, two by Chida-
vaenzi, one by Kousu, and Herbert Chitepo's epic Soko Risina
Musoro—all in dual Zezuru (Shona) and English texts on
matching pages. Two maps, drawings and geneological charts
plus extensive biographic and bibliographic information. *ZIM-
BABWE is a nationalist and esthetic event.* xv plus 276 pp.
LC No. 74-7822
ISBN 0-914478-00-1 (Hard) $14.50 ISBN 0-914478-02-8
(Soft) $6.00

CRITICAL PERSPECTIVES ON AMOS TUTUOLA

Collected and edited by Bernth Lindfors, editor of *Research in
African Literatures,* University of Texas at Austin. Book
reviews and critical essays on Nigeria's first great novelist from
1952-1974. Covers in detail *The Palm-Wine Drinkard* and all
subsequent works. 220 pp.
ISBN 0-914478-05-2 (Hard) $12.00 ISBN 0-914478-06-0
(Soft) $5.00.
Publication: February 1975

THREE NOVELS OF THOMAS MOFOLO

Newly edited texts of English translations from Southern
Sotho by Gideon Mangoaela, professor of African literature,
Howard University. *Moeti oa Bochabela, Chaka* and *Pitseng*
appear between two covers for serious study of the develop-
ment of Africa's greatest writer in an African language; with an
analytic-historical essay on pre-colonial literatures of Southern
Africa and bibliographic essays on each work by the editor.
400 pp.
ISBN 0-914478-07-9 (Hard) $14.50 ISBN 0-914478-08-7
(Soft) $7.00.
Publication: Spring 1975

BESIDE THE FIRE

Two satiric novelettes by Igbo writer, Obioma I. Eligwe

Each story is full of cruel twists of fate, heroic, if rather
unusual deeds. The stories speak on several levels—the traditional narrative one—and the allegorical political one reflecting
today's Africa. 83 pp. $2.00
LC No. 74-1441 ISBN 0-914478-01-X

Jordan Ngubane

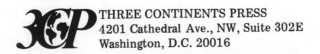

THREE CONTINENTS PRESS
4201 Cathedral Ave., NW, Suite 302E
Washington, D.C. 20016

FIRST EDITION

Second Printing 1975

Copyright © 1974 by Three Continents Press

International Standard Book Numbers
0-914478-03-6 (Hardcover)
0-914478-04-4 (Softcover)

LC No. 74-18755

Library of Congress Cataloging in Publication Data

Ngubane, Jordan Khush   1917-
Ushaba: The Hurtle to Blood River

PZ4. N5687Us
[PR 9369.3. N5] 823

Cover design by H.S. Clapp

DEDICATION

TO

Bernice Marie Wardell,

whose commitment to Africa
made this effort possible.

The plot, the characters, and the dialogue are fictitious; together they constitute the imagery of action, the stuff of an experienced world here re-experienced.

USHABA:

THE CHALLENGE

OF BLOOD RIVER

Isigemegeme sehle mhla kuzalw'uShaka!

Siguqe,isithole sak' oLangeni
Kwadum' izulu,ilanga latholoza.
Umhlaba uthuthumele
Kwaqhekek' amathun' emindeni,
Kumagebe kwagqamuk' amalangabi,
Kwabhenguz' izivunguvungu.
Ubuhanguhangu bushis' amahlungu,
La kusuk' uKhahlamba,
Kwaye kwahanguk' Amachibi Ezindlovu!
Nanamuhla indaba basayizeka kwaNgoni!

Athe eseqana amalangabi
IBhunu laqwal' uluNdi,
Ladilikela kithi kwaZulu Sihlangu.
IBhunu belingathwali maphand' emkhonto;
Beletshath' induk' embi, itsakamlllo.
Ushaba lusuke lapho ke,
Kungqwamana iklwa nesibhamu.
INcome ibheje yagelez' igazi;
Izidumbu zazintaba.

Kazi yintombi yakoBani
Eyozala oyocima lôl' ubhememe,
Avimbe izikhukhula zalol' ushaba!

Earth had never seen what happened
When the Langeni daughter knelt
And Shaka was born!

The heavens so thundered, the sun was scared;
The earth so trembled, violent winds and billowing flames
From the gaping graves of ancestral clan-founders
Gushed to scorch the green hillsides
From where uluNdi (Drakensberg Mountains) first took form.
And northward the fires raged
And set the Great Lakes of the Elephants on fire.
To this day, the Angoni stand in witness!

The flames still leapt, one on another,
When the Boer crossed uluNdi
To challenge Zulu, the Armed.
The Boer carried no bundle of spears;
The lethal fire-stick he bore.
Ushaba, the continuing calamity, began
When the spear clashed with the gun.
Crimson floods hurtled down the Ncome (Blood River)
As corpses piled into mountains.

Whose daughter will give birth to the man
Who will extinguish the flames
And stop the floodwaters of this ushaba?

TABLE OF CONTENTS

USHABA

Foreword

In the literatures of Europe and the Americas it is unusual for an author to commence a work of fiction with a lengthy introduction. The departure is dictated by the subject of the present narrative, the setting of the story, and inadequate white understanding of the African experience—all of which call for some explanation.

Black and white in South Africa are caught in an ugly conflict of minds. The ideal of fulfillment which the Africans translate into experience clashes with the philosophy by which the whites give meaning to reality. Race and colour are merely the vehicles for the collision at the level of fundamentals; they are not in themselves the causes of conflict.

The preoccupation with race has produced elements of tragedy which cannot be described adequately, in so far as the African is concerned, in literary forms developed in the English language. The polemical essay and the novel have their limitations. The English novel, whether employed by an African or a European, distorts the African way of perceiving reality and limits his freedom and style of describing it. While learned dissertations on race have their use, they tend to reduce the blacks and the whites involved in the race quarrel to emotional ciphers.

Translations of works written in African languages present difficulties which destroy much of their message. A valued friend some time ago urged me to translate into English my own Zulu novel, *Uvalo Lwezinhlonzi* (His Frowns Struck Terror), published in South Africa in 1957. I realised, after working on the first few pages, that the organization of images and situations and their transposition from one cultural milieu to another called for explanations which threatened to reduce the translation to a massive paraphrase of little value to non-Zulu readers of the English text.

Culture conflict stood in the way. The tradition developed by the ancient Greeks, Romans and Hebrews, which the whites in South Africa upheld, regards the human being as a creature while the *Buntu* evaluation of the person, on which the African experience is founded and which inspires most Sub-Saharan cultures, recognises him as a living ideal in the process of becoming.

1

The ideological conflict assumes interesting forms at the racial level. If the African insists on the validity of his perceptions of reality or of his perspectives, he often runs the risk of being laughed out of circulation in the literary world of the whites or of having his bona fides denied. Creating in new forms or in those rooted in his culture, his patterns of expression and the understructure of his very cultural self may all be misunderstood or even found "incomprehensible." African understandings of the truth are often rejected for stylistic or other so-called aesthetic reasons while black observations are dismissed as propaganda, exaggerations or worse.

This is done, and has long been done, not only by the white supremacists but also by many of those whites who regard themselves either as liberals or as sympathisers with the cause of the black people. Where the advocate of apartheid uses race to establish white supremacy, the white liberal sets out to entrench cultural supremacy. The effect is a peculiar white consensus on the inferiorisation of the African.

At the literary level, the African revolution seeks to smash this consensus. It addresses itself as much to the geopolitical and socio-economic aspects of white domination as to the purely cultural. The African insists on the legitimacy of his ways of doing things and of his manner of thinking about them. He recognises the white men's right to adhere to their culture but insists on the recognition of his right to adhere to perspectives which are uniquely his and to develop vehicles for his thought which may revitalise his culture.

In my search for a satisfying vehicle through which I could tell at least part of the tragic story behind the vicious power-struggle between the African and the Afrikaner in my country, I eventually turned to the patterns of story-telling which my missionary teachers had condemned and rejected as heathen and barbaric. In the pages which follow I have adapted the *umlando* form of narrative as used by the ancient Zulus when they talked to themselves about themselves. *Umlando* was a vehicle for developing the collective wisdom or strength of the family, the clan or the nation; it is the form of narrative the Zulus employed to translate into action the principles that *inkosi yinkosi ngabantu* and that *injobo ithungelwa ebandla*. (The king rules by the grace of the people, and that the collective wisdom of the citizens leads to the truth.)

I have chosen the Zulu involvement in the crisis of "colour" in South Africa because I understand the Zulu experience best; I was born into it and it has made me what I am.

The *umlando* genre, which the Zulus developed over thousands of years, as their poetry shows, is essentially a story of ideas in action. (There is evidence that the vehicle had a place of its own in Sotho, Xhosa and most Sub-Saharan poetry produced before the advent of the white invader.) It regards the idea as the pivotal link between the human being and his performance. The genre is unique in that it concentrates on the peculiar, almost intangible relationship between the person as a living ideal and the way he operates; it views him as having a composite personality; he is an incarnate spirit-form, a citizen of the community of the "dead," the living and the unborn, a performing self and the achieving spirit-form which creates destiny, all rolled into one. He expresses himself in ways so subtle, sometimes, it is often impossible for most whites to comprehend what he is doing.

The narrator or *umlandi* is a witness of history. As a rule, his authority rests on the fact that he was present at the critical moment when history took a new turn. His audience expects him to *landa* (narrate) what he knows and to do that according to rules cherished down the centuries. But *umlandi* must be confused with neither the European historian nor reporter. Where the historian and the reporter are supposedly objective and concern themselves with bare facts and where the historian seeks to deal with events and their causes and effects, the *umlandi* is creatively subjective. He deals with idea-forms, the subjective moulds in which events are first cast. These vehicles for the translation of motivating urges and feelings into action or objects are believed to have one remarkable quality: they congeal into transposable images. In *ukushaya umoklo* (focusing cosmic power), the Zulu woman churned up the female force of procreation and cast it into an idea-form to create the situation she desired. The poet uses the corresponding elemental power to vest the person with the eternity of mountains or the king with the power of lightning. His heroes and villains, like his planets, animals and plants are congelations of idea-forms. What the whites regard as witchcraft is the simple skill of manipulating cosmic forces.

In *Izibongo* or *Eulogia*, in which the traditional poet built poetic monuments to achievement, the Zulu artist clothed known fact in imagery. In the following stanza from *Izibongo zikaShaka*, which is sometimes attributed to Nomxamama and sometimes to Magolwane kaMkatini Jiyana, the idea-form (the king's majesty) is transposed or made to congeal into an armed buffalo:

Inyathi ejame ngomkhonto phezu koMzimvubu
AmaMpondo esaba ukuyehlela.
Nani boFaku,nani boGambushe, ningamhlabi!
Nothi ningamhlaba,
Koba senihlabe uPhunga, nahlaba uMageba!

(Poised on Mzimvubu river's banks,
The spear-wielding buffalo hurled challenges.
Frightened, the Mpondo dared not descend on him.
"Be ye warned, ye Fakus and ye Gambushes too,
Do not take up arms against him,
For, should you take them,
You will have stabbed Phunga himself and Mageba!")

3

The present is not an essay on the appreciation of Zulu poetry, but it might contribute to the understanding of *umlando* to describe briefly the poet's basic techniques. First, he has cast the stanza in the classical, five-part *Bunono* form. The word *ubunono* describes the procedure for the creation or doing of something in ways which accord best with the demands of neatness or which express a feeling for beauty or exhibit a pleasing regard for method or the rules. The person who is careful about his appearance or dresses neatly is known as *inono*. At the same time the Zulu people speak of *incwadi ebhalwe ngobunono*, a letter or book (in olden times a bead pattern) which pleases because it is written or composed beautifully or methodically or according to the rules. We refer to cultured or principled or decent behaviour or clean living as *ukuziphatha ngobunono*.

The poet employs the breath-bar as the mechanism by which to align his ideas or images or even to express the beauty or power of sound. The breath-bar is the period of exhalation into which the poet crowds a given number of syllables. A breath-bar might be a single sound extended over the length of the exhalation; it can also be a cluster of syllables or words. Most of the time, it is a sentence.

As a rule, each stanza has five parts which correspond to the five principles of becoming. The principles are symbolised by the five fingers of the hand and are regarded as vital idea-forms. We Africans like to touch each other or our children or those we love or like. In doing this we transmit to each other the cosmic power locked in the person or the vitality the idea-forms convey.

In the stanza under discussion, the poet states his theme in the first line, develops it in the second and reaches the catastatic moment in the third. He adduces the argument for the climax in the fourth line and concludes his message in the fifth. In stating his theme, the poet alludes to an historical fact: Shaka's invasion of the land of the Mpondo. Because *umlando* is a story of ideas, it is a convenient vehicle for political themes. To be a work of art, however, it must be based on historical truth. The development of the theme is clothed in images which are aligned to convey the subjective meaning in the poet's mind. These images could be decoded by every Zulu educated in the culture of the poet's times.

The skill of the poet thus lies not only in the quality of his ideas and the power of his language, but also in his choice of images and in how he aligns and crowds them into each breath-bar. It lies, also, in the cadences he creates by harmonising the tonal indices or pitches which govern the meaning of the Zulu vowel.

The poet acts in a timeless continuum. He transposes his images and symbols from the present to the past or the future in such a way that to the initiated his message can have an eternally valid meaning. Mpondo and Zulu ancestors are treated as though they are living persons. He is bound to do this or is freed to do it by the logic of

4

continuity which issues from his view of the cosmic order and to which we shall come shortly. The ancient poet is not unique in concerning himself so much with the eternal. The builders of Egypt's pyramids, like the Rozwi Mambo architects of Zimbabwe, it has been said, built for eternity. The Zulu court poet spoke to the ages.

To appreciate the poet's concern with the eternal and, therefore, to appreciate *umlando*, the reader has to have some familiarity with the poet's *weltanschauung*. Without it, the non-Zulu reader in cultures based on the Graeco-Romano-Hebraic evaluation of the person might sooner or later find himself despairing of understanding *umlando*. He might then find himself agreeing with the well-known Afrikaner authority on *Zulu Izibongo* who, after years of study, finally dismissed them as the ramblings of an undisciplined mind. What the Afrikaner was not trained to understand was the composite personality and why and how the Zulu poet moves action freely from the present to the past and the future with what looks like a total disregard for the time-unity. In his culture, which is rooted in the Graeco-Romano-Hebraic tradition and has a bias for analysis, the concept of timelessness made no sense and whatever made no sense to the white man was invalid. *This closed mind is one of the basic causes of conflict between the African and the Afrikaner.*

To the Zulu, timelessness makes a lot of sense. The poet concerns himself with what he regards as the essence of things; he insists that it is this first cause which must be understood in order to attain clarity on its individualisations. Where the historian or scientist arrives at the truth by analysis, by compartmentalising reality and trying to understand it through the study of its isolated "constituents," the creator of *umlando* uses what we shall, for lack of a better word, call *synalysis*. He regards all things as totals of totals. Nothing exists of itself, by itself and for itself. All things are clusters of subtler substances or forms of spirit-energy; each of them can be understood only where there is clarity on their essence. All things "begin" in this essence and exist in it as idea-forms or clusters of vibrations.

In the present adaptation from *umlando*, a Zulu vehicle has been "reconditioned" to convey into the English milieu ideas conceived in a Zulu framework. Incidents which took place mainly in South Africa have been arranged in a particular sequence to provide the historical basis for the story. The plot, the characters and the dialogue are fictitious; they together constitute the "imagery" in which the author clothes his story.

As *umlandi*, I have been involved all my life in responding to the challenge of being human in the *ushaba* (the continuing provocation or the proliferation of crises) which is steadily moving black and white in South Africa to one of the ugliest bloodbaths in human history. Because ideas determine social action, *umlando* deals directly and realistically with their effects on the person in every department of life;

in politics, culture, the economy, etc. In the present narrative *umlandi* concentrates on a limited area of South African life: the interplay of "racial" ideas.

The reader who follows events in South Africa will almost readily recognise many of the incidents on which the present story is founded. A South African prime minister was assassinated in mysterious circumstances after the Sharpeville shootings. A white nun was murdered and mutilated in Port Elizabeth in conditions the government has not wanted to see explained to this day. A white opponent of apartheid was executed for placing a bomb which exploded in the Johannesburg railway station and led to the death of a white woman. A well-known Johannesburg lawyer was visited by the security police at about two in the morning. The police found documents which indicated that he had received large sums of money from Ghana to finance the purchase of guns for guerrilla activity in South Africa. Instead of arresting him, the police took his word that he would present himself at the charge office when the courts opened for business. By sunrise, he was in Swaziland. Police involvement in sexual relations across the colour line is a continuing scandal in South Africa, while the disloyalty of some black police is a fact of South African life. An African policeman warned me of the ban the government had issued against me and gave me information which set me on the road to exile.

I mention these incidents because it is not inconceivable that people who are not familiar with conditions in South Africa might regard the story in the pages which follow as bizarre and, possibly, exaggerated. I would understand this. Many good men and women, many decent people and many law-abiding citizens of Free World countries regarded the stories of Hitler's atrocities against the Jews as bizarre exaggerations, until disaster overtook the world. Events are moving to another explosion. The collapse of the Portuguese dictatorship and the emergence of India as a nuclear power gives an altogether new complexion to the race problem in Southern Africa. The one is bringing the borders of Free Africa to South Africa's boundaries while the other places the nuclear bomb in the hands of a non-white power which is involved directly in South Africa's crisis of colour. South Africa has a permanently settled Indian community of about 700,000. In this setting the government in Pretoria gradually loses the initiative to set the pace of events. This creates the atmosphere in which the gun will increasingly become a political argument.

The bizarre character of white policy in South Africa is stressed by the contradictions in apartheid which constitute the reality into which the African is born, in which every moment of his life is affected by them and in which he finally dies. What, for example, would be more bizarre than to make it a crime for an African, in his own Africa, to be a child of his parents or to want to respond to the challenge of being human? What could be more tragic than the frustration of life's purpose for a whole race? At this level apartheid cuts wounds in the being of the African which are too deep to be comprehended fully even by the most committed white liberal or Coloured or Asian. The walls which separate the races are such that even with the best will in the world, the most committed white or Coloured or Asian opponent of apartheid identifies himself vicariously with the African in the labour-breeding paddocks known as the urban locations and the rural reserves.

In these conditions the white writer cannot help seeing the effects of the South African tragedy on the African from white perspectives and, in interpreting the African experience, to filter it through white perceptions of reality. He concentrates on specifics like segregation, the Pass Laws or influx control and tends to ignore the universals which interplay in the crisis of colour; universals like evaluations of the person and ideals of nationhood. The problem here is not one of integrating the African in the white man's society; black and white are caught in a complicated clash of conflicting ideals of fulfilment. The refusal to accept this definition of the race problem goes a long way to explain the fact that the United Nations Organisation has, for about a quarter of a century now, been going round in circles without producing a solution.

Enough has been said about the structure of *umlando* to warrant a brief reference to its use as a vehicle for ideas during one of the most exciting periods in Zulu history. As a genre, *umlando* was developed in response to the demands of crisis situations in Zulu history and was meant for a given type of audience. It was used extensively in the conditions created by the revolution which Shaka the Great led. In this upheaval Shaka set whole communities moving violently to a new destiny in Africa south of the equator. In his view, the ideal of rising to "heavens beyond the reach of spirit-forms" was a compelling challenge; it drove him to create the society in which the person would be enabled and seen to make the best possible use of his life, and, in that way, realise the promise and the glory of being human.

Zulu citizenship, Shaka insisted, had nothing to do with race, colour, blood, status or antecedents; it involved commitment to a particular ideal of nationhood. He demanded that this commitment should transcend every other loyalty.

The reward for total surrender was membership in a responsible society in which it was not a crime for a person to be the child of his parents. The great Mdlaka, for example, was a rehabilitated cannibal who rose from this situation of humiliation to become chief of staff of the Zulu armed forces. Shaka made it clear to those who objected to Mdlaka's appointment that merit and mind-quality were the basic qualifications for Zulu citizenship. Shaka married iron to discipline and set large parts of Southern Africa on fire in the bid to translate his ideal into reality. Almost without warning the Shakan revolution thrust the

Zulus into a situation where they found themselves the centre of attention in a turbulent conglomerate of peoples and cultures which stretched almost from the equator to the southern tip of the continent. *Umlando* was one of the vehicles by which they tried to understand the turbulence they had created.

The clash between black and white has thrown Southern Africa into another situation of turbulence. The Africans are challenging the ideal of nationhood on which the whites founded the Union of South Africa in 1910. As a result, the pillars of white power are cracking and as they collapse a leadership vacuum emerges which the Africans plan to fill with the ideal of nationhood they adopted at Bloemfontein in 1912.

The changes in the black-white power balance, however, are related, ultimately, to the shift in the centres of power from the North Atlantic states to the nations whose shores are washed by the Indian Ocean. The shift has left behind a leadership vacuum at the international level. Under the strains imposed on them by the proliferation of black, brown and yellow nations, the philosophies by which the whites guided the course of world events are cracking and losing ground; they cannot give a satisfying meaning to life among the coloured races. Democracy, capitalism, and communism concentrate power in the hands of the privileged few and thrive on the perpetration of crimes against the weak of all races and colours. Christianity is fatally overburdened with the sins of involvement in or connivance at slavery, colonialism and race discrimination.

These events occur in the context provided by the most spectacular revolution in human history: the emergence of the portable nuclear bomb with a limited explosive potential, as an answer to the gun and as a weapon of protest. By placing each deprived individual or each person punished for his race or colour or sex in the position where each can ultimately become his own private army, the "people's bomb" changes mankind's notions of freedom, justice, the state and property and promises each deprived person the power to blow up the Congress Buildings in Washington or South Africa's Union Buildings in Pretoria, whenever he is able and feels inclined to do this. The prospect has frightening implications. At the same time it is stimulatingly challenging; it creates an altogether new balance in the dispositions of black and white power. *Umlando* has been adapted to respond to some of the demands of this balance.

Jordan K. Ngubane

Washington, D.C.
May 25, 1974.

USHABA

I. Moment Of Vengeance

Mazibuye emasisweni!

(It's time to call your loans!)

The word is on the lips of people everywhere: history, it is said, took its moment of vengeance on the Afrikaner when the Africans in the former Portuguese colony of Mozambique became independent and brought the frontiers of Free Africa to the borders of South Africa. The change brought the Afrikaner face to face with the challenge of belonging to Africa. He had always dreaded facing it; he had done all in his power to put off the evil day when he would face it; he would rush to the laager or the parapets of race when he suspected danger and would shoot any threat while it lurked in the buffer states of Angola, Mozambique and Rhodesia. His first lines of defence have collapsed, creating a security vacuum which the African is preparing to fill.

The Afrikaners have not panicked as yet; they still regard their guns as the decisive factor in the new crisis. At the same time they are worried, very deeply, by the course events are taking; so worried they attach importance to every rumour in the wind. And Pretoria is full of these. The security police spend endless hours investigating the report that a submarine of the Nigerian navy was seen off Richards Bay in Natal. This leads to the question: why did the Nigerians not disband their army after the civil war if they did not have an eye on Southern Africa? There are stories that the police have arrested the driver of a huge petrol delivery truck which was full of guns from Lourenco Marques to Johannesburg. The Russians and the Chinese are rumoured to have established military training bases in Central Africa against South Africa. Pretoria quietly makes it known that the two resisters murdered in Botswana were on their way to China. The report which upsets all the whites, however, is that a band of one hundred black guerrillas crossed the border of Northern Natal and raped the white daughter of the postmaster at Ngwavuma. The whites tremble with rage as they discuss the story. All the kaffers assaulted the girl, they say; yes, all one hundred of them. These things were bound to happen; the worst is to come, say the smartest prophets of doom.

Rumours circulate in the African community also. The

presidents of Zaire, Tanzania and Zambia, it is said, are going to China to prepare the defences of Central Africa. Hundreds of Chinese military officers, the rumours continue, have arrived in a number of Free African states to train Free African armies in readiness for the explosion in South Africa, now that the world is free at last to devote all its energies to the citadel of race discrimination.

On the surface of things, there is no visible excitement in the black community; not even among the Zulus who are regarded by most whites as the curse God inflicted on South Africa. Pretoria is not taking any chances. The huge military base in the Ngwavuma district of northern Zululand has been reinforced; radar equipment has been installed to monitor activity in the Atlantic and Indian Oceans from the Argentine to Bangladesh to persuade America to sign a naval-military treaty with South Africa. On the face of it, the treaty is designed to keep the sea lanes between America and Europe on the one hand, and the Middle East oil fields on the other, open. In the process, of course, America and her NATO allies will provide a protective shield for white domination in South Africa. India counters with the manufacture of nuclear explosives. China increases the merchant navy ships she owns jointly with Tanzania. The Russians did a magnificent job in the former colony of Mozambique when they placed their Strella anti-aircraft missiles at the disposal of the African guerrillas; they have already established a powerful radio station in Central Africa to beam messages to South Africa.

The Africans see no point in America rushing to form an alliance with Pretoria at the moment. If a South Atlantic Treaty Organisation is needed, now is not the time for it. It might be in the American and West European interest to move carefully; the day might come when America and Western Europe might want the black southern states on the Atlantic and Indian Ocean sea coasts in a larger treaty organisation. Pretoria does not want black states in a Southern Atlantic treaty with the United States. America treads warily because whatever she does in the new balance in black-white power in Southern Africa is watched closely by the Americans of African descent. America obviously wants to avoid the fatal internal polarisations which the Vietnam war created.

Beneath the surface, the Africans prepare quietly for the moment of confrontation; the day of decision for which they have waited and suffered for more than three hundred years. In the view of most of them, the coming confrontation has a profounder significance than a mere clash of colour; it is a conflict of worlds; history is taking a new turn—the black South Africans prepare to enter the international community. The world of the white man is at last on trial, the Africans say. It has been built on arrogance, larceny, lying and hatred for the African. Go anywhere in South Africa, on the continent, in Europe or in the Americas. What limit of ugliness, what extreme of filth has not been conceived, said and done against the African for no crime other than that he was the child of his particular parents? Which African in all the world has not been cut to the small intestines, as the Zulus say, or wounded to the depths of being by those who stole his land, his freedom and even tried to steal his soul? Most of the people who committed these crimes against Africa and her children were christians; they were men of God; they held the bible in one hand and told the African to look up to heaven while they stole his land, destroyed his governments and lined the pockets of the whites with the gold, the diamonds, the iron and other wealth of his land.

The white man projected himself as a model of human perfection; he could plunder and rape and kill in the name of civilisation and Christ. The trail of iniquity stains the history of Europe and spilled out to Africa, the Americas and Asia. The Zulus say their land died when the white man stole it from them; its children cried out, mourning the death; their tears were the soft moisture which would one day summon to life the germ which will reactivate the land.

Nowhere is the collapse of Portuguese rule hailed with a greater feeling for history than among the Zulus whose land has contiguous borders with Mozambique. For more than a hundred years now, their name has been a swearword in most white homes while their achievements were dragged in the mud. Their history could not be taught in their schools; to do that was treason, heathenism and communism all sandwiched into one. Zulu children were taught about Herodotus, Julius Caesar, Metternich and Washington. What on earth, the Zulus protested, do we have to do with these white men? We want our children told about the revolution which Shaka the Great led; about the problems which forced Dingane the Magnificent to execute Piet Retief and his band of land-grabbers; we want our children to understand that Cetshwayo did not want the war with the British in 1879; that the war was forced on him to prepare ground for the formation of the Union of South Africa and the entrenchment of white domination.

For more than a hundred years now, the history of the Zulus has been written in letters of blood and tribulation which have been carved on their hearts; they preserved it in their bosoms and passed it on to their children when the missionary and the policeman were not looking.

A thousand years before Shaka, they have been telling their children in the last hundred years, the various Zulu-speaking clans lived, prospered and then crowded in Natal. They belonged to a large number of big and small clans which, under the pressure of overcrowding, continually fought each other. The insecurity which developed threatened to destroy the peoples of Natal. Many of them clamoured for a more satisfying ideal of nationhood which would stabilise conditions in their part of the continent. The poetry of the period is full of the cries for a relevant concept of nationhood. In it the Zulus speak to themselves about themselves; they tell each other who they are, what life means to them and what they live for. They tell each other that they have been around from the dawn of antiquity, when stones cried if pinched (*amatshe esancinzwa akhale*). They have been around, as they are, for a purpose; they are here to create the society in which the person shall be seen and enabled to make the best possible use of his life in the light of his abilities. The eighteenth-century Court Poet to Senzangakhona described the aspiration in these terms:

> Masiphoth' intamb' ende
> Menzi ka Jama,
> Siy'emazulwini
> Lapho nezithutha zingey' ukufika;
> Zobasakhwele,
> Zephuk'amazwanyana!

> (A cord of destiny let us weave,
> O Menzi, scion of Jama,
> That
> To Heavens beyond the reach of spirit-forms
> We may climb.
> So long must the cord be,
> The spirit-forms themselves will break their tiny toes,
> If they dare to climb.)

Shaka the Great set out to translate the aspiration into action. He founded the Zulu nation on the poet's injunction. His ideal was a state and a society in which the person would be enabled and seen to face successfully the challenge and realise the promise and the glory, of being human. He developed the revolutionary concept of the nation-state and used it as a vehicle for translating his ideal into meaningful deeds and reorganised the army to give permanence to his ideal. If the whites say anything about Shaka the Great, it is to tell Zulu children that he was a bloodthirsty tyrant. When the young Zulus grow older and read the history of revolutions in Europe, they realise that revolution is bloody wherever the oppressors of their fellowmen refuse to adapt to the demands of change. The hearts of the Zulus bleed when they see their children taught the lies about their ancestors and their place in the community of nations. That is what defeat means, each father passes the word to his son.

The world holds its breath as black and white move to the moment of confrontation. The Afrikaners mobilise white racial, political, economic and military resources to crush probable African revolts. This is what they have always done in the three hundred years they have been in South Africa. After defeat on the battlefield, the Africans

12

changed their strategies and concentrated on building up their brain-power as the weapon to use against the white man's gun and material power. Each side moves slowly to its chosen position in the confrontation. It moves, however, in such a way that there can be no going back; there is little or no room in this ancient quarrel for mistakes. As a result events move slowly; nobody knows where and how the Africans will strike when they start walking barefooted against the Afrikaner, as they say. Some whites in Europe and America still talk about non-violence, to which the Africans answer that modern arms have no fears for them; that no amount of radar can monitor activity in the fortresses of the mind.

Events suddenly take a new turn on the December 16 holiday when this story begins. For different, although equally historical reasons, the Africans and the Afrikaners regard the Day of the Covenant as the most important holiday in South Africa. On this day, each side takes up emotional arms and fights the Battle of Blood River all over again. The Zulus and the Afrikaners emotionally dig up the bones of their dead and crack each other's political skulls with them. They hurl defiance at each other, bombard each other with the humiliations and glories of the past, gloat on each other's defeats and bare to the winds the painful wounds which they cut into each other and stoke history's accumulated hatreds.

On these occasions both sides put aside the master-servant relationship and treat each other as real human beings who can be very dangerous to each other. No compliments are paid in these exchanges, except obliquely in the forms of bitter denunciations and mutual insults. The Afrikaners in particular and to a lesser extent the Africans, transport themselves emotionally to December 16, 1838, when the Boer ancestors of the Afrikaners crushed King Dingane's army at the Battle of Ncome (Blood River). The Afrikaners vowed then that on every December 16 they would go on their knees in thanksgiving for the victory over the Zulus. They subsequently named the holiday the Day of the Covenant and erected the Voortrekker Memorial outside Pretoria to keep alive the memory of their ancestors.

Although they had the guns, to which the Zulus did not have access, the Boers did not break the spirit of the Africans; they did not destroy the African people's will to rise to "heavens beyond the reach of spirit-forms" in their quest for a satisfying destiny. About forty years later, the Zulus were locked in armed conflict with the British Empire. Once more, the white man's guns crushed the Zulu army. About a generation later Bambada led an armed protest against taxation by a government in which his people had no say. Four thousand Zulus perished in the rebellion. But not even these disasters, following so closely upon each other in less than three-quarters of a century, killed the Africans' yearning for a satisfying destiny. In 1912, Pixley ka Isaka Seme, a Zulu barrister from the Inanda mission station near Durban, called a conference of the representatives of all the African communities of Southern Africa to consider a collective response to the White Problem. The delegates met at Bloemfontein and resolved to march together as a new people in history to "heavens beyond the reach of spirit-forms." From that moment onward the Africans have met every year on December 16 to rededicate themselves to the destiny their representatives accepted at Bloemfontein.

On the Day of the Covenant the Afrikaners dress like their Voortrekker (pioneer) ancestors and flock to churches or cultural or political rallies. In the old days the Africans travelled from every part of the land to Bloemfontein where they held political, religious, cultural and professional conferences. The Afrikaner-imposed laws stopped the Africans' political assemblies, but without killing the Bloemfontein spirit. Deep in the psyche of the African a wound gaped and bled, to heal only when the Africans reached the "heavens beyond." Deep in the heart of the Afrikaner, also, a wound gaped in clamours for a place in the African sun. Two wills of the wounded emerged from the clash and, in the last hundred years, the African and the Afrikaner have been moving inexorably to the moment of decision at Blood River. They have reached it on the Day of the Covenant under discussion. The country has been transformed into an emotional inferno as a result; everywhere it is as though the land has been struck by a cataclysm.

*   *   *

After the ceremonies in the shadow of the Voortrekker Memorial, at which he had spoken, Dr. Helvetius van Warmelo, the prime minister of the Republic of South Africa, drove to Waterkloof to have lunch with his daughter, Marietjie, and her husband, Dr. Piet du Toit van der Merwe, private secretary to the Minister of Forestry, Willem Adriaan de Haas. The prime minister is particularly devoted to his daughter, not only because she looks very much like him and tends to share his outlook on life but also because she did one thing exceptional in a woman; she married the right type of man. Piet is not only the scion of a famous and well established Afrikaans family; not only is he handsome and brilliant and not only does he promise to become a future premier, he is also a valuable channel of communication between the head of the government and his maverick minister of forestry.

De Haas is a large thorn in the prime minister's flesh. He tells all with ears to hear that he has an appointment with destiny which he is determined to keep. The intensity and consistency of his commitment have given him a towering stature in the Afrikaner community. But he also has his weak points. His doctors warn that his heart is strained by his intense lifestyle. He is so disciplined, however, that he believes his will shall prevail over the cardiac complaint. He does not

14

smoke and has never drunk anything stronger than water and milk in his life. He refuses to pollute his body with tea and coffee, because of their oriental origins; he cannot stand the smell of rice for the same reason. He will not touch intoxicating drinks because liquor, like black women, defiles the body of the white man, saps his vitality and corrupts his kultuur. He does not go to bioscopes which he regards as purveyors of morally disruptive pornography. He hates all sport and spends his time at work or in his den cleaning and oiling his guns, or viewing films of life in Hitler's Germany and reading Afrikaner history books, or magazines and newspapers of the Nazi period.

He believes, with a faith no power on earth can shake, that the Afrikaners were commissioned in heaven to be the beacon of white civilisation in savage Africa. Every word he utters on the race question, every thought in his mind, and every principle to which he adheres, is pickled in acerbity against the Afrikaner's enemies. This is not political posturing, as his English-speaking critics naively swear it is; the bitterness is a reaction to what he regards as the immoral frustration of the Afrikaner's right to fulfilment.

The chief culprits are the kaffers (the niggers), the Asiatics (Asian connotes equality and he refuses to use it) and, of course, the scum of the earth in the white community: the English liberals, the Jewish communists, the foreign hypocrites and other good-for-nothings who try to stop the Afrikaner's legitimate march to his destiny.

He is particularly bitter against the whites who advocate race equality and see nothing sinful or outrageous or criminal in a white woman stripping in the presence of a black, brown or yellow man and allowing him between her legs.

But his worst venom is reserved for Winston Churchill and Franklin Roosevelt; they ganged up with that Asiatic coolie, Josef Stalin, to spread the miasma of communism in the world. His recipe for the salvation of South Africa includes the liquidation of the communists, the eradication of obnoxious foreign influences, keeping the nigger in his place, and guaranteeing the permanence of Afrikaner dominance. He has never read any book or article on communism; he claims he was born into a communist-dominated environment, graduated from communist universities and is surrounded everywhere in his country by the communists: the white liberals. The obnoxious include protestant missionaries from America, Britain, Scandinavia and West Germany in particular and, in general, Roman Catholic priests and nuns from abroad. His cure for the spirit of rebellion in the black community is the castration of the leaders of African resistance before they are either hanged or locked up for life in the maximum security prison on Robben Island.

If the forestry minister's style inflames African passions, he does not hesitate to tell them in so many words that if they do not like the Afrikaner's attitude to them, they should get out of South Africa.

If, on the white side, the liberals and most English-speaking people think him an ogre, his views and the brutal candour with which he states them makes him the terror of all moderates in his community and the idol of Afrikaner youth. All these factors go beyond making de Haas one of the most significant leaders of Afrikanerdom or a likely prime minister; they give him the dimensions of a phenomenon in the hierarchy of Afrikaner nationalism.

The prime minister accepts the basic assumptions behind de Haas's programme but rejects his forestry minister's strategy because it extends the area of the Afrikaner's isolation in the world. Forebodings of catastrophe crowd into van Warmelo's mind when he contemplates the tide of African nationalism rolling southward to subvert the authority of the white man. His excoriation of the white powers for granting independence to the black child-race has steadily been falling on deaf ears in London, Paris, Brussels and The Hague. In spite of the instability of the first decade of independence investor delegations continue to flock to the free states of Africa, where the main attractions are the surfeit of cheap labour, the proximity to Europe and America, the low taxation on profits and, above all, the fact that Africa has metal, oil and other mineral resources which have barely been touched. The exploitation of these resources could make Africa the continent of the future. With the exception of the Soviet Union, the industrial countries are about to deplete their supplies of the resources which abound in Africa. Besides, there always is the irritating presence of kaffer delegations in international assemblies where they use their voting power to support their brothers in South Africa.

These prospects raise the danger of Afrikaner isolation on a number of vital planes. Isolation might harm the country's economy at different levels. The coming depletion of gold necessitates the development of the country's productive potential and the cultivation of foreign markets. South Africa cannot look to Europe and America for the volume of trade which would keep her economy viable; the Western nations manufacture almost everything they need in so far as South Africa is concerned.

She cannot turn to Asia because Japan, China and distance stand in the way. South America offers limited markets for South African manufacturers, partly because Brazil and Argentina are likely to supply most South American markets in the twenty-first century. Africa remains the main region to which South African manufacturers can seriously turn their eyes. Besides, every African capital is within a day's flight from Johannesburg. But the Free Africans are hostile to the Afrikaner's attitude to the black people in South Africa and are not likely to start the stampede for goods manufactured in that country. All these dangers call for a policy of caution in dealing with the Free Africans and for conciliatory attitudes to the Western countries. But it is precisely at this point that de Haas gives the prime minister no end of sleepless nights. His aggressive racism combines with his penchant for opening his wide mouth on the wrong subject, at the wrong time and in the wrong way, to stand the premier's entire foreign policy on its head.

The head of the government cannot do much about this problem; he is the prisoner of his position. The heroic mould in which Afrikaner politics is cast limits his power to discipline a phenomenon like Willem Adriaan de Haas.

Piet du Toit van der Merwe, the prime minister's son-in-law, enters the picture at this point. He is a genius at reconciling the angularities which preserve the distance between the prime minister and his minister of forestry and which can split Afrikanerdom and bring its government crashing to the ground. Piet's job, which gives him tremendous influence in his community, involves no real conflicts of loyalty; apart from having a good head on his shoulders, he functions as a two-way conduit. His father-in-law uses him for negotiating with de Haas as freely as the latter employs him as a conduit between himself and the prime minister. Afrikanerdom acclaims this role and proclaims Piet a paragon of Afrikaner manhood.

* * *

Zandile Makaye is employed as a cook and a housemaid in the van der Merwe household. Marietjie has packed parcels of delicacies into an *ilala* (a species of palm) basket she bought on her recent visit to the land of the Zulus. These include strips of mouth-watering *biltong*. These are pieces of salted, pickled and dried buffalo meat which are eaten either as they are or in vegetable stews. The prime minister loves to eat them in their dry form. They are cut into thin shavings and chewed as snacks or appetisers. Some people say there is no better accompaniment to beer. Piet shot the buffalo during the culling season in the Hluhluwe Game Reserve and had the meat cured and railed to his house. Marietjie, ever thoughtful, bought a long-necked Tonga decanter and had it filled with palm wine and sealed for her father. These vessels are made of burnt clay and are marvels of beauty. The Tonga, who live in northern Zululand and southern Mozambique, etch delicate patterns on the outside of the decanters to make it a pleasure to drink from them. A kind, sensitive and generous people, the Tonga fill the vessels with the palm wine and regard it as a privilege to present these to visitors. The prime minister cultivated the taste for palm wine in his younger years, when he was Native Commissioner for Natal's northern Ngwavuma district.

Zandile has walked through the back door to the front gate near where the prime minister's car stands and is packing the provisions into the boot of the car when the prime minister emerges from the front door, surrounded by the members of Marietjie's family. An

African in the white, red-bordered uniform of a garden or kitchen servant stands against an electric pole, not far from the gate. He takes off his hat, shoves it under his armpit and runs to open the gate for the prime minister. There is nothing strange in a black man acknowledging the supremacy of the white man in this fashion; on the contrary, white society approves of what it regards as a declaration of loyalty. On country roads in the Orange Free State it is still the custom for an African to stop his business and open the gate for any white person. Nobody thinks it strange that a "kitchen-boy"—the title is used to describe adult, black, male servants—wears a hat together with his uniform. The gesture of rebellion is cancelled by the declaration of loyalty. As the prime minister walks through the gate, the African draws a revolver from his hat and fires three shots between the prime minister's eyes before he is overwhelmed by the security police guarding van Warmelo. As the head of the government collapses the African shouts:

Sharpeville is avenged!

* * *

II. War Of Minds

Unya lwabasha luyaphindana.

*(In a fight between equals, the side defeated
to-day might retreat to fight on another day.)*

Wherever possible, most Africans in the locations stay at home
on the Day of the Covenant, just as the English-speaking, who include
the Jews, prefer to do. The holiday is not a day of rejoicing for them.
The white police, who are overwhelmingly Afrikaans, are usually in a
bad mood on this occasion and the wise man or woman keeps out of
their way.

Zandile and her husband are wise people, but both of them
have no choice on how they spend the holiday. Zandile has had to be at
Waterkloof to cook lunch for the prime minister while her husband,
Pumasilwe, had to sit behind the wheel of the municipal bus. After the
tragedy, she offered not to return to the location where she lives with
her family but to spend the night in the tiny cubicle in the backyard
which every white employer uses to accommodate servants. Marietjie
would not have it; on such an occasion she insisted Zandile should be
with her husband and family, if to assure them that everything is well
with her.

Bus Number AZ 1021 is not as overcrowded as it is on working days. While every seat is occupied, there is plenty of standing room
as it roars out of its Pretoria terminal. The letter A indicates that
Atteridgeville, the African location outside the capital, is its destina-
tion. The letter Z stands for Zulu and means that this particular bus
goes only to the section of Atteridgeville reserved for the Zulu-speaking
Africans. Government policy goes beyond segregating black and white;
it separates every African language group from every other in order to
create a balance in black-white relations that will guarantee white
security.

The evil has its compensations, some of which are precious
beyond price.

Isolated, the African turns inward to himself for those beacons
by which to light his path in the mazes into which the white man has
thrown him. This revives and reinforces the traditional group-
consciousness which industrialisation and the location system corrode

and transforms the consciousness into a spiritual fortress in which he can take shelter against the tyranny from the white side. Each of the language groups is organised on the basis of what the Zulus call *umteto wesintu*, the African law or principle of fulfilment. The law is a body of ideals evolved by the African down the centuries and is the foundation for the self-disciplining initiatives which each group has developed. While the initiatives differ considerably in the Sotho, Xhosa and Zulu groups, all of them respond to the basic ideal of fulfilment. The philosophy provides a dimension of experience in which they find themselves speaking the same moral and ideological language. No white missionary is allowed to live in the locations and, as a result, *umteto wesintu* is less exposed to subversion by christianity. The black clergymen are punished as harshly for being black as the ordinary people are; their advocacy of christianity does nothing to protect them against race discrimination. On the contrary, it projects them as the agents of a subversive religion. To survive and preserve their credibility, they challenge the government to base its policies for the black people on the christian teachings of love, equality and brotherhood. But where black and white see each other from the perspective of Blood River these teachings threaten the position of the white man; he regards them as revolutionary and draws no distinction between them and the dialectical materialism of the communists. This serves to give point to *umteto wesintu*. With it as a basis, ancient techniques of communication are revived and used because the white man can neither comprehend nor understand these.

A world is emerging in the locations to which the humblest African feels he belongs and within which he realises he has a value as a person which no power on earth can take away. Disillusioned with the hypocrisy of the white man, the educated are turning in their numbers to *umteto wesintu*; they are turning their backs on the individualism of *umteto wesilungu*, the white law or principle of fulfilment and now agree with the humblest that earth can offer no possession more precious than the friendship of the next person; that the person's neighbour's presence, security and contentment are the most reliable guarantees of his own survival. They have re-learned the truth that the joys and sorrows of one's neighbour are one's personal concerns. By enabling the privileged and the humblest to feel they belong together, *umteto wesintu* has brought the black community in every part of the country to the moment of rebirth into a new destiny. Each person is coming to feel, as his ancestors did down the ages, that he is a human being in his own right and not an individual by the grace of the white man; he is coming to realise that fulfilment lies in creating for himself the world he desires for his children and his people. His blueprint is no longer *umteto wesilungu*, the white man's code of ethics and criterion for achievement; it is the *Larger Truth* revealed in the principle passed on from generation to generation.

The convergence of attitudes which *umteto wesintu* encourages expresses the anger of the black people. They are shocked and outraged by the things the white man does to them. Now and then the police swoop on the colleges and arrest the most militant student leaders. These young people are not treated as political prisoners. They are presumed to be criminals even before they are tried and are not locked up in the cells for prisoners awaiting trial; they are driven to the special cells for the most hardened convicts who make sexual assaults on them every night. When the students defend themselves, the convicts beat them up and often murder them. The police then announce that the students threw themselves out of windows under interrogation, or while awaiting trial.

If it is a crime for the African to be alive, it is also a crime for him to be educated. Throwing him into the dens of the convicts brings him to the limit of humiliation; his soft skin, clean body and properly nourished physique arouse the most violent sexual urges in the convicts. They think only of ravishing him as they would a woman and night after night they attack him. Some students break under the assaults and commit suicide; some are so shocked they never want to talk about their experiences in jail. Mixing them with the convicts is designed to break their will to oppose white domination. A few survive the assaults and emerge from jail swearing that there can be no atonement for the crimes perpetrated against black humanity by the white power-structure. They swear every day of their lives to know no rest before avenging themselves and their people.

In these practices against them, the students and growing numbers of the educated see the ugliness of the white man's system of values; the wickedness of the theory that the person is a creature. They agree with the heathens in their communities that the person is his own creator; that he is not indebted to any power outside of himself for what he is; not to God, not to any idol and not even to the spirits of his ancestors themselves. He is himself the conscious cause and the determinor of his destiny. The students are turning more and more to Zulu lore for texts by which to understand the Zulu experience. Cakijana, who is the embodiment of intellectual excellence in Zulu lore, is becoming the hero of the young people, precisely in the way he was in the days of Shaka the Great. There was not a problem Cakijana could not solve. It was said of him that while still a foetus he knocked on his mother's womb impatiently, shouting:

Hurry up, mama, and deliver me! I have an appointment to keep and a problem to solve!

Cakijana symbolised the person freed from ignorance. Limited awareness, *umteto wesintu* teaches, is ignorance. The person is endowed with the mind to find his way through the mazes of the cosmic order. The ignorant person regards his neighbours as his inferiors; he wants for himself what he will deny those with whom he inhabits the world and

21

arrogates to himself the position of being the only custodian of the truth. *Umteto wesintu* enlarges the human personality; while it rejects the view that the person lives to carry out a mandate, it emphasises the enduring obligation to be responsible; to respond every moment of his life to the challenge of being human. It teaches that he is fulfilled when he sees to it that his neighbour makes the best possible use of his life in the light of his choices and his abilities. The enduring obligation to one's neighbour is the hallmark of a civilised person. The savage, the barbarian and the primitive think only of themselves, like most animals; they go through life with a deep-seated sense of inadequacy and need props to enable them constantly to prove they are superior; they are always afraid of the morrow. Wherever they go, they build walls within which they become the prisoners of their fears.

Events in Angola and Mozambique accelerate movement toward the moment when the Zulus and the other Africans will be able to tear down the white man's walls of fear and free him from himself. This is the point the prime minister's assassin was driving home when he fired the fatal shots. The Afrikaner has to be forced through a painful shock, to cure his fears and to enable him to see his neighbours of all colours through adult eyes.

In the evenings, the people in the locations celebrate the sending of the traumatic signal to the Afrikaner, when van Warmelo was shot, by singing the great war songs of their ancestors. To the Zulus, van Warmelo's assassination marked the beginning of the return to Blood River. One of the songs runs:

> Wathinta thina,
> Wathint' iziqand' ematsheni!
> Uzaukufa!

> (Be warned, O enemy!
> If you touch us
> You touch wasps among rocks!
> Death is your fate!)

*   *   *

In the conflict between *umteto wesintu* and *umteto wesilungu* meanings have a crucial importance. Each concept which the white power-structure attacks must be defined in terms which no exegetical skill evolved in the Graeco-Romano-Hebraic experience can cope with. At all times the African must avoid fighting on ground chosen by the white man; in every situation of conflict he must *xina* the white man; he must confront him with a larger truth than any he knows.

Umteto wesintu enlarges the personality in ways which guarantee the availability of larger ideas in every crisis. This quality gives it the dimensions of a larger truth and transforms *umteto wesilungu* into a smaller truth. As a result, the African is able to live within the white experience and be fulfilled outside of it. In the underground the paradox is called the Black Bombshell or BB or *bibi*, a species of African squirrel; it is the secret weapon by which to *xina* the white man. In the locations, as in the white man's towns, BB also stands for Brown Bread. The concept can be signalled in a variety of ways. The two fingers are raised in the V-for-Victory sign used by Churchill during the second world war. In situations of extreme danger, it is enough for the person merely to raise both his hands in the way some African communities do in salutation or, simply to sneeze or cough and place the nose or the mouth between the two fingers forming the V sign.

Although most of the passengers in the Atteridgeville bus are in their Sunday best, they are not gay. Most of them prefer not to speak to anybody, not even to their neighbours. A few souls, either incorrigibly naive or just stupid, talk in whispers. Now and then, the general silence is broken by violent bouts of coughing and sneezing, with people taking care to conceal their two fingers in handkerchiefs and when a bout starts many people turn their eyes to Zandile. Many know her and all die to talk to her about the events in front of Piet du Toit van der Merwe's house. But to be seen to know her or to say a word to her is to play games with lightning. People content themselves with pressing their handkerchiefs to their nostrils or mouths. Zandile does not acknowledge the gestures of identification, not so much because she has in mind the presence of the security police, but because it is only then that some events fit together and suggest a pattern too horrible to contemplate.

Uppermost in her mind is that dreadful morning, two years earlier, when a location policeman stood at her door. At that moment, fate crashed into her life. A policeman anywhere around one's yard was an evil omen; more often than not the presence preceded endorsement out of the location, the loss of a job and condemnation to a future of unspeakable deprivation in an unknown rural reservation. A particularly terrifying aspect of the endorsement was the manner in which a family's tiny children were torn away from their parents because the law said they were economically unproductive and had to be sent to live with indigent relatives they did not know. The rural reservations had become vast human rubbish heaps where men, women and children the white man did not want in his locations were dumped; where they could starve, die and rot in order to make South Africa safe for the white man.

Frobenius van Maasdorp, the location superintendent, wanted to see her before 5 o'clock that afternoon. The policeman did not need to remind Zandile that this was a command.

Zandile Makaye. Is that your name?

Yes; it is.

The white man's face had turned a little red behind his

dark-rimmed glasses. The black policeman who had ushered her into the superintendent's office had put his hand to one side of his mouth and had whispered:

Girl, did your mother not teach you how to speak to the lords?

She felt like slapping him on the face with the back of her hand but repressed the impulse before it got out of control. She would carve the insult on a stone, as her people said. She turned to the white man.

Yes, lord, Zandile Makaye is my name.

Are you employed in the city?

No, lord. I'm a housewife.

A friend of mine, a very important lord in the government wants a hard-working, reliable and first-class cook and housemaid. He's secretary to the Minister of Forestry. My policemen say you can do the jobs better than anybody in your section of the location.

But, lord, I have two young children and am expecting a third. The two are too young to be left by themselves in a location. The first is seven and has just gone to school and the second is five.

I'm not interested in how many piccanins you have. You know the law. Either you take the job or you or your children are endorsed out of the location and out of Pretoria.

I understand, lord. But, I also have a husband; I cannot give an answer without discussing your offer with him.

Be here at nine o'clock to-morrow morning to tell me your decision. Remember. . . the law.

That night she and Pumasilwe had sat talking until the first cocks began to crow.

Take the job, Mother of Landiwe. I cannot bear to live without you and the children here. I do not earn enough to maintain you in the Valley Of A Thousand Hills and myself here. But, above all, who knows, our ancestors might be giving us the opportunity to *xina* the white man in a way nobody can.

Two years seems a long period and in that time events have moved curiously in a series of uncomprehended zigzags to land her in the centre of a calamity whose effects on black and white not even the wisest can foretell.

* * *

Zandile does not enter her house by the front door; she hurries to the back verandah, into the bathroom, where she throws off her clothes, bites a piece from a dried root of the *siqunga* grass, chews it and sprays the medicated saliva into her bathwater.

The Zulus believe that a dead body radiates dangerous vibrations and that the *siqunga* root neutralises these. Babies are particularly sensitive to these vibrations and a nursing mother has to give herself a full *siqunga* bath before she enteres her house or touches her baby, if she has been in the presence of a dead person.

She hears voices of men as she washes herself and recognises some of these. Dillo Mareka and Sefadi Masilo sit opposite each other with her husband and three or four other men around her round dining table. A small bottle of brandy is being passed round. The men do not rise to their feet as Zandile enters her dining-sitting room. Custom in her part of Africa requires that they should salute her by shouting the second name of her father or by reciting the patronymic poem which is appended as a title to every African family name. In the old days Zulu law stated that the woman must not change her name when she married; she remained the daughter of her father and retained most of the rights which went with this. By repeating her father's name her neighbours acknowledged her right to remain the daughter of her father. The white missionaries opposed this recognition of the woman's equality with the man; it was a barbarous custom. They forced the Zulus to adopt the civilised customs of the white man; on the day of her marriage, a girl abandoned her family name and adopted her husband's, as though she were owned by him.

In the isolation of the location, people feel free to live not as the white man says they should but as they believe right.

Welcome home, Queen of the House, her husband cries out. Is every bone still in its place?

She touches a few joints on her body and replies: Yes, I think. The men join her husband in congratulating her and then rise together and leave.

I do not understand all this, Father of Landiwe? Are they afraid of me now? Why do they all leave so suddenly on this particular day?

Don't you see the point? This is to protect you and me; you don't know who's standing outside with cameras which take pictures in the dark or listening devices.

Let me hope things are as you say.

You question their motives? But these are our friends; you know them; you are as safe with them as with me.

I don't know; how can I? When the world spins in crazy dives and crumbles around me? When I first went to school my teacher told the story of the orphaned young elephant caught in a hailstorm. Help, everybody! Help, it cried; the skies are falling! There was nobody around to help. Then it turned to the earth and stamped it with its feet and cried: Crack open, O Earth, that I may hide! Well, the heavens are collapsing on me and I wish the earth could swallow me.

You are one experience older.

Yes, I am; but I think there are things you have to explain to me; I am so upset and so afraid, do please try and understand if I speak as though I am in a dream. Tell me, Father of Landiwe, what is going on between you and Maggie Kuboni?

Why? Maggie? I thought you had understood why the security police found me naked in her bed . . . . Otherwise I would be on Robben Island to-day. She had to play the role of a prostitute to give credibility to my story that I was in her bed when the bomb exploded in the offices of *Die Aanslag.*

I did understand; but what I don't understand is why you wear that ring which she has on the same finger of her left hand where you have yours.

That is difficult to explain, Mother of Landiwe. But, take my word, your ignorance, because of your employment, is the main guarantee of your safety, my safety and our children's safety.

The price of that safety is dangerously high, I'm afraid.

Why don't you come to the point?

Are you involved in the assassination of van Warmelo?

Mother of Landiwe! How dare you say such a thing?

She opens her handbag and takes a ring out of it which is similar to those worn by Maggie and her husband and hands it to him.

Where did you get this?

It dropped out of the assassin's pocket and rolled beneath a pansy plant. The whites were too busy helping the old man or mauling the African to notice it. When they left, I picked it up.

You understand what is happening now; from this moment, you do not know this ring; you have never seen it anywhere—not on me or anybody and not on Maggie, either.

Are you protecting her?

Why don't you join the underground, to understand the laws on which people operate there?

If that will keep our family together, I will. But I don't see where assassinations will help. If you continue to fight on ground chosen by the white man, you invite defeat . . . .

What do you know about war?

It was to a woman, Mnkabayi ka Jama, that the Zulu nation turned in the turbulence of the early days of the revolution which Shaka led; Mnkabayi served, not only as regent; she became supreme commander of our armed forces! Think of it; when this nation reached the crossroads; when it reached the dividing line between disaster and survival, it turned to a woman.

That is why we have turned to Maggie!

I do not trust Maggie; the only relationship she thinks of when she sees a man is the horizontal one. And, my instincts tell me that she is a police spy in your ranks.

Come over to Macedonia and help us!

III. Afrikanerdom: The Miracle

Inyoka kayilandelwa isisemgodini wayo.

(He is a fool who follows a snake into its hole.)

Intrigue is the grease which oils the wheels of Afrikaner politics. At the level of historical experience, the Afrikaners are nearer the Africans than the white nations. But unlike the Africans, they do not have those cultural anchors which stabilise because they have their roots in antiquity. Apart from being an amalgam of European ethnic groups and cultures they are still a young people lacking the poise of mature nationhood. From the eighteenth century onward, the Afrikaners had turned their backs on that Europe which they regarded as decadent and tyrannical and had ventured into the African interior where they were finally cut off from significant contact with the main stream of European civilisation.

Their only real link with their continent of origin was the bible which they regarded as the source of all the truth the race of Man needs to know, for survival. In their isolation, they interpreted the christian ideology in terms which were valid only in their experience; every other interpretation was alien, heretical and seditious. If that widened the gulf between themselves and the English-speaking on the white side, it left the Afrikaners in a cleft stick; in danger of being crushed by African numbers or by the cultural and economic supremacy of the English-speaking. A split mind developed in which they saw a threat to their survival in every situation of challenge. Truth had biologic associations, if not origins; it expressed the unique genius of a race. The christianity which inspired the Afrikaner experience was not the christianity of the Anglican Church or the African Pentecostal Church In Zion.

Afrikaner christianity could go to war with African or English-speaking christianity and glorify God by destroying both. The validity of the christian truth lay in the armed might of its adherents and in its ability to move them to their destiny. By rejecting this interpretation, Europe ganged up with the Afrikaner's enemies and she, too, had to be repudiated. In his isolation, the Afrikaner treads the earth with uncertainty and fear; whoever is not on his side is an enemy.

27

But he defines himself in a way which makes outside identification with him impossible; outsiders are all condemned for being the children of their particular parents. De Haas plays on these fears to project himself as the champion of the Afrikaner's cause.

In the months after the prime minister's assassination the dream of a South Africa dominated by the Afrikaner has been shattered. Voices have been raised pleading for a more realistic assessment of the dispositions of racial power in South Africa. The Afrikaner, it is said, must come to terms with one or the other of the two giants in the South African scenario; he must strike a deal with either the English-speaking or the African majority. Helvetius van Warmelo favoured a deal with the English-speaking because they are white. After winning them over, he planned to move from this position of strength to try and strike a deal with the Americans and to persuade them to take sides with the whites to stem the tide of African nationalism rolling southward. He explored ground cautiously because most of his people still did not see how on earth they could come to terms with the English communist-liberals who humiliated, oppressed and fought them right up to the end of the nineteenth century or with the communist-liberals in Washington who do not mind if their daughters strip before nigger males. These fears produce conflicts in the mind of the Afrikaners which give a peculiar fragility to their solidarity. Van Warmelo's death has deepened the contradictions.

* * *

Lukas Meyer lifts the telephone on his desk in the head office of Die Christelike Nasionale Party (The Christian National Party) or CNP on Church Street in Pretoria.

This is the Telephone Exchange. We have a long distance call for Mr. Lukas Meyer. Is that Mr. Meyer?

Meyer speaking.

Please stand by for a call from Excelsior in the Orange Free State. Mr. Cornelius Beetge van Schalkwyk wishes to speak to you.

Lukas Meyer is an important man in the CNP. As chairman of the party caucus, he supervises the arrangements for the special session at which the caucus will elect its new leader who will, in turn, be South Africa's next prime minister. Equally important, on a different plane, is Cornelius Beetge van Schalkwyk, the Free State wheat magnate. Apart from being president of the wealthy and politically influential Free State *Koringboeresvereeniging* (Wheat Farmers Union) or KBV, van Schalkwyk is chairman of the Free State section of the CNP. For fifty years now, the Free State KBV has been the kingmaker of the party and in the last ten years van Schalkwyk himself has been unchallenged master of the CNP in his province. The two men represent a new type of Afrikaner; the man who reads stock exchange reports with the

28

devotion reserved for the bible in a more pious age. Meyer is chairman of the economically powerful *Volksversekeringsmaatskappij* (the People's Insurance Company) or VVM which has spread its tentacles into almost every branch of secondary industry. Van Schalkwyk owns the largest bakery organisation in South Africa and has been granted the monopoly to supply bread in the locations. With bread a staple item in the diet of the locations, van Schalkwyk is making more money than he can ever hope to use for his comfort and needs; it has become an instrument for the accumulation of power.

Lukas, says the voice at the Excelsior end of the line, this is Beet. How's the weather in Pretoria?

As fine as wheat farmers would like it at this time of the year.

Lukas, I shall be in Pretoria to-morrow night to see you, if you will be about.

I was supposed to fly to Rustenburg to-morrow morning to meet the branch executive there, but if you're coming this way the sun can stop in the heavens until you come.

You and your kaffer slang! Christians don't speak of the sun stopping in the heavens. See you to-morrow then, Lukas; I'll call you from my hotel after arrival. And, Lukas, you understand, don't you? This is between the two of us.

O.K.! O.K.! Herr dokter!

*   *   *

Willem Adriaan de Haas has been affected deeply by the prime minister's assassination; so badly at times that he has had to be admitted into a nursing home. Everything has been done so secretly very few people know about it. At one point his doctors recommended that he should retire from politics. He travelled by train to Durban and spent a fortnight at the Haelstadt Hotel which he owns jointly with his brother-in-law, Karl du Plessis. The Haelstadt is unique in one important respect; it is the only hotel in Durban and, for that matter, in the province of Natal, which does not accommodate Jewish guests.

The rule in South Africa is that inferior breeds like the Africans, the Asians and other non-white peoples should not be accommodated in white hotels. The position is somewhat different in the Free State where de Haas was born and where he lives when not at work in Pretoria. There, the Jews are accorded the status of second-class whites in some of the towns. There is no hard and fast rule about their inferior status; only, a consensus exists which defines the Jews' place in white society.

In the smaller towns of the Free State, the Jew has no chance, for example, of being elected mayor. Kroonstad, a fast-developing city in the northern part of the Free State once considered the idea of electing a Jewish mayor to attract investment capital. The group of businessmen who had proposed the name of Israel Greenberg had to retreat in a hurry and explain, quite unconvincingly, that the whole thing had arisen out of a misunderstanding. They did not have much of a choice; the Dutch Reformed Church had brought some of its guns into action against the prospect of a Jew being chief executive officer of a christian city and, in the Afrikaner community, the Dutch Reformed Church is a power to reckon with not only in spiritual matters but also in politics, economics and the cultural life of the Afrikaners.

De Haas has cut short his secret holiday in Durban and returned to Pretoria in the midst of a cloud of rumours. One of the English-language dailies in Durban had reported that de Haas was convalescing from a heart attack and the English press in the rest of the country had taken up the item, splashed it on their front pages with banner headlines. Some commentators stated bluntly that there practically was no chance that de Haas would allow his name to be on the list of candidates for the leadership of the CNP. In a violent counter-attack *Die Aanslag* charged that the campaign was part of the English-Jewish-capitalist-communist-liberal conspiracy to destroy Afrikanerdom.

The weakest partners in the "conspiracy" are, of course, the Jews. They are a cowed and frightened community which knows its place in the hierarchy of whiteness.

Although none may hold office in the leadership of the CNP because, as Bokkie, the columnist of *Die Aanslag* puts it, of the *Abraham-factor*, many of them are members of Die Christelike Nasionale Party and, in some cities, are the financial backbone of the party. As a result they lead a complicated life of conspicuous invisibility which draws blame on them from all sides when things go wrong. As whites, they are members of the aristocracy of colour, but because of the Abraham-factor, they are punished for being the children of their particular parents. This leaves them perpetually in a cleft stick out of which they try to escape by identifying themselves with the Afrikaners in one mood and with the deprived peoples of colour in another.

The impossible choices they have to make in this setting have developed an ambivalence in them which makes them suspect when they are friends, suspect when they are enemies and suspect when they are neutral. The African hates them for giving financial support to the CNP. The Afrikaner hates them for having produced the largest number of liberals and the ablest communists. And, when they avoid identification with any group they are called parasites whose loyalty to South Africa is determined by shekels. They cannot identify even with the English, whose language and culture they have adopted; the Englishman hates them because they compete with him in the accumulation of shekels.

The treatment of the Jews by the CNP is but one of the many

contradictions in the complicated role race plays in South Africa. The Afrikaner does not trust the Jew although both are driven by the imperatives of survival to cling to a group consciousness which works for their isolation; he does not trust the English because they humiliated him and control the economy. He does not trust the Africans because they own the land and could regain control of it the day they have access to the guns. In this setting the Afrikaner is projected in the role of a business manager of an estate owned by the English (with their Jewish allies) on African soil. As the Africans put it, he lives in a stolen world. A triangular conflict has emerged which involves the Africans, the Afrikaners and the English, and which operates in a complex, peculiarly South African way.

Each group fights the other two in different ways. The Afrikaner imposes an inhuman form of deprivation on the African, whom he regards as the most dangerous enemy, precisely at the time when he offers him independence in the black reservations in the endeavour to drive a permanent wedge between the African and the English. At the political level, the Afrikaner makes it clear that he must remain unquestioned master; that he will tolerate no interference from the English and that he expects them to keep strictly to their place. If they behave he gives them the latitude to collect shekels and dominate the economy.

The English smart under the inferior place and accordingly adhere to a liberalism in racial matters which is designed to create an African-English front to smash the political dominance of the Afrikaner. At the same time so many privileges and rights go with the white skin the English will throw their weight on the side of the Afrikaner in the face of African truculence.

The African fights race discrimination from the Afrikaner and the English; he stresses human values not only because his outlook on life gives him no other choice but also because these evoke a response from the English which gives to their alliance with the Afrikaner the character of a marriage of convenience. The African works as hard to crack the Afrikaner-English united front as the Afrikaner does to widen the gulf between the English and the African. For their part, the English dread nothing more than a political coalition between the Africans and the Afrikaners.

In this type of conflict race loses much of its significance as a determinant of policy; what matters are the reserves of power each of the three groups controls and the nature of the alliances it can make either to preserve its dominance or to dictate the pattern of South African nationhood.

Race was an important unifying factor on the white side as long as the world was dominated by the white race. Then, the Afrikaner and the English had exclusive possession of the guns. The second world war extended the area of freedom on the globe. Black, brown and yellow nations emerged to give reality to the danger that the Africans would one day have access to the guns when they would smash white domination and drive the whites into the sea.

In the fifty years from the formation of the Union of South Africa, the black people have been evolving the *xina* technique to create voids in which white domination could not survive. To *xina* is to create a vacuum in which no living organism can live.

By day, the African works in the city and serves the white "lords"; when the sun sets, he retires to his world in the location where deprivation forces him to concentrate on the refinement of the *xina* technique. He has reached the point where he feels he can even dispense with the gun in the fight with the white man; he has won the war of minds; *umteto wesintu* and not *umteto wesilungu* has once more become the main determinant of African attitudes. This creates the climate of thinking in which the black peoples can respond in identical ways to similar provocations. They see the day coming when they will withdraw their labour and bring the white man's economy to a stop in every part of South Africa. The gun is becoming increasingly irrelevant as a guarantor of white dominance or even as the decisive factor in the overthrow of white rule. For a long time the white man rejected the African; now, the black man has disciplined himself sufficiently to contemplate rejecting the white man. The moment of decision approaches with the inevitability of growth.

Thoughtful Afrikaners are concerned about the changes taking place among the deprived; the less thoughtful are frightened. Shooting clubs, even for women, are being organised all over the country; the whites have become a community permanently mobilised for war. Events move relentlessly to predictable catastrophe; they are developing a momentum which precludes rationality in the ruling community. The whites have been taking up positions for the final confrontation. Everybody expected the Africans to strike violently and in that way fight on ground where white power was decisive. The assassination shows them doing precisely this.

* * *

Nine hundred members of the caucus of the CNP sit in semi-circular rows in the auditorium of the Groot Kerk in the centre of Pretoria. The Afrikaners are an exceptionally disciplined people. Although they have once more come to one of the moments of decision which characterise their history and while they are very tense, they are so orderly one would think the meeting was a funeral service. The caucus is made up of the members of the cabinet and of parliament, provincial presidents, secretaries and treasurers, branch chairmen, secretaries and treasurers and representatives of cultural, women's, students' and young people's organisations. About ten thousand men and women, mainly young people, crowd in the galleries.

Lukas Meyer, followed immediately by the four presidents of the provincial branches of the party enters through the main door. The eleven thousand people rise to their feet and resume their seats when the chairman has taken the chair.

I do not need to remind any Afrikaner of the gravity of the occasion which has brought us together, he says. Once more we have come to the crossroads; once more we have come to our moment of decision. It is on such occasions that the finest qualities which make us the miracle of history that we are shine brightest . . . .

The house breaks out in thunderous applause, giving him time to wipe his face and steady himself for what everybody knows is the moment of trial.

And, as we once more create history with our own hands we remember our beloved leader, one of the finest statesmen the Afrikaner nation produced who, if you will allow me to say this, died on duty . . . .

The crowd cheers, but not as mightily as before.

His death is a challenge to every true Afrikaner to proceed from where the great leader fell. We can pay him no finer tribute, in this, our hour of trial, than to close our ranks behind the leader you will choose tonight, no matter who he is. My hope and the expectation of *die volk daar buite* [the people outside there] is that you will elect a man who will heal the wounds which could divide us in the face of the dangers which we face. My only regret and I know this is yours, too, is that one of the finest sons of this nation is not with us. As you have seen in the papers, Willem Adriaan de Haas is in hospital. I shall ask this house to rise and, for a moment, wish him speedy recovery. We are the losers by his absence. But then, men appear on the stage of history only to disappear again while the Afrikaner nation goes on . . . .

After loudly reading the single item on the agenda, the chairman calls for nominations for the post of leader of the CNP. Cornelius Beetge van Schalkwyk rises amidst applause from most delegates on the wrong side of fifty and proposes the name of the chairman. A student delegate stands up from the back of the hall and proposes the name of Willem Adriaan de Haas. The chairman rises stiffly to his feet.

According to the rules of this caucus any person nominated must be present in person to accept nomination. Through illness, as we all know, Mr. de Haas has been unable to attend. I contacted the hospital and was told that his condition would not allow of his getting out of bed.

After two other names have been proposed and accepted van Schalkwyk moves that the nominations be closed. The chairman suddenly seems stunned; he pays no attention to what the president of the KBV is saying. His eyes are fixed on the phenomenon coming through the door. Willem Adriaan de Haas marches briskly, his head high, down the aisle to the rostrum. The ten thousand people in the gallery rise to their feet and hurl the bars of the Afrikaner national anthem, *Die Stem Van Suidafrika* (The Voice of South Africa) into the tense atmosphere. When the singing dies down the student at the back raises his hand and, failing repeatedly to catch the chairman's eye, marches down the aisle to the centre of the hall, from where he is in full view of the gallery.

Now that Mr. de Haas is here, may I ask him through you, Mr. Chairman, if he would allow his name to go forward for nomination.

That is not the way we usually do things, but in view of the exceptional situation in which we find ourselves, I shall grant your request. Mr. de Haas . . . .

De Haas moves to the microphone.

I want to explain one or two points before dealing with the question put to me . . . . Savagery has struck once more at the Afrikaner people, aided as has always been the case in our history, by its communist-liberal allies. Dr. Helvetius van Warmelo would be with us to-day if, in our drunkenness with power and greed for money, we had not compromised with some of the enemies of Afrikanerdom. We Afrikaners, who forgot that the tree bleeds itself to heal the wound on its bark, could unwittingly be responsible for the cowardly murder of our leader; we, who ceased to see black-white relations from the perspective of Blood River, could be political accomplices in the assassination.

The blacks have one unchanging end in view: to isolate the Afrikaner, crush his power and drive him into the sea. In the era of the wars, they fought to exterminate us; their policy has not changed. After defeat, they clamoured for integration in the white man's structure of society. They demanded race equality not because they loved justice; they had been forced to lay down their spears but were determined to fight using different weapons. Integration would enable them to master the use of the white man's weapons, and armed like him, they would proceed from where the white man stopped them at Blood River.

Winston Churchill, Franklin Roosevelt and Charles de Gaulle ganged up with that Asiatic coolie, Josef Stalin, to destroy that Germany which would have made the world safe for the white man; they set the miasma that is communism free on the earth. Let us be under no illusions, communism is a diabolic Asiatic plan for the subversion of the white man's position of leadership in the world. Race equality has been evolved by the blacks to serve the same purpose. The blacks and the Asiatics are in league in international assemblies to destroy the Afrikaner; this is the message of the assassination.

In these conditions, conciliation is suicide and compromise madness. You, ladies and gentlemen, know as well as I do that there are people in this hall whose knees quake at the thought of putting the niggers in their place to ensure that they never again dream of laying their hands on a white person. They want us to go the way of the Portuguese in Mozambique. I came here to let all with ears hear that I am not one of them; that I shall allow no nigger to touch a white person! I will stand for nomination only on this condition.

The house rises to its feet and claps hands, roars out cheers and stamps on the floor while many sob and weep until the ten thousand in the galleries swing as one frenzied mass developing a momentum which threatens to crack the beams which support the galleries.

That night, Willem Adriaan de Haas leaves the hall of the Groot Kerk not only a phenomenon, but he has become Afrikanerdom's man of destiny.

*   *   *

IV. Three-Eyed Giants

Akuqaqa lazizwa ukunuka.

(The polecat does not know it smells.)

Afrikanerdom has spoken once more in tones of thunder and lightning. Once more it has summoned its sons and daughters to the parapets. Once more, it tells itself that it is threatened and that survival lies in withdrawing into itself. In the face of danger, its ancestors surrounded themselves with their wagons and from behind these, as walls or *laagers*, mowed down the Africans with gunfire.

* * *

Like most Afrikaners, Piet and Marietjie du Toit van der Merwe adopt a peculiarly ambivalent attitude to the African. In one mood they fear and hate him because of history. In the era of the wars, the African often brought the Afrikaner face to face with the prospect of extermination.

King Dingane of the Zulus is represented in Afrikaner mythology as a monster in human form. As long as an Afrikaner lives, there seems no possibility that Dingane's name shall be forgotten. Stress is laid on how Dingane ordered the murder in cold blood of Piet Retief and his followers after Retief had returned to Dingane the cattle Sigonyela had stolen from the Zulus. The Zulus teach their children that Dingane paid the white people in their own coin.

Retief had invited Sigonyela to a party and, when the Pedi warlord was off his guard, had him arrested and handcuffed. Sigonyela was freed when he offered the Afrikaners the cattle which Retief took to the Zulus. Dingane, however, had taken the precaution to send his intelligence officers with Retief to keep an eye on what he did and, in particular, to make mental notes of what transpired between Retief and his "friend" Sigonyela. When the Afrikaners betrayed their friend, the Zulu spies rushed to the Zulu capital where they reported what had happened. Matters were not improved when Zulu guards responsible for the security of the Zulu capital of Umgungundlovu reported Retief's maneouvres by night which were designed to enable the whites to encircle the capital and hold Dingane to ransom. Dingane, the Zulus say, would have been unworthy of his high office if he had not snuffed out the nest of white traitors in his own capital.

After that the relations between the Zulus and the Afrikaners were so bad, an Afrikaner delegation to the king demanded hostages and seized Bongoza the son of Mefu, a distinguished Zulu jurist, as a guarantee of safe conduct through Zulu territory. To ensure that Bongoza played no dirty tricks on his white captors, they tied a leather thong around his neck and led him by the side of their horses on their way home. In the O'Pate Gorge, Bongoza complained of pains in the stomach, fouling up the air with loud rectal explosions. He begged the Afrikaners to allow him to relieve himself behind a boulder. His captors were suspicious; they showed him a boulder which they covered with their guns. The spectacle of a kaffer defecating in front of the white lords was more than the Afrikaners could bear. Behind the boulder, Bongoza gave the signal, whereupon the Zulus fell upon the Afrikaners and, except for one young man, wiped them out.

Against these experiences from history, Piet and Marietjie are often puzzled by the valour and humanity of Bhadama Ntuli, the young Zulu they employed as a gardener when they lived in Joubert Street, in the house Piet had inherited from his father. The sprawling bungalow had a long passage with rooms on either side. During a thunderstorm one night, a bolt struck the house setting it on fire. Piet and Marietjie were awakened by the flames and dashed to the passage to rescue their children, aged five and three in the next room. But the flames were so high and the smoke so thick neither Piet nor Marietjie could run through them. Piet's clothes caught fire and Marietjie dragged him to the front door where he collapsed as she tore the pyjamas off his body. Marietjie ran around the house to the children's room screaming for help. The window was too high from the ground for her to climb into it; at the same time the flames were billowing furiously out of one side of the large window.

Just then, Bhadama emerged out of the darkness, climbed the wall, smashed the windows and brought out the younger child first and then the older. By this time his clothes had caught fire. He held on to the wooden frame of the window and tried to climb out of the inferno; the wood, already in flames, crackled and collapsed. Bhadama fell to the floor and was a lump of charred and crinkled flesh when the fire brigade discovered his body under the debris.

By a happy coincidence Zandile comes from Empangeni in Natal, the town in which Bhadama's people paid their taxes and made their purchases. This has created a bond between Piet and Marietjie and their cook which goes a little beyond the master-servant relationship which Afrikanerdom insists upon when it comes to dealings with the African. More often than not, Piet and his wife generally feel little or no embarrassment when they lower the protective barriers they have to raise in dealing with an African. Zandile, for her part, is not only a very pretty woman, she also has very pleasant manners and performs magic in the kitchen.

The last quality is particularly pleasing to the van der Merwes, now that Piet is private secretary to the prime minister and has moved to Waterkloof, the exclusive suburb where Afrikaner magnates, members of parliament and foreign diplomats have their homes. Marietjie has won fame in the diplomatic community as a hostess. During the hunting season every year Piet goes on leave and spends his holiday in the Hluhluwe Game Reserve in Zululand where he satisfies his passion for using the gun in killing game. On these occasions the family takes Zandile along. Adept at the preparation of biltong, the dried, pickled and salted beef which is so dear to the Afrikaner palate, she cuts up buffalo, elephant and rhinoceros steak, cures it and dresses it in such a way that to look at it is enough to make the mouth water. A dinner invitation from the van der Merwes is something which every gourmet in the upper brackets of Pretoria society looks forward to. Piet is proud that he has achieved good relations with the Malawi diplomats; so good, in fact, all of them, from the ambassador on down, call him by his first name, which he found difficult at first, but which he is now glad to reciprocate.

Paul Kunene, the ambassador, is a short, portly man with a ready smile and few words. An engineer by profession, he likes to talk about buildings, about Cape Dutch architecture and bridges and roads—that is, when he condescends to open his mouth. The prime minister finds it impossible to conceal his dislike for the Malawian diplomat. To start with, Mr. Kunene has a face so black and a skin texture so fine the prime minister is almost certain the Malawian gives his face a shine with black boot polish each time he goes into the bathroom in the morning. The ambassador was educated in Holland and speaks Dutch with a fluency most Afrikaners envy. This does not mean that they love the language; actually they feel no strong attachment to Holland. But they marvel at the ease with which the African has command of a white language; they never thought it could be so beautiful. The ambassador's thick lips and broad nostrils impart a resonance to the language which is most pleasing to the ear. To the prime minister, who does not speak Dutch at all, the African's mastery of it is affectation, pure and simple. What gets on the prime minister's nerves above everything is Kunene's reserve. The prime minister thinks he is the most spoilt kaffer he has ever known. He never has any dealings with him and at official gatherings he spends the shortest time possible with the Malawian, allowing his Minister of Foreign Affairs to have all the time with the African.

Ambassador Kunene has a soft spot for the van der Merwes and he thinks Marietjie is one of the finest white persons he has ever met anywhere in the world. When she talks to him she uses the etiquette he is used to in his own country. For example, she does not refer to him as Your Excellency or as Mr. Kunene; she addresses him by his family title, Mtimande. When he passes her a salt cellar she does not say: Thank you, Mr. Ambassador, as most whites do. She stretches both her hands and receives it with: Mtimande! That melts the ambassador's heart, as he often says about her. That child is so well trained! he never tires of saying.

Piet's closest friend in the Malawian embassy is Dumakude Kumalo, the first secretary.

How comes it that you have Zulu names, he asked the Malawian when the friendship started.

Do you read Zulu history?

Well, er, I grew up in the Free State where the majority of the Africans are Basotho . . . .

I understand. During Shaka's revolution all sorts of things happened. He and his brother sent armies as far north as the tropics. Some of his generals deserted, conquered the peoples near the equator and established their own empires. Zwangendaba fought his way through Mozambique, smashed Portuguese opposition and finally settled in Malawi where his people are known to this day as the Angoni, the same word as your Ngunis of Natal and the Transkei. Some of these people trace their ancestry to the Zulus. We do not speak the Zulu language, just as you don't speak Dutch. But we retain many words from the language; that's true also of some of our names.

Dumakude is almost as black as the ambassador, but unlike him, he has a warm and likeable personality. A chemist by training, he was educated in Germany where Piet also went to university. Both are at home in German. The friendship is so close the van der Merwes and the Kumalos visit each other whenever the time permits. Marietjie surprised the Kumalos the first time they came to her house by welcoming them with the salutation: Mntungwa!

The architect of the van der Merwes' success in dealing with the Africans is their cook. Zandile never gets tired of answering Marietjie's endless questions while the latter relays the answers to her eagerly receptive husband. Over the years, the Afrikaner woman begins to note, timidly at first, that in some things she can deal with Zandile on a woman-to-woman basis and that she can even trust Zandile.

This man you were telling me about, what is his name, Zandile?

Dillo Mareka is his name, O Nooi.

And you say Kritzinger gave him the electric treatment?

Yes, Nooi.

That Kritzinger is a brute; he makes me sick! Is Dillo a friend of your family?

We are neighbours on the same street, Nooi. You know how we Africans are; people living on the same street form more or less a large family.

Do you know why Kritzinger burnt him with the electric

wires?

Ever since the death of the Ou Baas, your father, the police have been doing all sorts of things in the location.

Ah . . . .

They don't trust anybody. They search everybody, everyday, everywhere.

They search you, too?

They search me in the morning as I board the bus for work and they search me when I step off it in the evening.

That is ridiculous, just like Kritzinger. Just because he is police commander in the Pretoria area he thinks every black person was involved in my father's death. As a matter of fact the assassin, Theodore Darikwa, is not even a South African by birth; his parents came from Rhodesia. He grew up in Pretoria and regards himself as a Shangane. I think he was influenced by the English and the Jews to do that stupid thing. Poor boy; he will lose his life while the people who misled him escape.

The minds of the foolish are tools in the hands of the wise . . . .

I'm glad the prime minister intervened personally in the Darikwa case and took him out of Kritzinger's district. The brute would have killed the murderer before we knew all we could about the conspiracy.

Indeed, Nooi.

Some people find the prime minister a little difficult to understand; but he is such a nice man; so honest and so loyal to his people. You would love him too, if you were an Afrikaner.

Indeed; indeed! I hope they don't return the poor Darikwa to Kritzinger.

Never! The prime minister himself gave instructions that he must not be kept in one jail more than a month and ordered that instructions should be given to every prison where he is sent that the superintendent of the jail will be personally responsible for Darikwa's safety. Let's see . . . . It's August now and he's in Alberton; in September they'll send him to Heilbron, Vereeniging in October, Rustenburg in November and Standerton in December. After that, they hope to be ready to bring him up for trial.

I am not sorry for that stupid boy!

If you ever get into trouble with Kritzinger's police, let us know immediately. I nearly said you shouldn't tell his police you work for us . . . . He doesn't like Baas Piet.

Why, Nooi?

Well, Piet had been engaged to his daughter but changed his mind to marry me. Kritzinger thought his daughter had been rejected because she was the daughter of a policeman while I had been borne by the prime minister's wife. He called Baas Piet a chancer and hates him

41

like poison; he doesn't like me either and I don't care for him. Then, after a pause, that Dillo Mareka, Zandile? His is a Pedi name. How does he come to live among the Zulus?

    His mother is a Zulu; he grew up in Natal and married a Zulu.

    So, he's happy among the Zulus?

    His wife is; so is his mother; I hope he is.

    Women are the same in every nation, Zandile. I hope he's happy.

*   *   *

V. The Pope And The Colour Bar

Izingane zasisu sinye zahlukaniselana intethe.

(In a famine children born of one woman will share even a locust.)

The African, the Afrikaner and the English are three-eyed giants; each uses the first eye to watch where it is going, the second to keep a look-out on the one opponent and the third on the other. Most English-speaking people have been shaken by the Groot Kerk choice of Willem Adriaan de Haas as prime minister. Nobody is shaken more violently than the Roman Catholic Archbishop of Pretoria, Reginald Postlethwait.

He is convinced that dark times have descended on the church, not only in South Africa but in the whole of the continent on his side of the equator. He has been a keen student of Afrikaner politics and in the preceding twenty-five years has been warning the church against the rise to power of an Afrikaner phenomenon like de Haas.

His theory is that the Afrikaner is unique among the peoples of South Africa. If the English lost their position of economic dominance, they would lose their money, but still be free to emigrate to other parts of the English-speaking world. The Africans have lost their land and freedom but survive because of their numbers and will win in the end because history, Free Africa, world opinion and numbers are on their side. The Afrikaner has political power; if he lost it he would lose everything. He has nowhere to go, for Holland would be too much of a foreign country for him to survive in.

People, the archbishop insists, are like animals; they are most dangerous when fighting for their lives. He thinks it is unrealistic for the church to define itself as antagonistic to Afrikaner aspirations. That will give phenomena like de Haas the reason they need finally to extirpate Roman Catholicism in South Africa.

The church is under siege in the whole of Africa; a generation of African leaders is emerging which is hostile to all forms of authority on the white side. These people argue that the Roman Catholic Church is the historical enemy of the African people; that it blessed slavery and ordered the seizure of African lands in the fifteenth century; that it was the ally of colonialism and is the handmaid of white supremacy. The

43

pope, they say, is a partisan for white financial, political and military power; in the changing dispositions of power in the world, he is ultimately on the side of the white race and the white government in Pretoria. That is why he straddles the fence on South Africa's colour problem.

Postlethwait says the Africans are perfectly correct when they say that the church is a white institution. It was set up to uphold moral values developed in the white world; these values produced the "finest" civilisation history had ever seen and in a world where black, brown, red and yellow pagans proliferated, the time would come when the white races would have to stand together against the non-white pagans of the world.

He speaks of a *White Consensus on Africa* as the only guarantee of white survival in all Africa. He sees the Roman Catholic Church as being uniquely placed to be the catalyst that would accelerate movement toward the formation of a united white front in Southern Africa against communism. No other organisation is as united in its operations in this part of the world as the church.

The pope is the supreme commander of the forces of the church in Angola, Botswana, Lesotho, Malawi, Mozambique, South Africa, South-West Africa, Rhodesia and Zambia. The various peoples in this part of the continent might speak a thousand different languages, but those of them who are Catholics are bound together by one supreme loyalty: their commitment to Rome. This is power, the archbishop always says; call it moral power or spiritual power or political power or cultural power; call it what you will, it is power in any language. Postlethwait urges that this power gives the Roman Catholic Church bargaining advantages which raise the prospects of a deal with Pretoria.

De Haas must be made to realise that Roman Catholicism can be an ally of Afrikaner nationalism against communism; that it can even be one of the guarantors of Afrikaner survival.

At this stage he thinks it would be imprudent to play up the role of guarantor. The Afrikaners are a proud people, stubborn Calvinists who see their relations with the Catholics from the angle of the Inquisition. Their fears of race equality and communism, however, are so deep-rooted and their need for allies almost so desperate as to awaken their interest in the use of the Roman Catholic Church as a catalyst in bringing together the English-speaking in South Africa, Botswana, Lesotho, Malawi, Swaziland, Rhodesia and Zambia, the Germans in South-West Africa and the Portuguese in Angola and Mozambique in a single united front led by the Afrikaner.

Ten years earlier, Postlethwait had convened a conference of the hierarchy of the church in Southern Africa, ostensibly to redefine the role of the Roman Catholic Church in changing Africa, but, in fact, to sound the reactions of the cardinals, the archbishops and the bishops to his proposal.

Helvetius van Warmelo had been so impressed with the idea he had personally intervened and put pressure on the city council of Pretoria to allow the Roman Catholics to hold a rally in the Groot Saal (Great Hall) of the city hall which was attended by Catholics of all races. At the time, the hierarchy expressed interest in the idea but advised caution in implementing it. The churchmen had not made up their mind on Free African attitudes to domination by Rome. But van Warmelo thought the interest significant enough to justify the granting of permission to the Catholics to establish Boreneng mission, outside Atteridgeville, to preach the word to the kaffers and, at the same time, keep an eye on the communist agitators.

The prime minister's conciliation of the Catholics raised a storm, first in the cabinet. Willem Adriaan de Haas charged that every-thing precious in the Calvinistic protestant tradition and everything valuable for which the Afrikaner had shed his blood had been thrown down the drain. At the time he rejected the idea of a white consensus; he did not see how the disciplined Afrikaners could form an alliance with the easy-going, garlic-chewing Portuguese who spent a lot of their time in dalliance with African women. He took his objections to the caucus of the CNP where it divided the party sharply in two and threatened to bring the Afrikaner government crashing to the ground. At this point his opponents stood up, one by one and demanded that he should state clearly where he stood; if he was an agent of the English-Jewish-capitalist-communist-liberal conspirators, he would split the CNP and shatter Afrikaner unity. His friends rallied stoutly to his defence. Press reports of the time tell of blows exchanged on the floor of the conference room, for the collision of phenomena is quite a spectacle in the Afrikaner community. De Haas retreated, to fight on another day.

Postlethwait's victory gave him tremendous prestige in the Catholic hierarchy. He was invited to Rome and returned with the title of archbishop. With De Haas at the head of the government, he now thinks he should waste little time to rally the hierarchy behind the banner of a catalyst and to make concrete proposals to De Haas. His theory is that the evolution of an Afrikaner prime minister follows a fixed pattern. He starts from the extreme right in the CNP, breathing fire and brimstone and talking in tones of thunder and lightning against the *enemies* of Afrikanerdom. English economic pressures come into play first to isolate him in the CNP and finally to force him to break away from the party and retreat into the political wilderness where he starts from the bottom, rallying rural Afrikanerdom to his banner with jeremiads against the Black Peril, the English Peril, the Jewish Peril, the Indian Peril and, sometimes, the Brown (Coloured) Peril. A tornado of feeling rises which sweeps him into the prime minister's office in Union Buildings. Then, the responsibilities of office come into play, bevelling off the angularities of the phenomenon.

Yesterday's fire-eating extremist, at whose roar mountains quaked, becomes the suave realist whose main concern is the internal balance of African-Afrikaner-English reserves of power. Postlethwait argues that de Haas is moving toward coming to terms with reality; the tide of African nationalism rolling southward gives him enough headaches to make him more amenable to reason on the White Consensus idea. The archbishop has gone on the offensive once more and has called a second conference of the Catholic hierarchy in Southern Africa.

The doyen of the Catholic prelates in Southern Africa is Dom Bartolomeo, Cardinal Machado de Marandellas, whose headquarters are in Lourenço Marques in Mozambique. He is a politically colourless man with opaque views on every major issue affecting Southern Africa. Friends and foes concede, however, that he is a wizard of an administrator. The cardinal is a key figure in the power alignments which Archbishop Postlethwait has in mind. He has the ear of powerful personalities in the Curia and the Foreign Office of the Vatican and is the confidante of the Portuguese head of state in Lisbon. In addition, he has a high regard for the work Postlethwait is doing in Boreneng, right under the nose of the Dutch Reformed Church in the South African capital. For this reason alone, he is inclined to give a lot of attention to Postlethwait's views. The cardinal has a passion for pomp and ceremony and the archbishop has moved heaven and earth to flatter this aspect of the cardinal's vanity.

The archbishop's residence is built in the style of a Texan ranch house in Waterkloof. Its two occupants are the archbishop, who is in his early fifties, and his twin sister, Adeline, a former nun. Tragedy has crashed into Adeline's life. She holds doctorates in education from the best universities in Britain, Holland and the United States. For many years she headed the prestigious St. Mary's College for Girls in Johannesburg and sat in commissions appointed by the Smuts government to inquire into different aspects of education. Then she was appointed head of the Secretariat for Education of the Roman Catholic Church, with headquarters in Bloemfontein. Her main interest was the education of the poor of all races and her work commanded the admiration of most members of the Smuts cabinet. De Haas has always regarded her as the Catholic-kaffer fifth column in South African education and his government has accordingly been creating all sorts of difficulties for her. Her health has broken down as a result and she has just been released from a mental hospital, at the request of her brother. She is making some progress, though she sometimes has occasional losses of memory.

The archbishop's African cook-housekeeper is a devout Roman Catholic in her early sixties who lives in a two-roomed structure in the archbishop's backyard. She is concerned about the strain on Adeline's health during the conference of the church heads and one morning confronts the archbishop.

Monsignor, with so many people around during the conference, don't you think Sister Adeline should be taken to a quieter place in the country?

The African is standing inside the half open door.

I have been thinking, too, that so many people around . . . .

I thought something sinister was in the offing, screams Adeline from behind the cook. She almost bangs the door against the cook and crashes past the African to confront the archbishop behind his large desk.

Look, Adeline darling, you don't have your slippers on; you remember? Your doctor said you should never expose your feet to cold!

I don't care what he said. I'm expected to remember things designed to humiliate me . . . . And to lose my memory when your important friends are around? I've just had enough of all this . . . . And, I suppose that Dr. Hastings will be around again to drug me with sedatives, soporifics and other poisons . . . . I never expected this from you, Reggie!

She turns sharply, glares at the African and screams:

And you, too, Linah, after saving your son from the executioner's rope!

She storms through the door and leaves the archbishop and his cook staring at each other.

* * *

Pretoria is a city of rallies; the Afrikaners are fond of mass gatherings, parades and similar assemblies. They want constantly to be assuring each other that they stand together. Every year, they drive from all parts of the country to the capital to celebrate Kruger Day. December 16 is, of course, the event of the year. But no gathering in living memory excels in its size and the quality of the pomp the Catholic rally in the City Hall. The Groot Saal accommodates 50,000 people and another 10,000 have gathered on the square around the main hall. Seven cardinals, two of whom are black, lead the procession which is headed by Cardinal de Marandellas. A white page carries a huge, brightly-coloured umbrella to shade the cardinal from the heat of the sun. A score of archbishops and bishops make a long procession of the princes of the church. The 50,000 in the hall, most of whom are black, rise to their feet as de Marandellas walks in; the thousand-voice choir welcomes the princes of the church with the *Angelicus*.

That night, the princes are hosts to the leaders of the government, the members of parliament who live in Pretoria and the ambassadors of foreign powers. The dinner is largely a business gathering at which de Marandellas will make an important announcement on behalf of the Southern African hierarchy, and is attended by men only. The prime minister and Cardinal de Marandellas sit at the head of the table, in front of a small door. After dinner, Archbishop Postlethwait calls upon the senior prince of the church to convey to the prime minister the decision of the conference on the communist menace and the dual role of the christians in the situation of change in Southern Africa.

The cardinal is in the middle of his speech proclaiming that Catholicism and Afrikanerdom are allies with the same mission in Southern Africa when the door opens behind him. Adeline, naked from the top of her head to the soles of her feet, walks briskly to the cardinal's vacant chair and seats herself next to Willem Adriaan de Haas. In the consternation which follows, her brother rises quickly to his feet, makes a beeline for her and throws his cloak around her body and tries to pull her away gently. She rises to her feet, pulls the cloak off her body and throws it on the floor.

I'm not getting out of here, if that's what you're trying to do, she says quietly but firmly.

Cardinal de Marandellas orders Postlethwait to leave her alone and to pick up the cloak, which she picks up herself, covers her body with it and returns to the cardinal's chair. When the cardinal is over with his speech he descends the podium and de Haas is about to speak when Adeline rises to her feet, throws the cloak on the floor and protests:

I just can't stand him; not that man; not de Haas!

She walks angrily through the little door and leaves it shut.

* * *

VI. People With An Untidy Conscience

Yisilima esihle esizazi ubuwula baso.

(He is a wise man who knows his limitations.)

Pumasilwe's health has been failing from shortly after the assassination of the prime minister. His doctors have not been able to diagnose his troubles. He has been complaining of a persistent headache and, sometimes, palpitations and dizziness. Zandile has noted that he is becoming increasingly hysterical. She took him to the best doctors in her community and when these failed she tried the whites, who seemed to make his condition worse. Some of his friends have told her that it is possible one of Pumasilwe's ancestors has set dangerous vibrations around Pumasilwe's life and that she should not rely wholly on the medicine of the white people, which contains more poisons than curative principles. In the end she urges him to go to his father's kraal in the Inanda mission station near Durban to get expert advice on what to do with his condition.

Hezekiya Makaye is a wiry old man of medium height in his mid-seventies, with an agile and restless mind. There never is a moment when he sits down to enjoy the company of his friends or to sip tea or even to sit down under his verandah on a hot summer afternoon to rest or stare vacantly into space. If he is not mending something, he is in the fields with his hand hoe removing the weeds between the rows of sweet potatoes or batata, for which he is famous. He returns to the house at about five, has a cold bath, attends to the mail and then settles down to read the English morning paper published in Durban. By the time he is through with all this, supper is ready. Every dinner is a party in Hezekiya's house. While he and his aging wife are the only inhabitants of the sprawling house built of stone, the table is set as though for six people. Hezekiya likes it that way; it makes him proud to know that any stranger can move into his house and have enough food. If there is nobody to join the couple, why, there always are the spirits of the Makaye family hovering around and who set the right vibrations in motion when they see their son take so much care of his family.

Pumasilwe arrived in his father's house shortly before lunch on the day when his parents enter this story. The arrival of a relative is an important occasion in the life of every Zulu community. Members of the extended family, friends and neighbours come in to greet him and to hear of their own sons and daughters in the Transvaal. Some bring gifts, mainly food items, and many collect messages, letters, parcels and money from their relatives in Pretoria and Johannesburg. The process of greeting took the whole afternoon and Pumasilwe is tired. When dinner is over Pumasilwe's mother helps the girl who cooks for the family clear up the table to enable the father and his son to talk business freely.

You do not look well, Puma; what is wrong?

I can't tell, father; one of the diseases of the city, I think.

Do you know the woman?

You get me all wrong, father; venereal disease is not involved here.

We who live in the country think of venereal disease when people talk of city diseases.

There are tuberculosis and kwashiorkor in the city?

Yes, there are.

And, of course, the stress diseases, like *fufunyane*. I think my nerves are giving in.

Have you been working very hard of late?

As you know, I have always been a hard worker; I don't know what has gone wrong. I thought that I might come to you and we talk things over. I want to go and see a specialist of my own people; a sangoma, to diagnose my condition.

A sangoma, my child? And you say that in my own house?

That is why I came down to see you. Pretoria is a long way, father, and it costs a lot of money to travel from there to here.

Witchcraft is forbidden in this house; I never thought the day would come when my own son would turn to witchcraft in his hour of need. I am a Christian; I am serious about my religion and I intend to remain serious about it. No member of my family will go to a witch-doctor; not while I live!

Not even when my health is involved?

There are first-class doctors in Durban. I never preached faith in witchdoctors to any of my children. I have never been to a witch-doctor! What would your mother say if I told her you had travelled all the way from Pretoria to see a sangoma? What would the people of Inanda say? How would I face the world? How dare you say a thing like this, son?

Hezekiya resists with difficulty the tears which swell in his eyes.

Mother of Puma, come and hear this!

The old lady walks into the dining room and sits on an ancient armchair against the wall, from where she can see the faces of the two men.

Puma, tell your mother the nonsense you've just told me.

Tears roll down his mother's cheeks as Puma describes his illness and how, in desperation, he and his wife decided that he should consult a sangoma.

But we have never had any dealings with witchdoctors; we do not know their ways, Puma. Where did you learn about them? From your wife?

No. Suffering taught me that I could solve all my problems only if I used resources which belonged to me and which were controlled by me.

Child, you are tired and your father is upset; his health too is not so good. Why don't we all retire for the night and rest, so that we can talk when fresh to-morrow?

Hezekiya opens an obviously overworked bible and reads a few passages and then goes on his knees. Instead of leading in prayer, he is silent for a while and then calls out:

Pray, Puma!

Puma has not done this sort of thing in all the years he has been in Pretoria. But this is not his only difficulty; Puma is no longer a christian. He coughs a little, plotting a way out of his troubles.

I said pray, Puma!

All things commenced with the intention to do good end well. May it be so in these difficult times. Amen.

Puma, you have changed a lot, son. You no longer are the person I knew you to be. You, too, have become an enemy of Christ?

Would you say I have changed? I think I have grown, in body and mind, mother.

Growing backward? Growing toward superstition? Growing toward darkness? Growing away from the Lord and the light? What growth is that? You can't even pray? Your father was right. We did not bring you up to do these things; we did not send you to school, we did not deny ourselves so many comforts to develop your brain so that you should forget prayer!

It no longer matters to me whether or not I am an enemy or follower of Christ. He and I are not going the same way; I know now that he and I are moving in opposite directions. He is the Lord of people who steal persons and destroy souls; he is the Lord of people who steal other people's lands; he is the Lord of people who fulfil themselves in self-defilement. Whoever he is, he can't be my Lord. And, in any case, mother, I don't need a Lord. All I have to do is to look inward, as deeply as I can, into myself and there I will find that I am my own Lord!

Then, why can't you cure yourself?

Because I am ignorant.

Why can't you free yourself?

Because I am ignorant.

51

When will you know, son?

The sangoma will tell me.

Hezekiya rises abruptly, makes an angry clicking sound, flings his glass-case on the table and walks into his bedroom. His wife collects herself and beckons to her son. She speaks to him in a lowered tone.

Come, son; sit next to me so that we should not make noise. Father is tired and he wants to sleep . . . . But tell me, have you turned your back on the challenge of being a christian?

I have outgrown the white man's superstition. I am now a free man; I see things through my own eyes; I explain them on my own terms where, before, I saw them through borrowed eyes and understood them through borrowed perspectives. Now, mother, I am the person I should like to be; I am not the person the whites want me to be. Only he who is free from the white man's superstition is ready for freedom in his society and his country. This is what the quarrel with the whites is all about.

What did your wife say when you first told her these things?

She bought a goat, called in a Pedi witchdoctor, had me kill the goat and we called in our friends to celebrate the moment of liberation!

This freedom you constantly refer to . . . what is it that you really want to be free from? From the white man who brought the Word and Civilisation?

I want to realise the promise and the glory of being a person and not a creature. I have to take the white man out of my mind, to take his superstition out of my system, before I can summon the powers in me as a limb of God, a hand of God, an eye of God, call it what you will. Then, I can cure myself; then I can restore to my people and myself that which was stolen from us.

Curing yourself? You never were an arrogant boy. Science has most of the cures for the diseases that afflict us . . . and science was invented by the white people. But there is no cure for any illness that is more potent than the grace of God . . . and the white man brought God to us . . . .

Mama, I am tired to-day. We can talk about that until sunrise. But I want to say one thing: Have you ever thought of an alternative to the germ theory of disease?

How can you have an alternative to science? You negate the person himself; you destroy all meaning. But since yours is only one mind, you only destroy yourself with the illusion—like the hunted monkey which plucked a leaf, put it against its eyes when cornered and believed it had hidden itself safely.

You were a teacher at Inanda Seminary for a whole generation, mother, and yet you never said a thing about vibrations. Everything vibrates and therefore is alive; conversely, everything is alive and therefore vibrates. The ignorant concentrate on treating the germ and not the vibrations which make it dangerous and which give it form. Vibrations are the key to the understanding of all things. One day, we shall know enough about vibrations to use them to cure every disease. Who knows more about vibrations and their effects on our lives than the sangoma? I came down to seek the fount of real knowledge . . . .

His mother rises from her chair slowly, without looking at him and moves heavily toward her bedroom.

Have a restful sleep, son; we'll talk to-morrow.

Good night, mama.

* * *

The seer's kraal stands on a hillock in the valley of the Mzinyati, about two thousand feet below Inanda. Hezekiya leads the way, followed by Puma and, after him, a nephew of Hezekiya's. The old man now and then mumbles something inaudible to himself and then shakes his head vigorously. Uppermost in his mind is how he will face the world with a sangoma consultation in his life. Everybody in Inanda and in the valley knows him. He was schools inspector in the district for twenty years and is deacon of the mission church at Inanda. He has never spoken to Mazani Lukele, the sangoma, though he has met her several times in the buses. He has never liked her because she represents the forces of darkness; she leads his people away from the light which the white missionaries brought from across the seas.

Mazani's place is more than a kraal; it is a village in its own right. White-walled rondavels surround a cattle enclosure filled with oxen, milk cows, donkeys and four horses. By every standard, Mazani is a woman of substance. Stories circulate that she has a bank balance which runs into thousands of rand. Hezekiya starts believing these stories against the affluence which meets his eyes. A beautiful hedge surrounds the village and, to his surprise, roses blossom around some of the rondavels. As custom requires, he stops at the gate, raises his walking-stick and announces his presence with salutations:

Hail, Daughter of Wisdom! Hail, Lukele!

A young girl, wearing only a skirt made of beads, opens one of the doors and is walking toward the gate when she recognises Hezekiya. Her breasts tell her age. They stand out like quaking cones from her chest, announcing that she is beginning to be conscious of her womanhood. She races back to the hut.

Mother! The inspector is at the gate!

Don't be silly! Are you awake?

Yes, mama; he's there, with two men; two mission people, to judge them by the way they're dressed.

Her husband sits on a low carved stool, sipping coffee from a large mug.

53

Father of Pasiwe! Do you hear what Pasiwe is saying?

Yes, I do; but what does it matter if Makaye is at the gate?

The inspector! To be received by a child? You are out of your mind. What would the world say if we sent a child to receive him?

He's obviously in trouble and is not coming here so early as a former inspector.

Go, father of Pasiwe and stop arguing!

Her husband gulps his coffee and walks to the gate. Hezekiya goes through the formalities and is led to a large rondavel covered with leopard skins. This is the consulting room where Mazani receives patients and dignitaries. Pasiwe sneaks in behind the men with small, ceremonial grass mats and spreads each on top of a leopard skin for the three men to sit on. Apart from the expensive skins on the floor, there is no furniture in the room except for a low stool near a set of drums on a rack by the side of huge black pots covered with grass mats. A small drum starts beating to the accompaniment of male and female voices outside. Mazani walks in, covered with furs and beads and followed by about a dozen young men and women. After the formalities each of the young takes a drum and they form a semi-circle behind Mazani. Her husband opens the proceedings by reciting the praise-poems composed in honour of Mazani's ancestors down the centuries, followed by a short homily by Mazani, addressed to the former inspector.

I am aware, Inspector, that you might not be familiar with the procedures adopted in seeking the wisdom of our ancestors, whom most people refer to as the dead. All is life in the cosmic order and there can be no death where all is life; there can be no beginning and no end, for all things are forever responding to the call of the morrow. Life is spirit; it is consciousness. It exists only to express itself; to create and radiate vibrations and to transform these into thoughts, ideas and phenomena. I am a phenomenon, just as you are, Inspector; just as the stone, the tree, the bird and all living and "dead" creatures are. We differ from each other because of the concentration of the vibrations in each of us. Because the stone, the piece of glass, the plant and the animal are all individualisations of the consciousness, they communicate with each other, through vibrations. We can talk to a dog and be understood, not because the canine is aware of the meaning of words but because we set in motion vibrations to which it responds. We can set up vibrations to which the stone, the piece of glass, the tree and the animal will respond. Do you understand me, Inspector?

I think I do, so far.

Good. If all things vibrate and if all things communicate through vibrations, there can be no secrets of nature or mysteries. Only the ignorant and the superstitious have secrets or believe in mysteries. For, how do you hide vibrations? They are always being emitted and hurled into the air; everything is always speaking through them. Those trained in the law of vibration decode the messages for the uninitiated. It is my privilege to have been trained in reading the vibrations for the purpose of helping my fellowmen. Do you still follow, Inspector?

So far, so good.

That brings us to health. We say the body is healthy when harmony exists in the vibrations emitted by every organ in the body. Ill health comes in when the harmony is disturbed; it can be disturbed, first, by the person himself harbouring thoughts which produce harmful vibrations or by the strong planting evil vibrations into the weak or the untrained or by dangerous vibrations in the atmosphere or by the "dead" setting up harmful vibrations. Disease is thus caused by wrong vibrations from no less than four different sources.

Am I allowed to ask questions, Daughter of Wisdom?

It is hard for a christian to understand; so ask them.

It can be shown that disease is caused by germs, by viruses and by upsets in the metabolic process . . . .

It is as you say, Inspector. But the white people concern themselves with beginnings and ends; they are aware only of the obvious; they do not know the intrinsic truth which inheres in all things. Germs and viruses are coagulations of the living consciousness and vibrate in ways that sometimes do harm to other substances. It might help to neutralise their activities with antidotes; but all these are crutches used because men are still ignorant. One day men will know the truth more fully and they will realise that the vibrations of cosmic and earthly forces are at the heart of all things; that they cause and cure disease. Then, the conflict between the germ and the vibration theories of infection will be resolved; they will be seen then as complements. The doctors of the future shall be trained in the nature, the functioning and the use of vibrations. Ordinary men and women will then be taught that for purposes of life on this earth, all things start and end with vibrations; that vibrations are power and that this power is locked in every person, no matter who he is, where he is or what he is. When people know the power in themselves, they will then no longer hate or fear or steal or kill or rape or envy or even die; they will have discovered that they have in themselves all the power they need to get what they want. What I am now going to do is to take the individuali-sation of the consciousness that is me out of the world of analysis to the world of perception in order to diagnose the trouble with the vibrations at work in your son, Inspector.

May it be as you say!

The instrumentalists start playing on their drums while Mazani goes through the first slow and graceful movements of the *sina* dance. The tempo of the rhythm becomes faster in response to the vigour and intensity of her movements. All of a sudden she sways round and round and staggers to her knees with the help of her husband. He stretches her on the ground and sits on the stool while the drums continue to beat. After about twenty minutes, she comes to and sits up. She speaks to Pumasilwe.

Son, I do not know you. Your father tells me you work in Pretoria. Your vibrations tell of a split in the conscience. You stand in the shadow of a white man; he is dead; he has his eye on a ring you wear. You are afraid, son; you hesitate and that sets up vibrations which poison your body. Why don't you do the right thing?

What is the right thing, Daughter of Wisdom?

Confront yourself with your real self; then you will not be afraid; that will normalise your vibrations.

How do I confront myself with my real self?

The ignorant person is passive and, therefore, weak; he regards himself as a creature who lives by the grace of God or the goodwill of the spirits of his ancestors; he is a prisoner of his evaluation of himself. The person who knows is positive and therefore strong; he is the creator who commands all the forces in the cosmic order; he has confronted himself with his own self and knows what he is. Knowing himself, he commands the earth to do his will, and, it obeys. But the confrontation of one's self with one's real self is a dangerous activity; it is like playing with lightning in a thunderstorm. In our present state of ignorance, very few people are advanced sufficiently to be entrusted with the power of lightning.

But for me to continue in ignorance is to drift to death. This is what I believe you've been telling me. I want to confront myself, for, as you say, I have a problem.

Remember, lightning is a deadly power and you might crack and kill yourself in the process of handling it.

Better die in the attempt than to die doing nothing.

Go home for the present and think carefully about what I have said. Return to me before the rising of the sun, seven mornings from to-day.

* * *

Puma's mother has set the table; she is nervous that her son has not returned. The night is very dark outside and the last bus has arrived at the Inanda terminal. Hezekiya reads his paper against the light of a bright gas lamp by his side.

Father of Puma, the boy has not returned and our cats have disappeared.

Where did he say he was going?

Durban. Puma is no longer the person I knew him to be. That business about the shadow of a dead white man—did he tell you anything about it?

No. He said he did not know what the sangoma was talking

56

about because he was not involved in the killing of any white man. He did say, however, that he had known the man who killed the prime minister.

Dead people perceive things more clearly than the living. Perhaps the dead white man knows about the friendship . . . .

No. I don't think there's much to bother about in what the witchdoctor said. It was all guess work. Puma comes from Pretoria and in her view everybody from that place must have been involved in the assassination.

Puma has not been home for three days and his mother has been urging that the absence should be reported to the police. Hezekiya dislikes contact with the police, at the best of times; he is in no mood to send them running around looking for his son. Somebody shoves a postcard under the front door one night. Hezekiya rushes to pick it up; he recognises his son's handwriting:

DON'T WORRY ABOUT ME, FATHER AND MOTHER. I AM SAFE AND IN GOOD HEALTH. WILL RETURN SOON. PUMA.

Hezekiya opens the door and sees the figure of his son silhouetted against Durban's lights. Puma is running toward the Mzinyati River. It is going for midnight when he reaches the point where the footpaths cross, just above where the Mngeni and Mzinyati rivers merge. Nearby is the cave which is his temporary home. Time is running against him; midnight is only half an hour away. He collects the firewood, the tripod and suspends the three-legged pot on his right arm and takes all these to the crossroads. Next, he throws the bag containing two animals on his shoulder and takes these to the crosspaths where he makes a fire above which he hangs the pot.

Twenty minutes later, the pot's bottom is white with heat. He takes a quick glance at his watch and as its arms indicate twelve o'clock midnight he grabs one of the cats in the bag, and hurls it into the white-hot pot, holding down the lid while the cat tears the stillness of the night with its frightened screams. Holding the lid while the cat makes the hoises is like an eternity in hell. Puma is so scared he thinks he is going insane. He remembers that Mazani warned him against being afraid when playing with lightning. He wipes the perspiration on his forehead, shoves his hand into the bag where the second cat, now terrified, is in no mood to give away its life without a fight. He finally grabs it and throws it into the pot, holding the lid until the animal is dead. He fills the pot with water. Then, he sits down by the fire concentrating on the self which overcomes fear. At about three, he takes the pot to the running water and empties its contents into the shallow water, opposite a previously marked point. During the next three nights, he sits in front of the cave and contemplates the moon until the early hours of the morning. On the morning of the seventh day, he takes a bath before dawn and then returns to the sangoma's kraal. The diviner sits in front of a fire in one of the huts.

Well, son! It is good to see you back with every bone still in its place. How did things go?

Those cats! They turned the nakedness of my conscience inside out. I have no conscience now. How shall I live with their memory?

Are you sorry you killed them?

Yes, I am; but if it had to be done, then I am glad it is all over.

Do you see what you have done? You have become the instrument of your own rebirth into a new destiny. But you must evolve beyond being an instrument, even of your own self; you must realise that you are the destiny; that all you need to do is to live out the destiny; be what you are—the incarnation of the infinite consciousness.

I, the son of my father, to kill a cat? In that manner! If my parents heard about it, do you know what they would do? They would disown me. My mother would and my father, too!

You have to outgrow fear; you must not be afraid of anything or any deed; not even of your parents or your own self. Your perform-ance with the cats enabled you to open the first door in your life, out of which you will kick fear. The infinite consciousness has no law outside of that which it is, itself. It does not have a conscience to be clothed in what you call decency; it does not know nakedness; it is just itself. The enemies of their fellowmen set out to capture and imprison the minds of their fellowmen; they invent the conscience and endow it with given qualities. This is a technique for the control of the ignorant mind. The mature person outgrows the prison of the mind called the conscience; he knows he is the individualisation of the infinity and because he is aware of this, he is responsible. Talk of nakedness of the conscience or of the body is a lie planted by the strong in the minds of the weak, like us, to make us the willing desecrators of our own sacredness.

But if we are all sacred, why do we suffer so much?

We are afraid, and, we fear because we are ignorant; because we are ignorant and are scared of our own selves we cannot command suffering to get out of our lives. See what I mean? We are prisoners by choice. Thieves and robbers descended on our country; they desecrated our soil with their presence and polluted the air with their breath; they pillaged the land and defiled the most sacred things in the human experience. Then our land died and we, all its children, are left to wander the earth like cadavers with no life. But nothing they could do could change the fact that we are the incarnations of spirit-forms; that the person, no matter who he is, has a creative potential, a power, which nobody can ever take away from him. There is locked in him all the forces in the cosmic order. He is invincible when he understands them and conquers when he controls them and gives them focus. This is the fortress of the soul handed down to us by our ancestors; we gave up this fortress; we surrendered it to the enemy; we accepted his definitions of reality and of the person; he planted an alien conscience in us.

Daughter of Wisdom, you are one of the few people who speak the truth that I understand. I see now what is wrong with my parents; they are unconscious hypocrites . . . .

No. Do not pass judgment on them; they are passing through a cloud of darkness—through a moment of ignorance. For, does it not strike you that serious, educated and intelligent men like the Inspector believe in the superstition about the son of God who rose from the dead? Bells ring every day calling millions to the superstitious ritual!

Where do we strike, to bring the whole rotten thing crashing to the ground?

At the personal self! That is where the enemy is ensconced!

How many thousands of years will that take, O Daughter? God knows we've shed rivers of blood in the defence of this land; wherever we go, the soil is soaked in it, a grim reminder of our tragedy. Must we start all over again?

Cool down a little, child. In the moment of absolute deprivation, when the person has lost everything and hopes for nothing, he discovers himself. Forced to the bottom of experience, he cannot sink lower; if he moves at all, it can only be to the top.

The bottom! That is where I am . . . .

Arise, then, for you have reached the moment of truth. Take the white man out of your mind and walk the earth as though he does not exist. Command the winds and the oceans and the mountains and the valleys shall obey. Set your mind on "the heavens beyond the reach of spirit-forms" and things will fall apart precisely at the moment when the white man thinks he is invincible.

Tell me, Daughter of Wisdom, why do you waste your time in these rural valleys? Preaching to people who will not restore to us that which is ours? Why don't you come to the towns? People in the locations have eyes and ears; they want to see and are ready to listen!

I have work to do here. I must speak in the wind so that all men may hear. There is calm here; there is peace here; not the peace of the bullet in the locations; the mountains, the valleys and the rivers can listen, here; so can the animals, the trees and the birds.

The first rays of the morning sun shoot through the crevices in the door signalling the arrival of a new day.

We've wandered off the things you had come to tell me . . . .

I did as you told me; every step, all the way.

Where's the evidence?

Puma shoves his hand into a coat pocket and pulls out a small parcel wrapped in a piece of newsprint. The diviner takes it, turns it twice in her hand and smiles:

Ah! This is what a man does, son! Take these two breastbones after I have treated them; they are your keys into everything; they are

59

the torches which will light your path through the mazes of experience. The one you will always keep next to your body and the other in a safe place, known by yourself only. The day you lose one, you will die. Did you hear what I say? So, take good care of them. These are only keys to release the power locked in you. If you want to proceed beyond this, you alone can choose.

Daughter of Wisdom I have joined the Caravan To Blood River; I can't stop here; I can't go back; I always have to be moving, always forward.

Are you sure you want to go forward?

May all the Makayes in their graves arise to witness against me.

You do not have to make oaths. When you understand, a Yes or a No is all you need say. Have you ever killed a person?

No.

Do you think you could kill one?

A white person? Yes, I would.

No. That would not help; he's your enemy. You've only torn off the cloak of darkness which covers your conscience; but now you must grapple with your conscience itself. Would you kill anybody you love? Your wife, your child, your mother or your father?

Isn't there another way for freeing myself from my conscience?

Of course there is, but it takes a lot of time and patience. You do not have the time, for you soon will return to work. Like Cakijana, you are in a hurry to keep an appointment with destiny. The shortest route to your goal is to confront yourself with the real self in your person. Men in a hurry to meet destiny sometimes take this course. But, be warned, son, he who takes shortcuts into the future plays with lightning. There is an alternative. If you want to, you can open yourself to the challenge of the morrow. But this involves a long, often painful struggle with your own self; you have to discipline every cell of your body and know each and everyone of them; you have to master the technique for aligning them and focusing them on your ideal in order to transform it into reality.

I do not have the time; we have waited too long!

Whatever choice you make, remember, that is your fate.

* * *

Akukho qili lazikhoth' emhlane.

(No man is so smart he can lick his back.)

Pretoria is a city of hate. It has been like that in all its history. In the old days, when Boer and Briton fought for the mastery of South Africa, the city was the citadel, the *laager*, into which Afrikanerdom withdrew in the hour of danger. It was the symbol of Afrikaner determination to resist British rule. Johannesburg was the commercial capital of the British-Jewish-capitalist-liberal establishment; it was the hotbed of vice used to corrode Afrikaner morals while Pretoria was the city of God from which nothing but the light and truth radiated.

Things have not changed much since then, except for the fact that the main contestants for power are no longer the Afrikaners and the British; they are the Africans and the Afrikaners.

Oh, it was much easier to deal with the British; they were white, a minority on the white side and the joke still does the rounds when Afrikaners get together to drink, which they do not often do, that like the Jew, the British will do anything and everything for money. Cut an Englishman's testicles, the joke goes, and give him money; he will take the cash.

The Africans are clay of a different kind; they are black, they own the land, are in the majority and are irrepressible. Above everything, their labour is the backbone of Afrikaner wealth and, strange as it sounds, they are also the Afrikaner's guarantee of survival. The powerful and booming economy which the British and the Jews have established is the magnet which attracts foreign investments and the Americans, the British, the French, the West Germans and others who have sunk their money in this land of gold favour changes in the political structure; they do not like the policies of men like de Haas, but if these men guarantee profits, it is prudent to forget the evil in their politics. The irrepressibility of the African keeps the Afrikaner's leaders awake of nights. The black man is the most dangerous animal alive to-day, they say. The white man builds all sorts of high walls with which to protect himself against the black peril. Sooner or later, the African climbs over these in the bid to destroy Afrikanerdom and

61

drive the white man into the sea. Constant vigilance is the Afrikaner's only guarantee of survival.

In the old days again, the gun, the policeman and the Pass were adequate as forms of protection. The Pass was used to control the movements of the Africans from the rural areas into the cities. Once inside the industrial areas, the black man could move with some ease because the police kept an eye on him. At the time, only black males carried the Pass. By keeping the numbers of the African within controllable limits, the Pass ensured that their influx into the urban areas constituted no security problem.

Black women were in demand as domestic servants and as factory hands; they were docile and provided cheap labour. Besides, it was an old-established Afrikaner custom, dating back to the days of slavery at the Cape, that a man had not attained real manhood before he had lain between the legs of a black woman. There was something mystical about the reputed sensuality of the black woman which attracted the Afrikaner male as powerfully as a naked flame did the insects in the African night.

The custom now creates all sorts of problems. Government secrets leak to the winds and before anybody knows what is happening, they are being bandied about in the streets of Moscow. A more disturbing aspect of the black woman's ability to attract the Afrikaner male is that she uses her legs to create lethal, dual-loyalty conflicts in the Afrikaner male who yields to the temptation to be embraced by an African woman.

There is the sad case of the Afrikaner officer in command of police troops ordered to quell a disturbance in Durban, which is still talked about in Pretoria. Instead of giving orders to shoot first and ask questions afterwards, he armed his men with batons and riot shields and teargas. He lost thirteen men in the clash with the Africans; nine of them were white. The commission of inquiry appointed to investigate the disaster discovered that the officer was in love with a black woman who lived with relatives in the riot area.

In recent years, the black woman, who was allowed free entry into the white man's cities and moved freely in them has turned out to be the African's Trojan horse inside the white man's urban laagers. A congenital member of the Caravan To Blood River, she is breeding men inside the cities at a rate which magnifies the very security dangers which the gun, the police and the Passes are designed to check.

These men, born into and nurtured in the atmosphere created by the Sharpeville massacres, know only one passion in life: to return to Blood River, cost what it may.

On the Day of the Covenant, they dress themselves like Zulu warriors and march up and down the streets of urban locations, singing the songs their ancestors chanted in battles with the white man. These are city Africans who have no connections with the rural reservations;

they cannot be easily endorsed out of the urban locations, where they are always a thorn in the flesh of the police.

One of these children's most annoying activities, everyone knows, is the distribution of anti-government leaflets, pamphlets and other seditious literature in the locations. As a rule, their only playgrounds are the streets, which they use with greater freedom after sunset when traffic is out of the way. It is almost impossible for a policeman to spot a black-faced child in the dark alleyways of the location as the little person darts from back door to back door shoving the literature through every crevice in the houses. Besides, the kids know all the ways of the police and how to fool them. The locations boast that an African child is able, by the time he reaches ten years of age, to smell a policeman ten miles away. The police who live in the locations are, of course, black and none of them wants to turn the communities against themselves and their own children.

Worse, those kids in the semi-dark streets are deadly with the *intshumentshu* (pronounced ee-nchoo-men-chu) in their hands. The *intshumentshu* is a piece of tough round wire about seven or eight inches long one of whose ends is as sharp as the point of a needle. The other is stuck into a stick. A short piece of stick is bored in the centre and provides the sheath in which the *intshumentshu* is concealed. The *intshumentshu* is a weapon of attack in the dark; a boy can run down a street and kill as many people as he likes without being caught. The secrets of the weapon are that it can be used with lightning speed and creates fatal internal haemorrhages. No black policeman in his senses wants to incur the wrath of the *intshumentshu* bands.

The Afrikaners in Union Buildings, the seat of the white government on top of a hill outside the old city, are concerned about the black Trojan Horse and, in the open spaces of South Africa, the people speak their minds openly; black and white attitudes are expressed with a candour which is as crude as it is brutal. People fighting for survival do not have time to waste on refinements. The men in the Union Buildings speak of *Operation Cork Stopper*, to change the population balance created by the fecundity of the African woman.

They tell each other that the white man must stop the trouble at the entrance to the womb and agree that the stopper must be the subjection of the women to the Pass Laws which will not only facilitate the control of their movements but will also classify them on the basis of their fertility.

One of the documents in the Pass Book is a health certificate signed by a government medical health officer, which has to be endorsed every six months for the woman to remain employed in an urban area. The health certificate contains a code giving her age, the number of children she has and indicating whether or not she is past the menopause.

Yes, the white police are particularly enthusiastic in their support of *Operation Cork Stopper*. The Immorality Law, which illegalises sexual relations across the colour line, will be reinforced by the Passes for black women. In the past, an African woman on the streets at night could not be stopped at will by a policeman because she did not carry a Pass; the policeman had little or no power over her. The proposed solution will give the police absolute power over every African woman. Pretoria is still shaken by the scandal involving the six white police who had sexual intercourse with an African woman. In court the first pleaded that he was acting as a trap; the other five swore that they had intercourse with her to provide corroborative evidence. Despite such commendable zeal, even the staid Dutch Reformed Church, whose women's sections drill their children, particularly their sons, on the intolerable smell which the African woman emits, was constrained to tell the de Haas government that the police were taking things a bit too far.

There are signs all over the country that the African women are determined to resist the proposed Pass Law; there are indications that the black men will stop work in support of the women. Paul Kritzinger, the chief of the police in the Pretoria district, for one, is particularly concerned about what could happen to the capital if the Africans staged a determined protest. Apart from paralysing life in the capital, the Africans could set the city on fire; every African man or woman employed in the city is, at least, a potential saboteur. Kritzinger has worked out a plan for countering sedition which promises to solve some of Afrikanerdom's problems in this regard. He outlined it in a paper, bearing the title: *Ritual Murder As An Instrument Of Political Protest* which he read before a special meeting of the Institute for Pan-African Studies. A graduate of a famous Afrikaner university, he holds a degree in anthropology and is at present making a special study of magic as an instrument for the control of the mind. His main thesis is that the African evaluation of the person, which regards him as a cell of an infinite consciousness, surrounds the person's existence with a dangerous aura of sacredness. It raises him to the status of a limb of God, without which God cannot do if he is infinite. God becomes the beggar beholden to the person for his wholeness. One human being taken out of the body of God leaves God a mutilated reality from which a limb has been torn away; since God always has to be whole, he cannot do without a single person.

Kritzinger points out that while he is not a student of theology, the idea of a God whose wholeness depends on the will of the person is particularly unacceptable to him as a christian.

As a scientist, however, he is interested in the implications and practical applications of the African evaluation. If the person is a cell of God, then he has all the attributes of God; he is power, truth and everything the mind of Man can conceive. He has a preciousness which cannot be determined in human terms; he is above sin and law. In actual fact, however, the person committed to this view of life lives like an animal; he has no spiritual values by which to guide his life. He lives in fear and relies on black magic as the prop to explain the mysteries of creation. He is confounded by the complex civilisation of the white man and falls back to superstition for explanations.

As the old ways die under the impact of civilisation, the black people become increasingly fearful about the future; they turn their backs on christianity and return to the ways of their ancestors and its superstitions. They revive ritual murder because every portion of the cell of the infinity is a dynamo of power; a piece of human flesh in the possession of a black man is more precious to the African than his wife or his child. He believes that it radiates powers which cannot be controlled even by the white man. The higher the status of the person, the greater the power in every part of his body. White people, because of their superior power, are believed to have a special value and, in the turbulence emerging in the land, each individual white person will defend, not only the values of his civilisation, but his physical body against mutilation for magic purposes.

The revolts planned against the Passes for black women, Kritzinger continues, will be used as an excuse for murdering as many whites as possible—for the acquisition of bits and pieces of their bodies. This should be a warning, he concludes, to those academic men from Afrikaner universities, now touring the country, to start a dialogue with the blacks on segregation, that the conflict lies, not in the clash between the Larger Truth and the Smaller Truth, but between white civilisation and black barbarism. The same Afrikaners who plead the black people's case against government policy will be the first to be murdered and mutilated by their black allies.

The Kritzinger theory has, in the space of a few weeks, become a subject of heated and sometimes violent controversy on both sides of the colour line. The rumours are that after the presentation of his paper, Kritzinger was invited to dinner with the prime minister where he explained that his thesis was designed, first, to discredit the black revolt in the eyes of the world—certainly, of the white section of it—and, at the same time, to discredit the Afrikaner intellectuals who have organised themselves into the *Universiteitsburo vir Rasseverhoudings* (UBRA, the Universities Bureau for Race Relations). De Haas is reported to have been excited with Kritzinger's idea, to have encouraged the police chief to develop it and assured him of all possible help. Since these rumours are associated with pressmen who have direct access to cabinet ministers, most Africans, like most whites, are inclined to say that there is no smoke without a fire. Reports also circulate that Kritzinger might be the next Commissioner of Police.

* * *

While the atmosphere in the capital city is tense, no incidents have occurred. The police force has been reinforced with recruits undergoing training at the Roberts Heights police college and the curfew laws against blacks tightened. Word has gone round quietly to alert the various reserve sections of the South African army. Because Pretoria is the administrative seat of the government, people in the capital are used to the tension. It is in Union Buildings that the plans are conceived and policies formulated for widening and deepening the gulfs dividing the Africans and the whites. All the storms which rage in the land eventually converge on Pretoria where they keep the tension alive every moment of the city's life.

The outsider is not readily aware of the tension; every African in the city, like every white person, knows that the calm is the peace which the bullet produces.

James Hawthorne is an accountant in the large firm of auditors founded and headed by his father, Felix. Like most wealthy Pretorians, the Hawthorne family lives in Waterkloof. The firm of Felix Hawthorne, Myburg and Myburg handles the books of cabinet ministers and the senior civil servants. Felix Hawthorne is a descendant of the British Settlers who landed in South Africa in 1820. His father fought in the Anglo-Boer war of 1899-1902 and, after the Peace of Vereeniging, bought a farm outside Pretoria on which Felix was born. Although the Hawthornes are English-speaking, they speak Afrikaans with the fluency of Free Staters. Now in his mid-sixties, Felix has come to terms with political realities in South Africa and takes the position that the British will never again recover the political power they have lost; that wisdom lies in active collaboration with the new Afrikaner masters of South Africa, as long as they allow the English to collect their shekels.

This bowing to the wind does not mean that Hawthorne accepts a future in which his people will be absorbed by the Afrikaner in the way the French Huguenots and the German settlers were swallowed up by the Dutch in the Cape. He sees to it that his children attend the most English of English schools in the land. James went to Michaelhouse, the crustiest high school for English boys in Natal, and proceeded from there to the University of Natal in Pietermaritzburg, which is crustier even than Michaelhouse.

Felix believes that the conflict between the Afrikaner and the English has shifted from power to survival; the Afrikaner is united sufficiently now to guarantee the permanence of his power in South Africa, if the Africans allow him to do this, and is strong enough to confront the English with the threat of absorption. At this level, Felix sees no room for compromise. He does not open his mouth too wide on this subject; as a matter of fact, he is so discreet the two Myburgs who are his partners and who are extreme right-wing Afrikaner nationalists get on fairly well with him.

But son James has youth on his side and is determined to see

Afrikaner power crushed before he goes to his grave. Unlike his father, he thinks the English can regain political dominance if they form an alliance with the Africans against the Afrikaners. Nobody in the capital hates the UBRA intellectuals more bitterly than James; de Haas himself does not hate them half as much. James has studied Zulu and Northern Sotho in order, as he puts it, to establish direct contact between the mind of the English and the mind of the Africans.

Father and son do not agree on the African-English alliance; Felix believes in the inherent inferiority and untrustworthiness of the black man and is certain that one of these days a political cataclysm is going to descend on Free Africa and send the black governments scurrying to Britain and France to ask them to protect them against the Africans they freed and whom they misrule.

The differences between Felix and James have not been allowed to come to crisis-point. Felix admires his brilliant son who, he hopes, will, when he is wiser, give the English the leadership that will save them from absorption by the Afrikaner. James needs the protection his father's name gives him; it has for years enabled him to preserve a perfectly respectable exterior while involved in complicated underground activity against the government.

On this particular morning he is driving up Church Street to the main railway station. The sun has just risen and in another twenty minutes the 7:40 non-stop train from Johannesburg will be in, bringing his wife from the Witwatersrand. For a while his mind is on the Kruger Memorial which has been removed from the front of the railway station to the centre of the city. Kruger is not one of his heroes; as a matter of fact, he has quite an assortment of nasty epithets by which he describes him when white company is not around. He is not unique in this; the Africans, the Afrikaners and the English each have a colourful repertoire of ugly names by which they call each other when feelings catch fire. The thought flashes in his mind and he remembers the African arrested urinating on Kruger's statue. Brought before a magistrate, his simple plea was:

Your worship, I have never been to school; I do not know the ways of the white man. I saw a lump of metal shaped like a man on a pile of stones and thought nobody would be offended if I hid behind the stones.

Then, there was that nasty story reported by *Die Aanslag* of the African who defaecated at the base of the Kruger statue and outran the police who chased him. No Englishman or Jew can afford to mention incidents like these in the presence of Afrikaners, but they are repeated with an infinity of variations and embellishments in English bars or at social gatherings when the English are with their friends. James cannot help laughing and shaking his head and saying to himself:

These Africans!

* * *

67

The main hall of the central railway station is crowded with Africans, Asians, coloureds and whites as James walks into the great hall of the terminal at the end of Church Street. Press reports indicate that the city council is discussing plans to make it illegal for the Africans to enter the station through the main entrance and to walk across the great hall to their platforms. The Africans resent the insult, but, as has happened so often in their history, their feelings bleed inward; as they say it themselves, the mills of their hearts grind good grain and rotten grain. James is a little too early and saunters leisurely among the crowds now thinning out of the great hall. The loudspeaker blares out the announcement that the 7:40 train from Johannesburg will be late by twenty minutes. James clenches his fist in his coat pocket and swears quietly to himself:

These Boer bastards! They can't even run their trains on time!

To cool his anger, he paces across the main hall, in which less than a hundred people, mainly white, linger. Maggie Kuboni comes almost trotting through the gate into the platform reserved for people of colour and walks briskly across the centre of the hall to the main exit. James knows her very well and has a high regard for her. In the tension which prevails in the city he feels compelled to protest against Afrikaner domination by identifying himself publicly with the African—even if it is a woman. Many English-speaking people have become shy of recognising their African friends in public and James is determined to stand out and be counted, even in the great hall of the central station itself. Besides, Maggie is by no means an ordinary woman. In the old days, when black and white fought together in the underground, it was a privilege to work with Maggie; there was no danger before which she trembled and no job so ugly she would not do. Her explanation of her attitude was that she had been exiled from a white farm into the city.

I was the first child in a family of five, she used to tell James. Three sisters came after me and the last-born in the family was a boy. My father, like his father and his grandfather, had been born on a white farm in Northern Natal. I, too, was born on a white farm. For six months in the year, father would work on the white farm in payment for the right to live on the farm with his family. He was allowed to own eight head of cattle—four oxen and four milk cows and was alloted two acres on which to raise food for his family. During the other half of the year, father would go to Johannesburg where he earned twelve rand per month with which he bought us groceries, clothed us and sent us to doctors when we became critically ill, which was not unusual. His greatest ambition was that his children should escape from the serfdom which kept him the white man's prisoner. His Pass betrayed him in whatever he did. It indicated when he was due for work on the farm, no matter where he was. Any policeman and, for that matter, any white person, could demand his Pass and arrest him if his six months' "leave" in the city was up. He would be brought before a court of law, fined and endorsed out of the city.

To escape arrest, father owned two Pass Books, one with his real name and the other with what we call a borrowed name. The legal document was used during the six months he would be legally away from the farm, when he would switch on to the illegal Pass. This endeared father neither to the farmers on whose lands we lived nor to the authorities in Johannesburg. As a result, we moved from farm to farm, doomed always to be expelled when father's delinquency was discovered. Much of our time was spent on the road. The law required that an African should be expelled in winter. We could not go to our relatives or to our friends after these expulsions, lest we endangered them.

It was while we had been expelled and when we were on the road one winter that we had a snowstorm. As a rule, snow does not fall heavily in Natal; not even in Northern Natal, except on top of the Drakensberg mountain range. But once, in fifty or seventy years, we have a snowstorm. My part of the country has nothing more dreadful than a snowstorm. We were marooned on the roadside without food and fuel for nearly two weeks. Occasionally, passers-by brought us a little food if they were black.

Most whites did not bother to stop to find out what had gone wrong with us. They knew what had happened and were delighted to see nature punish us for our impudence. It was during the storm that mother gave birth to my brother and was so cold and hungry after the event she fell sick and died on the roadside. Day after day father moved from farm to farm to get a piece of earth in which he could bury my mother and no farmer would allow us to bury her on his land. It was a serious crime to bury her on government land on either side of the road. One afternoon, father called me aside. Child, he said, we shall have to drag your mother out of the house during the night and let the dogs eat her . . . .

I was stunned and cried so bitterly my younger sisters rushed from beneath the ox-wagon we used as our home. I remember father saying: Child, we have no choice. I cannot afford to be arrested and taken away from you. I remember I blurted out something like: We shall bury her; it does not matter if they arrest you; I shall look after the children and the cattle. We buried mother and the police arrested father . . . . The rest is a long story. Luckily for us, we were too young to carry Passes. We sold everything father had on the roadside and walked the thirty miles to Ladysmith, the nearest town, where I got a job as a nanny. Our home was a hole we dug into a bank of the Klip River . . . until I had my first pay when I looked around for a spare room in the backyard of an Indian . . . .

And, in that way, I graduated into womanhood . . . . You see? I had no choice. I just had to go forward into exile in the white man's city. Father was a spoiled kaffer, as the whites called him, and that brought me to where I am. I was only twelve years old then. I had always dreamt that one day I would be a medical and surgical nurse and, with that in mind, I walked into the white man's world.

James would ask her if she was not afraid and she would answer that she had been a woman so early in her life, she had lost the capacity to be afraid. One night both had been assigned to paint slogans against the government on the walls of the Groot Kerk in Pretoria. They belonged to the same underground cell and had just finished the job when Maggie spotted the violet flashlight of a police car at a light two blocs down the street. She told him to follow her, ran down a darkened lane, tearing through space like an arrow, jumped over a fence into a huge, private swimming pool. He hesitated for a while and then followed her. The police searched the area for about forty minutes and it occurred to none of them that the black woman and the white man were in the water.

Maggie was happiest when she struck at the white power-structure. James remembers the occasion she organised a reception for the Chief Bantu Affairs Commissioner for the Witwatersrand and served brown bread sandwiches! Kritzinger was called to police headquarters where the Commissioner of Police gave him a piece of his mind. Subsequently, the Minister for Bantu Affairs issued a circular to all Chief Bantu Commissioners to the effect that they should not attend receptions in their honour in the locations. All because of B.B.

Maggie organised a loyalty deputation to the permanent secretary of the Department of Bantu Affairs. There were two types of deputations in the locations and the rural reserves at the time: the loyalty deputations when African delegations called on government officials to ask them to convey their thanks to the Great Elephants (cabinet ministers) in Pretoria for what they had done for the blacks. Then, there were the obnoxious protest delegations which no government employee wanted to see. Maggie confronted the permanent secretary:

Sir, what we want to know from you after the ban is how best we might demonstrate our loyalty to the government or express our appreciation of what its officials do for us!

The secretary was touched by this simple expression of loyalty and went off guard for a while, confessing, in the heavily guttural Afrikaans of the rural Free State:

Well, woman, I don't know what to tell you. I am sure opportunities should be provided for you to show appreciation of the many good things the government does for your people.

Hawthorne runs across the centre of the hall to Maggie and when he catches up with her, touches her on the shoulder. The African stops suddenly, turns sharply around and recognises Hawthorne, whom she gives a wilting look. As quickly, she gives him her back and walks away.

Pardon me please. I'm Jimmy Hawthorne; aren't you Miss Maggie Kuboni?

I know who you are! But listen, I don't want to speak to you!

But . . . Maggie! Miss Kuboni, what's wrong?

She stops suddenly as he catches up with her and turns toward him again. Maggie is not screaming; she talks in low, though unmistakably angry tones.

I told you I did not want to speak to you, you dirty Boere gatwyser!

She spits in his face, slaps him sharply on the cheek, and walks away. In Pretoria, a demonstration like that is a challenge to the entire white world; every true Afrikaner son of his father would want the whole army brought to the station to surround this single woman who hits a white man in public. Some white males present cannot control themselves and they surround Maggie, who turns round and attacks:

And what are you standing around me for?

Why do you hit a white man?

How brave of you! To surround a woman in order to defend the man she hits! Why don't you ask him why I hit him? He knows.

With that Maggie turns away and leaves the whites looking at each other, some swearing at her and others swearing at her victim. A few Afrikaner women have gathered behind their men and some of them make their feelings known:

She iss quite right! Quite right! These men forget themselves sometimes. Any animal in a skirt they think iss a woman!

The attack emboldens some of the Afrikaner women to come brutally to the point—at least as closely as Afrikaners can in dealings across the colour line in these matters. The women scream at the circle of men:

Leafe her alown! Leafe her alown!

That disorganises the circle of men and as it melts away, some of the women gloat:

That serfes him right!

There usually is a black policeman in the hall of the main station whose job is to handle the Africans in such a way that there are no scenes involving black and white. The railway station was built in the old days of the Boer republic in the Transvaal, when Pretoria was a sleepy rural village which was dominated by the Indian departmental store owned by the Coovadia family. The main hall then was large enough for the capital's needs. But Pretoria has grown since. In the old days there was no location around Pretoria; very few Africans used the railway station. Now, every morning, thousands of Africans enter the city by train to work in its offices, stores and factories. Thousands of whites from the suburbs do the same and, in the South African setting, the crowding of black and white creates all sorts of ugly situations. In a

71

collision between black and white, the Africans promptly gang up with the black man and attack the white man together. These are not isolated clashes; if a black man and a white man fight anywhere in the city and there are no police about, the Africans join forces, hit the white man and then go to the man they are supporting. They put to him a question which indicates how they have judged the case:

Wakithi (person of the house to which I belong), that animal you have just beaten, why did he attack you?

The black man tells the story and, as people say in the locations, gives his "witnesses" the line. When the police arrive, the African and his witnesses are ready. This sort of behaviour is not confined to Pretoria. In every large South African city, with the possible exception of the Orange Free State, the Africans give each other the "line."

It is also in situations like these that the passes become useful for the whites. When the "line" forms, the police go on the offensive and demand the production of the passes. The "witnesses" then either have to keep away from fights across the colour line or be jailed for irregularities in their passes. At this level, the pass ceases to function as an instrument for the control of African labour; it becomes a weapon of white defence in situations of physical conflict across the colour line. The policeman's role in this setting changes; he ceases to be the arm of the law and becomes a soldier in the front line of the white man's defences against the African. This just adds to the tension between the blacks and the police for the Africans naturally regard the police as an army of occupation.

In the old days, every police station in the country had black and white constables. White officers were in charge of the police stations inside the locations. But the locations were African territory and the people who lived in them wanted no army of occupation around. They used the *intshumentshu* effectively as an argument which convinced Pretoria that the white officers had to be withdrawn from the locations and blacks appointed in their places. A new relationship has arisen between the location communities and the black police in their midst. The police are grateful that the *intshumentshu* argument has pushed out the whites and forced the government to appoint them to positions of real authority. At the same time they have a very healthy respect for the *intshumentshu*. That makes them as superficially perfect an arm of the law as the police can be in any part of the world.

As a rule, most people in the locations are pleased with this new attitude on the police side. The police are not only the white man's first line of defence, they are the influence which guarantees that the African-Afrikaner-English balance continues to function. In the old days, when it was rewarding for the black police to side with the power-structure, the black constables distinguished themselves in beating up African strikers, rioteers and other agitators who attacked the white power-structure. Things have since changed; the *intshu-mentshu* has transferred much of effective power from the white police to the black in the locations. To the Africans, the change means that in future confrontations with the white power-structure the prospects of other Sharpevilles will be reduced. This is a shift of power which gratifies the locations.

The black policeman who keeps order among his people in the main hall was conspicuous by his absence during the altercation between Maggie and James Hawthorne. In the old days he would have rushed to manhandle the black woman and arrest her for disorderly conduct. He has no authority to arrest a white person; he quietly vanished from the hall. When everything is over he makes a conspicuous appearance, tightening his trousers belt ostentatiously after the tactical visit to the lavatory. He marches across the hall, carefully avoiding the eyes of the angry whites, to the African platforms.

Maggie is sitting on a bench, with her eyes on the floor. The policeman strides up to her, assuming the stance of a Zulu gallant. They understand these things in the locations. They know, for example, that a Zulu woman is queen when it comes to matters of the heart. To be a queen is to have power and her whole education stresses the fact that there is no influence on earth which can take this power from her; that it is her right to demand that this power should be recognised. For example, the Zulu girl feels insulted if no head is turned or nothing is said by any group of Zulu men she might be passing. Every Zulu who has been taught *umteto* must recognise the presence of her majesty. Among orthodox Zulus it is barbarous for a man to let a woman sit alone in public, particularly if she is not married. Any man worth his salt is expected to keep her company; to recognise her majesty's presence. When the policeman adopts the stance of a gallant, he pays homage to the queen of her heart.

Hail, *mntanethu* (woman it would be an honour for me to marry)!

Every Zulu woman has had scores of men say this to her, unless, of course, she knew of very good reasons why they should not address her in this fashion. In the old days, the girl who had been taught *umteto* would acknowledge the greeting politely because she did not know the man she would marry. But, in the conditions created by contact with the white man, men no longer observe the requirements of *umteto* in their dealings with women; like the whites whom they emulate, most men want to crash into the personality of the queen; they have adopted the white man's barbarous ways. The woman has had to adapt to this fact of life. Maggie acts as though she did not hear the policeman's greeting.

Mntanethu, I am talking to you!

What are you saying?

The policeman looks around to see if his superiors are seeing him and then braces himself, assuming an authoritarian stance.

That dog you slapped in the hall . . . you struck a blow for all of us.

What do you want from me?

Just to say you did what many of us would like to do, but do not have the courage to do it.

You want me to tell you things, so that you can tell your Boer masters, so that they might promote you?

My apologies if that is how you see me. I am a black man like you, though in uniform; there are many like me who would honour you for what you did. More power to your hand.

The policeman walks up the African platform. Maggie is still sitting on the bench. Her working day has been spoilt. When the white men surrounded her, she saw the floods of Blood River. She knew that she would be arrested for one of many crimes manufactured to ensure that South Africa remains safe for the whites. Maggie is not the type of person who would give the whites or their police something to crow about. To get into the train and leave the station would have been a retreat. The word does not exist in her vocabulary; as people who have worked with her say, Maggie goes through life only in one direction . . . to Blood River. There, she tells them, she will find her mother waiting for her. She sits on the bench to give the whites and their police the chance to arrest her. The African policeman is now coming down the African platform.

Whose daughter are you, to do the inconceivable?

My father's!

Indeed, your father's daughter! I wish I could shake hands with him. He produced a fine soldier for the Battle of Blood River!

That softens Maggie, who has kept her eyes on the floor all along as an indication that she does not want anybody to speak to her. Now she turns her face to the policeman, without looking him in the eyes. Only cheap girls look men in the eyes; men look in the eyes only those they despise. Friends do not look each other in the eyes. The only people to look straight in the eyes are the gatwysers and when the African is really angry, all white men are gatwysers, the animals through whose ears the sun shines.

Yes. I am going to Blood River. You see, my parents did not have a son for a long time. I was the oldest child. I herded the cattle and drove them to the dipping tank. I can handle my own sticks in a fight like any man; I fought every boy in our neighbourhood and not one hit my head and not one sent my sticks flying out of my hands!

Your deeds speak for you. What had the transparent-eared animal done?

Your walkie-talkie equipment ready?

I am a policeman; yes I am; but I am a soldier to Blood River.

That white man . . . . He is one of those hypocrites I hate so much. He poses as a friend of the Africans and an enemy of the CNP. For a time, I was a fool; I believed that he was a friend and ally. Events have made me wiser. I resent bitterly the fact that I once believed and told my own people that the white liberals were our friends; that the white christians were decent people. I know now that they are not; that they are the friends and the allies of Willem Adriaan de Haas! Our enemies . . . .

That is strong language. Some whites are decent; take the nuns at Boreneng . . . .

As individuals, some whites are decent. But remember, I mentioned groups. You remember the *dumdumu* [a celebration in which drums are beaten] when de Haas sat, conferred, ate and drank with Cardinal de Marandellas? Why do you think de Haas the Calvinist and de Marandellas the Roman Catholic put their heads together?

Well, they are white.

You said some white persons are decent . . . .

Ha! Ha! Did I say *mntanethu* when I greeted you?

I told you that I herded cattle.

Your deeds speak for you; they tell the story. Alright then, some whites are decent as persons and some white groups are rotten.

You are now talking sense, as my father would say.

Where is he?

With his ancestors now.

Why did he die, before I had shaken hands with him?

You'll meet him at Blood River.

May it be as you say . . . . But our enemies . . . . Did you say the white liberals, Christians and the like are on the side of de Haas? I mean . . . do you seriously believe this?

In my days of darkness, when I saw the truth dimly, as through smoked glass, I believed that they were on our side; that they seriously upheld the ideals they preached and which I tried to translate into meaningful action in my life. At the *dumdumu*, they came out in their true colours; they advocated white supremacy; de Haas did, so did the Roman Catholic; the one uses race to perpetuate white supremacy, the other uses values to achieve the same end. See what I mean? Differences arise only in their strategies. It pains my heart and hurts me grievously to know that I trusted the liberals, the christians, the radicals and similar white groups for so long and collaborated in my own humiliation . . . .

It was not until the *dumdumu* that I saw the truth in the clearest light possible. But, as my father used to say, wisdom does not come to the person in one instalment; one grows into it . . . . I grew into it and the process is very painful. That white man I slapped on the face is a Roman Catholic, a christian! You should have seen how thrilled he was during the conference! How he loaded scores of Africans in his car ... to and from the *dumdumu* ... when the kaffers were needed to give mass to the power of the white man .... He still is a christian, a Roman Catholic. The thought of hypocrites like him makes me vomit!

The policeman is continually looking around to make certain that his superiors do not see him. A white constable comes up the African platform. The African policeman collects all the frowns he can place together on his face and pointing a menacing finger at Maggie and speaking in Afrikaans, shouts:

Answer my question! What are you doing here? You were sitting here when I went up the platform; you were sitting here when I returned ... and (looking at his wrist watch) how many minutes have I spent here asking you one question?

Maggie pouts her mouth in the way a hostile Zulu woman does and turns her face away from him. The white policeman walks past them, up the African platform. When the white man is out of earshot the black constable lowers his voice and speaks to Maggie in Zulu again.

I understand now, sister; you were provoked.

You must go now. There'll be trouble when that animal with transparent ears comes down. But before you go, do you know why I now hate these white hypocrites? They preach love and justice ... they define love and justice and demand that we accept these definitions .... They judge us according to white values; they are the enemies of our values. Their hatred of our truths is the common link which binds them all, de Haas, the CNP, the Roman Catholics, the white christians, liberals and radicals and every white group which seeks our destruction or works for our permanent subjugation.

* * *

As a rule, the English-speaking whites, like the Jews, are too far removed from the African, in terms of history, to feel the subtle beats of his political heart. Wherever it serves their economic interests, they use the African as the battering ram by which to smash Afrikaner political power. They do not hesitate to use the Afrikaner in a similar capacity to smash African reserves of power. Situations often arise when the power dispositions on the African and the Afrikaner sides reach an equilibrium which threatens to make the English irrelevant for the purpose of determining South Africa's future.

Whenever this balance emerges, the English shout themselves hoarse in demands for a Bill Of Rights or some such document to preserve their rights and protect their interests when the African restores to himself his land and freedom. The younger Africans in the locations oppose all talk of Bills Of Rights. The whites, they say, stole the African's land, stole its wealth, stole the African's freedom and stole his soul. It is absurd to the point of being insane for any African in his senses to lend support to anything like a Bill Of Rights. Such documents, the young argue; merely legalise the retention by the whites of the things the whites stole from the African. If people want any Bill Of Rights, let them accept the Buntu evaluation of the person, the young say.

James Hawthorne thinks the young Africans have a case when they reject race as a determinant of policy and confront the whites with a different system of values. The African alternative, he is steadily coming to believe, is an acid test for the white Christian, liberal and radical. If they mean what they preach, they must stand out to be counted, to lay the foundations for a meaningful dialogue between black and white on an alternative ideal of nationhood. He agrees with the young Africans that the great conflicts of the twenty-first century will centre, no longer around blackness or whiteness, but on the clash between the *Buntu* evaluation of the person and the one developed mainly by the Greeks, the Romans and the Jews. He wants to keep his channels of communication with the location open, as evidence of the readiness to be counted. He drives to Dillo Mareka's house.

Dillo, I am in trouble, he blurts out.

What's gone wrong? The police . . . .

No . . . .

What's your trouble, then?

Gatwyser! I've never heard the word before! It sounds terrible!

You were born in Pretoria and you do not know what gat-wyser means?

I know that *gat* means arse; that *wys* means show. I have some idea of what the combination might mean—but, well, I want to understand what it means.

Somebody hurled it at you? Said you are *umhadaveyisi!*

Er . . . yes.

The African laughs loudly, not realising that he hurts James.

Man, somebody did plaster you with shit! Gatwyser means somebody who goes around the world showing his anus to the sun and doing this as an act of fulfilment. Remember, we Africans were originally a rural people. After conquest the white man took our land and forced us to work on his farms. The Afrikaner on the farm thought he owned us and punished us as he liked. He would kick a person with enough force to send him spinning into the air . . . that is, until the African saw his backside. Surely, you've heard the Afrikaners say: Ek sal jy jou gat wys (I will show you your arse) when angry? Our ancestors thought the farmers liked talking about or seeing the arse and so the Boers became the gatwysers!

But, how do I become a gatwyser?

An African called you that?

Yes. Maggie Kuboni.

Maggie? Well, you're in trouble, boy.

77

She slapped me on the face and spat on me in the great hall of the main railway station this morning.

Up to now the African has been taking Hawthorne's excitement as a joke. Now he knows that something serious has happened.

Maggie did that to you?

Why?

It's the times, Jim; they're changing. Are you still a Roman Catholic?

Yes.

You remember the Boreneng conference of the Roman Catholic hierarchy?

But what does that have to do with me? Everybody knows I'm against bartering the conscience of the church for political breadcrumbs.

Don't you see what's happening. The whites are ganging-up against us; they're taking up positions . . . for war . . . against us. *The bible and the gun are ganging-up, as they have done all along, to keep the nigger in his place.* The nigger doesn't like it . . . .

I can understand that. But how do I become a gatwyser?

By not knowing what you should know. There was a time when I thought you white people were smart people. I have since changed that view . . . .

The African pauses for a while, as though in deep thought. His remarks hit Hawthorne like a blow between the eyes; he has known Dillo from the days before the Sharpeville shootings. Both of them were students at Cape Town university. Dillo worked in the underground then, as he does now, organising the strike after the shootings. James had been with other young whites who drove trucks with food, secondhand clothes and medical supplies into Langa location when the Africans struck in protest against the shootings.

There had never been a period in his life when every moment was crammed with so much meaning; for the few weeks when the strike lasted, he had temporarily ceased to exist; he had lived. The locations were the place where the action was. It was a glorious thing then to be a white radical or communist or socialist or liberal; one became a fighter by definition. There was nothing like seeing an African in tattered clothes on the streets, raising his open right hand in the Pan-Africanist salute to greet a white man.

For a moment, many young whites in Cape Town caught a glimpse of the coming revolution; they saw history being made and saw themselves creating destiny. Many distinguished themselves in the great collision between what they regarded as Boer tyranny and the freedom movement. Wherever James had gone, he had been hailed as a hero, a liberator. He remembers the experience because he was very much in demand in liberal parlours in the white suburbs of Cape Town. There was no end to the demand for the stories he told about the Africans.

Suddenly, the black people had become human; they had become subjects of serious conversation in white lounges in every South African city. African students ceased to avoid white students.

Dillo Mareka had left the university to become a teacher in Pretoria. Years before, Chief Luthuli had spoken in Pretoria to a mixed audience. White hoodlums had rushed into the hall, beat him up and sent everybody scurrying for shelter. The spectacle of strong white men, beating up African, Indian and white women in the meeting converted Dillo; he became an ardent liberal. He himself had introduced Maggie to a number of whites, including James Hawthorne.

Oh, yes, things had changed since then. Black and white had fallen apart. Christianity, liberalism, socialism, communism and all the isms invented by the white man were not able to hold the races together. On the day of this story, Dillo Mareka is no longer a liberal; he no longer teaches; there no longer is a political party which accepts black and white members. Above all, Dillo is no longer anxious to meet any white man. If he can help it he never does. He and Sefadi work in the underground, burning factories and helping prisoners escape. When he laughs with one nearby, there is scorn in his voice and contempt in his eye. Hawthorne looks around the tiny sitting-room—all rooms in location houses are the same size, same shape, with doors and windows in the same position. The furniture he knew in the old days has not changed; the cheap gadgets salvaged from secondhand dealers in Pretoria are still there. In the chilly atmosphere of the sitting-room, he feels as though a whole ocean stands between him and Dillo; the familiar objects are like ruins reminding him of a past that seems not likely to return again.

I don't think we are all that smart, Dillo; we should have known better. But what happens to people like me? If my family could, they would reject me. The whites reject me and the Africans reject me; where do I belong?

To Waterkloof; you belong to Felix Hawthorne, Myburg and Myburg.

Come off it, Dillo! You know I don't belong there.

It's a fate you can't escape even if you wanted to. It so happens, you belong there by choice . . . .

How can you say that, Dillo?

You breakfasted on bread, bacon and eggs this morning . . . and I, on mahewu. You know the fermented porridge we drink. That is the difference between you and me now.

I don't understand.

When the time comes to defend your sources of bread and bacon you will be at Waterkloof; that's what I'm telling you. I'll be here, possibly in jail.

We were together in the underground. We had the same enemy then; he is the same enemy to-day.

I thought so then; I know better now; we do not belong together. The whites are ganging-up to destroy African independence across the border ... and you remain a Roman Catholic. You're committed to the white man's system of values when we are rejecting them. You're committed to the white man's culture because you think it superior. De Haas is committed to the supremacy of the white skin. Supremacy is the common factor; that is where the lines are drawn.

But, Dillo, I can't help being white!

Can I help being black?

Well, what do we do about it?

Don't ask me; that's no longer my problem.

Do you mind if I say it's mine?

You're over twenty-one, aren't you?

James feels like dashing through the door; everything he has stood for is in a shambles. He cannot go back to his family and admit that he was wrong to attack the establishment or that he was slapped in the face by an African woman; he does not even want to mention the fact that she spat on his face. He can imagine his father nodding his head, saying:

She would do a thing like that, son. I told you; they're all like that; ungrateful, treacherous and unpredictable. But ... I told you they'd do that to you. Imagine, a white man spat upon by a nigger!

But James has worked sufficiently with the Africans to know that if he leaves in the way his instincts dictate, Dillo would never talk to him again. Dillo knows too many things; a quarrel with him could be dangerous. Dillo might be arrested any moment; under police pressure he could break down and tell stories which could hurt Hawthorne. A walk-out would, above all, be a defeat, a flight from the black world. As the Americans would say, he decides to tough it out. The scorn in the African's voice and the contempt in his brown eyes leave James hanging emotionally somewhere in space, feeling no real bonds with the white world and rejected by the African.

But things can't go on like this forever, Dillo.

We know our weaknesses ... and our points of strength. All this sounds depressing, doesn't it?

I guess it does.

That is the Native Problem; from this moment in history watch us tackle the White Problem. That's what Maggie was telling you. Your people and mine are now caught in a war of civilisations.

There was a time when we thought we could come to terms with your civilisation. The white man kicked us in the teeth and proved to us that we do not need it.

Now, we know we do not need it. We don't need his Christ. Our ancestors did without his civilisation and survived; we too are now determined to survive without the infamy.

Are you being realistic?

80

I told you, you don't understand. Realistic? What do I care if you think I am not? Please yourself and what you do does not matter any longer. We have taken the white man out of our minds—never again to have him there. Though he can pass all sorts of laws to humiliate us and force our women to carry the pass, all that does not matter any more. We've set our eyes on a star of our choosing and before he stops us, he'll have to kill all of us . . . .

Dillo, there are things some white people can do to stop the extermination . . . .

It's too late. Their police won't allow them to do that. And, in any case, I'm no longer interested in what the white people do; I am concerned about what the black people do. You go to the university and sit as you do next to Paul Kritzinger in the anthropology class. Anthropology sees us from white perspectives; all our enemies do that. All our enemies tell us they love us; they shoot us and take our land; they love us even when we do not want to be loved. *They left their continent to come and love us and we were so loved they wrote Sharpeville into history. Did any African go to Europe or America to ask any white people to love him?* Damn it, man! Let them stick their love in their arses!

Hawthorne rises to his feet. He can leave now, without shutting the last door to future contact with the Africans in the location. Dillo, too, rises to his feet.

Well, Dillo, you and I can't say we were glad to see each other. But, I'm glad I came. I want to tell myself that I shall again be allowed to see you . . . .

See me you will . . . at Armageddon.

The white man forces a wry smile and shrugs his shoulders slightly.

I'm not going there.

Let me tell you one thing, before you go. If you were caught in a riot and my people were killing whites and they wanted to kill you, I would defend you . . . against my better judgment.

For a moment, the two men look each other in the eyes without winking. For a moment, two worlds clash in emotional space.

Yes, I would . . . against my better judgment . . . because I know that unlike most whites, you want to face the challenge of being human!

* * *

To give to his life a meaning chosen by himself; to shock the whites into awareness of the disasters they are creating for themselves and to commit a supreme act of identification with the Africans and in doing this send a signal to them that not all whites are sub-human, James Hawthorne makes a bomb which, after two months of planning, meditation and considering alternatives, he places beneath a bus-stop bench, reserved for white people, near the Kruger monument.

Jennifer Huggins, a white woman in her sixties, sits on the bench beneath the monument, before moving into the main railway station to catch the next train to Johannesburg. Jennifer is tired in body and mind. She spent the day in Pretoria to try and get the Department of Native Affairs to grant permission for a white pediatrician to serve at the Zenzele Orphanage which she founded for African infants for whom nobody could care in the locations. The orphanage now has about a thousand little black people. Zenzele is in an area marked out for the Africans and no white person might enter it without the permission of the Native Affairs Department. Government policy frowns on white people working in an African location. The belief is that as a rule, such white people are either liberals or radicals or communists who plant subversive ideas into the minds of the Africans. As a rule again, the Department treats them as the scum of the earth and places every conceivable difficulty in their way.

Jennifer Huggins occupies a place of her own in the "scum" community. She is the only child and heiress of the late Sir Alastair Huggins, the famed South African multi-millionaire, who made his millions in the days of the gold rush. He left most of his wealth to his daughter. A militant philanthropist, she sunk most of her inheritance in the construction of the Zenzele Orphanage in memory of her father. The hundreds of little black human beings for whom and among whom she lives call her *Mama*. Jennifer is too busy looking after her large family to bother about a public image. She does not even have a car of her own and, like the Africans with whom she has identified herself, travels by bus and train. Pretoria views her work with particular suspicion; she is regarded as bringing up the little Africans in an atmosphere of communism. The law says it is a crime for black and white to have normal human relations; black children should not say *Mama* to a white woman; that reduces the African's respect for the white person and only communists want this respect destroyed. Evidence of the destruction is not lacking. The security police in Johannesburg and Pretoria have bulging files on her. All of them attach importance to the fact that wherever she goes in the locations, the black people receive her as one of them! They call her the Mother of the Children. That is communism, pure and simple.

Jennifer is still on the bench watching a group of white children march past. The bomb explodes, killing her and wounding some of the children.

* * *

VIII. Stolen People, Stolen Souls

Mhlathi owazanayo, hlangana!

(Keep together, O jaws which belong together!)

The Kritzinger theory on ritual murder as an instrument of political protest has received considerable attention in the Afrikaans community. The popular press uses it to explain every delinquency in the African group; scholarly journals hail it as the discovery of the century. The clamour for more research by the Afrikaners on the subject is raised from every side, including the powerful Dutch Reformed Church. The church is particularly keen to get scientific explanations for its support of the government's policies. It is under attack almost from every christian organisation in the world for its policy of punishing people because they are the children of their parents. Nowhere is the church's support of race exclusiveness attacked with greater aggressiveness than in Holland.

Generations of Dutch scholars have been taking the view that the Dutch Reformed Church in South Africa is in error when it calls itself christian and when it quotes the bible as its authority in the justification of race discrimination. Some of the most distinguished Dutch scholars devote much of their time to proving that there are no scriptural foundations for the attitude of the Dutch Reformed Church in South Africa. The Afrikaners are particularly sore about the attitude of the Hollanders; some of their roots are in Holland and, in their position of isolation in the world, they need friends and expect Holland not to be at the head of campaigns against their policies.

For her part, Holland does not stop at dynamiting the scriptural foundations of the Afrikaner philosophy; she goes on record as one of the countries which raise funds to finance the black revolt against Afrikaner domination. One of her queens has made a secret donation to provide medical and related facilities for the victims of CNP policies. These wounds cut deep into the soul of the Afrikaner. The Dutch theologians are blamed to a very large extent for forcing the Dutch Reformed Church in South Africa into a position of isolation from the rest of christendom in the world. The Afrikaners insist that this is not a new development in Hollander attitudes; they blame history for it. Holland did little to reinforce the Afrikaners in their struggle against the British toward the end of last century. In the moment of defeat for the Afrikaners, their leader, Paul Kruger, could find no place in Holland in which he could hide his head; he could find no friends in Holland to champion the cause of his sorely tried people.

Oh, yes, he roamed the European continent, a defeated, embittered, broken man, to die in the obscurity of a tiny Swiss village.

At every turning-point in the history of the Afrikaner, Holland has almost been invariably on the opposite side. In the first world war, many Afrikaners took sides with the Kaiser and wished him success; some even organised rebellion and one was executed as a result—not by the British, but by a South African government headed by Jan Smuts, himself an Afrikaner. Holland was neutral in the first world war and showed no sympathy with the Afrikaner rebels. In the clash with the Nazis, Holland and the Afrikaners were once more on opposite sides. This strained the relations between The Hague and Pretoria in such a way that after the hostilities Holland refused to accept an Afrikaner ambassador who had identified himself with the Nazi cause during the war. The campaigns organised from Holland against the South African Dutch Reformed Church's interpretation of the scriptures combines with the Dutch queen's support of the opponents of the CNP to rub salt and acid into festering wounds.

Partly as a result, the government views with thinly disguised hostility the employment of Dutch nuns as teachers, doctors and nurses at Boreneng mission, outside of Atteridgeville. This creates complicated difficulties for Archbishop Postlethwait. He first wanted British nuns and priests, but dared not argue his case too enthusiastically in this direction. When government policy favoured the substitution of British investments with the American, Postlethwait pressed for the appointment of American nuns.

The idea horrified everybody in the headquarters of the Department of Bantu Affairs; not one official was prepared even to discuss it. No Afrikaner would allow undisciplined American women to teach in a location school or to work in a location hospital. They have no pride of race or colour; they feel no sense of shame when they shake hands with black people and seem to take pride in their pictures being taken with black people or photographed holding kaffer piccanins in their hands. (Little Africans are not children; they are piccanins.) Every one of them, Postlethwait was told, is a communist-liberal agent. But the indomitable archbishop had a trump card. When government officials advised him to have African nuns and priests at Boreneng, he replied that Boreneng had been established to keep an eye on communist and other anti-christian activity in Atteridgeville. Did anybody in the government seriously believe that it would serve this vital purpose for both the Catholics and the CNP once it was controlled by the black people? His solution was the importation of Dutch nuns and priests. Pretoria did not like the idea very much, but the Hollanders were decidedly better evils than the British or the Americans.

* * *

Zandile leaves Atteridgeville every weekday about 5:30 in the morning and reaches Waterkloof about an hour later, when she prepares breakfast which Piet du Toit van der Merwe insists on having exactly at 7:30. At first, the van der Merwes said she should come in also on Saturdays. But the quality of the service she has given them persuaded them that she had a case when she pleaded with them that they should allow her not to work on Saturdays, in order to have a little more time with her family. After breakfast she cleans the house, trots with the basket behind Marietjie to do the day's shopping and returns to prepare lunch. More often than not, Marietjie helps with the cleaning, but in recent weeks has been showing signs of increasing indolence; her temper, which is usually placid, has tended to spark at the slightest provocation. A new development in her changing mood is that she wants to sit down where Zandile is working and converse with her.

Ag, Zandile, I feel so miserable!

What is wrong with you, nooi?

If you mess around with a man, this is what he does with you, she says, pointing to her bulging belly.

That is the way of all decent women.

You say so . . . . Tell me, Zandile, I've been wanting to ask you this question for some time now. Are you a Roman Catholic?

Why, nooi?

Well, Catholic people are such horrible bigots. I often wonder why the government allowed them to establish Boreneng mission so close to Atteridgeville. I don't think they're there to do anybody other than themselves, any good.

I am not a Catholic and am not a christian, either. But my children go to Boreneng day school; it's the best school for my people in the Pretoria district.

I don't understand you, Zandile. You're not a Catholic, you're not a christian and you send your children to a christian school?

I couldn't establish the type of school I wanted, even when I had the money. Government policy requires that no black child should be taught by anybody, anywhere, except by teachers in licensed schools. It is a crime for anybody to teach an African child without a licence; this is what the law says.

Are you telling me that you can't teach your own child?

Not that; but of what use is that right when I leave home before sunrise and return to my children long after sunset? For five days in the week, I do not see them at all.

If a friend of yours were to gather the children of her friends during the day and keep them away from the streets by teaching them

85

in her house, what would happen?

She would be arrested, charged, fined and possibly endorsed out of the location, if she did not have a government licence to impart knowledge to the children.

This is nonsense, Zandile. Does the prime minister know about it?

I don't know if he does; what I know is that this is the law.

You didn't tell me why you're not a christian.

Nooi, why do you want us to talk about these things? They're not pleasant.

Believe me, I would not if I could help it. But I want to know how you live, how you feel about things. You see, I am afraid, Zandile; all of us are afraid; most white people do not trust black people; we do not know what is going on in your mind; we're doing everything we can for your people, but all we seem to be getting for our pains is a kick in the teeth. Your people, we are told, are not grateful. But you are so different! Why are you not a christian?

Christianity makes me a smaller person than I want to be; it gives me a smaller mind, a smaller heart and leads me to a smaller world in a smaller future.

Aren't you afraid of what will happen to you when you die? When you face your God?

Afraid? No, of course not. I am a limb of God; he can't do without me any more than I can without him.

You mean . . . you mean that you practise witchcraft?

I never understand what white people mean by witchcraft.

I mean, things like bewitching people, digging dead bodies from their graves, ritual murder, worshipping ancestors and things like that.

Our wise men down the centuries taught that life is a response to a necessity that is immanent in our nature. I do a certain thing because it is necessary for me to do it and not because it is good or evil. If it was necessary for me to bewitch people, I would do it; if it was necessary for me to dig up dead bodies, I would do it. For the same reason, I would commit ritual murder and I do the things you call ancestor worship. And I do not think we are unique in doing these things. If you go to our cemetery, you would see something there that would possibly break your heart. Most of the graves there are of babies and infants. In my community, we say that an infant has no business to die; we took that from our ancestors. The white man came and said infants must die. That is witchcraft. He was burning his own women on the stake in Europe in the days your ancestors came to this land. That is witchcraft. For, what is witchcraft? It is the evil thought translated into action to hurt the weak. The thought is the important thing; how men translate it into action depends on their culture, their history and their environment.

You should have been a schoolteacher, Zandile, and not a housemaid.

It so happens, I am a teacher; I have a Master's degree in Education.

And what are you doing in the location, then?

I love somebody and am a mother; that's why I'm there; it makes me feel my personality grow.

You mean ... you mean that your personality is enlarged in the location?

That is precisely what is happening just now .... Nooi, I thought I would ask you to let me go home earlier to-day. I'd like to do a little shopping and rush to Atteridgeville. We have company from home.

Is it your papa or your mama?

No, nooi; it is a witchdoctor.

What? A witchdoctor ... in the house of a university graduate?

Yeah!

* * *

The South African location is a self-contained little world, sealed against contact with every outside influence which does not serve the ends of the white rulers. As a rule, it is surrounded by a high steel fence; entrance into it is through one main gate which is generally patrolled by police twenty-four hours of every day of every year. The law requires that any stranger entering the location should have a permit to be inside it; before the permit is issued, the outsider must state in the clearest manner possible why he enters the location, who it is he wants to see, whether or not he knows such person and if he knows him, to indicate the length of time he has known him.

As a rule, black visitors are allowed to stay inside a location for seventy-two hours. Whites, Coloureds and Indians may not sleep in the location.

The male children of a family have to get a government licence to stay with their parents when they reach the age of eighteen and start paying the poll tax. Beyond that age, it is a crime for a child to live in the house of his parents, if he is a male. He is presumed to be productive as an economic unit when he reaches eighteen and is expected to enter the labour market, instead of staying in his father's house.

The law discourages visits by whites or Coloureds or Indians to private homes. Non-Africans, for example, may not attend a party in a location home; they may not attend dances at night in location halls. The law of entry into locations is strictest against black diplomats. Although they are Africans, they are accorded the status of whitemen, second degree, and, as such, may not enter a location by themselves.

The people who move fairly freely in and out of each location are the leaders of the various separatist sects because these are, as a rule, not connected with any missionary group or any obnoxious foreigners or any other whites. As a rule again, they have strong views on the race question and do not take too kindly to contact with whites or Coloureds or Asians.

Next on the list of the privileged are the medicine-men. The class is made up of people committed to different professions.

At the top of the list are the seers or soothsayers or diviners. These are generally sensitive women with exceptional leadership qualities who are trained to be constantly in contact with the spirits of the dead. Their main function is to diagnose illnesses by studying the state of the vibrations each person emits. After years of study, some of them proceed to master the ancient art of healing, but many of them are quacks and charlatans. The practice of medicine is dominated by the herbalists, who have become a wealthy class in the locations.

In a class by themselves are the bonethrowers, who are mostly males and are generally regarded as the worst charlatans of the medical profession.

Then, there are the physicians, surgeons and nurses trained in the white man's schools who man the hospitals, clinics and health centres. Most African doctors prefer private practice which protects them against the daily humiliations for being black.

The location is unique in one other aspect: every person inside it is the legal equal of his neighbour. The wealthy trader or rich doctor has no rights which his neighbour, the gravedigger, does not have. The African who seeks distinction will not get it from the white side; he looks to his own people for all rewards. The levelling power of the location has created a vigorous democracy in which there is no class and in which wealth is sometimes a distinct handicap in that it isolates the rich man from the main stream of life in the location. The isolation has a multiplicity of dangers. As a result marriages across economic or social lines are by no means exceptional. This bevelling of social angularities, however, has frightening political implications. In the democracy of the location, the equality has developed a feeling of security in the person which militates against the exclusive group consciousness which tribalism was designed to stimulate. Although the various language groups are segregated in each location, the equality develops a feeling of security which extends the area of solidarity at the group level. No longer threatened by the other language sections, each group sees fulfilment for itself and guarantees of survival in identification with the other groups. The diversity of languages and customs has been transformed into a source of strength.

Each language, each culture, is accepted as one more eye by which the Africans might discover their way through the mazes of creation.

Stress is laid on the excellence of Basotho diplomacy and no longer on the fact that they once ate horses; on Xhosa perspicacity and no longer on what was once known as Xhosa untrustworthiness. If there is a tough job to be done, the staying-power of the Zulus has come to be accepted as a pillar of strength for the black people. People pay less attention to what was once believed to be the stupidity of the Zulu.

With group solidarity cemented by the rigid segregation, each community has become a compact, self-organising unit. There is no longer any need for political organisations in the location. The subtle and not so subtle checks and balances which preserved stability and promoted viability in traditional societies have come into play once more, creating a rhythm in the lives of the communities which is beyond control of the white authority. It is no longer necessary for mass meetings to be held when the police get to know the dangerous men. The locations argue that all that is needed is to *speak in the winds.* This means that a message passed to a Zulu is broadcast to every Zulu; that the Basotho and other groups behave as the Zulus do. In this setting stress has come to be laid increasingly on *ubuntu*, the essence of being human, which is the common foundation for all African cultures in the locations.

While the children in the Basotho, Xhosa and Zulu schools speak different languages and are taught different histories, each grows up regarding *umteto wesintu* in its own language, history and culture as its alternative to the white man's law; *umteto wesintu* evokes identical responses from all the language groups. To relate things to *umteto wesintu* is what has come to be known as "speaking in the winds."

The practice has two advantages: it transmits messages to the educated and the illiterate Africans in symbols both understand; at the same time these symbols cannot be readily identified or understood or legislated against in terms of white perspectives. Maggie and the women organise a *brown-bread* sandwich party for the chief of the chiefs of the Bantu, the Chief Bantu Affairs Commissioner for the Witwatersrand; the women insist that this is an act of loyalty to the government; that they use brown bread simply because it is the cheapest on the market and that as poor people, they cannot afford white bread. Maggie and the women of the location do not want the Chief Native Commissioner for the Witwatersrand to enter their location. They suffocate him with profusions of loyalty and force Pretoria to say, in effect, that senior white officers should not enter the locations. How, in terms of English or Roman or Dutch law, is an African professing loyalty to be arrested for being loyal? Perceptive Afrikaners are aware of the trap they have laid for themselves; some of them dread its implications. Piet van der Merwe and his wife are some of the people who fear the things going on in the location.

The emphasis on *umteto wesintu* has created a revolution in black political life. From the beginning of the nineteenth century, when the British came to South Africa, they had gradually developed techniques by which they used the chiefs as instruments by which to control the Africans. The Afrikaners had taken over the techniques and used the chiefs as tools by which to gain African acceptance for white policies. The chief was almost invariably appointed by the government or, in the case of members of royal families, approved by Pretoria. The chiefs relied on tradition to uphold their authority. As a result, they were constantly in conflict with the educated Africans or the urban workers. These clashes corroded their authority in the black community and forced them to identify themselves with the government to preserve their positions of influence.

This suited Pretoria; the chiefs were given more power over their people so that they should collaborate more effectively in making South Africa safe for the white people. This created cleavages in the African community which militated against an effective African united front. Pretoria committed itself to the maintenance of African traditions, languages and cultures—as interpreted for the Africans by the Afrikaners. The commitment split the Africans on the one hand and, on the other, destroyed English influences among the black people. The educated had gone to English schools and had cultivated English attitudes to South African history at given levels.

Things have been moving splendidly for the CNP in the rural areas where the chiefs have been steadily clamouring for power and having it rationed out to them in proportion as it kept them tractable. Agitators in the locations are "endorsed" out of cities and thrown into the reserves where they become a headache for the chiefs who, in turn, are given more and more powers to deal with the *vermin from the locations*. But the ferment in the locations, resulting from re-evaluations of *umteto wesintu* has filtered through to the rural reserves. More and more people have spoken in the winds as more and more chiefs listened. These upheld *umteto wesintu*; they upheld its values, preached them from church pulpits and taught them in the schools. At first, the government was thrilled; the black man was at last accepting the policy of developing along his own lines as the Afrikaners had always said he should.

By slow degrees, the rural chiefs find themselves no longer treated with contempt by the educated; they receive invitations from the urban locations where they are received by thousands not only of their own people but by men and women from all the main African language groups. To reinforce their position and counter the spirit of revolt emerging in the locations, the chiefs are even told that if they want independence, they can have it. Care is taken, of course, to see to it that the land on which black states are established is so small it will be impossible for the blacks to maintain themselves as viable communities. They will be forced, as Malawi, Botswana, Lesotho and

Swaziland are, to export their cheap labour to South Africa where they will have to accept all sorts of humiliations to scrape a living. It is at this point that the government's difficulties have started.

It has become increasingly clear to the chiefs that the type of independence they are being offered will be real on paper only; that the idea is to saddle them with the government of starving populations which will have a vested interest in their liquidation. More and more chiefs have been attracted by the prospect of using *umteto wesintu* as the bridge over the language chasms which divided the black communities. To make things easier for them, the government established a college for the sons of chiefs in the expectation that a class of born rulers would emerge which would always deal with the white man on his terms.

In the strains and stresses created by CNP policy a consensus on *umteto wesintu* has emerged to bring together the black intellectuals and the educated chiefs. The bases of the new understanding are the *ubuntu* evaluation of the person, the build-up of power to guarantee the restoration to the African of his land, the creation of the conditions which will force the whites to negotiate and confronting the whites with an alternative ideal of nationhood.

The traditional African view of the person is the crucial factor in the regrouping of urban and rural forces; clarity on it enables the urban workers and the rural peasants, the educated and the illiterate as well as the rich and the poor to respond in identical ways to similar provocations.

With ideological unity established, the segregated institutions for the government of the blacks can be manipulated in such a way as to create a dual authority structure of black-white power: that is, to have a legal black administration opposing the white government. The advantage in that setting would be with the African, who has the numbers and carries the white economy on his shoulders. He would withdraw his labour and paralyse the white man's economy; it is difficult to see how Botswana, Lesotho, Malawi and Swaziland could supply cheap labour where the black South Africans had thrown black and white into a situation of confrontation.

Both the rural areas and the urban locations feel that the moment when their hearts will beat at the same rate is not far. And, as the urban locations turn their backs on the white man's world and as they take him out of their minds, they hunger more for clarity on the values which give meaning to their understanding of reality. It is in response to this yearning that Puma and Zandile have invited Mazani Lukele to visit them in Pretoria.

About twenty men and women crowd in Puma's sitting-room. They sit on sofas and chairs and empty wooden boxes, forming a circle on either side of the diviner. She sits on a leopard skin she brought with her from Natal. She spent the whole day meditating in her room and

91

her face glows with vibrancy.

Hail, Children of the House to which I belong!

The ancient salutation electrifies the air and transports people's minds to a past which they never thought they would see again. It gives them feelings of union with one another in the small room and of being simultaneously in the past, the future and the present. When they have recovered from the experience they return the greeting:

We feel as you do, O Daughter of Wisdom!

We are being reborn into a new future; I came here to see the rebirth. People had told me about it. Now I see it with my own eyes. I had been told that a new spirit is at large among our people; that we who had borrowed the meanings we gave to life had ceased to be borrowers. I understand that some of you are university men, medical practitioners, lawyers, leaders of our people. What a beautiful people you all are!

I never thought the moment would come in my life when all of us, the schooled and the unschooled, would, as people say in my part of the country, grind together like the jaws which belong to one skull.

Now, we are doing it; the moment is beautiful.

Mazane chooses every word she utters. She has never had the chance to speak to a group of educated Africans. In the old days, when the English dominated the economy and politics, they established schools where the African was forced to see reality from English perspectives. Fulfilment for him, he was taught, lay in being a good, black carbon copy of the white man. The black people were divided into two categories: the "civilised" and the pagan. The "civilised" African read, wrote and spoke English; he worshipped the white man's gods and prayed for blessings from the ancestors of the white race.

Ah, yes, it was beneath his dignity to speak to or associate with the pagans. While he never was accepted as the equal of the white people, he had some of their privileges. In Natal, for example, he could be issued with a certificate which exempted him from the laws which regulated the lives of most of his people. He did not carry a pass and could not be prosecuted under curfew laws.

A black middle class emerged which bought land and built houses in the white man's cities. These people could, if they wanted, marry white women. In the Cape province, black men even had the vote; they elected members of parliament and the provincial council.

Walter Rubusana had been a member of the Cape provincial council. The anglicisation of the African had produced handsome political dividends for the English. The "civilised" Africans had consistently voted for English representatives in the legislatures and did all in their power to weaken the Afrikaner. The balance in black-white relations then was based on the division of the Africans into hostile groups, a cultural-political alliance between the English and the "civilised" Africans, the isolation of the Afrikaner and English dominance of the government and the economy. A fierce nationalism had developed in the Afrikaans community which set out to smash the African-English alliance and establish the political dominance of the Afrikaner.

It used the white skin as the bond of unity on the white side and bribed the English with economic privileges into siding with the Afrikaner. While it punished the African savagely for being the child of his particular parents, it corroded the English influences in his education and his churches and passed laws to ensure that he developed along "his own lines." Since then, a new balance in the relations between the races has emerged; where, before, merit fixed the position of the individual in South African life, race and colour determine it now. Afrikaner political power has been allied to English finance-power against the African.

But now a fierce black nationalism is developing which seeks to smash this balance. Educated black men are turning their backs on the values which the white man's culture translates into action; they are digging into their past, to discover that larger truth which their ancestors had for thousands of years used to give meaning to reality. If this is breaking down the barriers which separated the "civilised" Africans from the pagan, it has awakened a consciousness of belonging together which makes it possible for the educated to want to hear Mazane Lukele explain the principles of the *Buntu* philosophy.

Rebirth does not mean that we are a new people; it only means that a set of scales has fallen from our eyes; that we see the truth in clearer light.

For, we have been around these mountains and valleys from the dawn of antiquity; we were around when stones cried if pinched and shall be around when the stones have crumbled into dust.

We shall be around because the person is a living ideal in the process of becoming; he is real and lives on forever as he has always been in existence. Because he is the individualisation of the power from which all things derive their being, life's purpose for him is to project himself into the future. He does not need any God, any Christ or any ancestor to do this. He moves eternally into the future. His ancestors have been around here, before him; they understand his problems and live in the future; they guide him. But he and he alone determines his life. The eternal person has in himself all the power he can ever need to be what he wants to be. There is an infinity of paths into the future and each person is one such path. Some see the way more clearly than others; some run while others walk or limp along; the great thing is that all are human. Some are black or brown or yellow or white; what does it matter? All are human! We, who have been around from the dawn of antiquity dare not forget this truth . . . .

Some of the educated people shake their heads. They have

been punished so cruelly for being black and have been so drilled in white values they have begun to identify race with principle, like the whites.

I realise that it is difficult not to strike back when you are hurt. I am for striking back . . . but with weapons of my making. The larger truth is our weapon; we have not borrowed it from the white man; he can't take it away from us. It teaches that society exists to enable the eternal person to make the best possible use of his life. See what I mean? You and I are all-of-us. Let us, therefore, open ourselves to each other, explore each other and, ultimately, lose ourselves in each other.

When we have done that, we shall know that no man is good or evil; that each responds to the necessity which inheres in him as the eternal person. When we do this, we shall realise that virtue consists in aligning the responses; when we know how to do this we shall be ready for freedom; the walls with which we have surrounded ourselves will fall apart. The tree does not need the gun to crack the rock in which it buries its roots; it simply acts as though there was no rock. The tree does not go to other trees to heal the wounds on its bark; it exudes its own gum. Men might call us all sorts of names; they might say we stink; they might say we are primitive. Whatever they say merely reflects the levels at which they think.

The answer is to take them out of our minds; to act as if they did not exist and to walk boldly into the future. All you need to do this are your heads and your bare hands, for, in the final analysis, no person has what his neighbour does not have; every person achieves in the light of his choice. This is the challenge, the promise and the glory of being human.

So, the jaws worked. Those were the words!

* * *

IX. The Anniversary

Faka induku emqubeni 'ze ilunge mhla idingeka.

(Keep your fighting stick in a manure heap for use when needed.)

A year has gone by since the murder of Helvetius van Warmelo. In those twelve months violent storms have raged in the Afrikaans community, threatening to smash the unity which van Warmelo worked so hard to establish. In the fifty years after Union, the Afrikaner has been migrating from the countryside into the cities and cultivating the poises and habits of thinking of the city-dweller. Out in the open spaces, everything belonged to him as long as he had his gun.

Life had only one major challenge; to defend himself against the Africans or the British. His only weapon of defence was his gun. The next equipment he needed was a patriarch or *volksleier*; the man who would dispense the law, arbitrate in disputes, and lead in the moment of crisis. Piet Retief, whom the Zulus executed for espionage in 1838, was one such volksleier; Paul Kruger was another. In the chronicles of the Afrikaner, these men are accorded the reverence due to deities. When that African who urinated on the Kruger statue was brought to court, he had to be accompanied by an armed police escort. Some Afrikaner youths felt so insulted they wanted to cut off his penis.

Beyond the gun and the volksleier, the Afrikaner anchored his soul in the bible. He believed it was the source of all wisdom; the beginning and the end of all truth. He was not prepared to accept any fact outside of those defined by the bible. In some of his universities, the teaching of evolution was a heresy for which a professor lost his job. Everywhere, the Afrikaner built walls and laagers by which to protect the truth as revealed in the bible. Gold and diamonds and industry brought the cities into being and confronted the Afrikaner with the danger of extinction from every side. Like the African he did not know the ways of the city and was largely illiterate. Almost as poor as his black urban neighbour, he settled in the cheaper parts of the large

95

city where poverty made him the equal of his black neighbour. The humiliation of being the equal of the black man cut wounds which have not healed to this day. From the wounds, a hatred for all outsiders developed which fuelled his nationalism.

But the African was not his only problem. The city was dominated by the English and the Jew; these controlled the economy; they dictated cultural standards and political goals. The Afrikaner had to fit into patterns of thinking and living laid down by the economic and cultural aristocracy of the cities. His white skin was no advantage; as a matter of fact, it exposed him to forms of contempt which he could never forgive or forget. It projected him as the scum of the white world; the vermin which had to be wiped out or allowed to die out in order to preserve the purity of white, Anglo-Saxon culture.

If an Afrikaner made a mistake, he was taunted with the remark that not even a kaffer would do things as he did them; wherever he turned, he was made to understand that he was a disgrace to the white race. No English or Jewish girl dared to marry an Afrikaner if she had all her senses in their right places. From the wounds cut by the English and the Jew on the one side and the fear of being swamped by the African on the other, there developed a bitterness against outsiders which committed the Afrikaner permanently to isolation and exclusiveness.

He turned inward, to himself, for that strength which would enable him to transform South Africa into the land after his design. He set out to generate forces in himself before which nothing could stand; he was going to use every weapon, every means and everything on which he could lay his hands to get himself to the top and, once there, to keep himself there forever. Willem Adriaan de Haas represents this approach.

He comes face to face with problems for which he had never prepared himself when he gets to the top. For example, he discovers that real power lies, not in the heroic approach to reality but in aligning the resources controlled by the different groups which constitute society. If he controls the government, the English have the economic know-how while African labour is the backbone of the economy. In the old days, when the white race dictated the destinies of nations, he could use colour and the gun to keep the black man *in his place*. He could use the mineral resources of the country to buy his way to acceptance by the white powers.

But things have since changed, as van Warmelo so often warned. Black men and brown men and yellow men have risen to positions of power and influence in the world; it has become a risky business to kick a kaffer until he sees his rectum or to call an Asian a coolie. In the good old days a white man could shoot any number of recalcitrant kaffers and nobody in the world would say a word about it.

To-day, it is enough for a policeman to slap a black man to get the whole world screaming as though God had been murdered in his heaven. This is not the world to which the Afrikaner wants to belong; his problem is that he cannot withdraw from it for there is nowhere to go in the world to-day. Every piece of land on the face of the earth is owned by somebody. To survive, he has to fix a place for himself which is dictated ultimately by black, brown and yellow men.

Some Afrikaners are trying to come to grips with the implications of this fact. People like Lukas Meyer, the chairman of the CNP caucus and Cornelius Beetge van Schalkwyk, the Free State wheat magnate, believe that Afrikanerdom must strike a deal with the black, brown and yellow peoples of the world now, while they are still weak and when they can accept a compromise on the Afrikaner's terms. They argue that the first step in this direction is a dialogue with the rural and urban leaders of the black people in South Africa which will lead to a negotiated settlement of the colour problem. They insist that the fact that the Afrikaner controls the government gives him a freedom to influence events which the black people do not as yet have. To hesitate to act decisively at this stage, they warn, is a clear invitation to disaster. They tremble each time an African talks of the dual authority structure of power which the CNP has created in South Africa and are under no illusions about what would happen to South Africa if the Africans finally decided to withdraw their labour from white industry.

No phrase has a greater terror for them than the *irresistible momentum of floodwaters rushing to the sea*. Each time they see three Africans putting their heads together, or come across BB scrawled on a wall, they see the momentum developing irresistibility. One of these days, these men agree, the black men will set South Africa on fire and the conflagration will be such that no power on earth will extinguish it.

The views of men like van Schalkwyk and Meyer are shared by a number of Afrikaner academicians in the universities. These have formed themselves into UBRA and once every year, during the summer vacation, they travel in groups all over the country having consultations with black leaders in the bid to agree on a basis for a negotiated settlement of the colour problem. The funds for enabling the professors to move around are provided largely by Afrikaner businessmen who think de Haas and his supporters are leading the country to disaster. For his part, the prime minister regards all these people as chicken-livered traitors who must be crushed by fair means or foul. If they are not, he fears, they will poison the minds of young Afrikaners in the universities and encourage them to come to terms with the black peril. The compromise, he warns all with ears to hear, can be arrived at only over his dead body.

A political quarrel in the Afrikaans community is as spectacular as a war among elephants. Baobab tree trunks are ground to pulp when the denizens of the forest resort to force to drive their points home. De Haas mobilises every resource at his disposal to discredit the professors, including the secret police. The university men are at an advantage at the intellectual level. Professor Japie Geldenhuis speaks for them all when he says:

The dice become loaded against the Afrikaner each day we delay a settlement. We are a small people; if it were not for the gold in this land and for the attractive investments opportunities we offer the industrial countries, not one Western country would care a damn about what happened to us. But these advantages are controlled ultimately by the black people; they provide the cheap labour which makes us prosperous.

The day the Africans withdraw their labour, not one of our friends in the West will raise a finger to defend us.

They won't have much of a choice. Nationalism has reared its head in the world. The Arabs recently turned the world upside down by withdrawing their oil from the markets of the world. If that did not do greater harm than the entire American stockpile of nuclear bombs, I do not know what it did. But the industrial nations have almost depleted their metal and many other mineral resources. Our civilisation cannot survive without most of these. Africa has some of the largest deposits of metals and minerals we shall have run out of in the next seventy years or so. Think what would happen if the Africans decided to use their metals and minerals as a political weapon against South Africa. Think what would happen if the Africans and the Arabs ganged up and used their metals, oil and other minerals as a political weapon against us. Show me one country in the world that would come to our help! If America and Russia have nuclear weapons, the Africans and the Arabs control something incomparably more dangerous for the white race here!

* * *

In Pretoria, the celebrations of van Warmelo's death include a short memorial service in the Groot Kerk to be attended by the prime minister, his cabinet ministers, members of the diplomatic corps, heads of government departments and other dignitaries. The service in the Great Church is to be followed by the laying of a wreath on the grave of the late prime minister.

The Africans, too, celebrate the anniversary. Three uniformed African police, one of them driving, accompany two white men in a jeep with a Pretoria, government-garage number-plate. They park in front of the office of the chief warden of the Standerton jail. The two white men step out of the car and walk around, admiring the flower garden in front of the jail. Both of them speak Afrikaans with the accents of Free Staters. Their manner and bearing suggest that they are men accustomed to giving orders. The older man, in his early forties, walks to the main office, his hands shoved aggressively into the pockets of his trousers. Prison wardens are uniformed in South Africa and are organised along army lines; their officers carry military titles.

Warden, I am Brigadier De Villiers Swanepoel, chief of the assassinations division of the Security Police in Pretoria and this is Captain Jooste van der Horst who's in charge of the case involving that kaffer who shot the prime minister.

The warden, who had risen from his chair as though his spine ached has suddenly straightened and is all smartness in the presence of the mighty from Pretoria. The two men present their identification papers. The warden is so shaken he glances quickly at the documents and returns them ceremoniously to their owners.

Where's the superintendent?

He's in Johannesburg, meneer; on government business and won't be back for three days.

And the assistant superintendent?

He's in his office, meneer.

Tell him Brigadier Swanepoel and Captain van der Horst from Pretoria want to see him.

Ja, meneer.

Swanepoel lights his pipe and blows clouds of smoke which almost fill the tiny reception office. He walks noisily around the room to let everybody know that he is the cock that crows first in the morning at that moment. The assistant superintendent comes down the passage to meet the officers himself. He is a tall, wiry man with a voice which rumbles like distant thunder. He is a man of few words; so few, in fact, he gives the impression every word he utters costs him money.

Captain van der Kemp, did you say?

Ja, meneer.

Well, Captain, do you know Theodore Darikwa?

He's treated like an English lord around here.

Well, it's time he went to another manor; here are his transfer papers.

Van der Kemp goes through the papers slowly, to the end and then starts all over again, pointing every word with his finger as he reads it aloud.

Everything seems alright to me. And, in any case, I don't want the sight of the man around here. You'd think he was twins with Dingane.

Nobody laughs; everybody understands what the reference means.

Did you get anything new from him?

Not much, I'm afraid. You people in Pretoria don't understand the kaffer mind. That nigger knows we can give him the works only up to a certain point and not beyond. He knows we don't want to kill him. I suspect he knows you made us responsible for his safety.

You gave him the wire treatment, of course?

You could try it with that nigger; he just passes out, almost at will. It's native magic, you see. The district surgeon and all his psychiatrists can't do a thing.

In the electric bath? How did he perform?

Same. If a man faints in electrified water, if you're not careful, he'll die and our orders, from the prime minister himself, are that under no conditions must he be allowed to die before he's told everything you people want to know from him.

Well, Captain, you can't do better than your best.

Van der Kemp goes to a pigeonhole and brings out a sheaf of papers, some of which he signs and hands over to Swanepoel. While the latter goes through them van der Kemp gives instructions through the intercom for the delivery of Darikwa.

He'll be here in another two or three minutes, Brigadier. At least I'm glad he's out of my hands. I've never seen a stubborner kind of nigger . . . .

It'll soon be over, Captain.

You people in Pretoria have more power than we do. But I tell you, if I had had my way, I'd have beat hell out of his arse!

Wait until you hear what we do with him in Pretoria!

My best wishes!

Swanepoel rises to his feet and puffs heavily at his pipe as he moves toward the door, shouting out the names of the African police.

Jakob! Samuel! Jinja! Here!

The Africans jump out of the jeep, run to the main hall of the prison where they stand stiffly at attention. Swanepoel emerges from the passage, followed by van der Kemp and van der Horst. The Africans salute. Two white wardens bring Darikwa down the other end of the passage. He is still wearing the kitchen-boy's suit; he does not seem to have lost much weight; he is in shackles. Swanepoel turns red in the face when he sees the black man, rushes to him and slaps his face and kicks him on the thigh. Darikwa loses his balance and falls.

Get up! You dirty communist murderer! I hear you think you're too important to talk! Wait until we get to Pretoria, my boy! There, *ek sal jy jou gat wys*! Hear?

The African does not answer.

Take him into the jeep!

Brigadier, says van der Kemp, I understand your feelings. Quite frankly, I think that man is better dead than alive and I would like to kill him with my bare hands.

You did a good job, according to your results. I'll remember that when I get to Pretoria.

Thank you very much meneer! Thank you, Brigadier! A safe journey, Brigadier!

* * *

It is about three in the afternoon when the ceremonies are over at the cemetery. At that time of the day, van Warmelo would have said he had done enough for the day. Not de Haas. He insists on being taken to his office in Union Buildings. He has no sooner sat down than Piet du Toit van der Merwe enters by the side door.

Meneer, the Commissioner of Prisons and the Commissioner of Police wish to see you on an important matter.

What is it? Do you know? Why both of them?

I cannot say, meneer.

Bring them in.

The two officers march in.

The Minister of Justice is out of town, Mr. Prime Minister, and because we have a report that deserves your attention, we decided to bring it over to you directly. The Commissioner of Prisons will communicate it to you . . . .

Mr. Prime Minister I have just received a report from Standerton jail that Theodore Darikwa escaped from prison at eleven o'clock this morning . . . .

What are you telling me?

Two white men, disguised as security police officers from Pretoria produced forged papers and took him away.

That damned fool, who let him go . . . . Where do you think they took him?

Mr. Prime Minister, says the Police Commissioner, I have given orders to every police border post to be on the look-out for the refugee.

For a while everything seems a cruel nightmare; de Haas buries his face in his hands. After a long pause, he raises his head.

Alright, gentlemen, you may go.

* * *

X. The Zulus Are Coming!

Izinyembezi zamaqhawe zidiliza ilanga.

(The tears of heroes can bring the sun crashing to the ground.)

Days of the Covenant have come and gone, each with its own events. This particular one falls on a Sunday. Chief Bulube rose before sunrise to give medicine to one of his favourite Jersey cows which had given birth to twins, both of them female. It had had difficulty in delivering them and the chief had spent half the night in the special cattle kraal with two of his friends, helping the cow. Although the sun has risen over the faraway Inanda hills, Bulube is still asleep.

The times have changed. In the years gone by Bulube would by now be in church for the first service of the day. But now, he sees no reason why he should worry about being the first to enter the church building, which his father built. Now and then he catches himself wondering if the money spent on it was not wasted. The values taught from the pulpit, he tells himself, have proved disastrous for the African people. The missionary came with the bible, preached love and told the Zulus that they should turn their eyes to the skies, to heaven, while the white man stole their land. For many years he believed that those whites who took their christianity seriously could be reasoned with and talked into agreement on the resolution of race conflict. Steadily, events have proved him wrong; he knows now that the christians in whom he had so much faith were white men first and christians afterwards. When some of his closest friends ask him why he is losing his faith in christianity, he says the load it places on his conscience is more than he can bear.

His friends know that one item in the load was the death of Dr. Mpini Magasela, the brilliant professor of physics at Ndulinde university college. Mpini means Man-in-the-War. The young man had been a child prodigy; by the time he was twenty-five he had obtained his Ph.D., degree in physics from a distinguished centre of learning in the United States. One night, the security police knocked on his door and arrested him. For months nobody knew where he was or what was happening to him. Then, one day, the police came to his father, Professor Dazinkani Magasela, who heads the department of

geno-politics at the university and told him that his son had committed
suicide in Johannesburg. Their story was that Mpini had thrown himself
from a sixth-storey window of a building at police headquarters in
Johannesburg while being interrogated.

Hardly a year goes by without one or more such "suicides" in
the largest police stations in the land. Bulube has not recovered from
the young man's death, which he regards as a national disaster; equally
painful to him is the personal bereavement. Bulube regarded Mpini as
his own son. Bulube has been shaken by the silence of his white
christian friends when it comes to the "suicide." With the exception of
one or two maverick clergymen who have asked awkward questions in
press interviews or have written letters to the prime minister, the white
church acts as though nothing had happened.

The people who reacted sharply the moment news of Mpini's
death was made public were the students in the black universities and
colleges all over the country. Everywhere they came out in
demonstrations while hundreds went on hunger strikes. The police
opened fire on some of the demonstrations, killing dozens of
demonstrators. Near Durban, for instance, three thousand young people
were coming down Syringa Avenue toward the centre of the city when
they were stopped by the police who had placed machine guns across
the street. The police ordered the students to disperse and when the
young Africans refused, the police opened fire. Bulube had been in
Durban and had seen the shootings with his own eyes. Those who stood
close to him say they saw tears flow down his cheeks; they say they
heard him groan:

How long, O Lord? How long?

* * *

Bulube's wife was up early, to keep an eye on the cow while
her husband rested. She is making herself a cup of coffee in the kitchen
when she hears human voices in the distance. She rushes to the window,
pulls the curtain aside and sees thousands of Zulu men in national attire
marching toward Bulube's kraal. She runs to her bedroom to wake up
the chief.

Siluba! We are a dead people! An army is on the yard around
the kraal!

The Zulu wife does not call her husband by his first name. If
he is a chief custom does not allow her to call him even by his second
name. If she addresses him, she has to use the name of one of his
ancestors. Bulube jumps up and sits by the side of his bed.

What is it? What has happened?

An army! Coming up the road; I have never seen anything like
this!

She rushes out of the room and starts calling in her children and the people around the chief's kraal. Bulube pulls aside the heavy curtains. He cannot see the figures clearly because of the dust. He presses his binoculars to his eyes. Yes, indeed, it is an army. His wife runs into the bedroom again and shouts:

The Zulus are coming, Siluba! What shall we do?

You and the children and everybody around here, come into the house. Sit still here, as though nothing has happened. I shall go to the people coming; I shall meet them outside the gate.

Shall I call the police?

No. You do as I tell you.

Bulube dresses quickly, covering his body in the traditional attire of a Zulu gentleman. He takes his ceremonial shield and his staff of office and walks out of the front door. His three sons, the youngest of whom is only ten, are waiting for him under the verandah with three of his hunting guns. The sight overwhelms him; those three little boys, the oldest of whom is fourteen, are ready even at that age to die by the side of their father. He stands still for a moment, holding back the tears of pride and then turns to the boys.

Do you know who those are?

No, Siluba, says the oldest boy.

Do you know what they want?

That disorganises the boys, who look at each other without answering their father.

You take those guns into the house and make yourselves useful to your mother.

The boys slink away while Bulube marches to the main gate. His personal bodyguard has already taken positions near the gate. The mass of men comes slowly, up the incline toward Bulube's house. These are difficult times for the African people everywhere in the country; Bulube cannot be certain about what is in the mind of the thousands coming up to his kraal. As the Zulus say, the moderate African leader always carries his life in his hands. The people often want him to create situations of confrontation and when he takes a strong line, the government mows them down with gunfire. If he buys the time to build up more power, the people say he is scared or that he has been bribed by the whites or that he is otherwise weak. The Zulus can tolerate a fool; they can throw themselves into the flames of hell itself if they think their leader is brave, but one thing they cannot stand is the leader who is afraid. The militants, led by underground leaders like Dillo Mareka and Sefadi Masilo sometimes criticise his moderate leadership in tones which suggest that they think he is afraid.

The thousands are now about half a mile away from Bulube's kraal; they are singing; the tune is that of a famous resistance song:

Thina sizwe . . . .
. . . . .Thina sizwe esinsundu
Sikhalela . . . .
. . . . Sikhalela Izwe lethu
Elathathwa . . . .
. . . . .Elathathwa ngabamhlophe
Mabawuyeke . . . .
. . . . . . .Mabawuyeke umhlaba wethu!
Malibuye . . . .
. . . . .Malibuye ilizwe lethu!

(We, the nation all so black
Forever mourn the land we lost;
The land stolen from us by whites;
Let them clear off our soil!
Let our land be restored to us.)

The chorus leader chants the syllables of the breath-bar while
the thousands respond massively. They are about a quarter of a mile
from Bulube's gate now. He starts marching down the gently sloping
road, toward them. His bodyguard follow him, with their battle axes.

Do not follow me, he orders them.

The captain of the men is the son of the man who was captain
to Balube's father. He cannot imagine his chief walking into the midst
of the marching thousands who are armed with sticks and are singing a
resistance song, while the guard stand watching at a safe distance.

Siluba! How can we not follow? What will the Zulus say if
anything happens to you?

See that the children are safe!

Bulube continues marching to the thousands until he is about
two hundred yards from them, when they stop suddenly and roar out
the Zulu royal salute:

Bayete!
Bayete!
Uyizulu!

Show us the enemy!
Show us the enemy!
Thou, O essence of the heavens!

That throws Bulube into a rage; it is treason; he throws down
his ceremonial shield and his staff in protest.

How dare you . . . . he shouts. How dare you throw dust on
the king of the Zulus? There is only one man in the whole world whom
you can ask to show you the enemy and that is the king of the Zulus. I
am not even a member of the royal family! Have you come to bring

about my ruin . . . .

Professor Magasela emerges from the thousands while Bulube is talking and jumps forward in the *giya* dance. In the days when the Zulus ruled their land, the heroes challenged each other in the *giya* dance. Magasela has donned the regalia of a commander of the Zulu army and, after the dance, pulls a broad-bladed *iklwa* (stabbing spear developed by Shaka) from a long pouch sewn inside his large oxhide shield. It is a crime for a black man to possess any type of weapon without the permission of the police. And even when the permission has been granted, no African might carry a spear in public. The law is so strict an African housewife has to have a government permit to buy a bread knife in a hardware store. The white authority wants to take no risks with the security of the whites. Long before the start of the guerrilla war in Rhodesia, the police warned the government that constant vigilance against home-made guns would be necessary. And a simple warning had rallied white dealers in kitchen hardware or cutlery behind the government. The guerrilla war in Angola, Mozambique and Rhodesia had confirmed the white man's worst fears. Magasela concealed his spear in the pouch on his shield.

The professor occupies a unique position in the Zulu community. At the university he teaches what he calls geno-politics, which is the study of the peculiar relationships which arise and produce conflict in situations of contact between black and white. His enemies call him a Zulu chauvinist because he preaches that situations arise in the history of nations when a powerful ideal of nationhood knocks at the walls of the womb of history demanding that it should be born. Such a situation arose among the clans which spoke Zulu during the thousand years before Senzangakhona, the father of Shaka the Great. The ideal was finally born in the eighteenth century, when the court poet to Senzangakhona defined the destiny of the Zulu people as rising "to heavens beyond the reach of spirit-forms." Nandi, the mother of Shaka, suckled the infant prodigy and nurtured him on the ideal; she brought him up on the teaching that he had an appointment with destiny; that he was the one man in Africa who was to create the type of empire and society which mankind had not seen before. And, when Shaka became a man, he created the society he had been born to establish.

At this point, the professor adopts a hostile attitude to Shaka. He says Shaka developed into an idealist and set out to establish a society in which mind-quality was the basic qualification for Zulu citizenship. Cannibals left their caves in the Drakensberg mountains and went down to Dukuza where they were rehabilitated and given positions of power in the Zulu army. Albinos through whose ears the sun shone sailed into Durban harbour. Shaka admired their brains, their skill and their guns and set out to establish diplomatic relations with their king in England. The English served him right; they cheated him,

107

lied to him, sabotaged his plan and finally jailed his emissaries in the castle at Capetown. Magasela does not refer to the white people as whites; he calls them the albinos. Does it surprise anybody that after defiling the destiny of the Zulus in the way he did, he was assassinated?

But, Magasela continues, Shaka was not the only traitor. Seme was like Shaka. He rejected what Magasela calls Zuluism and dreamt of a larger nation or community of peoples which would include everybody—the Afrikaners and all sorts of good-for-nothings. The professor has no word ugly enough to describe the leaders of the African in the fifty years after 1912 who "humiliated" the Zulu people by trying to persuade the whites to accept the African ideal of nationhood. The attempt was bound to fail disastrously because black and white are like water and oil; they have nothing in common, except to meet each other on the banks of the Blood River.

After the Indian riots in Durban, the government appointed a commission of inquiry to determine the cause of the explosion. When asked for his views on the Indian question, his single answer was: Aren't there any more ships anywhere in the world to take the Asians to India? His solution for the white problem in South Africa is to blast them out of the country. He spent all the money he had on the education of his son, Mpini, to enable him, one day, to manufacture a portable nuclear bomb with which to bring the white power-structure crashing to the ground. He never said a word about his intention to anybody, not even to Bulube himself. The only person who knew about it was Mpini and that was only when he returned to South Africa with a Ph.D. in physics. When alone, the professor tells himself that he knows precisely why the police killed his son; they found an uncompleted nuclear explosive in the workshop he had built in his father's backyard. To Magasela, the death was not just a bereavement; it was the collapse of a vision—the end of a world. He believed, however, that he still had a trump card which would at least ensure that he reached the end in a spectacular blaze of defiance.

*   *   *

Magasela has laid the spear on his shield, indicating by this his real mission. He has already pulled out of his pocket a scroll parchment which he also lays on the shield. Bulube is still uncertain about what the professor's intention is. When he laid down the shield, everybody realised that he was declaring his peaceful intentions. But when he produced the spear, which Zulu could think of peace? The scroll, well, that mystifies Bulube; the Zulus did not have scrolls. Besides, people know the professor as

UMgaseli wezinseshenseshe,
Ubagasele ilanga liphuma,

Wabaxosha liqopha;
Lize lashona esabagadulisa.

(The pursuer of people with straight hair;
He attacked them when the sun rose;
He was still chasing them by noon;
He was after them when the sun set.)

These little poems or patronymic legends are prized by the Zulus; they are social recognitions of achievement. When Magasela is dead, his grandchildren will be proud of them; each of them will inherit the title Mgaseli (the attacker). He was awarded the patronymic legend for his contributions to the Zulu cause at the university, where he told students that each civilisation or culture or nation or people or clan is the translation into social action of a given ideal of fulfilment. Some ideals can be reconciled, others cannot be; when the latter collide, wars arise. He has devoted his life to the study of the ideal which the Zulu experience translates into action and has produced a galaxy of scholars from Ndulinde who are doing for the Sotho, Shangane, Swazi, Tonga, Tswana, Xhosa and other African experiences what he has done for the Zulus.

He teaches that there has to be clarity on the ideal each experience translates into history, culture and action; that the reconciliation of these ideals is the only real basis of unity in Africa and the only answer to the challenge of tribalism. One day, all the peoples of Africa will attain clarity on the ideals behind their cultures and their histories; when that day comes, the wise men of Africa will put their heads together, each proud of his people's ideal, history and culture and each knowing clearly what it has to contribute toward the enrichment of the African experience as a whole. When that day comes, Africa will lead mankind along safer routes to a better future.

Magasela attacks those Zulus who speak of a *race* problem. He denies that there is such a thing as colour conflict. Like its Zulu counterpart, the Afrikaner experience translates a given ideal of fulfilment into action. The people who accept this ideal believe in its validity; they believe that it gives a satisfying meaning to life; that it is a guarantee of their survival. The important thing in this regard is not whether they are right or wrong in their belief; what matters is whether or not their ideal can co-exist with those accepted for thousands of years in South Africa before the coming of the white man. If it cannot cope with the demands of co-existence, the white man either has to abandon it or clear out of Africa. If it can be reconciled with the African ideals, the white man has every right to remain in Africa. When the Africans enter the white world, they live there as the white man dictates. If the whites want to remain in Africa, they should live as the African dictates.

For years now, the professor has been attacking those people who, he said, wanted to be carbon copies of the white man; who agitated for race equality and for the integration of the African in the white man's society or way of life. The integration of a conquered majority in the society of the conquering minority means the rejection or the repudiation of the ideal of fulfilment which inspires the African experiences and the recognition of the white man's ideal as the thing to live for; it is an African declaration to the world that the meaning the Africans have given to reality and life down the ages is invalid. This, Magasela has always argued, is nothing if it is not the repudiation by the African of his own humanity.

At the level of race, equality has a valid meaning. Each race like every other, has its geniuses and imbeciles; each is ruled by statesmen at one time in its life and by crooks at another; each has all the vices and the virtues to which the race of Man is heir. Integration is a negation of equality. One race arrogates to itself positions of superiority; the weaker acknowledge the superiority by fighting to be recognised as the equals of those whom they acknowledge to be their superiors, on terms laid down by their conquerors. They end up upholding the pattern of life which has brought about their ruin; they become slaves by choice.

The Zulus, Magasela continues, reject the invader's pattern because it destroys life's meaning for the black race. The white man cannot help destroying life's meaning for those he comes into contact with; the rot is deep down in his evaluation of the person. Each African group has to save itself by reaching agreement on fundamentals; by defining the ideal its experience translates into action in the clearest terms possible and then in reconciling the definitions to produce a larger consensus. That is the only answer to what Magasela calls the fragmentation of the African's personality; to "tribalism," to white domination and to Free Africa's hunger and groping for a valid meaning of independence.

Bulube and Magasela are of one mind on the reconciliation of conflicting perspectives as an answer to race problems in mixed societies. They differ, however, on the strategy by which to move to the moment of reconciliation. Magasela argues that the Zulu ideal is the only one that the Zulus can claim to understand fully and that this enjoins on them the duty to develop it to the limit of its excellence. This cannot be done for the Zulus by other peoples and the Zulu himself cannot develop his ideal as long as he is not free or as long as his universities are dominated by self-serving invaders and foreigners. The Zulu must walk out of the society of the white man in order to be free to think clearly and to challenge the white man as an equal, from positions of strength. Only when he is free can he have the independence and the power to make his ideal a viable basis for determining policy.

Bulube says it is not enough to see the world narrowly from Zulu perspectives because the Zulus are not the only people who inhabit the earth. If the validity of each racial or ethnic experience is acknowledged, the next, obvious step must be the reconciliation of the ideals of fulfilment not only behind the various black ethnic experiences but also behind the African and white experiences. Bulube wants African wise men and the wise men of the Afrikaner, the English, the Jew, the Coloured and the Asian to put their heads together to study each other's ideals and to work out a formula for their reconciliation. His hope is that a larger ideal of fulfilment might emerge from the mutual consultation which could provide a solution to the race problem; a solution the African, the Afrikaner, the English, the Jew, the Coloured and the Asian could all accept because all would have put something into it. The larger ideal would satisfy, among other things, because it would stand the best chance of having the same meaning among all the peoples of Southern Africa.

But Bulube sees beyond the race problems of Southern Africa, to the quarrels which afflict the international community; to the conflict between the political power now controlled by the black, brown and yellow races and the domination of the world's economy by the white races; to the clash between the so-called underdeveloped nations and the industrial nations over the exploitation and use of resources and to the changing power dispositions in the world.

The Zulus cannot turn their backs on these developments as the Afrikaner once tried to do; they cannot live outside of the international community; they belong to the world and the globe's problems are their headaches. Each people's concept of nationhood must be viewed as a part of what can be developed into a larger concept of fulfilment for the human race. Each concept expresses the same basic urges which motivate thought and action among all members of the human race. Improved communications call for pan-African and world strategy which will move events toward convergence, while undue stress on the particular conduces toward polarisation. For this reason, Bulube warns, the Zulu has to be fastidious about the independence the whites offer him; he must always draw the distinction between the vassalage the whites offer as independence, and which Magasela in his anger and frustration is prepared to accept, and true freedom.

* * *

The great debates on nationhood which go on in the African community are, as a rule, not reported in the white press. The Africans charge that white reporting on events in the black community is crisis-oriented; that it is at all times slanted to serve the goals of the

English and the Afrikaner in the balance based on African labour, Afrikaner political power and English dominance of the economy.

The Africans complain, bitterly, that the white reporters cover crisis situations, filter their perceptions of African realities through white assessments of the African and report developments out of their context. The English have been doing this from the day they first published a newspaper in South Africa; they have closed their mind to African realities ever since.

The Afrikaners behave exactly as the English do. This is what the Jews do to the African. The Afrikaner has developed the closed mind to unusual extremes. He sets out to tell the African what it is to be an African; he appoints Afrikaner principals and senior staff to African universities in the bid to interpret the African to himself. In Government propaganda which is distributed extensively in the West, the African is presented to the world from the point of view of the Afrikaner. Afrikaner scholars ghost-write books for illiterate Africans which are foisted on the outside world as African interpretations of the African experience by the Africans.

But the closed mind is not confined to the whites in Southern Africa only. One comes across it in every white country. The Russians are as bigoted against the Africans almost as the Afrikaners are. Just the other day a group of Soviet scholars put together what they passed as a history of Africa. They saw nothing wrong in referring to the peoples of Africa as "tribes." Some contributors wrote superciliously of what they termed African "backwardness." At this level, the communist view of Africa is almost as distorted as the capitalist is.

The first thing that strikes the African visitor to Washington is the fact that the American capital has virtually the largest concentration of African embassies in the world. To this is added the fact that at least one-tenth of the American population is of African descent. In spite of all this, the American press, television and radio treat Africa as though she is on the outer periphery of the international experience. Africa seriously gets to the communications media when a crisis erupts in one part of the continent or another. Through the long years when the Africans grapple with the great problems which afflict contemporary mankind or which affect the lives of millions of American citizens, Africa is usually forgotten even by some of America's ablest commentators; or, she continues to be seen from the Tarzan perspective. American corporations with interests in Africa buy TV time to show the wild animals that live in the African bushveld as though Africa were inhabited solely by savage beasts. And yet America depends so much on Africa's cocoa, chrome, oil and other materials, all grown, or mined, and shipped by the labour of *men!*

Magasela's march to Bulube's kraal receives no attention from the white press, whether racist or liberal, although five thousand African young men and women have marched more than thirty miles from the Durban locations to Bulube's Mkambati kraal in the Valley Of A Thousand Hills. The only white people who are giving attention to the event are the police who continually fly helicopters and spotter planes to ensure that nothing gets out of control. While Magasela's differences with Bulube have been discussed widely in the Zulu community, the white press has acted as though nothing was taking place. All African newspapers have been taken over by the whites, who dish out to the black readers what they consider good for the people they have conquered. The controversy between Bulube and Magasela is regarded as political dynamite and therefore receives little attention in the white-controlled press. In these conditions, the Zulus have fallen back to the means of communication and political organisation used by their ancestors during the revolution which Shaka led. One of these is *umbimbi*, a Zulu way for "passing the word."

The African lives in his own world, in which he is free to take the white man out of his mind. The whites also live in their own world in which they try hard to keep the African out of their minds. The only real connection between the two is the white man's determination to exploit the African's resources. As a result, most whites live in a make-believe world, playing games with each other to assure themselves that they can keep the African forever on the outer periphery of South African affairs.

The press, as a rule, works hard to create this illusion. Just the other day, most English papers gave publicity to what occurred at a church meeting in Durban. Black churches are now almost the only really organised institutions in the black community and as such their leadership is becoming increasingly important. The two presidential candidates for a laymen's organisation which raises funds to establish black schools held conflicting political views; the one supported Bulube while the other was Magasela's follower. The young men who believe in Magasela invited the Bulube candidate to lunch where they drugged him with liquor, just before the elections. He did not turn up to give the election speech. Thirty minutes after the election session had started and while his rival was on the floor, the Bulube supporter crawled on all fours into the conference room. When he stood up, the front part of his trousers was facing backwards.

The white press had a lot to say on the incident, which had its own appeal as news, but ignored the important endorsement of the Magasela proposals by the conference.

* * *

Bulube stands, waiting . . . .

Magasela holds the scroll in his hand. An attendant hands him a portable loudspeaker and, after a short speech explaining that he has come to enlist Bulube's support for the demands in what he is about to present, he reads:

RESOLUTION ON INDEPENDENCE

WHEREAS

   i. White South Africa's racial policy is a programme for the systematic extermination of the black people, to make South Africa safe for the white people;

  ii. A law compelling the African woman to carry a Pass would be a standing insult to every person with African blood in the world;

 iii. The Christlike Nasionale Party, which governs South Africa to-day, has on several occasions informed the Africans that it is ready to grant them independence if they ask for it;

 iv. The Party has further announced its intentions to the world;

  v. The government's new intention changes the character of the race quarrel and calls for corresponding responses from the Africans;

 vi. The collapse of the Portuguese dictatorship has destroyed the foundations of the white united front the government in Pretoria established in Southern Africa and in doing this the collapse has created a political vacuum in this part of the continent;

 vii. The political vacuum in turn establishes a new balance in black and white power;

viii. The balance eliminates the value to the whites of Angola, Rhodesia and Mozambique as buffer states between Free Africa and white South Africa and leaves the way open to an armed clash between the peoples of Africa and the whites in South Africa;

 ix. The availability of Zulu soldiers on the side of Free African armies will reinforce the African side and,

WHEREAS

  x. The centres of world power have shifted from the white nations of the world to the black, brown and yellow peoples whose shores are washed by the Indian Ocean;

 xi. The shift has created a new balance of power in international relations which calls for a positive response from the nations of Africa in general and the Zulus in particular;

 xii. The shift in the centres of power combines with the power build-up in the Indian Ocean to give strategic importance to the coasts of Zululand and the Transkei on the western approaches to the Indian Ocean;

xiii. The changes listed above call for an altogether new approach to Southern Africa's problem of "colour,"

BE IT THEREFORE RESOLVED

> That the Zulu Territorial Authority be instructed, as it is hereby instructed, to open immediate and direct negotiations with the government of South Africa for the independence of Kwa Zulu.

The five thousand marchers roar out their approval in a long breath-bar thus:

E-LE-E-E-THU!
(We agree!)

Magasela hands the scroll to Bulube which the chief takes with both hands. Bulube stretches his hand for the loudspeaker and addresses the thousands.

I take it, Professor Magasela and enemies of oppression who accompany you, you will allow me to respond to your instruction . . . .

E-LE-E-E-THU!

As all of you know, I am for independence. But before we demand independence or decide on the next course of action, now that the white united front in our part of the world is collapsing, let us be sure that we mean the same thing by independence, for there are types and types of independence. We can have a type of independence given on terms which serve white interests; we can also have an independence whose terms are dictated by us. Independence on white terms would keep the ownership of the gold, diamond, coal and iron mines of our land in white hands; it would leave 87% of our land in the hands of the white people who make up only about 20 per cent of the population. A white oriented independence would exonerate the white invaders from the payment of reparations. In my view, an independence which crowded us into barren rural reserves, with a population density of 117 per square mile is no independence at all; it is vassalage . . . it is the legitimisation of larceny.

E-LE-E-E-THU!

If the government honestly wants to let us have our independence—for we are tired of being on the white man's back when we have never asked him to carry us—and if you seriously think Pretoria wants meaningful negotiations with us, I have an alternative. I suggest

115

that we reject the independence which will make us the vassals of the white man . . . .

E-LE-E-E-THU!

I suggest that we persevere in the struggle. The white man is thinking of independence to-day not because he loves us. He has never loved us; he loved our resources. He thinks of independence now because we have made race oppression ruinously expensive for him. Remember we fought him when we stood alone . . . we used our brains and these bare hands. We did not retreat when all we had were our bare hands. We have friends and allies now; we have isolated him . . . with these brains and bare hands. We and our brothers in Angola, Mozambique and Rhodesia, in Botswana, Lesotho, Swaziland and Zambia have cracked his united front . . . with these brains and bare hands. Must we then retreat when victory is in sight and let him keep the things he stole from us?

NO! NO! NO!

If we want our own type of independence let us continue to operate the segregated institutions he has created for us to build our power and consolidate our unity. When we established the united front of our territorial authorities, he offered areas to the Transkei which he had said he would never yield. The Transkei now has more land because its leaders were powerful in our united front. If all of us stand together, we will recover all the land of the Xhosas. If we stand together all the black peoples will eventually regain all their lands. If we in Natal stand together with our brothers in the other provinces, even when this means rejecting the independence offered us, we shall restore to ourselves the boundaries of the Zulu state before the Great Trek!

BLOOD RIVER! BLOOD RIVER! BLOOD RIVER!

When the shouting dies down, the Zulus break out in the war song their ancestors sang at the battle of Blood River:
>Wathinta thina,
>Wathint' iziqandi ematsheni!
>Uzaukufa!
>(Touch us not, O enemy!
>If you do, remember,
>You touch wasps on boulders.
>Death will be your fate!)

116

Magasela does not sing; tears are trickling down the wrinkles on his face. The battle of Blood River has always been a living experience in his life. He lived for avenging the defeat; Mpini was the stick he drove into the manure heap, as the Zulus say, for use against the enemy at the opportune time. When the security police murdered Mpini, they confronted Magasela with another Blood River; with another defeat. But when he sees the five thousand young people who have marched on foot all the way from Durban to support him, he sees himself rising from defeat and marching once more to Blood River, for there can never be an end to this march, before the land of Zulu is free. Bulube, who is a very much younger man, continues his speech. Turning his face toward Magasela, he says:

I am moved when I see the tears of a hero, for, from the days of my youth, I have always been told that the tears of heroes are a nation's most precious possession; that they can bring the sun crashing to the earth. Now, I know what the wise men meant when they said this. The challenge to us is to persevere; to use the segregated institutions and build up a dual authority situation. We must use these institutions to build up our organised power; to confront white power with our power; to place ourselves in the position when we can use our labour as a political weapon to paralyse the economy with a national strike and smash once and for all time white South Africa's reputation as a lucrative investment field . . . . When the white people's chamber pots are not emptied; when the garbage is not removed from their cities; when the fires in their factories are not stoked; when their crops rot on their fields, the white people will know then that we mean to be free. Please know that if epidemics break out, it is we who shall die first; if the economy is paralysed, it is our children who will starve and die; if the crops rot on the fields, it is we who shall suffer most. But speaking for myself, I would rather face all these tribulations to restore to you what was stolen from you . . . .

E-LE-E-E-THU!

When the white man's cities are filled with the smell of rotting garbage and the corpses of dead people; when his factories have gone up in flames, he will be obliged to want to talk to us; to negotiate with us on our terms. It is then that we shall teach him what it is to be human. But we must go beyond that. We must build a larger nation, a larger society, to ensure that no enemy shall ever again set foot on Africa to steal that which belongs to us. We must build a nation stretching from Angola, Zambia, Malawi in the north to the Cape of Good Hope in the South; from the Indian Ocean in the east, to the Atlantic Ocean in the west, that, my brothers and sisters, is what I call independence!

* * *

117

XI. Die Kafferpolitiek

Kucabeka amahlathi empini yezindlovu.

(Forests are razed to the ground in a war of elephants.)

South Africa is a land of grave fears and complicated hatreds. The Afrikaner is afraid of the African, who is the historical owner of the land and has the numbers on his side. The Afrikaner is honest with the African at this level; he does not apologise for the fact that his hostility to the man of colour, like his racial policy, has its roots in history and in the fear that if given the opportunity the African would push the Afrikaner into the sea.

The fear is so deeply ingrained the Afrikaner would sooner see himself spat upon by the international community; he would sooner have the ugliest name in the comity of nations; his students would sooner be neutrals in the great struggle between the demands of justice and white arrogance, than accept the African as an equal. People call the Afrikaner names, they analyse his obsessions with race in a world of proliferating black, brown and yellow nations and even compare his attitudes with Australia's changed policy toward the coloured peoples of the Pacific and the Asian mainland, and end up despairing of ever seeing him do the sensible thing in his relations with the black people.

But there is a harsh logic behind the Afrikaner's attitude; so harsh he dreads to think about it loudly enough to explain himself to the rest of the world. His history combines with events in Southern Africa to make the African the ultimate guarantor of the Afrikaner's survival in South Africa.

The Afrikaner might boast of the miracle he has performed by rising virtually from the ashes of defeat at the turn of the century to become the master of South Africa which is the richest and the most powerful country in all Africa. When, however, he contemplates his position from the perspectives of history and the future, he realises that, in the final analysis, he holds what he has ultimately by the grace of the African; that he is strong only to the extent that the African is weak.

The Afrikaner's fear is compounded by his unique position in the white world. He is a creature of the beauty and the ugliness of

119

South Africa; while he is a white man, his psyche has been affected profoundly by the African, to the extent that he has substantial African blood in his veins. He went to Africa as a white man; Africa swallowed him and transformed him into a marginal white man. He cannot escape his position; wherever he goes he realises that whether or not he likes it, he is the plastic clay in African hands. The atrocities he perpetrates against the African, his bitter hatred of the black man and his suicidal disregard for international opinion are the terrible rejections of a fate he feels he cannot escape.

If he were to leave South Africa, he has nowhere to go; his identity would be destroyed. This explains his preoccupations with considerations of survival. To keep his identity, he has to remain in Africa . . . a prisoner of the African. But living in the shadow of the African casts a menacing shadow over his entire future. So he sits in the shadow, his gun in his hand, looking to a future about which he can never be certain. As a Calvinist he accepts his fate dourly and tells himself that if he is predestined to lead a marginal existence in the white community while he is threatened by the Africans, he will do that at least heroically.

But the African, too, has his own fears. On the face of it he is afraid of the white man's gun. In the centuries of contact with the white man, nobody knows the number of Africans who perished at the tip of the white man's bayonet or at the point of his gun. Nobody will ever know, for the bloodshed continues in the quiet most of the time. Now and then it erupts into massacres as in 1920 when Mgijima's followers were mown to the ground on the commonage outside Queenstown or the bloody suppression of the revolt of the people the Afrikaner calls the Bondelswarts of South-west Africa or the Sharpeville shootings or the killing of South African, Botswana and Lesotho miners at Carletonville in September 1973. The African is afraid because he is not armed. The fear finds expression in the commitment to non-violence and the reluctance to use arson as a political weapon.

But the African's fear has made him a realist. It has made him refuse to fight on ground chosen by the white man and has forced him to evolve his own weapons by which to meet the white challenge. Above all, it has developed in him a capacity to survive defeat which is almost without parallel in our times; it has enabled him to shift the fight against white domination to the intellectual plane where he has transformed it into a fierce war of minds, and where he has at last seized the initiative to give leadership in thinking on South Africa's destiny. While the war of minds rages at this level, he keeps his options open; he tells himself and his children that the weakness is a passing phase which they must survive. One day, he believes, he or his children will have the guns to avenge the wrongs of Blood River and correct the injustices of history.

The African is not afraid that the white man will one day

succeed in wiping him off the face of South Africa. The numbers are on his side. But there is something he fears more than anything else: he is afraid of himself. He fears that under pressure from the white man's ideal of fulfilment or evaluation of the person, his personality might be fragmented and his identity shattered; beyond, he would see the end with both his eyes. White policy drives him to this end. It has split his people into the traditionalists who are mainly in the reserves, the men and women committed to the syncresis of African and white cultures who come from the mission stations and the urban locations, and the Africans on white farms who are the weakest and the most cruelly oppressed of the black people.

In addition, the Africans are divided into christians and "heathens," the educated and the illiterate, the rural and the urban, the rich and the poor and the resisters and the conciliators. Each of these segments has its own little identity and redefines fulfilment in terms of its particular experience and has developed its own little personality. The African fears that the fragmentation produced by oppression might force him to lose his real self in the forest of identities created by the whites. He could survive both conquest and the seizure of his land by the white invaders; he could even adapt to the demands of defeat and enslavement—but what he dreads most is the fragmentation of his personality because he does not know what would happen to him if that disaster were to overtake him. Professor Magasela addresses himself to this fear, just as Bulube or Father Maimane does.

To the African, the danger is real and constant. People point to the case of a Coloured family reported in the English press to illustrate the dangers of fragmentation. Herbert and Ethel Knox had been married for seventeen years and had originally owned a house in a white suburb of Capetown. Herbert was a white man and an accountant in a large departmental store owned by Jews and which served the growing Afrikaner middle class. While Ethel had a fair complexion and readily passed for a swarthy beauty from Southern Europe, she was, in fact, a Coloured. She and Herbert had met in Port Elizabeth where she had lived as a Coloured. He knew and loved her as a Coloured and both were married in Port Elizabeth. Herbert was subsequently transferred on promotion to the Capetown head office of the departmental stores. He bought a house in a white suburb and settled down to rear his family. Ethel, a teacher, was appointed to the suburban school.

The family started to increase. The first three children readily passed for white and went to white schools. Then, tragedy crashed into the lives of the Knoxes. Ethel gave birth to twins, a boy and a girl. Aggie was white while Christopher was black. Herbert quietly sold his property and bought a new house in a middle class Coloured area. Ethel asked for and got a transfer to a school nearest her new home, which happened to be white. In those days Capetown was racially the most liberal city in South Africa and continued to defy some of the racist laws of the de Haas regime. The University of Capetown had students who distinguished themselves in fighting race discrimination. At the time people said Capetown was an oasis of humanity in a desert of race hatred.

Herbert's mother, a wealthy widow living in Rhodesia, had taken the twins after birth and had looked after them on her farm. Things went well with the Knoxes while the de Haas regime tightened its hold on the country. People started talking, in whispered rumours. In a situation charged with fear rumours are the social currency. People's feelings are bottled up in insecurity. And whenever overcrowding sets in among animals, cannibalism develops. This is true also of human beings. Crowd the human beings socially or emotionally or psychologically, and you transform them into social cannibals; they tear each other down and devour each other's reputations. Stories about the twins in Rhodesia drifted until they reached the security police. Herbert lost his job; shortly thereafter, the school board dismissed Ethel.

Herbert was a brave man who was determined not to allow the racist wolves to devour his family. He struck back. In terms of the law, Ethel could go through complicated and humiliating procedures to get herself declared a white person in order to live with her husband and family. The authorities pointed to one snag after another. Ethel lived in a Coloured area and although she had taught in a white school, that did not establish the fact that she was regarded as white because in Port Elizabeth she had identified herself with the Coloured community.

Herbert was determined to go through hell itself to keep his family together. The law said he could be declared a Coloured if he associated with them and conducted himself as a Coloured. Up to the time of his dismissal he had associated with the whites; his pension and other benefits were calculated on the scale which applied to the whites only.

Then, the police moved in. One night Herbert and Ethel were arrested and charged for violating the country's most sacred law: the Immorality Act which prohibits mixed marriages and makes it a crime for people to love across the colour line.

You are out of your mind! Herbert exploded when the police showed the warrants of arrest issued against him and his wife. He pulled their marriage certificate from the safe.

Look at this! We were legally married in a christian church in Port Elizabeth before the Immorality Act became the law. We are professional people! We love each other; we love our children and we are clean-living and law-abiding citizens. Is it a crime . . . I mean . . . we are christians . . . . Is it a crime for a christian to love another christian in a christian country?

The police were not interested. Aggie and Christopher, who were twelve by then, were home for the holidays when their parents were arrested. Herbert and Ethel were out on bail. One night

Christopher walked into their bedroom.

Daddy, am I really your child . . . and yours too, mama?

Yes, son . . . and both of us love you so much.

The child was quiet for a while; the world of the adults bewildered him.

The police arrested you and mama because I'm your child? The white boys in the park beat me and call me half-and-half or a kaffer. The Coloured girls in the park beat up Aggie and call her a white monkey . . . . Why?

Alright, if you're not happy in this cursed place, we'll send you back to grandma where you'll be happy.

But I want to stay with you, here . . . .

Herbert and Ethel looked at each other silently. As was her habit, Ethel woke up long before sunrise. In the bathroom she found Christopher's body hanging from a waterpipe fixed to the ceiling.

* * *

Nowhere are the fears of personality fragmentation more fiercely expressed than in the locations. It is a clear invitation to trouble for any white person who is not known to enter some of the largest locations. In Johannesburg a group of liberal young whites drove into one of the vast locations and stayed with their friends until after sunset. As they were leaving the location, they were stopped by a group of young Africans who dragged the two girls out of the car and raped them in front of the five young men who had been with them in the car.

Nowhere, also, do people react more violently against what some militants call Magasela's chauvinism. His teaching is viewed as endorsement of the de Haas policy of separating every South African from every other; of turning the black communities against each other and doing the dirty work for the white man. In South Africa, the people in the location are in the front line of the conflict between black and white; urbanisation is destroying some of their cultural values. Crimes involving violence have assumed frightening proportions. Many of the location residents have the direst forebodings for the future; they are frightened when they see the violent elements in the locations tearing the community to pieces.

As a result they are afraid; they are fiercely hostile to anything which threatens to increase their weakness. They see in unity their only guarantee of survival and hate Magasela passionately because they believe he creates polarisations in the black community when the most urgent need is for unity and co-ordinated action. It would be different if he preached the narrow nationalisms and procured the guns to settle the race quarrel. In Atteridgeville, Maggie Kuboni, Dillo Mareka and Sefadi Masilo take the position that if Magasela ever set his foot in the location, they would set the boys with *intshumentshu* on him. People are not concerned with his revolutionary theory for the reconciliation of conflicts in the African community. African unity has become a slogan bandied about as a cure for all racial and political evils; nobody wants to sit down and spell out what it is or what its basis is.

But if Mareka's militants reject Magasela's insistence on principled unity as tribalistic and therefore divisive, they oppose Bulube's policy of negotiating from positions of strength. Building up what they call black power will take another fifty years. Revolution is what they demand. None of them seems to have the clearest view of how the Africans can organise a successful revolution in an industrial society where the whites are united and control national life with the backing of a first-class army.

The militants are not opposed to building up African power; they protest, however, that the process is too slow. When Bulube points out that the slowness is, in fact, an index of African weakness, they lose their temper; how can a loyal son of Africa waste time weighing African weaknesses; that damages the morale of the masses, they say. Attack! Attack! Attack, they clamour. Attack what, Bulube asks. Attack the white power-structure; do not collaborate in working the segregated institutions; call the workers out on strike; tell it like it is to the white people; do not work with the liberals. Attack! Attack! For goodness' sake . . . attack even if it is for the sake of attacking!

In their bewilderment and anger the militants want a complete break with the past; they do not want to have anything to do with being a Zulu or Xhosa or Pedi or Sotho; they do not even want to call themselves Africans . . . they are blacks . . . the vanguard of the new, liberated humanity which is creating a new world and which must, in order to do this, repudiate the labels which link them with the past. That past has no meaning for them; they are progressive and look to the future of human brotherhood.

Magasela is, in their view, the high priest of black reaction; Bulube is a stooge of the white people even when he says he wants to negotiate in order to buy the time to build up the African's power to paralyse the national economy. The confusion in the Marekites arises from their fears, from uncertainty about their values and, above all, the realisation that in spite of their weaknesses, they provide the third pillar of the African-Afrikaner-English balance—labour. They know they are a potential power to reckon with and yet feel powerless to transform the potential into reality. Their confusion and anger are the inflammable ingredient in the South African situation which arouses the Afrikaner's worst fears.

But if the Marekites are not the only militants, the government and the police are not the only whites concerned about the turbulent debates going on in the African community. South Africa has a tradition of communist involvement which is almost as old as the Union of South Africa. In spite of race conflict and exploitation, communism has not been a vigorous plant in the South African setting.

An obvious handicap, which the communists never want to discuss, is their commitment to scientific materialism which defines reality and the person in terms which are the exact opposite of those of the *Buntu Ideal*. The other weakness is, inevitably, the communists' doctrinaire commitment to the class-struggle approach. The ideological conflict between the philosophy of the Christelike Nasionale Party and the *Buntu Ideal* is never discussed; African Nationalism is dismissed as a black bourgeois aberration and stress is laid on socialism and the worker. That forces the African nationalists to retort: Communism is another white man's creed! It so happens the ideals which inspire the revolt against white domination are not Marxist; they have their roots in the African experience.

Economic laws are ignored in South Africa or distorted to serve white racial ends. The contradictions which arise cannot be clearly explained in Marxist or Graeco-Romano-Hebraic terms. Marx gives no clue on how to tackle the problems which arise because the majority of the workers in Europe were not Africans when he developed his teachings.

Above all, the real custodians of the communist tradition have never been the Africans. The ablest communists have come from the white, privileged side. The small Indian community has produced the next most important communists. The Africans have produced a few outstanding communists who were forced to speak the language of nationalism which was not wholly acceptable to the white, Indian and Coloured communists. As a result, many white communists in the South African underground adopt Gandhian attitudes to violence; that is true also of the Indians. They have a problem here; if they advocated violence, the Africans would, in situations of confrontation, draw no distinction between a white communist revolutionary and a member of the de Haas party.

Their problems have been complicated by the ban on the Communist Party, the tightening of the laws against political contact between black and white and, of course, China's involvement in Central and East Africa. As a rule, most white communists in the underground have a pro-Soviet orientation. China counters by playing up the race issue, which is foremost in the minds of the Africans. China shrewdly avoids the big-brother stance in her dealings with the Africans, where the Russians do not hesitate to throw their weight around; she adopts the attitude of supporting African initiatives and that places her in the position not only to be accepted but also to influence events far more effectively than the Russians.

In the underground, the communists have preserved a small but highly disciplined core of operatives. But as the guerrilla war spreads southwards, anti-white feelings take deeper root in the African community and define the coming struggle in largely racial outlines.

125

The Russian support of guerrilla movements is certainly appreciated in the black community, but it does not do much to place Russia as clearly on the map in the conflict with the CNP as the white communists would like.

The Africans regard China's membership of the United Nations as a valuable weapon for them. China can be persuaded, through the African states who are friendly to her, to create polarisations in the Security Council which would make the United States think twice about intervening openly in the collision between black and white which now seems imminent in view of the collapse of the white united front in Southern Africa caused by the collapse of Caetano's dictatorship in Portugal.

The communists like neither Dazinkani Magasela nor Chief Bulube—nor even Dillo Mareka—because all insist on the assertion of African leadership initiatives. That is a serious obstacle for the African communists in the underground. Some of them remember the days before Sharpeville when communism advocated multi-nationalism in South Africa. History plays people strange tricks sometimes. Today, the de Haas government is the most determined advocate of multi-nationalism. Professor Magasela's comment is: Both have their origins in the Graeco-Romano-Hebraic evaluation of the person; both are materialistic—the CNP uses race to concentrate power in the hands of the few while the communists use the economic class to serve the same purpose!

The whites are like the children of one mother and one father, both of whom are supremacists. The missionaries loved us so much they destroyed our system of values and imposed their religion on us. The liberals so loved us they destroyed our political traditions and forced the white man's notions of authority on us. The communists are like the missionaries; they want us "free," but only on the basis of socialism; they preach the white ideology and reject the African's political beliefs. The white racists say the white skin is a hallmark of excellence. All these people are committed to supremacy! They define our struggle in white terms; they deny the validity of the ideal we translate into experience. Is anybody surprised the United Nations cannot evolve viable programmes against race discrimination?

Underground communism has not as yet found a way of dealing with the African's fear of fragmentation; they would not want to be involved in splitting the Africans like the government, but they fear the unity emerging in the locations.

Nowhere are some of the Marekite militants' fears expressed more clearly than in their hostility to Magasela's readiness for independence for the Zulus even on terms initially dictated by the white man or to Bulube's preference for an independence based on strength.

Consider what would happen, Maggie declaims, if the Afrikaner cracked under *xina* pressures! He would not lose anything because he would still be in control. The African would be free only to become a slave by choice. A smart successor to de Haas would cede the whole of Natal to the Zulus and with that single move split the Africans from head to foot. The Boers think the Zulus are the gravest threat to white domination; that God made a mistake the day he created the Zulus; they are always scheming to overthrow white rule; they are incapable of accepting defeat. Take any major African rebellion in the fifty years from Union; we have been there! What would suit the white man better than to isolate the Zulus in Natal? The Boer would lose nothing; Natal is English country; it is Indian country—both thorns in the Boer's side. Negotiation? Not for me!

Maggie reinforces her argument against negotiating by saying history shows that if the Afrikaners got rid of the Zulus, they would at last establish for themselves the place they want in Africa. Cetshwayo had stood in the way of the whites; he had sent emissaries to his contemporaries urging the creation of a military alliance which would declare Southern Africa a collective security area and drive the whites into the sea. The British fought a major war to frustrate his intentions while the French lost the Prince Imperial in the conflict.

Twenty-five years after Cetshwayo's defeat, Bambada was on the warpath against paying taxation to a government whose authority he did not recognise. Four thousand Zulus perished in that rebellion. Six years later, Seme went to Bloemfontein and created a new nation from the ashes of defeat. The Afrikaners had crushed British political power when Albert Luthuli internationalised African resistance and won the Nobel Peace Prize in the process. No African group has as large a surfeit of Western missionaries as the Zulus; last century, practically every major missionary society involved in Africa was keen on making Zulu converts. In spite of all this, the Zulus have not been tamed.

Maggie cannot take the Afrikaner out of her mind; whenever she discusses Natal she sooner or later returns to what the Afrikaners might do. An Afrikaner politician might emerge, and this is not as crazy as it sounds, she repeats, who would negotiate directly and seriously with the Zulus; he would want allies; he would set himself the goal of striking a deal with the Zulus and offer to return to them the province of Natal, which was part of their empire.

The Afrikaners could do this without hurting their pride. Their roots in Natal have never been deep; the province is an English preserve. To hand over Natal to the Zulus would almost destroy the remaining vestiges of English political influence in South Africa, and transform the Afrikaner into an unchallenged master in white politics. At the same time, the move would split the Zulus to start with.

Many of them would find it almost impossible to resist the temptation to accept independence in part of their own territory, even if that meant the temporary abandonment of the Bloemfontein commitment. Zulu acceptance of an independent Natal state would be viewed as an act of betrayal in the other African communities. Afrikaner diplomacy could then go around telling the Xhosa, Basotho, Shangane and others things like:

We have always warned you against the hegemonistic intentions of the Zulus. They only used you to get Natal restored to themselves. See what they'll do, now that the Afrikaner has given them what they have always wanted.

A Zulu state in Natal would offer other attractions. It would solve Afrikanerdom's Indian problem. The Afrikaners have no liking for the Indians who were brought to Natal by the British, mainly as indentured labour in the sugarcane fields of the province. The Afrikaners inherited the Indian problem from the British and could see some benefits in saddling the Zulus with it—now that India is a nuclear power. With the Zulus placated, Afrikaner statesmanship could think in terms of a military alliance with these warrior people, to guarantee the Afrikaners a secure and permanent place in the African sun. All of this sounds unbelievable; but when one considers the lines of conflict between the Africans and the Boers, nothing is impossible with the Afrikaner.

Accordingly, whenever Bulube mentions a negotiated settlement, his opponents promptly think of the guarantee to the Afrikaners. Maggie does not hide her feelings; she makes it clear that negotiations with the Afrikaner will be conducted over her dead body. What Maggie wants is to cleanse the soil of her land of the white pestilence; one white person remaining on South African soil, she shouts, is an eternity of the evil.

The Marekites agree with Bulube that vultures are already flying over the besieged Afrikaner but, Mareka warns: *Ha eshoa, ea raha!* (The beast kicks most violently when it dies). The possibility that in his troubles, the Afrikaner might smash African solidarity calls for the readiness to *seize the moment* and give Afrikaner domination shoves so massive it will go crashing into the past. The Afrikaner is vulnerable at so many points that the African is at last free to attack where he likes, he says. The African has soaked the soil of South Africa with his blood from the formation of Union to win this freedom. And to negotiate now, when he can strike the white man where it hurts, is to vote for the legitimisation of larceny. There can be no negotiation with thieves of the soul; there is no basis for trying to reconcile *umteto wesintu* and *umteto wesilungu*. Violence of every form, on every plane, is the only language the Afrikaner is capable of understanding.

The only Afrikaner that I love, Mareka tells his closest friends, is a dead Afrikaner! How beautiful they look in the pallor of death! But, dead or alive, I don't want the sight of the pestilence; I wouldn't allow anybody further to desecrate our soil by burying them in our land. There are sharks in the sea; they might enjoy a party in which

Afrikaner steak is served! The only sensible thing for the Boers to do, after the mess they have made of our lives, is to QUIT AFRICA! We are mobilising our forces slowly, and painfully, for the final kill.

Marekite strategy seeks to enable the African to control the mind of the white man. Violence is the only means of doing this. The white man must be given no moment to relax or to enjoy his life or to have peace of mind or to put away his gun. The black burglar who leaves the location by night and invades white territory is hailed as a hero; he is placed in the vanguard of the Caravan To Blood River. Mareka's followers approve of the burglary into white homes; the burglars, it is said, are doing no more and no less than to recover that which was stolen from their people. The murder of whites on such occasions avenges the dead whom the white man has been killing in the three hundred years he has been in South Africa.

The chief value of the burglaries, however, is that they force the white man to become the prisoner of his gun; Dillo wants him to think only within the range defined by the gun, to accelerate his own destruction. In the suburbs the white man has been forced to go to bed with his wife with a gun under his pillow cushion. Conception takes place on top of the gun and the white woman gives birth to her child in the shadow of the gun. Dillo and Maggie tell every young man who is willing to listen to sneak out of the country as best they can in order to join the guerrillas in Central Africa.

We regard the guerrillas as important, Dillo explains at numerous divining sessions conducted by the army of witchdoctors in the location, not because we think the war of the races will be decided on the Zambezi. We would be fools to imagine that it will be decided there. The chief value of the guerrillas is that they extend the area in which we *xina* the white man.

Our numbers and his stand in the ratio of 4:1. If we keep the bushfires burning on the Zambezi, we force him every year to withdraw so many thousands of the cream of his manpower and to tie down these valuable young people in unproductive military employment. In a country where our colour shuts us out of skilled jobs, the absence of the young whites affects industrial production and could, in the long run, reduce the Afrikaner's ability to pay the high profits which attract foreign investments and threaten to buy alliances. We have thrown the Afrikaner in a cleft stick at this level and we are determined not to allow him to escape; he fights on the Zambezi while his need for foreign investments requires that he should abandon the industrial colour bar. Now, we are taking over the jobs formerly reserved for whites. That is one of the advantages of controlling his mind; we force him to hurt himself and when he retreats, we take over. That is the essence of the *xina* strategy.

Force the Afrikaner to hurt himself and when he retreats, take over—this is the principle around which Maggie's whole life is built. In the old days, she did not spare herself and learned all she could from the English-speaking young whites in the underground movements before the Sharpeville massacres. Now, she is an ardent prayer woman in the Zion Pentecostal Church, one of many christian sects which thrive in the locations. The joke in white christendom in the country is that the Black Zionists read the bible upside down. They have no time for the new testament and do not mention the name of Jesus Christ. Their exemplars are the prophets of the old testament. They take care, though, not to pray to the God of Abraham, but to the God of Shaka and Dingane and Palo and Mshweshwe.

They meet almost every night in long prayer meetings which combine declamations against injustice with prayer, community singing, drum-beating and traditional dancing.

Men, women and children dress in white in these sessions. Maggie is a medical nurse in the location clinic and leaves work at five, when she puts on her Zionist cloak and spends almost every night in one or the other of the wakes. She is a power to reckon with in the location. It is said of her that there is so much force in her prayers she can command a million African men to march barefooted and unclothed into the furnaces of hell itself. The black security police prudently avoid getting into her bad books or in those of her *intshumentshu*-carrying co-religionists.

As a student-nurse in Durban, Maggie spent most of her free time on the night train to Zululand. Asked why she did this, she explained that she was "in love with a married policeman" in Stanger whose wife was employed permanently on night duty in a sugar plantation hospital near Stanger. Maggie would book a compartment for herself and pack boxes of matches and cigarettes in her travelling bag. She would light a cigarette as soon as the train entered the canefields in the Avoca district, just outside Durban, place its other end against the heads of the match-sticks and shut the box so tightly it held the cigarette firmly against the phosphorus heads. At the opportune moment she would throw the burning cigarette and match-box into a lush canefield where the explosion would set the inflammable sugarcane leaves on fire. She would leave the train at Stanger and return to Durban.

People tell other stories about Maggie. One of the most popular centres on the prayer she gave at a funeral of a young man who had been shot by the police in a strike. As the black Americans would say, Maggie told it like it was, to God himself. That did not please the security police keeping an eye on the burial. Hauled before a court of law, Maggie put up a simple defence:

Your Worship, I did tell God one or two things about the evils of race discrimination. I told him that he makes a mistake by allowing it. If I can't be frank with God, to whom can I open my soul in all its nakedness, Your Worship?

The story is told very largely in the thousands of drinking

parties organised in the location during week-ends, where it draws this comment from the men:

Man! That Kuboni girl! She *xinas* the white man as nobody does!

While the argument about being frank to God got Maggie an acquittal, the police do not think the magistrate was smart enough. Maggie has become a problem for the police. While she is an ardent prayer woman, she mixes religion and politics so well the police are not sure about what to do with her. For example, what do the police do when she sends a seditious prayer to God? If the police try to put pressure on her to say the right things to God, Maggie gets on to hilltops and starts screaming about the police coming between her and God. And Maggie knows how to scream in the right way, in the right place and at the right time. Sooner or later rumblings start in sections of the Dutch Reformed Church; some Afrikaner clergymen make it clear that it is not only the christian's right to open his conscience to God, it is his duty to do this. Preoccupation with the race issue has become the cleft stick in which the Dutch Reformed Church is caught. The Church cannot afford to see christianity discredited beyond a certain point in the African community. Maggie argues that hers is a christian national attitude, just as the attitude of the Dutch Reformed Church is christian-national. She insists that the Pentecostalists have as much right to work for the African people as the Dutch Reformed Church has to support the Afrikaner cause.

Maggie is popular with neither the married women in the location nor the police. The latter try hard to enlist the support of the wives by spreading rumours to the effect that Maggie is generous with her body. That sort of characterisation certainly does nothing to make her popular among the wives. But Maggie works so closely with their husbands in the underground that wives find it difficult to attack her and possibly jeopardise their husbands' position. When the women attack her, Maggie replies:

"The skunk conquers with the power of its smell. . . ."

The police do not trust Maggie; they believe she does a lot of politically dirty things. But the blacks in the police force admit that if she does anything at all, she commits crimes in the cleanest manner possible. Pretoria is, for example, very concerned about the report that the independent state which was formerly Mozambique allows plutonium from Niger and weapons from China to be conveyed overland to the Zulu rebels in northern Natal. This portion of Natal has become the most sensitive area in South Africa; the Zulu Territorial Authority has developed the swamps which abound there into lush ricefields, with the aid of Chinese experts from Taiwan. The Zulus look forward to developing the swamps into one of the largest rice-producing regions of the world, when they are free. Pretoria asked them to invite experts from Taiwan. The Zulus were only too glad to bring in the Chinese. Complications developed when Peking suddenly became interested in the Zulu rice scheme. Radio Peking took care to give progress reports on the rice scheme, which, everybody in Pretoria agreed, was unusual. Peking never cared to praise Taiwan's achievements anywhere. Some of the smartboys at security police headquarters suggested that it would be a wise thing to keep a sharp look-out on the Taiwanese on the ricefields. Some of them might be military instructors or physicists from Peking working secretly with the Zulus on the plutonium from Niger, which comes through Lourenco Marques.

One day, one of Maggie's sisters, who married the man who is now the mayor of Lourenço Marques, died. In her last days she had expressed the wish that she would like to be buried at Kwa Mondi, an African settlement outside Eshowe, in Natal, where her father's parents were interred. Maggie goes to Lourenco Marques and subsequently joins the mourners who travel overland to Kwa Mondi. The security police plant some of their men among the mourners and as soon as the hearse and the cars accompanying it reach the border between Mozambique and northern Natal, the uniformed South African police stop the hearse, seize the coffin and take it to the charge office where they open it, search its contents and run the geiger counter over the corpse in the belief that plutonium might be concealed in the dead body. When Maggie protests to the Afrikaner officer in charge, he apologises politely and then adds:

"The government feels that it can't take chances with the Zulus."

The police find no uranium or plutonium or arms in the coffin. And when news of this reaches Pretoria word goes round in the African locations that Maggie has done it again. The Africans have a way of talking about these things to themselves which cannot be comprehended in white terms. The Commissioner of Police warns his Minister that there is some form of collusion between the black security police and some of the underground groups in the location. At this stage, the Commissioner adds, there is no concrete evidence, only, it seems strange that the black police do not come up with reports on which to base charges.

* * *

In the locations, the clash between the African and the Afrikaner is referred to as the war between two mountains. The collision is defined in terms which preclude compromise and sentiment and moral law. The one mountain is determined to level off the other. The millimetre-by-millimetre progression to the final confrontation has developed a momentum in which respite is neither possible nor expected nor asked nor granted.

As the minority groups sometimes say, the African and the Afrikaner hold each other by their throats and have reached the point where they can allow neither the English nor the Coloureds nor the

Indians to come between them. If any of these minorities try to do this, they risk being bruised or hurt or crushed. But the war of the mountains is such that no group can afford to be neutral in a conflict where non-involvement can mean destruction. The African and the Afrikaner hold each other so tightly they have transformed their fight into a death-struggle; each side strikes to destroy.

Bulube and Mareka might disagree on strategy but both are of one mind on the urgency of organising African labour in such a way that one day the black people should organise a strike that will bring white rule crashing to the ground. The white man's answer has, in the sixty years since Union, been to make it illegal for the Africans to organise trade unions.

De Haas has reinforced the answer by pushing a law through parliament which empowers the white police to shoot first in situations of conflict and to ask questions afterwards. Strikes are defined as situations of conflict.

But the fight goes on on every plane. For nearly a generation now the CNP has used Afrikaans as an instrument for bending the will and controlling the mind of the African. The first thing the Africans do when they gain control of the segregated administrations established for them in the rural reserves is to smash the moulds in which the Afrikaner seeks to cast the mind of the African child. Bulube and Mareka work with equal zeal to smash the moulds.

A situation has arisen in which the white people live in uncertainty about when and where the African will strike; the only thing they are certain about is their gun. Mareka says their thinking must be tied down to the gun, no matter what it costs the Africans. Bulube takes advantage of the white man's preoccupation with the gun as a guarantee of survival to translate traditional values into modern political concepts and programmes in the bid to give a new quality of leadership no longer merely to the black people, but to the brown, yellow and white.

Colonel Prinsloo now attaches the greatest importance to this development, to which he has given the code name *Process TNT*. In a secret memorandum to the Minister of the Police, Nienaber Gaehler, and which bears the heading CRISIS OF SURVIVAL, the Commissioner argues that there has been a fundamental shift in the balance of black and white power and that this development has implications which strike at the very roots of Afrikaner survival.

Events, he argues, have destroyed the power of the gun as a guarantee of Afrikaner security. It is only a matter of time before the free states of Africa have contiguous borders with South Africa when they will transport guns to the black population of the republic.

Yes, a prominent social welfare worker was recently arrested for speeding on the main Johannesburg-Pretoria road. Her car crashed into a pole and she was taken to hospital where she was kept under guard. The hospital authorities noticed that she was losing blood rapidly from a vaginal haemorrhage. The cause, it was found out, was a broken glass test tube in her vagina which contained a secret message to a black conspirator giving a list of the military equipment a named African government was sending to the black guerrilla fighters on the Zambezi.

Evidence of Free African involvement in the organisation of an armed revolt in South Africa accumulates, Prinsloo points out. He then proceeds to criticise as unrealistic all talk of an alliance with the United States, to which the prime minister gives a lot of attention. There has been a basic shift in the balance of power from the white race to the black, brown and yellow peoples. A security vacuum has emerged which reduces America's significance as an ally.

Beyond this, there always is the possibility that one day the Arabs and the Africans might present a united front and use their metals and oil against the whites in Africa. These developments have a direct bearing on black politics, Prinsloo argues. The leaders of the rural administrations have rejected the government's offers of independence.

Nowhere, nowhere ever in the world, has a colonial people refused independence when it was offered. The leaders of the black people feel that they have the potential now to settle the race problem on their terms and are translating that potential into political realities. It has taken them more than sixty years to build up the potential.

Now they know that if they want to give the stock exchange a bad shaking and send foreign investments flying out of the country, they have to stage a politically motivated strike and force the police to shoot them.

The black administrations in the rural areas are in the position, finally, to control the flow of labour from their areas and to persuade Botswana, Lesotho, Malawi and Swaziland one day to withdraw the cheap labour they export to South Africa. The meaning of these developments is that the African can withdraw his labour if and when he likes; that he can strike at the white man where and when he pleases.

In plain terms, he is reducing the white people to the position where they will rule South Africa while he determines the country's destiny. To give himself as many options as possible, he refuses the independence which the white man offers him; he is convinced that he can get his freedom on his own terms at the right moment.

Time is his most powerful ally; he has forced the Afrikaner into the position where the Arabs placed the Jews. In this setting, to force the African's women to carry Passes is like playing with dynamite. What Afrikanerdom is up against is no longer the control of the black people's movements; the Afrikaner is up against the spirit of a whole people.

The answer is a peace treaty which will reconcile the black people's desire for fulfilment with the Afrikaner's yearning for a secure place in the African sun. Isn't there anybody with enough brains in the

Union Buildings, Prinsloo concludes, to read correctly the implications of these changes and to start negotiating with the Africans?

*   *   *

XII. The Child Race

Inhlamba yezithulu kayinamatheli.

(The deaf hear no evil.)

Union Day is a holiday which falls on May 31 to commemorate the formation of the Union of South Africa in 1910. The driving power behind this development was Britain's greed for South Africa's mineral wealth. The Afrikaners, who controlled the Transvaal and the Orange Free State had lacked enthusiasm for the unification. They feared that Union would mean the consolidation of British economic power and this is precisely what happened.

They feared, also, that Union would lead to the welding of the various African language groups into a single racial bloc in opposition to the whites and this is precisely what happened.

Now that they have snatched political power from the English and are using it to transfer economic dominance to their side, it becomes increasingly clear to the perceptive few that Union was a white elephant for the Afrikaner.

While de Haas never tires of telling all with ears to hear about the miracle that is Afrikanerdom, on festive occasions, the professionals in UBRA argue that the real victors when the Union of South Africa was formed were the black people.

They had the numbers one day to seize political power from the Afrikaners and do to the latter what the Afrikaners had done to the British; they are marching to a future in which they will use their numbers, first, to seize political power and eventually to use it to transfer control of the country's wealth to themselves. This creates an atmosphere of uncertainty about the future which gives the Afrikaner no peace of mind. In his bitterest moments he blames it all on the British; if they had left him alone, he would have created the world in which he would be sure about the future he was marching to. In this mood, some Afrikaners adopt attitudes of ambivalence toward Union Day.

Piet du Toit van der Merwe attended the military parade on Church Square in the centre of the city where Afrikanerdom flexed its muscles. After that, he returned home. Marietjie's health is becoming

137

increasingly fretful. The death of her father affected her so badly her doctors have warned that a miscarriage could occur. Whenever possible, Piet wants to be by the side of his wife. He is sitting on his favourite chair while Marietjie knits a baby's shawl when Hantie, aged seven, runs into the sitting room, almost out of breath.

Papa! she taps his knee excitedly, there's a kaffer outside; an old nanny; she wants to talk to you!

A kaffer wants to talk to me!

Ja!

Tell Zandile to talk to her.

The child seems puzzled and does not move. After a few moments she races to the kitchen. Zandile walks into the sitting room.

Baas, the old lady has something to say to you personally.

If she won't tell you what she wants, tell her I'm too busy to see her just now.

I think it is important that you should see her; she has the letter you wrote to her . . . about . . . .

Me? Write a letter to a black woman?

Marietjie stops her knitting and gives him a puzzled and vaguely hostile look. He rises somewhat angrily from his chair and walks heavily to the back door. Marietjie follows him. He stands under the verandah . . . to keep the distance between himself and the African who wants to see him. She is in her seventies and stoops as though she carries the woes of the world on her shoulders. She holds on to a long staff to support her weak legs and has covered her shoulders with a tattered blanket. A strange light shines from her brown, deepset eyes; she seems to be seeing through everything and to know that she does this. This look, which is characteristic of all the Africans he has met, angers Piet; he believes it to be the look of defiance directed at the Afrikaner. Most of his people believe this. Marietjie, too, does not like the glow in the old woman's eye; it conveys an arrogance which seems ridiculous on a face scribbled all over with defeat, humiliation and grief.

Zandile stands on the lawn by the woman, to help with the translation. Piet is the first to speak.

Yes? What do you want?

The old woman disentangles a knot on the scarf on her head and does this so slowly Piet loses his temper.

Tell her, Zandile, that I can't stand for a thousand years here, waiting for her to speak. If she won't talk, I have other things to do.

Zandile passes the message. The woman remains unruffled.

Tell him, child, that he has to have the time for me.

Zandile does not pass the retort to the whites. Black and white in South Africa, as in many parts of the world, are like two deaf men engaged in a violent, mutual swearing and cursing fight. Each says the ugliest things against the other while the other does not hear. Zandile realises that the woman is beginning to be angry with Piet's manner, just as he is with hers. The old lady turns to her again.

Don't these people have any rules of behaviour? Any law of decency? Aren't they even trained in manners? They're all so rude you'd think they were borne by one loose woman. Doesn't he see I'm untying this knot? Tell him what I'm saying.

Piet has lost a good deal of patience and starts pacing up and down the verandah. It is Marietjie who breaks the silence.

What's she saying, Zandile?

She's talking to herself, nooi.

The lie does not sound very convincing, but Zandile is determined to play the role of diplomat in what she regards as a clash between the Zulu and Afrikaner worlds. The old woman sees the white man from her exclusive perspectives and behaves toward him in terms of the etiquette used in her society. The presentation of a subject must be done according to the rules and the black woman is not going to be rushed to violate them, not even when the white man thinks her a beggar in his backyard.

These rules require that she should prepare the ground for the statement of the theme, develop her subject, establish her point, relate the point to prevailing conditions, and then conclude her presentation. These steps are based on the movement of the person through life on this earth and represent birth, growth, maturity, decline and death. The fingers of the open right hand symbolise each stage and birth starts with the shortest finger.

To shake hands with the next person is to communicate to him vibrations wishing him the happiest passage from stage to stage in life. Children and younger people are touched with the open right hand to pass on to them the vibrations calculated to give them good health, to protect them and set them on the road to success. Refined conversation must be divided into the five parts symbolised by the five fingers. Every statement, every story, every speech, every dance, every form of action must be conceived in five parts. The cultured Zulu casts his conversations with the humblest and the exalted in the form just described.

The old lady has known no other tradition; the impatience and brashness of the white man offend against good taste; in her view, he behaves like a primitive barbarian; he has not been trained in the law of polite conversation. She would like Piet to know what she thinks of him, but Zandile does not think she should oblige. The old woman finally pulls an ancient-looking piece of paper from her scarf and hands it to Zandile.

Give this to him; tell him to read it.

Piet reads it quickly and then turns to his wife, beaming.

Do you know who this is? Bhadama's grandmother. Where do you come from, old woman?

From the land of Zulu. I have been on the road for three

months now.

You walked all the way from Empangeni to Pretoria? Incredible! Why did you do it?

I am looking for Bhadama; I want to talk to him.

But I told you in this letter that Bhadama had died and that he had been burnt so badly only his ashes remained. We buried them. I told you this, old woman!

I want to talk to the ashes.

For a moment, Piet does not understand and he stares at the woman not comprehending what she says and not knowing what answer to give.

How can you talk to the ashes?

For a moment, the African does not understand how the white man cannot follow what she is saying; for a while, she does not know how to answer. She half blames the patient, self-controlled Zandile.

You, white people, you do not understand; I see now that you are only a child-race. We black people were around when the stones cried if pinched. That was long, long ago. We have grown in the understanding of the person; we know how to handle the eternal in him . . . .

The old woman pauses for a minute, which looks like a millennium, turning her head first to the whites and their children who are intrigued as much by her queer manners, her slowness, as by their father's reactions to her. The woman then turns and stares at Zandile as though to warn her that disaster is about to descend on the scene. Piet is so tense he stops pacing up and down the verandah and glares at the woman not knowing what could be in her mind and, at the same time, not knowing what to do. If she had not been Bhadama's grandmother, he would have walked away; but, Bhadama's grandmother is a different class of kaffer. If she has come all the way from the land of the Zulus to put him through a test of nerves, he prepares himself for the confrontation.

What you do not know is what the person is; you do not understand that Bhadama is a part of me; not just a part of my flesh, but a part of my spirit. He is the part of myself which belongs to the future. I gave birth to his mother three months after her father's death and she died giving birth to Bhadama. I brought Bhadama up with these bare hands of mine. One day, he grew up and became a man; he worked on the white man's farm for six months and for the rest of the year came here to work for you. Bhadama was a man; a man among men; he worked hard, saved his money and sent it to me. He did not squander it with the women of the location as some young people do. I kept it for him; then I bought him cattle. One day, Bhadama would get himself a pretty girl and found a family. I lived for that moment; then, the fire in your house came . . . . Now, I am left alone; I am old and the world is collapsing on me. I want to go to Bhadama's ashes, to his grave, to ask him to tell me what to do . . . .

Tears trickle down the wrinkles on her face. Marietjie steps closer to Piet and holds his hand.

I know how she feels. Poor thing.

Marietjie, you don't understand the native mind; you just have to be patient and let her work off the steam. I still don't know what she wants me to do. A good twenty minutes have gone . . . wasted!

Shall I get her something to eat? She looks hungry.

Zandile will do that when we know what she wants.

While Piet speaks to his wife, the old lady staggers to the ground and sits on the lawn, readying herself for a long talk.

What do you want me to do, old woman? You can't talk to a dead person!

Forgive me, for sitting on your lawn. Being on the road, walking every day for three full months is more than the body of an old woman can bear.

Were you not afraid to be alone, on the road or by night?

You do not understand; you cannot understand. Your wife does. A person has never lain across your middle; your body has never known the experience of passing life to your neighbour; to the future. See it this way: the future is always beckoning to the present, through woman, to pass life from the past to itself. Woman is the custodian of life, she must respond when life calls. I am here to look for a part of my life; for a piece of my flesh; for the umbilical cord I buried when Bhadama was born. It is the cord which links me with the past and the future.

Think of how old I am and how old you are; how old every living person in the world is—old, not in terms of years, but of ages.

The ages are telescoped into each person; successions of umbilical cords linking generations of me and you with antiquity. You and I are not things of the moment; we are eternal persons, linked directly to the beginning of the human experience. See what happens? A part of the umbilical cord drops off the navel of the baby; we dig the soil and bury it. The baby lives and grows up while a part of himself lies buried in the soil. The reason for this is that there is no death; there's life only. We live in death and, dying, are reborn into another dimension of existence. The cord in the earth does not die; it merely changes into earth-stuff or life and vibrates through the soil into the roots of the plant whose grains sustain human life. See what happens? That which is "dead" sustains life. It was like that at the beginning of things; so it is now, as it always will be. That is why I am here. The future is always calling out to me and to you to grow into it. You understand what I mean?

Piet does not answer; he turns his face and looks at his wife, who has her face turned to his. They hear words and feel the power of the thoughts behind them, but do not understand what the woman is

141

talking about. It is as though they hear a voice in the dark, from another planet; she talks to them from one level of experience and they hear her from another and neither side understands the other.

I see; you do not understand. Bhadama now belongs to the past, which is also the future. He calls out to me and I have to respond when he calls; I have to rise up and heed the call, even when it means I have to walk barefooted around the earth. For, I must heed the voice of the part of me that is in the soil.

What do you want me to do?

I am old now and too weak to work for the white man who owns the farm on which I live. I have no relatives to work for him in order to have a roof over my head. He says I should leave his farm if I can't work; he says a lot of hard things; you would think his heart was made of stone. He says he'll take my cattle; Bhadama's cattle, to cover my rent for living on his piece of earth. If I tell him that the cattle are the pillar which keeps me alive, he says my life is my business and not his; that he came alone into this earth and shall be alone in death. If I ask him where I shall get food when he has taken my cattle, he says I should ask the government. I went to the white government in Empangeni; they told me that the law says I should go when a white man says I should get out of his land.

There are scores of Bantoe reserves in Natal. Can't you find a place in any of them?

Child of a white woman, have you ever been to a reserve? Those places are overcrowded; people live like cattle in a stockyard! I thought you would do better than tell me about the reserves. The government cannot take any more people into them because there's no more place for them; that is what the chiefs tell me. See what this means? If there is no place for a black person, then we must no longer bear children. I asked the Bantoe affairs commissioner how he would solve the land problem, since people would continue to be born. The women must push a cork stopper into their genitals. That is what he told me. But, even if I were to find a place, I could not take my two huts on my head and carry them to a reserve. I would have to sell the cattle in order to build a new house and I would be left with nothing to give me food.

You have your customs; you share things; your neighbours would share their food with you.

You do not understand. How do you grow food on over-crowded land? Who ploughs the lands, because you take our men from their homes; you want them to work for you in your towns. Those reserves are places where people starve, die and rot. Bhadama used to tell me that you are one of the white lords; that you work for the chief of the white people; that the chief makes the laws for the white people. I have come to ask you to help me; I need your help. I came to you because I believe you are the only white man who can understand; Bhadama stood by you too, in your hour of need. I don't say pay me for that: I ask you to understand . . . . I need a place where to hide my head.

She has a point, Piet.

Marietjie! You don't understand! How on earth can an Afrikaner prime minister force an Afrikaner farmer to accommodate a kaffer on his farm, whom he no longer needs? Put aside the political implications which I, his secretary, dare not even consider. Think what the principle does; it strikes at the very roots of Afrikaner survival.

But this is a special case. Our children . . . .

Don't repeat liberal sobstuff to me. All you need to do is to get the opposition paper in Johannesburg, the *Rand Post*, to publish the story that a black woman shed tears which melted the prime minister's heart. See what would happen? You can't expect me to shatter the prime minister's image! I, his own private secretary, to be involved in a thing like that would be a scandal with which I could never live.

Piet shoves his hands into his pockets and steps heavily up and down the verandah while Marietjie disappears into the house.

If you were younger, I would ask you to come and work for a friend of mine in the city here; then, you would have the right to rent a municipal house in the location. But then, you are too old to help yourself. And, if a Bantoe affairs commissioner says his reserves are full, I can't do much to help; the law ties my hands just as it ties his.

Was that law made by human beings, for human beings?

That riles Piet; he takes his hands out of his pockets and, glaring at the old woman, shouts.

Who do you think made it? These trees?

They are too understanding to do that.

Well, if that's what you travelled all the way to tell me, talk to them!

You are such handsome people; look at your pretty wife, as beautiful as a budding flower on a spring morning. Look at your children; look at yourself, a pillar of strength; manliness at its best. Such handsome people! Does it not hurt your conscience or anything decent in you to make yourselves ugly by enacting ugly laws which make life ugly for other people? Don't you ever sing or dance or open your lives to your neighbours or lose yourselves in the beauty of all the people with whom you inhabit the earth?

We are a different people.

Indeed, you are. But, don't you get tired of remaining a child race when all the people around you are growing up? All the other people ask is that you should grow up and learn to live with them as adults do. An adult is a civilised person and to be civilised means wanting nothing for yourself which you will deny your neighbour. That is the law enunciated by our ancestors when the stones were so soft they cried if pinched.

143

Zandile was happy to translate all of this.

* * *

Bus Number AZ 1021 is not as crowded as it is on workdays. Zandile leads Bhadama's mother to a seat for two.

Child, now that we are alone, tell me: How do you live with those barbarians?

We do not live with each other; we just watch each other. When we are hungry, they give us jobs; when they have work to do, they need our labour. We know where they are strong and weak; they know where we are weak and strong; we work where we are weak and watch where we are strong. They do the same.

How long will you go on like that?

How long did you think you would go on when Bhadama went to his ancestors?

That white couple for whom you work! There's nothing human in them. They couldn't even shake hands with me, just to express gratitude for what Bhadama did for them!

No! They wouldn't shake hands with you. They don't shake hands with me or with any black person, except the diplomats from the land of the Nyasa. The Afrikaners do not shake hands with black people; that is their law.

What do they lose when they shake hands?

They know best.

That white man again! Did you see the way he eyes you? I don't blame him. You are such a pretty child the sun itself hides its face when you look at it. You make him feel deeply human; he desires you; he can't control himself.

Sometimes he says silly things.

Watch out, child. I once was a pretty girl, too.

He told you that he is a prisoner of the law; the law controls his passions.

Now, I want to see your husband. He must be a very handsome man to have a wife with such a beautiful spirit. How shall I express my thanks for your offer to keep me in your house until I have seen Bhadama's house. May more be added to everything you want in life.

I'll tell you one thing, mama, about my husband. He'll be hurt, very deeply, when you tell him that those *gatwysers* would not shake hands with you even after Bhadama had given his life to save their children.

Well, let me not tell him, then. The white people are a child race; they do not know how to handle the most beautiful, the most precious and the most sacred thing on earth: the human personality. It does not matter who has it. Let me hope that you townspeople do not allow the diseased mind to contaminate yours. For, what shall we be the day our minds are diseased, like the white man's? There won't be a single black person left on this land. To save yourselves and all of us, you have to refuse to punish a person simply because he is the child of his parents.

My husband finds it hard to live according to that rule.

Child, he has to abide by it not because he likes the white people but because he is different; the rule is one of his guarantees of survival. The day he throws *umteto wesintu* out of his life, he will walk the earth like a disembowelled shell of flesh, without *ubuntu*, without a sense of direction and without a future. The white man said they are different; we, too, are different from them. If they handle the human personality with untidy hands, we prefer to handle it with clean hands.

* * *

By May, autumn has said its farewells to South Africa and winter, windy, cold and dry, is round the corner. People no longer walk leisurely from the bus terminal to their homes; they run. As a rule, the door of a normal African home is never shut by day as long as there are people in the house. In the locations, however, crime is rising in such a way that people open the front doors only when they are in the living-room. The open door is a signal that human beings live in the house; being human means that the people who live behind the open door want nothing for themselves which they would deny their neighbour. In the old days, the doors were shut only on cold, rainy or windy days.

In spite of the cold, Pumasilwe stands in front of his main door, waiting for his wife. He rushes to the gate and opens it and helps her with the groceries. The old lady smiles approvingly. She has heard that the people in the towns have adopted the white man's lifestyle and have lost their regard for privacy. Men, she has been told, will smoke in a room where women are present. Husbands and wives embrace and kiss in public. When people talk to each other, they look each other in the eyes. In her culture only crooks look people they are talking to in the eyes; uncultured people, too, do this. Crooks are uncultured people; they have no sense of decency. Boys and girls kiss in the presence of older people. A flash of fear passes through her mind; suddenly, the meeting with Zandile's husband might be an encounter with white backwardness in the black community. Pumasilwe does not kiss his wife and she does not in any way indicate the readiness to be kissed in public. A well-bred Zulu youth or girl knows that people in love kiss in their bedroom. In the old days, when a boy or girl reached puberty, a private hut was built for him or for her so that he or she should have the privacy to express love to the loved one.

Why do you stand in the cold? Zandile is speaking.

Waiting for you.

Good news, bad news?

Good! It had to be good. I know you don't have much time for Maggie, but she did a good job.

Alright, father of the children, you'll tell me more about her later.

They walk into the house and settle down for the evening. In their bedroom that night Zandile asks her husband about the good news.

Maggie contacted Paul Kritzinger's cook. Yes, the Kritzingers hate the van der Merwes—as bitterly as the hen hates the wildcat. If the women are planning a showdown with the government on the law forcing them to carry Passes, in Pretoria, at least, we shall be fighting a police force with a split mind. Our tactics will be based on the quarrel between Kritzinger and Piet van der Merwe on one side and, on the other, on the conflicting views between de Haas and the Commissioner of Police. You did a fine job, Mother of the Children.

It was all a waste of time . . . .

Procuring information on the heads of the government? How can that be a waste of time? How else can you control the mind of the white man if you don't know what he is doing?

From to-day, Father of the Children, I feel I am a changed woman. I grew up being told that there are millions of paths to Blood River and that each person is one of these. I thought I understood what this meant; I was ignorant; that was my undoing. I could not have understood; all the education I have reduced me to a carbon copy of the white man. I saw reality as he dictated. He told me who and what I was. I accepted his definitions of the truth and made myself his consenting slave. I told myself that love is the only thing to live for. Since I loved you, I sacrificed my personality at the altar of love; since I loved our children, I became a slave to the family. To keep it together was the thing I lived for. The family had been transformed into the prison of the mind in which my real self was locked. Society's mind was locked in that jail. People regarded the family as so sacred, it was an unforgivable sin to do anything to shake its foundations; people lived in fear of the consequences of shaking the family. But the fear was one more instrument the white man used to control our minds and manipulate our lives. From to-day, I shall never again be a slave by consent!

What is happening to you? Are you telling me that the doors of your heart are now shut to me?

No. I love you; but now I am a custodian of life and I love you as such. Those white people for whom I work . . . they wouldn't shake the hand of a woman like Bhadama's grandmother! That Bhadama who died saving their children. I was so hurt, I asked myself: Zandile, what is it that you live for? Forever to be spat upon even when you do good? Forever to be spited for being the owner of your land? Forever to be despised, just because you are the child of your parents, in your own Africa? No, I told myself; I live to be a woman; the custodian of life

146

and the destroyer of life . . . .

Pumasilwe still does not think he understands what is going on in his wife's mind. The hot tears from her eyes warn him that mud has been stirred at the depths of her being. Each time she does this in reaction to treatment by the whites, which is not infrequent, he feels pangs of guilt. He asked her to join the underground, to collect information on the whites at the head of the government and he knows that he cannot make much use of it. He, Mareka and Masilo plan strategies based on it which do not seem to hit the white power-structure where it hurts.

They meet and manufacture home-made bombs and occasionally blow up small bridges and electric pylons, but never strike where the white man will be forced to realise that the black people are determined now to restore their land and its wealth to themselves.

If the tactics of the underground leave Zandile frustrated, she leaves her husband in no doubt about her feelings on the futility of blowing up electric pylons in the hope that this might inconvenience the whites and frighten them into quitting South Africa. And each time she says this, she makes it clear that the underground is, in the final analysis, delaying the struggle's march to freedom. Pumasilwe knows that she no longer has the confidence she once had in the underground.

She stays on her job out of love for him and Puma is not the type of man who is not affected by this. She collects whatever bits and pieces of information she can because she loves him and sometimes he hates himself for placing her in this position. And when she breaks down and cries, he finds it difficult not to feel guilty.

In such moments, when he does not know what to do, he turns to the breastbone of the cat and holds it between his fingers. That steadies his nerves and gives him at least a feeling of security. He has it between his fingers as his wife talks; it has become the prop he turns to in moments of challenge. He and his wife sometimes quarrel badly over even this prop. The bone, she tells him then, will not do the thinking for him.

Do you know what happened, Father of the Children?

I am listening.

In one short encounter, that old woman taught me what I had not learned in all the years I had been in the white man's schools: she showed me what it means to take the white man out of my mind. She spoke to the whites in her own language, according to the rules observed in her culture and at a level beyond their range of thinking. The whites just did not know what to do or how to handle her; she dominated the scene. Their arrogance, superior knowledge . . . all that ceased to have meaning in the situation she created. Piet's final answer was to lose his temper. The old lady was not ruffled; she never stepped out of her world. He raved and ranted and there the old custodian of life sat on the lawn telling him that he was a handsome man who defiled himself and plastered his personality with ugliness. In effect, she told him to stop being silly by inflating his personality out of all human proportions. You should have been there, to see how calm she was, even when the gatwyser was red in the face . . . . I realised then what the poet meant when he cried out: "Arise and march, O ye bones which lie buried on the banks of Blood River!"

That was some experience, her husband agreed.

I said I am a changed woman? No; that is the wrong word. I became an experience older; I grew up. If woman has the power to create and destroy life, that power is not given to her by the white people and cannot be taken away from her by any force on earth or in the whole of creation. The old lady used the power which inheres in the woman to create a situation to which the whites had to respond, regardless of whether or not they liked it.

I still do not know if I understand what you are telling me.

I'm telling myself something. If I can create and destroy, I can destroy to create. If the whites pass the law which forces us to carry passes, we can crack their psyche; we, the women of Africa, can use the power which inheres in us as the custodians to create the situations in which we shall crack the stoutest Afrikaner heart. That is the lesson the old woman taught me. I never thought of it . . . .

As she speaks, her face brightens as though it is illuminated by an invisible, inner light. She looks as though she has suddenly been lifted to a higher plane of consciousness. Puma notes the change; Zandile radiates an aura of beauty which is no longer of this earth when she is ovulating. It is then when she loves him best; when she is irresistible. But he knows that she is not going through the most beautiful cycle in the life of a woman and, at that moment, she is not thinking about love; she has her mind on the things that hurt a black person; the things that drive black and white to war. The woman thinking of war is not a woman in love. Puma is puzzled and whenever he faces a problem he cannot solve, he takes refuge in his prop. He shoves his hand into his pocket and strokes the breastbone of the cat.

Zandile is now quiet. Her mind wanders back to her childhood days; to the moments when she would live on her grandmother's lap, to have the nits picked out of her hair. Those, she always tells herself, were the most precious moments in her life, when her grandmother explained the mysteries of existence to her. The old lady had been born toward the evening of Zulu power. Two years after she was born, the British had declared war on the Zulus, forced Cetshwayo into a war he had not wanted and crushed the Zulu empire in order to establish the Union of South Africa, dig up the gold and the iron and the diamonds in the lands of the Africans and ship these to the lands of the white people. Grandmother had grown up in the shadow of defeat and humiliation; she had seen the man she was to marry recruited and forced to work on the road and then the railway line from Durban to

Johannesburg; it was like conscription; armed police roamed the countryside hunting for young men to be conscripted into the labour gangs. People died by their hundreds in the filthy compounds in which they were locked at night. Those were the years of the hated *isibhalo*. That was what defeat meant; the white man sent his police and came with the gun to force a man out of his home, to work for the whites.

The defeat had stirred up an unprecedented desire for changing defeat into victory. The Zulus realised that the collapse of their power meant that they had to fight the white man with his own weapons. All over Natal, people sent their children to school; mastering the white men's techniques was the most powerful ambition of the times. The head of grandmother's clan, wise old Chief Ngangezwe, was the subject of this panegyric poem:

> UNkulunkulu mkhulu,
> Emkhulu kangako uSomandla,
> AkangangoNgangezwe,
> Umgqwabagqwaba omile emandulo,
> Waqhakaza ngalêna kwe phakade.
> Umkhulu Ngangezwe!

> (God is indeed great;
> Although he has all the power,
> Ngangezwe is greater;
> He is the tree rooted in antiquity
> And grows and flowers on the other side of eternity.
> Thou art great, O Ngangezwe!)

Ngangezwe had forty wives and two hundred children; his cattle were as many as the sands of the Tukela River and it was said that there was enough gold in his great house to outshine the sun. Ngangezwe fought in the war of 1879 against the British. After defeat he returned to his kraal, which was a town by itself and made up his mind to adapt to the challenge of defeat. One morning, he loaded half a ton of gold on one of his ox-wagons and led one hundred of his children to the mission school.

Take these Zulus, he told the principal, and teach them the wisdom of the white people!

These were the times in which Zandile's grandmother had grown up. The old lady denied that the human being was created; he had emerged, she insisted, from a cleft reed in a primeval swamp; his entry into the earth was an act of his will. He owed his life to nobody other than himself; he was not owned by any power in heaven or on earth. That had been reassuring to Zandile; she had grown up feeling at home in the cosmic order.

One day, little Zandile went to school, where they told her

149

about genesis. That introduced conflicts which shattered her feeling of security in the world. The missionaries and the teachers taught that God had created the person; that he had the copyright on the person's life; that he owned her! If he owned her, his representatives had the right to own her. The feeling of being owned distorted Zandile's personality and filled her mind with fear. She became uncertain about her position in the cosmic order; that made her a prisoner of the white man's God; the whites punished her for being black and God created her to be punished; it was a crime for her to be alive. The old lady tried to reasure Zandile:

Child, do not worry; it is not a crime to be an African; the race of men has not as yet been born which shall say it has conquered the African. See, child, you can take all the soap there is in the world and wash the black skin ... it won't turn white. There is a power in us which makes us endure what no other race of men has endured. We grow and keep growing. The white man builds his jails, crowds us in the locations, steals our land, starves us and builds all sorts of walls within which to confine us and when he has done everything, we outgrow it all and keep growing. How do you conquer a people like that?

Zandile remembers how some of the things her grandmother told her were puzzling and how she would ask endless questions.

Grandma, does it mean that the person does not really die?

Yes, he does not die.

But people do die!

Yes, they do die.

Zandile would sometimes be angry with grandmother's abstruse explanations of the truth. There was so much the little girl wanted to understand about life and there were not many grandmothers to appeal to.

See, child, we human beings are still ignorant; that is why we die. We are not as yet aware of the power of emergence locked in us. One day we shall be aware of it. We still concern ourselves with the physical aspects of our lives and ignore the cosmic influences which shape our bodies and affect our health or love or hatred. Medicine treats the physical in us; it has not as yet been developed to control the cosmic forces and focus these on the treatment of disease. Our ancestors had mastered the art. In his ignorance the white man called the art witchcraft. But, one day, things will change; the white people shall grow out of ignorance .... Then, people shall not die!

As Zandile sits next to her husband, these thoughts enter her mind. To her, the behaviour of Bhadama's grandmother translates her grandmother's teachings into experience.

Think of it, Father of the Children! The power of emergence! I can move out of the owned slave-self that I am to become the self-determining self on my own steam! By an act of pure will! Nobody has any copyright on my life; that old woman, Bhadama's grandmother, showed how this is not so! The white man's God doesn't have this copyright and not even the white man who stole my land. Grow out there on the plain by myself; stand out there alone in order to strike the Boer where he is weakest! Boy! Shall I not strike!

I thought people like Bulube called that the *xina* technique? You create the situation in which you seek to make it impossible for white domination to survive . . . even if it takes you a thousand years to create it . . . .

I don't see how the underground is doing better. Blowing up an electric pole here, cutting fences there and burning an old deserted house and wearing a particular type of necktie or not cutting your hair or wearing long beards and blasting white power out of existence with the irresistible might of the conference resolution! You call that fighting? I don't!

You can't fight if the good-boys are around, the quislings and their allies stand in the way. You have to get rid of the enemies of freedom so that the masses can march to freedom.

Then, why don't you kill the good-boys? Why don't you kill the quislings and their white friends?

That will play into the hands of the enemy; it will split the masses . . . .

Excuses! Excuses! Always excuses. He who is determined to be free strikes with every weapon within reach; with his bare hands if nothing else is available and, if necessary, with his body or freedom or life.

You have to prepare the masses . . . .

Rhetoric! More rhetoric! It all makes me sick! In 1912 our fathers went to Bloemfontein and told us that white domination is wicked. Since then, what have we been doing? Vying with each other in denouncing white domination; making great speeches, passing portentous resolutions, preparing learned memoranda, writing learned books, analysing white domination, planning action . . . in a desperate bid to avoid action. How much have our leaders spent in air fares, flying from one foreign capital to the other planning action, attacking white domination and all the time saying nothing new!

You have to fight wherever you can hit the enemy . . . .

I'll tell you what I think is wrong. The underground does not know what it really wants.

That's nonsense! Everybody knows we want freedom?

What is freedom?

The right to determine our lives.

The white man's definition again. You want what the white man has; you want what he says is good. Why not want something different? Something higher?

What is more precious than freedom?

I hate freedom; it gives all the scoundrels of the world the right to meddle in the lives of their fellowmen. I want to know where and how to hit to kill the enemy; I want to know how I can create a responsible and balanced society; I want to know how to feed, clothe, house, educate and cure every person. Freedom won't enable me to do that. In your great democracies, people are free to starve; in your people's republics people have enough food, though they are slaves.

In the name of goodness, what do you want, then?

To be like that woman I brought home with me; to have the white man out of my mind; to be able to say to myself and to all the people of Africa: Don't waste your time writing about the evils of white domination! Don't waste your words condemning the whites. They can't do better than what they are doing. Let them enact the Pass Law; let them please themselves; let them make our honour the plaything of any scoundrel in uniform. Cease to respond to their initiatives, for then they do the thinking for you and for us.

Zandile's voice rises scornfully. Then, I would tell myself: let them always have the power to keep the sun in the skies to give them continuing power; I would tell myself: Let the day never come when the sun shall set; for the black woman shall rise, draw the line and say: thus far, white man, and no farther! For when that moment comes, there shall not be enough tears in the world to wash the wounds we shall have torn into the body of Afrikanerdom. There shall not be enough tears to extinguish the fires which shall rage in this land.

* * *

The Sunday is the first Bhadama's grandmother has spent in Pumasilwe's home. Zandile and her husband understood that the most important business in her trip to Pretoria was to visit Bhadama's grave. She had lost most of the cattle he had bought and therefore had no money to buy a train ticket to Pretoria. She is old; but not even this stood in her way. She had to rise to a dimension of existence where she would do the things she wanted done.

She steps out of the house, into the car Pumasilwe has borrowed from Father Maimane of the Zion Pentecostal Church. Zandile and the old lady sit in the back seat. It is a momentous day for the old woman; night after night she has been meditating on this moment; she meditates on it as the car drives to the African cemetery. Sunday is, as a rule, burial day in some of South Africa's largest locations. Most people do not work on this day; they therefore are free to accompany their loved ones to their last resting place. Pumasilwe and the two women leave their car at the gate to the cemetery. Pumasilwe warns the old woman:

We will walk a long way to Bhadama's house. We shall take our time and do not strain yourself, Mother.

Every Zulu who has been brought up the right way refers to every woman about the age of his mother as Mother and she, in turn, calls him Son or Child. Zandile's guest moves nearer to her as the two walk slowly down the footpath to Bhadama's grave in the distance.

Did you say, child, that only black people lie in these graves?
Yes, mother.

So many graves? Of adults and infants? One would think there were no more black people left in Pretoria.

There still are many of us, mother.

I have never seen anything like this! So many people dead? In peacetime? This frightens me. You live in the midst of undeclared war; a very real war because people die.

She shakes her head and holds her stick tightly. After a long silence she addresses Zandile again.

Child, how do you live with these people, who live to destroy? How do you survive the peaceful war? These graves . . . they are the foundations on which white power is built; they are the pillars of the white people's rule. No wonder the whites are so thoughtless and so inconsiderate; their power is founded on death. Yes. The death of little children; the death of adults and the death of everybody and everything. I did not know . . . that such beautiful people can overload their hearts with so much wickedness.

She is quiet again; she wants to think of Bhadama, but the sight of the vast cemetery and what she regards as its implications for her race almost overwhelm her. She talks to Zandile again.

Child, you went to school and you send your children to school. Why do you do that? You learned the ways of the white man. You want your children to learn these ways; to be like him; to destroy life instead of preserving it. Why do you want your children to see the truth as he does? They will commit the mistakes which are his to-day. Are you not afraid, that when the death by which he lives has overtaken him, your own rule will be founded on the power of death? Look at all these graves! You want to have as many of them too when you rule? The thought frightens me.

The path to Bhadama's grave has taken a sloping bend and the old woman feels the strain. She stops for a while and turns her body downhill, to draw a larger volume of air into her lungs.

Graves! Graves wherever you turn! You want your children to learn how to send more people to the grave?

Not at all! We send them to school to learn how to survive the death. We want them to understand the mind of the enemy so that they should be able to fight to win. We must know where the enemy is weakest.

And now, you think you know?

Not yet, because they are still our masters. But that will not last too much longer. We know now that the truth by which they live destroys everybody and everything they come in contact with. That is one of their weaknesses; we must work harder to speed their march to self-destruction.

The old woman takes a deep breath and starts the uphill climb.

She walks for a while and stops again.

Graves! Graves everywhere. You are mistaken, child. You will not beat the white man at his game. You will become worse destroyers of your fellowmen . . . .

Zandile does not want an argument. The cemetery is not the place to discuss race politics. Besides, the old woman has touched on a point where most educated Africans are sensitive. They realise that they are people of two worlds; that for good or for evil, they see reality from two, often conflicting, perspectives. While they are aware of the truth as it has been revealed to their race, they also understand the white man's outlook on life. The African who has not been to school sees reality from one angle, like the white people. The bifocal mind has its advantages. Bulube has used it to create a synthesis of political experiences with which he has established a leadership vacuum in the country. He has created a situation in which the whites progressively lose their sense of direction at the time when their army has never been stronger and the market for gold has never been better. Above all, he has developed leadership initiatives which promise to lead South Africa along safer routes to a better future.

But the bifocal mind also has disadvantages. The educated Africans resist with difficulty the temptation to define fulfilment in terms which are laid down by the whites. Very many of them are still christians; they see nothing wrong with a philosophy which stresses individuality. If that works for the fragmentation of their society, just as it has split the whites throughout history, some of the educated hope that one day they will adapt christianity to the demands of a responsible society. They are not ready to face the truth that *ubuntu* and christianity are ideological incompatibles. The unreadiness develops an ambivalence which some of the educated would like to conceal.

Some even give interpretations of christianity which are so revolutionary that they have no place in the white man's religion. Largely as a result the African's political thinking is always in three directions: there always are the traditionalists who see fulfilment for themselves in burning the white man's cities and purifying their soil by driving every white person into the sea.

At the other extreme are the conciliators. Largely christian in outlook or background, they adhere to the concept of human brotherhood with a determination which nothing seems likely to crack.

Between the two is the majority which has blended African and white traditions and produced a syncretic culture based on the *Buntu Ideal*. Bulube belongs to this group. In the South African setting, every African has something of a traditionalist, a conciliator and a syncretist in him. At the same time the clash between black and white is so fundamental it works for the continuous clarification of attitudes in every walk of life.

Traditionalism, conciliation and syncretism exist in every walk of African life. The Africans who have not been to the white man's schools draw no distinction between the conciliators and the syncretists; all of them have, as the saying goes, licked the spittle of the white man and are regarded with varying degrees of hostility. When Bhadama's grandmother persists in questioning Zandile about the children's education, she expresses this hostility.

The old woman will not allow Zandile to retreat easily; in her view, people who send their children to school are the unconscious allies of the destroyers.

How will you push the whites to self-destruction, the old woman asks.

We shouldn't make them better human beings.

You do not understand, child. The whites are human beings; the human being grows; peoples, too, grow. As the child approaches puberty, he becomes aware of the tremendous powers locked in him. He has all the energy he needs; he believes human wisdom begins with him; all those who have gone before him are fools; he alone has a solution for every problem. He would destroy the world itself if he could . . . to prove his wisdom! The white people are reaching puberty in the growth of nations. In every nation, the child is not punished and rejected for growing into puberty; the older people understand. The whites are a young people; we are very much older; we should understand. Sometimes the older people will whip an adolescent child who makes a nuisance of himself; but the correction is based on understanding. We will go to war with the white man one day, to stop his habit of destroying. I would think we would fight because we understand. And what we understand is simple: the white man is too young to have learnt the habit of living with other peoples.

Pumasilwe now stands on the side of a low mound which has collapsed in the centre; the women come slowly toward him.

This, mother, is Bhadama's house, he says.

The old woman holds herself together and raises her right hand in which she holds her walking staff. She salutes Bhadama's spirit by calling out the name of the most famous Ntuli ancestor:

Mpemba!

She walks in circles around the grave reciting the poem in which the deeds of Bhadama's greatest ancestors are preserved. At the conclusion of the recitation she stands still near where Bhadama's feet lie. Torrents of tears rush down the massive grooves on her face. The recitation was a simple act of faith in and identification with the eternal person who lives beyond death. Her presence by the grave of her grandson defines the completeness of her defeat and the reality of both the irony and the tragedy of her life.

But the thousands of graves around her give a larger dimension to her tribulation; they project Bhadama's life as one of many destroyed by the white man. The ages rise and file past her mind's eye. History has become a depraved adversary, bombarding her with questions she cannot answer and reducing virtue to a cruel joke; it magnifies her tribulation into a punishment for her race; her suffering has become the epitome of her people's tragic experience. The blows are more than her frail knees can bear; she staggers unsteadily. Pumasilwe and Zandile help her kneel by the grave. She kisses the mound of earth and then picks a handful of its soil which she presses to her bosom. At that moment she feels the presence of her grandson.

In the old days the soldier who fell in battle was not mourned publicly. A special ceremony was conducted in his kraal to speed his socialisation in the world of the spirit-forms. A short lament was recited during the ceremony. After conquest by the whites, the Zulus no longer went to war. Young men left their homes to seek employment in the white man's towns. Some of them died in the white world. In orthodox homes, these young men are regarded as having died in action and are not mourned. To leave one's people and accept employment in a white man's town, hundreds of miles from home, is to go out on a crusade. The money is not the most important thing in his life; it is the means by which he will buy the cattle which will enable him to marry the girl of his choice, have a family, project the name of his ancestors into the future and rear the men and the women who will continue the march to Blood River.

History turned the wrong way at Blood River, every Zulu child is told; his most sacred mission in life is to return to Blood River to correct the error of history.

In the view of his grandmother, Bhadama died in action. The soil she presses to her bosom is a real part of her grandson. She buried the umbilical cord which tied him to his mother. With her own hands she did it; she was the witness of history. When he lived, a part of his body was in the soil; the whole of it is there now and she presses it to her bosom. She has composed this lament for the occasion:

> Wangenzake mntanomntanami!
> Wangenza ungazenzi;
> Wawuthi wenza ubuntu;
> Kanti ubenza kubantu
> Abangazi buntu!

> See the fate you brought on me,
> Child of my child!
> A fate you did not desire.
> You did the human thing
> To people who knew not
> What it is to be human
> (And that was my undoing!)

After the lament she speaks to the elements, in which Bhadama now lives, detailing her troubles and concludes the statement with this question:

Tell me then, scion of Mpemba, how shall I get out of my

tribulation?

She then rises to her feet, wipes her face with her tattered shawl and moves away from the grave without turning her back on it.

* * *

XIII. Revolution From The Countryside

Lapho ake ema khona amanzi
Ayophinde ame futhi . . . . *(John L. Dube)*

(Water will stop again where it once
formed a pool.)

In the white man's societies, the most successful revolutions tend to be led from the cities where overcrowding, boredom and deprivation have visible meaning in the daily lives of the poor. The revolution going on in South Africa is remarkable in one major respect; it is fuelled by political choices made in the rural reservations. This puzzles the experts on the race quarrel. The people whom the policies of the CNP hurt most are the dwellers in the locations. During the first fifty years after Union, political fashions were set by the urban Africans, many of whose leaders were "exempted natives" who believed they could establish a Buntu-oriented society through co-operation with the whites. This policy failed, among other things, because it ignored the ideological character of the race quarrel; it did not make adequate allowance for the conflict between the white and the African evaluations of the person. The more the African begged for co-operation with the white men, the more he fought race oppression on ground chosen by the whites; the more he used weapons borrowed from the whites, the greater the ground he lost.

The African did not have much of a choice at the time. The location, pass and educational systems made him the prisoners of the white man. They were used to controlling his thinking in ways which served white ends; they were visible provocations on which he was compelled to concentrate, to facilitate the control of his own mind. The African in the rural areas was not controlled in the way his urban brothers were; he did not live in an overcrowded, soul-crushing location. While the schools did their part in brainwashing him, history and his past were always real in the institutions which moulded his life in rural communities. These cushioned some of the shocks of defeat by the white man. Of greater importance, however, is the fact that conquest did not destroy his roots in the soil where his ancestors were buried. As long as this remained the case he regarded conflict between black and white as a collision between irreconcilable spiritual values. Since he was the incarnation of these values, he regarded race discrimination as an attack not only on his person but also on the meaning by

159

which he understood reality. In this setting the seizure of African land had a graver significance for him than the mere conquest of territory; it was a desecration of that from which he derived his being.

For him, the race quarrel was defined, less in terms of colour and more in terms of ideology; there was a direct relationship between race humiliation, the desecration of the graves of his ancestors and the land as a determinant of being. In the old days, he had suffered profounder shocks from defeat on the battlefields. The imposition of white rule had been like salt rubbed into the wounds of defeat. He had all the time to live out history almost in everything he did, whereas the urban African was too busy with the struggle for economic survival to have the time to think too much of history. The rural African supported the urban-oriented political parties more as a declaration of faith and an act of identification and less as a conscious act of determining his destiny in the light of his choices.

The older clan chiefs who went to Bloemfontein never tire of giving lengthy monologues on what happened after defeat by the white man, in the endeavour to establish the relationship between defeat and race oppression and in that way rally the young behind the political renaissance which the rural areas are leading. Revolutionaries from the rural areas urge their people to grab the opportunity to appoint their own representatives to the segregated rural administrations and to use these as the platforms from which to re-define the race quarrel and as the bases on which to build dual-authority situations as an answer to the policies of the whites. In the rural areas, people believe that segregation is a blessing in disguise; it forces the Africans to concentrate on the things which matter most in life instead of living for the tinsel which passes for wealth in the urban areas. Land is the most crucial of these. The Africans do not think of it as territory only; it is their mother. If woman is the custodian of human life, the soil is all life; the umbilical cord is buried in it to continue the cycle of life. The soil cannot be destroyed; it can only be desecrated. In African societies, no crime is more heinous than the desecration of the soil. The Zulu words for the crime are *ukukhanda inhlabathi* (restructuring the soil) and have cataclysmic connotations. He who interferes with the soil creates a cosmic crisis; this, in the African view, is what witchcraft is all about. Life is an infinity; it cannot be cut up into areas or acres or plots or periods of time; it can only be used to sustain itself and is not owned by any person. When the white man cuts up the woil and claims proprietary rights over it, he commits a crime against life; he practices witchcraft. The Africans laid down their lives in the defence of their soil, it is said in the rural reserves, they must die again in order to have it returned to themselves.

If the soil cannot be destroyed, physical woman can be—by the simple fact of desecration; by making her honour the plaything of any scoundrel in the uniform of a policeman. Woman destroyed is a people destroyed, old Chief Yedwa Zama tells his councillors in Natal's vast Valley Of A Thousand Hills.

First, it was the land; the white man tried to kill it; now, it is woman—he is trying to kill us; before he does it, cows shall give birth to human beings. First, he said we must worship a wraith called Jesus Christ; then he took our land and, finally, he has declared war on our women. He said polygamy was sinful and created a society in which each man could have only one wife. But which child in all creation does not know that more women are born than men; that men die sooner than women? The women who cannot have homes and husbands become prostitutes. See what his monogamy has done? It has brought prostitution into our lives. I am old now; I have shed my tears over the fate of our daughters. But I am glad about one thing; I have lived to see the dawn of a new day; the educated people are at last taking the white man out of their minds . . . .

Unlike most elderly chiefs, Yedwa believes with Bulube and Mareka that in the final analysis the conflict between black and white is a war of minds. He was a young man when the Bloemfontein conference met in 1912; people called him a young man because he had just been installed chief, his sixteen years notwithstanding. Clan warfare had erupted on such a vast scale in the Valley after his father's death the government had to accede to pleas that he should be installed as chief. Like a few other chiefs at the time, he attended the Bloemfontein assembly and never tires of telling about his experiences.

I was born in the sunset of African independence and grew up amidst the shocks of defeat. At the time of my birth the smell of gunpowder filled the air and our kingdoms were destroyed one after another. I saw the man who would get to the top of a hill by day or by night bringing tidings of the end. Ye who hear, he would shout, note that I am the last of the doomed! The white invaders had descended on his people and blasted them out of existence.

Then Seme came; he said there was no reason why destruction should be our fate; we could, if we used our brains, create for ourselves the world we desired. We would have to abandon the loyalties which made us narrowly Zulu or Sotho or Xhosa; we all had to be reborn into a new people: the African people. Rebirth would be painful and slow, he warned us; but after it, we would have a quality of power before which nothing would stand. From 1912 to the mid-twenties we toiled to make regeneration a fact of our life. Then, the era of the coalitions with the whites, the Coloureds and the Indians began. We hoped to persuade them to accept our ideal of nationhood. For a whole generation we formed alliances across colour or racial lines. But, viewing everything in retrospect now, the coalitions were doomed from the beginning. Our ideal gave us one set of priorities while the white liberals, the Coloureds and the Indians adhered to different sets. Instead of the coalitions developing into cohesive united fronts, they degenerated into ideological battlegrounds where each group strove to advance its ends at the expense of the others. There could be only one end to all this: the African people were split from head to feet.

The coalitions were doomed for another reason: to be good allies of the minorities, we had to abandon the traditional methods of organising ourselves which had been passed on to us by our ancestors and adopted the white man's ways. That was our undoing; the white authority picked out our elected leaders and silenced them, it proscribed our political organisations and isolated the masses of our people. But the greatest mistake we made was to take our mind from the Afrikaner; we were told and believed that our struggle centred around doctrines developed in Europe. We took sides in a quarrel that was none of our business. We believed that the European powers or America could become our allies if we showed them that we adhered to their ideologies. Our educated people said ideologies would be our salvation. We believed them and stopped evolving strategies based on our experience, culture and history against the Afrikaner. When we tried to speak to the Afrikaner in the language we were told he would understand, he wrote Sharpeville into history.

Chief Yedwa pauses at this point; the fire in his greyish eyes glows as though it encompasses the past and the future. Visions from the past flash in his mind and fade into the future. Men had come to the fore in this Valley, which stretches for miles in front of him, who said the firestick was the only instrument by which to open the footpaths to Blood River. Every tinsmith in the Valley became a gunsmith. On the roads which criss-cross the Valley one would meet women carrying pieces of steel water piping or see children running to shops with hens or cockerels under their arms to buy steel coil springs. By day and by night one heard the sound of the axe hitting the hardwood trees in the forests of the Valley. The community had been isolated from its leaders and had been shut out of the ideological struggle. In its moment of weakness, it had turned inward, to itself and its past in order to discover its own paths to Blood River.

Never, in living memory, had there been so many home-made guns in the Valley. Then, one day, the police got wind of what was happening; they swooped on the Valley and what they found shook white South Africa to its foundations. Every head of a family had a home-made gun; others had more for their sons and relatives. More than this, the police realised in time that the Valley Of A Thousand Hills was not the only rural reserve manufacturing its own guns; large numbers of them in Natal were building a stockpile of these crude weapons. When news of their discovery reached the Commissioner of Police in Pretoria, he promptly flew to Durban to organise campaigns for disarming the Zulus. The police went through every reserve with a fine-tooth comb.

Prinsloo's instructions were that nothing should be done to provoke the Zulus; there were to be no arrests; the police would enter the reserves quietly and move from house to house and kraal to kraal and cave to cave, searching for and seizing all home-made guns. Month after month troop-carriers roared into African reserves every day with police. The operation was carried out without a single incident. Police non-violence had paralysed the Zulus; it was contrary to their way of doing things to fight when the police talked peace and did not arrest anybody. And yet, deep in the heart of every Zulu in the Valley the police campaign was a moment of humiliation and when Yedwa stares vacantly into space until a tear trickles down one side of his face, the men around him understand.

Perhaps it is as well that the police took our guns from us, Yedwa continues. We were like a cleft reed; the people in the locations were quarrelling about ideologies while we in the reserves were arming to avenge Blood River. We were a nation whose mind was at war with itself. A cleft reed cannot stand in the wind. Chief Luthuli was a wise man who kept his ear to the ground; he told all our people to avoid violence at the time. I had told you in this Valley, I don't remember how many times, that you were fools to make those crude guns and hope to fight the white man with them; to imagine that you could use them against his flying-machines and his wireless. You did not listen; one day, the police swooped on this Valley. Most of you were in Durban or Pietermaritzburg at work.

Did you expect the women and the children to take up the guns against the police? he demands. The police were smart; you were fools; they could afford not to arrest you; they had better brains. For there is only one way to beat the white man: to have better brains; to do what he cannot do. If he survives on one loaf of bread per day, survive on one loaf for twenty days; if he works one hour, work twenty hours and if he reads one book to gain wisdom, read twenty books. That is the only way to beat him. Any other course is a shortcut to defeat . . . .

Some of the young men seated around the chief shake their heads; others start whispering to each other while three of the most militant rise to their feet, salute the assembly and walk away. This old man, one of the young men tells the other two in tones loud enough to be heard by everybody, contradicts himself. First he tells us that the Passes will expose our women to humiliation and then he turns round to say we must defend our women by putting on their skirts!

About twenty other young men rise and rush after the three.

Didn't anybody teach you the law? Did you not herd your fathers' cattle? That you should insult the assembly of men!

The twenty beat up the three, who are forced to return to the assembly.

That is one thing good the Afrikaner did to us, Yedwa says, pointing to the twenty. He rejected us. The missionaries and the English had transformed us into individuals with no sense of community. Rejected now by the new rulers, we have turned back to our own law and become human beings once more and not individuals.

* * *

163

Maggie was a student nurse in Durban toward the end of the period of coalitions. The Sharpeville shootings had signalled the beginning of the era of self-assertion. Those had been difficult years in the black community. No black girl dared to straighten her hair as had been the fashion during the era of coalitions. In the locations around Durban, bands of young men roamed the streets with scissors which they used freely to cut off any girl's straightened hair. There could be no greater humiliation for a Zulu girl than to have her hair cut, in public, by strangers. Maggie had never straightened her hair because she had less time for appearances and spent most of her time in the mailtrain to Zululand. But, once, she was involved in an ugly incident with the haircutters. She and another midwife were returning from delivering a baby when they were accosted by two young Africans.

Don't you know the law? one of them said, walking up to the other nurse.

What law?

The law of the people which says no Zulu girl shall identify with our enemies. Don't you have brains in your head? The white man is making a law to make you the plaything of every scoundrel in uniform. And you approve? You straighten your hair? You identify yourself with him? Well, if you don't know the law, we'll teach it to you!

The man held her by her hair and was readying himself for the first shearing when she plunged the needle of a hypodermic syringe filled with methylated spirits into his cheek. He screamed as never a man had howled before, and ran away.

Black sister-tutors were replacing the white in black training hospitals all over the country in a systematic bid to destroy English influences in the African community. The Afrikaner did not have enough trained nurses to take the place of the English, so he encouraged the training of African tutors—it was cheaper to train a black sister and had the politically desirable effect of projecting the Afrikaner in the role of a liberator of the black nurse. She was glad to assume control in the hospitals serving her people where before the English and the Jews had directed policy. The most spectacular change she introduced was first noticed in the maternity wards. After taking the particulars of an expectant mother, the midwife admitting her would ask her to describe the ceremony performed by people with her husband's family name when a baby was born. After delivery, the baby was put through the ceremony, with the nurses, the midwives and the expectant mothers awaiting delivery participating. That changed the character of the relationship between the hospital and the African community. Where before the former was regarded as enemy territory to which the African went only when face to face with danger, it became an integral feature of African life.

In the days when white matrons and sister-tutors dominated, the unmarried mother was treated as the scum of womanhood; she was the butt of cruel jokes and was accused of pulling down her bloomers before every scoundrel with something hanging between his legs. This changed gradually in those hospitals controlled by black matrons or with black sister-tutors. The student-nurses were taught that no baby and no human being can ever be illegitimate; that each was a master-piece of creation with as much right to live as any other; that only an unclean mind could harbour the notion that any baby could be illegiti-mate. Stress was laid on the link between the person and the soil, through the umbilical cord buried in the earth. The trainees were taught that earth does not have a sight more beautiful than a woman carrying a human being in her womb; the *big house*, womanhood was called.

Each woman who delivered a live baby was hailed as a heroine; she had carried her people one step nearer on the road to Blood River. Each baby born was a precious acquisition; through him the dead had risen from the many Blood Rivers and Sharpevilles in South African history to avenge the wrongs of the past. Each child was no longer an individual; he was a vital fragment of society; he lived, no longer for himself but for the community. The name which his parents gave him described a principle of fulfilment, as it had done before the days of conquest; wherever he was and in everything he did he translated the principle into action. His name and the ideal were one and the same thing; he was the living ideal.

Each person was an ideal; babies born during a particular season or amidst a particular combination of events were a total of ideas; they were blood brothers linked by their common origins, their umbilical cords in the earth, and their age. Their first duty to them-selves and to society was to translate into action and to defend together the total of ideas which they incarnated. The language group was the total of totals which created the conditions in which the person could make the best possible use of his life and project himself to the future to the best of his ability. The habit of responding in identical ways to similar challenges developed almost automatically in this setting.

As the child grew up, the range of his responses widened; he assumed greater responsibilities. The schools came in to prepare him for these. The language group assumed significance once more in the life of the person; it became the person extended into society. A message passed to the group evoked a collective response; a challenge posed evoked identical responses. In a crisis, the person no longer stood alone; he readily fell back to the values of his language group, which were his guide; these imposed disciplines which he could not escape. With language solidarity thus established, race discrimination transformed all the black people into a collective of totals facing the same challenge and responding in identical ways. The change restored to the person his dignity and sense of worth and to the chief his responsibility as the mouth from which no lies issued.

For the first time in three hundred years of defeat, people like Chief Yedwa, Maggie, Bulube and Mareka find themselves at last in the position where they can all understand the same thing when they say to each other:

Grind together, O jaws which belong together!

In the atmosphere created by the Passes For Women Bill, the slogan has a ring which most whites regard as ominous. If some think more and more of the gun, a few see in a negotiated settlement the only guarantee of Afrikaner survival. The urgency of action, either with the gun or around the conference table, is emphasised by the developing uncertainty on the African's answer to the Passes For Women law.

Each side has points of strength and weakness which create a somewhat unique balance of black and white power. The points of strength conduce to hope and point to a dialogue on final goals and a negotiated settlement. The weaknesses create a mood of pessimism and an atmosphere of doubt and suspicion in which the seismic movement toward the appointment on the battlefield increasingly becomes the fate neither black nor white can escape. The lives of most people on both sides have been distorted so cruelly for so long, to give added impact to the seismic movement has come to be the thing to live for. In this setting, the voice of reason or of morality has become the voice of the traitor. Each side regards itself as a world, threatened by the other and in a war of totals or mountains or worlds there is no room for compromise; there is no ground to be yielded. Every millimetre surrendered becomes a crack in the foundations, a defeat at the level of fundamentals.

* * *

Every year now, during the summer vacations, groups of UBRA intellectuals travel secretly around the country meeting African leaders of all shades. The factor which emphasises the importance of secrecy is the decision of Afrikaner business leaders who share UBRA's concern about the deteriorating relations between black and white to join the academic and professional men in the sessions with the Africans. De Haas is alarmed over the development; it is such a basic rejection of the traditional CNP approach it could split the party and bring his government crashing to the ground. Kaffers exist to serve the white man and to be shot when they refuse to do so.

The prime minister is alarmed for another reason; he cannot understand the quality of a white mind which can consider negotiating with a black man. The suspicion lurks at the back of his mind that the Afrikaners who think in terms of negotiation either have mixed blood or a liaison with black women. If no other reason existed for the Passes For Women Bill, this possibility makes it impossible for him to yield ground. He attaches particular importance to the UBRA group reported by the security police to be visiting Mkambati in Natal to talk to Chief Bulube. These men are led by Munnik Bierbuyck who professes political science at Stellenbosch University.

166

* * *

Chief Bulube, Bierbuyck opens the conversation, this is the third time we have met in three years. A lot of things have happened in the last twelve months and we do not seem to be moving anywhere ourselves. He stops.

We ourselves are moving somewhere. More and more people are coming over to the view that the only answer to de Haasism is the unification of all the black people of Southern Africa—from Angola, Zambia, Malawi and Mozambique to Port Elizabeth. Bulube smiles.

That is remarkable as an ideal, Chief; the reality at the moment is that whether we like it or not the great powers will not allow it and it is difficult to see how the whites in Southern Africa will allow it. As you know, we take up a sympathetic view of the problems of the free African states, but with the best will in the world, they are not as yet in the position to dictate a solution to Southern Africa's problem of colour. I don't see how America, for instance, can support a state of the type you propose which would control the oil fields of Angola. And even if time were on your side, black and white are heading for another Sharpeville, now that the Passes For Women Bill is before parliament. The immediate question before us is to establish a bridge of understanding between your people and ours; to create a communion of minds among people who think alike on both sides of the colour line. If you will allow me to put it this way: it seems to those of us in UBRA that a coalition of concerned people like you and ourselves would have the resources to drill a little more common sense into the head of the government.

You've raised points on which we could conduct a public debate for at least the next twelve months!

All the men laugh.

Our starting-point is that the attitudes of the great powers and of the white nations are irrelevant for the purpose of creating a union of the black peoples of Southern Africa. The only people we are concerned with are the Africans. For twenty-five years now everybody has had the opportunity to work out a solution to the colour problem. In that time nobody has come forward with anything feasible. One reason for the failure is that people have not been thinking in terms of alternatives to de Haasism. To press for the abolition of the colour bar cannot be an alternative; the demand is negative in the first place. As such it does not address itself to the Afrikaner's problems of survival.

Second, it is predicated on African acceptance of white values. In this regard it holds out before us a future defined for us in white terms. That is not acceptable to us. We want to create for ourselves and our children a world designed by us. For more than fifty years after Union we tried to persuade the white minorities to change their mind and create a society in which no person would be punished for being the child of his parents. They rejected our ideal; since we believe in it we have decided to march to it without the white people. What they do is their problem; not ours. Our people smashed the Central African Federation and the sky did not fall; I don't see why it should fall if the various reserve administrations come together in their own federation which will be the nucleus of the state we have in mind. That is more or less how the United States of America started on the road to unification.

And, talking about America brings me to a point raised earlier. I do not think the assumption is correct that it will always be in America's interest to have Southern Africa dominated by the whites. Washington's straddling of the fence on the conflict of colour should be as clear a warning as any the Americans can give that their real interests in Southern Africa require that they should have no permanent friends and no permanent enemies.

But, Chief, how are you going to convince the Americans that they do not need a friendly power controlling Cape Town, on the sea route to the oilfields of the Middle East?

That is not my problem at all. An African state stretching from the Indian Ocean to the Atlantic Ocean will dominate the approaches to Cape Town. If America opposed its formation, it would be up to her to decide if she wanted to transform Southern Africa into a second South Vietnam. But the point which is likely to determine American policy in the final analysis is not likely to be oil, which is a vanishing asset; it is likely to be nuclear energy. At the moment America has nearly 38 nuclear reactors which produce more than 5 per cent of her electrical power. The depletion of oil is likely to increase reliance on nuclear energy in most industrial countries and to increase the demand for metals like uranium and sodium whose sources have barely been touched in Africa.

Oil and metals aside, Chief, do you really think America will allow Russia to dominate the Indian Ocean?

I would not want to concern myself much with what America or Russia will or will not do. If they have not learned their lessons from the collapse of the Roman, British and French empires; if they continue to see world problems in terms of spheres of influence, the black, brown and yellow peoples of the world will have to evolve a consensus of their own for the purpose of by-passing America and Russia.

My own view is that America will eventually come to terms with Russia if she wants to remain a power to reckon with in the world; this is the message the American President was sending to the American people when he visited Peking and Moscow. If you can't beat them, join them; that's the American formula for survival. For us, this has this meaning: If America survives her internal and external economic troubles and, speaking for myself, I hope she does, for those brave people are trying out the most fascinating experiment in human co-existence within the framework of one ideal of fulfilment, our business will be to confront her with alternatives it will be in her interest to take into account. If the white people hold out the strategic position of Cape Town as a bargaining point, we must balance that with the strategic value of an African state stretching from the Atlantic Ocean on the west to the Indian Ocean on the east across the abdomen of Africa.

This is the first time Lukas Meyer has joined an UBRA team and it is the first time he has met an African at the level of intellectual equality. The Afrikaner press, church, universities and the CNP have created the impression in his mind that the African lives in a non-world; that whenever he talks about his problems he puts on a thinking cap tailored for him by the communists. The voice of nationalism, which he knows so well, and which he hears from the African, evokes a disturbing response. He cannot resist the impulse to probe into what he regards as a delicate area in the black mind.

I can understand how you feel, Chief, he begins. We Afrikaners went through the experience which has brought you where you are. Some of us, a few of us, realise that some of the things we are doing to you are the things against which we protested most vigorously in British rule. But difficulties exist which make it hard for all of us, on both sides of the colour line, to see peoples as they really are. Although we are white, we belong to Africa; like you, we regard ourselves as one of Africa's many children. You will tell me that, if we want to belong to Africa, we must do as the Africans do. I believe you will have every reason for saying that. But how shall I be assured that I am dealing with the African and not with China, for example? How can I know that I am dealing with the real African? What makes the real African? What is it that the African really wants from the Afrikaner?

It would take an additional twelve months to answer that!

The men laugh together again.

Our attitude to the outside world is determined by our needs and not the needs of the Chinese or the Americans or the Russians or any other peoples. Our needs determine our attitude to the Afrikaner. If these needs require collaboration with America or China or Russia or any other nation, we shall work with them. If collaboration hurts us, we shall not consider it. China has problems which make it imperative that all Africans, free and unfree, should regard her as an ally. She wants to have the security which will enable her to play her rightful role in world affairs; we want to be free to do this, too. We want to create a balance in black-white relations in Southern Africa which will make it impossible for any white person or group to punish an African for being the child of his parents. China has an obviously vested interest in helping us create this balance. That she is a communist country is none of our business; the American President did not become a communist when he visited Peking and Moscow! No communist is behind the Passes For Women Bill.

History has created all sorts of difficulties for all of us,

Chief . . . .

I don't think it is my business to go around telling the white people what they should do in Africa; I don't want anybody to dictate how I should live. I want people to make their own choices. My business is to outline the alternatives in our situation. Our present position has to be seen in the context provided by the momentum of events both in our country and in the world. The African and the Afrikaner are caught in a war of worlds; it is the momentum this war has developed which determines our strategies and not the liberals or the communists or the Coloureds or the Indians or the English or the Jews.

For fifty years after Union we strove to persuade the Afrikaner to work with us to create a society in which the person would be seen to make the best possible use of his life and where merit and not colour would fix his position in the life of the nation. We adhered to these ideals because we believed they were reliable guarantees of fulfilment for every South African racial group; our ancestors had evolved these ideals and tried them out for thousands of years all over the continent. They had evolved different types of societies in response to the challenge of these ideals.

We thought we could build a mixed nation because these ideals derived from our evaluations of the person; they recognised the person as a cell of the infinite consciousness from which the cosmic order derives its nature and form. As such, he was not only sacred and eternal, he was the essence of his neighbour cast in a different mould. This gave a validity and legitimacy to the experience of his community which could not be alienated. Believe me, gentlemen, it took us thousands of years of experimentation to understand all the implications of the validity and the legitimacy.

Our ideal of fulfilment worked for the continuous enlargement of the personality. The constriction is the basis of conflict between us and the white people.

I realise, Chief, that the lives of all of us are now in a horrible confusion. I do not think it does anybody any good to point fingers and I want to say how grateful I am to see that you concern yourself with principles. But the question I am asking myself is where I could start to aid movement to some form of agreement on final goals.

I do not think it is my business or that of any African to tell the Afrikaner where to start; that is a decision which he and he alone will have to make for himself. We have chosen our goal and are going to move to it in our own way, just as our ancestors have been moving toward it for thousands of years. If the Afrikaner wants to join the progression, that, gentlemen, is his business; if he wants to stand aside and be left on the roadside while African humanity marches into the future, that is his business, not ours. See the problem this way: As children, my generation was told and we also teach our children that in a war of worlds the first precondition for final victory is the ability to survive a fall; to rise from defeat. When we were rejected, we had nowhere to go; we turned inward to ourselves in order to develop those weapons evolved by our ancestors and to reassess those values which had always been their guarantees of survival.

If I understand you well, Chief, you are telling us that you are going your way and we must go our own way. But surely, somewhere, there must be the South African way?

I have no way of knowing this. What we say is that we are pulling out of the world in which we are not wanted and are going to create a different world for ourselves. In this setting whatever the Afrikaner does is irrelevant for the final realisation of our goal. We will reach it without or with him; he can't give us anything which we cannot get on our own if we persevere, as we have done these three hundred years, to move, no matter how slowly or how painfully, to our goal. And when we reach our goal, we won't defile our society by punishing the white person for being the child of his parents. We will open all doors to opportunity for him too, always provided he outgrows the habits of thinking which belong to the childhood days of the human species. In our world, it will be our business to tell people how to live with us.

But then, you open the door a little and shut it a little. You don't give us the opportunity to know where to fit in. Would you not agree that statesmanship would create ground where we can develop a communion of like-minded Afrikaner and African minds? These people would have the potential to sweep de Haas out of power! He is as much of a threat to you as he is to us.

I would say that such a coalition is either premature or has no place in our quarrel, now that we have chosen to leave the white man's world.

But you don't give us a chance, Chief!

We were not given a chance; we created it.

But that means war?

The Passes For Women Bill is, in fact, a declaration of war.

If you were a white man how would you solve the race problem?

I would return to Europe. . . .

But, Chief . . . you sometimes speak of a negotiated settlement?

Yes, I do; that is the tragedy of my generation. We speak the language of morality to people who do not know morality. One day a generation will arise which will speak the language the white man will understand. And when that day comes, God save the white man. My own solution is the momentum of disengagement. One day we shall bring every mine in this land, every factory, every farm, every seaport and airport to a dead stop, with these brains of ours and these bare hands. Most whites laugh when we say this; they laughed also when the Arabs said it. Let them laugh, Colonel. The conflict in South Africa is a

171

dress rehearsal for the coming clash between the African evaluation of the person and the white man's. We are a people walking painfully in the shadows of history. What do you think we are doing in the strikes, Colonel? We are exercising for the moment of decision and, *mark my words*, when that moment comes not one nation will stand with the Afrikaner. This is the position we have been driving him to in the years from 1912. If you understand this, you understand the race problem.

* * *

XIV. The Professor's Diary

Izinkomo azithunjwa linile.

*(The wise rustler drives away
no cattle when it has rained.)*

The prime minister's temper catches fire on the slightest provocation these days. While the Passes For Women Bill is making good progress in the House of Assembly, now and then voices are raised in the Afrikaans community which question the wisdom of the measure. De Haas is sensitive when Afrikaners question his policies for the black people. If the doubts spread too far, the Afrikaners could reject his leadership. This would not mean the pro-English Unionist Party would rise to power. Afrikanerdom does not think that way. De Haas would be rejected and be replaced by another Afrikaner. At the moment, the tide is running heavily in the direction of extreme hostility to the African; that places de Haas at the crest of the political wave. But, with the rise of the entrepreneur class in the Afrikaans community, the day might come when the Afrikaner's preoccupation with considerations of survival will give way to economic necessity as a determinant of racial policy.

De Haas is beginning to realise that Afrikaner omnipotence or *kragdadigheid* can be affected by developments in the outside world. He still rejects van Warmelo's policy of trying to come to terms with external pressures at given levels, but he realises that external investors tend to influence the political thinking of sections of the entrepreneur class. He has come to realise that time is no longer one of the Afrikaner's allies, that, as a matter of fact, it has become one of his main enemies. He feels under pressure to establish permanent foundations for Afrikaner security before the enemies of Afrikanerdom gang-up to overthrow the balance which keeps it in control of the government.

In these conditions the passage into law of the Bill has become an act of fulfilment for him; it will enable the Afrikaner to strike at the Africans where he is sure they are weakest. If black women carry passes, the government can have effective control of the African people's birthrate and, at the same time, bring in more cheap labour to produce the profits with which to buy Western democratic connivance at the inhumanity of CNP policies.

173

Speed is of the essence of success here. There are Afrikaners who warn that the time could come when the Africans would regard the Pass as an instrument of genocide. Then, the Pass would be a poor guarantee of survival for the Afrikaner. Many of the people who take up this position are in UBRA and no loyal Afrikaner thinks much of them.

The general view is that they are traitors to the cause of the Afrikaner and Afrikanerdom has too many urgent survival problems to limit its definitions of traitor. Honest dissent is not known in the CNP; and treachery is punished swiftly, harshly and effectively. But some of the people who show concern cannot be disposed of so easily.

One of these is Dominie de Villiers of the Groot Kerk in Pretoria. The dominie is chaplain to the cabinet and this gives him tremendous prestige in the councils of the Dutch Reformed Church. He rarely airs his doubts in public, but behind the scenes he is known to have criticised the Bill in ways which upset some people in the government.

The real spark which sets the prime minister's temper on fire, however, is the position taken by Lukas Meyer. At a recent meeting of the caucus of the CNP Meyer spoke of the need for fundamental adjustments in Afrikaner thinking on guarantees of survival. The changes taking place in the world, Free Africa and inside South Africa called for this change; the Afrikaner, Meyer had argued, should move out of the nineteenth century and fix a satisfying place for himself in the twentieth. It had been shocking enough for the chairman of the caucus to talk of adjustments in the caucus itself, but for him to tell the leaders of the CNP that his thinking had been affected by his contacts with the representatives of the black people has catastrophic implications.

For one thing, it is communism, whatever an Afrikaner understands by communism. Most Afrikaners are too isolated from the rest of the world to see anything wrong in *kragdadigheid*. If the black, brown and yellow nations are provoked by it, since when has it been the business of the white race to consider non-white sensibilities? But when Lukas Meyer demands change, the Afrikaner has to start worrying. Meyer is too fine and loyal a son of Afrikanerdom to be a traitor or to be influenced by the communists and their liberal allies. At the same time he is powerful enough in and out of the CNP and sufficiently independent to wreck de Haas's moment of fulfilment. The prime minister does not doubt that Meyer carries enough weight in the Afrikaans community to be able to split the party. If that happened, the English and the Jews would move in with offers of a capitalist-liberal alliance. History would blame him for failing to keep Afrikanerdom united; but that same history has placed him in the position where he has to dare to do the thing no Afrikaner prime minister found possible: to place the black woman in her place.

What angers the prime minister is that Meyer does not conceal the fact that he thought of fundamental adjustments after his conversations with Bulube.

Can you believe it, Paul, he tells Kritzinger, that Lukas Meyer sat there and listened while a kaffer told him of a black ideal of nationhood? I've never heard of it and I don't care a damn whether or not there is such a thing. The kaffer said the Afrikaner was irrelevant for the purpose of determining South Africa's destiny! And Lukas sat through all that nonsense! Don't you see what is happening? The kaffers have sewn a thinking cap for people like Lukas and Dominie de Villiers, the black agitators are defining the colour question in their own way and are forcing the white man to adjust to the definition! The black man is now to dictate the terms on which the Afrikaner must remain in Africa! Hear that, Paul! That is where your Afrikaner capitalists are taking us!

* * *

Nobody is certain about how the Africans will react to the passage of the Passes For Women Bill. There are rumours of a national stoppage of work. Already, strikes have been reported in Natal. Ugly events have occurred in some of the province's largest locations. During one of the strikes in Durban, for instance, people who ignored the call to stay away from work were waylaid, murdered and thrown into the sugarcane fields between the city and the locations. The fear now is that the strikes might spread to the Witwatersrand industrial area. The police are taking no chances; they have reinforced their positions in the country's largest locations. The white-coloured Saracen tanks and armoured cars used by the riot section of the police force are in evidence in the largest locations. In Pretoria the police claim to have unearthed a secret plot to poison all the reservoirs, grind bottles into fine powder and to burn white homes and factories, in a desperate bid to drive the white people into the sea.

The police allege that this plot has been organised by the *Shisa Shisa* underground movement. The members of the *Shisa Shisa*, the police say, have been trained in China and are adept at the use of knives. The whites are scared sufficiently by these rumours so that the Merchants Federation issues a circular to its members, who are all white, advising them not to sell bread knives and similar weapons to the Africans. If an African carries a walking stick in the cities, the police take it.

The scare is so serious the passenger trains from Durban to Johannesburg are watched very carefully by the police. As soon as they cross the Natal-Transvaal border the coaches for the Africans are sealed and every African in them is searched; they are searched again when they alight from the train. Every railway station in the main towns has a separate, guarded entrance for the black people. African men, women and children are searched on the streets of every major city. All public meetings have been banned, except bona fide church services. Church conferences come under the ban, except that a bona fide church assembly might be held provided the requisite permission has been obtained from the Bantoe affairs commissioner.

* * *

Bob! Bob! Are you awake? See that light on the window?

Forget those lights, Barbara! I want to sleep.

Robert Shawcross turns his back to his wife and covers his head with the blanket.

Bob! Do you hear the steps? Somebody's at the window.

Hm?

Bob sits up almost with a jump and switches on the light. Torches flash suddenly through every window and a knock is heard.

Open! Police!

Police? Hear that, Barbara? Police? What on earth would they want at this time of the night?

Perhaps an accident! Somebody we know?

I don't know. But . . . let's see what they want.

About a dozen men stand at the door. From the sounds in the dark, it is clear that there are men at the back door as well.

We are the police and have reason to believe that you have information we need . . . .

The leader of the security police shoves his identification card and the search warrant into Bob's hand and almost moves past him into the hall.

My apologies, Dr. Shawcross, for coming at this hour of the night . . . .

Two . . . in the morning?

We are interested in your research into the evolution of black leadership traditions.

Yes; but this is not the time and the place to talk to me about that.

We'd like to look around your place for a while.

What's all this about? You have no right to move into my house like that. I haven't committed any crime. This is outrageous!

Can you lead us into your study?

What do you want there?

Some of your papers.

Bob leads the police into his study. The police chief goes to a small bookshelf with about a dozen books and takes each of these and first shakes it and then opens it. A hole has been scooped inside the pages of one of the books; a key drops out.

That's the first thing we want, doctor, and now we go to the second.

The policeman moves to a steel file cabinet which he pushes

away from its position. A small hole shows in the wall and into this he pushes the key and opens a little door. He pulls out a large leather-bound book which looks like the ledger of a huge business corporation.

This is what we want, Dr. Shawcross.

But this is only a diary . . . .

A record . . . . For twenty-five years you kept a diary in which you recorded some very interesting things.

He opens the book at random. I see here that you have a note on Theodore Darikwa. That's a very interesting character. You understand, doctor, we'd like to know about him. You can tell us a lot about this man.

All I know is what's in there.

The policeman turns another page.

Sobukwe? In Durban, three weeks before Sharpeville? That's very interesting. What was he doing there?

The policeman speaks casually; he is pleased with his find and for the present is not interested in what Bob says. Even when he asks questions, it is to emphasise the importance of the diary and not to elicit replies.

You realise, doctor, that you have a goldmine of information on hundreds of people who threaten the security of the state. This diary will solve scores of mysteries. And, you are too valuable a witness to be exposed to the dangers of being left free. You'll come alone with us to the police station.

What have I done?

We'd like to ask you some things about what you've written here.

I don't understand! This is research . . . .

Very valuable research it is, doctor. Look at this: Sugarcane fields burnt in the Mount Edgecombe area! If you co-operate, nothing will happen to you. Everything is up to you. I don't see why a man like you should want to spend ninety days or one hundred and eighty in a cell.

Tell me. How did you know about this diary?

That's exactly what I want to do—to tell you how we got to know about it. But I'll tell you that at the right time. In the meantime, you are under arrest.

* * *

XV. Interpreting The African

Umuntu akalahlwa.

(There is no human being who is beyond redemption.)

The police jeep stops near Maggie's office in front of the building complex generally referred to as Atteridgeville hospital. Constable Bashise Busengi is alone in it, which is somewhat unusual. Policemen go about in twos these days in the location, even in a car. It is about eleven in the morning; it is a bright summer day; the sun smiles on the earth as brilliantly as it does only in the southern hemisphere.

What's happened, Busengi?

No trouble, Maggie. Relax; just one or two little things.

What does that mean? When a policeman comes to your office at about eleven o'clock?

Don't you know? When a policeman commits a crime, he does it in broad daylight, when everybody can see him.

Please sit down and tell me things the lords gossip about these days!

The lords don't gossip; kaffer women do. The lords converse. Maggie, Kritzinger would like to see the Busengi naming ceremony to-night.

How on earth did he know about it?

I was at his house last week-end. They had the braaivleis (beef-grilling party) on Saturday and Kritzinger's favourite kaffer-boys had to be around to chop the wood and drive the lords home when they were drunk. The kaffer-wives had to be around too, to wash the dishes. Kritzinger talked to me about the ceremony, now that the wife is out of hospital; he asked if he could be allowed to watch the Busengi naming ceremony.

I don't know how you and your wife feel about it. But I don't want any white people fouling up the air and setting up evil vibrations on such an occasion. We don't gatecrash into their holy functions. And, whatever the motive, it can only be evil. Besides, I don't think anybody wants to be responsible for the safety of a white man in the location at night these days.

Maggie, my job is involved here. Kritzinger takes his anthropology seriously. He's a man going places; he spends more time

179

in the prime minister's house than anybody in the cabinet.

Places or no places, one gatwyser is like every other gatwyser!

Wait a minute! Why do you get yourself excited about an ordinary Boer-boy coming over to see what the primitives do at night?

Because I don't want his smell around; these people have a smell I can't stand. I don't want to have anything to do with them. You know, I can't even eat in the presence of a white person. Their bodies have the smell of death. But then, the child is yours; if you and your wife don't mind. . . .

We'll look after the evil vibrations, of course.

How does Father Maimane feel?

He said he'd object if we did and . . . you did.

These are difficult times for us black people. What happens if an angry boy shoves an *intshumentshu* into Kritzinger's side?

He wouldn't be chief of the Pretoria police if he didn't know how to look after himself. Besides, when you work closely with these people, you find that some of them are ordinary persons like you and me. I see, you shake your head; you don't agree. But Kritzinger is a human being. . . .

An anthropologist! Like all of them he observes the primitives in order to evolve better rules for forcing them to fit into his political moulds. It's just that I'm tired of every white incompetent who can't make the grade in his society coming over to observe the black people, to study the black people, to research the black people and to interpret the black people. For goodness sake why don't they leave us alone? Why don't they go back to Europe and do these things to their own people? But, well, I shouldn't talk politics to a policeman.

You can talk politics to the wind; not to a wall for, you never can know these days, walls have all sorts of ears.

If you don't mind the vibrations, if the clergyman says everything is alright, well, I suppose I have to go with the majority.

Good girl, Maggie; we'll see you this evening.

As the policeman moves to the door he signals to Maggie to follow him to the jeep.

Maggie, some people are going to be in very serious trouble. Dillo Mareka is one of them and Sefadi Masilo is another. The Commissioner of Police's office has received the Shawcross Diary. Sensational is not strong enough to describe the document; it's a key into everything the black people have been doing in the last fifty years to overthrow white rule. And, I tell you, heads are going to roll; black heads, white heads, Coloured heads, Indian heads. There won't be a place to bury the heads! I have never seen the like of it. People crack when confronted with a whole list of their activities against white domination for years. All of a sudden, the police have almost a complete, ready-made file on every African leader. Somebody cracked and revealed that Dillo Mareka and Sefadi Masilo were with the white people who rescued Theodore Darikwa from the Standerton prison.

The police will arrest them at 2 in the morning.

Does the Kritzinger visit have anything to do with the arrests?

No. I don't think the local police know much about the Shawcross Diary; this is stuff for the big boys at security police headquarters, where it is a privilege for a kaffer like me to serve tea to the lords!

*   *   *

Darkness has descended on the earth and people who live for their religion are already beating their drums. All sorts of drums are used in the location, for each drum serves a specific purpose; each sound it makes sends out a message defined by each given culture. People talk through drums; they translate their deepest feelings into drumbeats; the drum is one of the physical bridges between the person and the infinite consciousness. The infinity is a living whole; to be alive means that it is always vibrating, sending waves of itself colliding in the heavens to produce thunder and lightning; it is always vibrating, drawing man and woman together into the only experience which merges them into that inconstant reality: the human being. It is only in the embrace of love that man and woman merge into the unity we call the human being. The infinity is always vibrating to keep the stars in orbit, to regulate the seasons, to guide the birds in their migrations across the globe and to regulate the glow in the next person's eye.

The vibrations are the language which creation speaks to itself; they are the medium by which the person communicates with the dead and the unborn, with the moon and the stars, with the animals, the plants, the birds, the stones and the soil itself.

When the African beats the drum he talks to creation; he loses his identity in the complex rhythms of the infinity; he sets up the vibrations which give meaning to life. An African theologian, trained in Europe, recently delivered a sermon in the Anglican cathedral in Cape Town and stated that the drum constitutes the key into the understanding of the African; that it is his bible, his theology and his ritual all rolled into one; that when he beats the drum, God arises in him. He told his white audience that what the white christians need most is to cultivate the capacity to respond to the elemental message of the drumbeat; to grasp the implications of the truth that when the African beats the drum, he issues a command to creation; when he dances in the streets, in his churches and everywhere, he involves himself in the process of commanding creation; in the elemental harmony which makes him human. This was communism. A fortnight later, the theologian was banned; it became a crime for him to preach from any pulpit or to attend any gathering of any type or to have anybody in his house other than members of his immediate family, his doctor or lawyer and, of course any policeman.

*   *   *

181

People are streaming into the football ground of the location and groups have lit small fires to light up the place. The flames show three white men standing together. They shift farther away from the light because it makes them conspicuous. Each time they move away, another fire reflects the whiteness of their faces. A procession, headed by Father Eliakimo Maimane, enters the gate into the football ground. Immediately after him are Bashise Busengi, his wife and their baby boy who are followed by the elders and the members of the Holy Pentecostal Church of Christ in Zion in Atteridgeville. The Pentecostalists are one of the many congregations which together constitute what is known as the *Zionist* movement in South Africa. The Zionists have nothing to do with Israel, except the conviction that they are God's chosen people. Their mission is to bring about a regeneration of the African race for the purpose of restoring to it that which belongs to it, they say. The restoration, the leaders of the movement are quick to explain, has nothing to do with the things of this world; it involves rebirth into a new spiritual destiny.

The African has to return to the ways of his ancestors, dig up the past, learn its wisdom and proceed from there to create his own City of Zion. The Pentecostalists are one of the most extreme sects in the Zionist movement; they don't touch a white person, do not stand in his shadow and do not want to have anything to do with him. No experience is more humiliating to a Pentecostalist than to be employed by a white person. The rule requires him to have a cleansing when he wakes up to go to work and another before he enters the house to wash off the evil vibrations from contact with the whites. The cleansing is a complicated and demanding process; the person first has to take an emetic to expel whatever contaminations his mouth and nostrils might have imbibed from contact with the white people. Once a week he has to wash the whole system with a purgative made from ashes and consecrated in the temple. Then, the person has to wash every part of his body from his head to the soles of his feet. He has to pay particular attention to the orifices and the dirt beneath the nails on his hands and feet.

The Pentecostalists do not drink anything fermented, avoid pork, do not smoke. The strictest of them do not take medicine at all and would sooner die than accept it. The only concession made is to pregnant women; these might receive medical attention, it being understood, of course, that taking medicine in this regard is one of the humiliations of being a conquered people. The woman holds an important position in the life of the sect; she is the custodian of life, the living link between the past and the future; she is the embodiment of all excellence and the regard shown her is almost indistinguishable from worship. Everything associated with her is sacred and precious beyond price. The teaching is that when a boy is born, a world comes into being, but God himself comes to earth each time a woman is born. This is what the Pentecostalists mean when they address womanhood as

The Great House, Indlunkulu.

The true hero of the Pentecostalist movement is the woman carrying a person in her womb; each birth is a moment of great rejoicing in the community. Polygamy is encouraged and every woman is regarded as a front-line soldier in the march to the City of Zion; the more the children she bears, the greater is her contribution to the power of the group which has evolved a complicated system of relations to protect her and her offspring. The protections wreak havoc on the white-led churches which preach the sovereignty of the individual and shout themselves hoarse against the sinfulness of sex. Location communities, as a rule, have a notoriously high birthrate.

One section of the location is known as the hostel area. In it are housed the thousands of men recruited from the countryside to serve Pretoria's industries. Women are not allowed in the hostels. Thousands of married and single men have to spend periods of from six months to two years in these without female company. Every major location in South Africa has these hostels; some of them, which are often a short way from the locations, are owned by the mining corporations. The batteries of masculinity locked up in the hostels give the locations an abnormally high birthrate, which de Haas seeks to reduce by controlling the movements of African women in the urban areas. Father Maimane and his followers launch savage attacks on the white-led churches for preaching a morality which is not related to the problems of the black people in the locations. They blame the woman for being *The Great House*, he declaims; our own people attack our own daughters, our own sisters, our own wives and our own mothers for conditions imposed upon us by the powers which support the white-led churches. In the Holy Pentecostal Church of Christ in Zion, we accept the challenge from which everybody else flees; to the black woman we say: Come into the house to which you belong; we love you when the weather is good; we love you when it is bad; we love you in good health; we love you when your body is covered with syphilitic chancres. We love you because we belong to you and you belong to us! We are but your own self cast in different moulds.

This approach has a tremendous appeal to women employed in Pretoria. The Pentecostalists provide a world in which the person is asked to make heavy sacrifices and to subject herself to harsh discipline and, in return, they offer her dignity, security and the opportunity to enlarge her personality. Largely as a result, the Pentecostal Church is a young women's congregation; the women, in turn, are the magnet which attracts young men. Father Maimane exercises a form of authority which no bishop in the white-led churches can ever hope to have. His official designation in the church is bishop; but the Africans are not sure that the borrowed title has the connotations which Father carries. Father, in all their languages, is somebody who is unconditionally on your side. The black clergyman or bishop in the white church, the Pentecostalists argue, is interested in making money out of you; if you pay your dues, you are a good christian; he'll visit you in hospital and bury you when you die and the chances are that you will pay him for doing that. But all he does for you is merely to appear; he is not interested in how you live, eat, sleep and struggle. He is an agent of the thieves of the soul who have brought us to where we are. Every penny you pay into the Pentecostal Church comes back to you; it is held in your name as a community; it is used to create for you the world in which you are wanted!

The Pentecostalists avoid politics as they would the plague. One of their arguments is that politics is a crooks' game on the one hand and, on the other, a business to be handled by adults only. Where the people have lost their soul, they are like sheep without a shepherd; every scoundrel is free to tear into them, to preach one type of political doctrine or the other in order to serve his own purpose and to slow down movement toward the City of Zion. What the African needs most is not to be divided into ideological factions; he has to be made to realise that the jaws which grind together are like irresistible floodwaters rushing to the sea, which carry everything with them. The way to develop the irresistible momentum is for people to rediscover their soul; only when they have done that can they be ready to involve themselves in politics. Rediscovery goes beyond merely returning to the ways of their ancestors; it entails the direct involvement of the person in the creation of the world he desires for himself.

The Pentecostalists are urged not only to be clean in mind and body, but also to be self-reliant and thrifty. They train each other in the use of their minds and hands. They prefer to be self-supporting if they can help it and tend to look down upon dependence on the white man; they make all sorts of things with their own hands, sell them and save their money.

They are not alone in doing this; all Zionist congregations preach and practice self-reliance. But at this level, too, they get into trouble with the established church. The clean mind, they teach, sees creation from clean perspectives. No person is good or wicked; in everything he does he translates into action the will of God whom he incarnates. Zionist theology creates all sorts of problems for the police in general, and for the CNP in particular. In one mood the Afrikaners are delighted with it because it advocates the rejection of the white man's ways, which, in the South African context, means English ways. At the same time the rejection has implications which hit at the very roots of Afrikaner survival in South Africa.

Unlike the English, the Africans belong to Africa and constitute the majority; it is from their side, more than any other, that the real threat to Afrikaner survival comes. The Pentecostalists avoid politics but proceed from this to preach a christianity in which it would be impossible for the Afrikaner to survive.

* * *

The Pentecostalists are all dressed in white, and have formed concentric circles around a small pile of wood. The men sit at the circumference of the circle; next to them are the older, married women. Young women and nubile girls stand in the third circle. Girls on the threshold of nubility sit in a group on one side of the pile of wood while Father Maimane and the elders sit opposite them. Every member of the congregation carries a grass mat on which to sit. Father Maimane himself sits on such a mat, on the ground. At the sound of a drum the group girls throw off the mantles in which their bodies are covered and sit naked in the full view of the thousands surrounding them. An old woman lights the wood while the drums beat. One by one the naked girls rise and dance in front of the fire to the accompaniment of the drums and clapped hands. Father Maimane raises his stick and all the young, married and single girls throw off the mantles on their shoulders, revealing the black skirts they wear and their bare breasts. Kritzinger turns to one of the men on either side of him:

Never seen anything like this in all my life; have you?

The other police officer is embarrassed.

No, meneer! Never!

Complicated people . . . these black people, Aren't they?

Complicated, meneer; very complicated.

Did you say complicated too?

Very complicated, meneer!

So complicated you can't keep your eyes off the magnets?

The two white police feel scandalised. The country has not recovered from the shock given it by the police who raped an African woman and pleaded in their defence that they were after corroborative evidence. Another white policeman raped the African woman he had been ordered to accompany to identify and arrest the man who had raped her. When the dancing stops, Father Maimane addresses the crowd:

Greetings to all of you, *bazalwane*, you with whom I was born; greetings also, to our white visitors. It was good of all of you to come over and support one of the most important ceremonies in our church. On an occasion like this, The Great House assumes its position as the pillar of the family. Maggie, the daughter of Kuboni will say a few words on what we have come to witness . . . Ma Kuboni!

I love the salutation Father used; You, with whom I was born! For me, it epitomises *ubuntu*, the humanity we have in common and which is our real bond. In our community, we say that a world is created when a boy is born and that God himself descends into our community when a girl arrives. So marvellous is the moment of birth. The baby is a complex piece of living clay. He does not know what life has in store for him. We plant the meaning it will have; we sow it into his life when we give him a name. The name we give him is the ideal by which he will guide his life; he can't separate himself from it. As the name, so the person! The naming ceremony is important because in the names the mother and the father give to their child, they project themselves and their hopes into the future. In our community the first name is given by the mother and this ceremony, therefore, is a women's ceremony. We have here the baby's grandmother on his father's side and her opposite on his mother's side. They will perform the ceremony. Arise, mother of Mamsi and name the child.

Bashise's wife hands the naked baby to her mother, who rises and raises the baby high above her head.

> *Behold the wonder of the ages*
> *O people!*
> *Busengi has returned!*
> *Busengi, uqobo nezinqotho!*
> (The Busengi reality in every detail!)

The father's mother rises and stands on one side of the fire while her opposite stands on the other.

> Zanabo Busengi!
> Do you hear?
> Zanabo Busengi!
> Stiffen, O Spine of a Man
> Thus to recover the heritage,
> Yours by birth!

She throws the baby over the flame to her opposite who recites the formula and then throws the baby over the flames to his maternal grandmother. The women throw the baby at each other three or four times, chanting with the gathering:

> Stiffen, O Spine of a Man!

Kritzinger turns to his bodyguard.

I suppose that is the end of the ceremony?

Yes, meneer.

There's every reason for a stiffened spine ... with all those magnets displayed before him.

The police laugh and walk away.

* * *

XVI. The Value Of A White Skin

Ophatha inomfi ubuya namaqubu.

(He who has birdlime on his fingers will collect feathers.)

For weeks now the security police have been asking Bob Shawcross all sorts of questions about people in many walks of life. Bob has stood up to the interrogation. The police are particularly interested in Theodore Darikwa and the people who rescued him on the one hand and, on the other, in the person who placed the bomb at the foot of the Kruger Memorial. Bob has been transferred for questioning to Pretoria. He is brought before Colonel Lamprecht, the officer in charge of interrogations.

Take a seat please, professor. I understand you've been having difficulty in explaining your notes to us. I probably would do what you're doing in your position. But, professor, you don't want to be hanging around here for the next ninety days or one hundred and eighty. And, if you don't talk you might wreck your career; in terms of our criminal laws you are liable to prosecution for contempt of court each time you refuse to answer the questions put to you by a magistrate. This would mean that you would be arrested and kept in gaol for a certain period and then be released, to be arrested again and thrown in prison.

The process can go on for as long as you live; there's no way of stopping it as long as you refuse to furnish the police with information they need. You can't even leave the country; you would be banned and subjected to house imprisonment when the police would keep your house under surveillance for twenty-four hours of every day of the ban. Not even the Natal University will keep you on their payroll if it means you have to stay in your house and see nobody without police permission for five years.

I ask you, professor: Do you deserve such treatment? From a man in whom you confided? Your friend, James Hawthorne? How do you think we got to know about your diary? Some people do not deserve the loyalty of their friends. Hawthorne is one of them. He's a free man, making his money and can leave the country any time he wants and here you are, almost at the end of your career. Why did he come to Durban? Who saw him, apart from yourself?

I have been asked these questions thousands of times. Jimmy told me he was on holiday and that is all I know. The people he saw were my family. . . .

Oh! Come off it, professor; you know better than that. You tell a man something in confidence and the police reproduce that exactly as you said it and you say that man deserves your trust?

I don't say that; I say I know nothing.

Even when your own records contradict you?

We live in an age of . . . shall I say, electronic miracles!

Some people are affected by long periods of interrogation and, believe me, professor, we want nothing from you other than the truth about Hawthorne. Are you feeling a little tired? We have the police health officer in the building. I'd be glad to take you to him. Come with me.

Colonel Lamprecht's door opens into a medical examining room. Two doctors stand at the far end, chatting.

Dr. Cilliers, this is Dr. Robert Shawcross; he's professor of history at the University of Natal and is an authority on the black underground movement. We are trying to get additional information on his studies. His health is not yet adjusted to the dry air of the Pretoria veld. Shall I leave him in your good hands?

Presies! [Certainly!]

After taking the particulars and making preliminary examinations, Dr. Cilliers shows Shawcross into a glass cubicle with a bath tub and a shower.

They don't give you much of bathwater in the cells do they? That's against the regulations, doctor; they can get into very serious trouble for that, you know? Go into the bathroom, doctor. . . .

Shawcross half fills the tub with water and as he steps into it, the glass door slides shut behind him. There is room for the tub only in the cubicle. A slight electric shock passes intermittently through the water.

Help! Help!

A new doctor rushes into the bathroom and stands opposite the glass door.

What's gone wrong, professor?

You know what's gone wrong. Get me out of here!

Are you ready to talk?

Nonsense!

Tell me when you're ready, doctor.

The new man slams the door and leaves Shawcross in the cubicle. The current starts flowing into the water.

Help! Help!

A third man, also dressed like a doctor, enters the bathroom and opens the sliding door.

I'm so sorry, doctor. The plumbing in some of these old buildings isn't what it should be.

He presses a button and two men push in a stretcher and carry Shawcross to the recovery room. Swanepoel sits behind a huge desk.

I'm sorry about the accident in the bathroom, doctor. These things happen in old buildings. Have you been doing any more thinking?

No.

Swanepoel presses a button and two uniformed police take Shawcross into the waiting-room outside which looks like an operating theatre. A woman now and then screams in frightening tones inside the theatre. After a while they carry her out, on a stretcher. The police order Shawcross into the theatre. A broad table covered with a sheet of wet white rubber stands in the centre of the room. One man stands next to the table, in the uniform of a police doctor; the five or six others, also in white, stand a distance away from him. He signals with his thumb:

Strip and lie on the table!

What's happening?

I said strip and lie here!

The men in the room pull off Shawcross's clothes and lay him on the table and fasten his feet and hands on to it with plastic clasps. The man in the doctor's clothes sprays a thin shower of water all over Shawcross's body and connects an electric clasp to the current. He puts on his rubber gloves, rolls the prepuce on Shawcross's penis backward and attaches the clasp to the lower part of the penis.

This is the sun-ray treatment, doctor, and you might have it for as long as you want to have it. It doesn't kill; it tones up the system and increases the potency of the rod! Are you ready?

Shawcross screams like the woman he followed. The current is switched on and off until Shawcross faints.

Take him to the recovery room!

Shawcross is in his cell when he comes to. He feels as though the world around him has been in a crazy whirl. Suddenly, things begin to clear up. He begins to ask himself if his life is worth much now. If he yields to police pressure, he will never live with his conscience again; if he stands his ground he might condemn himself to an eternity of torture. The torture, however, is not his real problem; he is sufficiently disciplined not to succumb to it; he thinks he can pull through even though the forms of torture are changed from week to week.

There is no regular pattern followed; for example, he never knows when he will be interrogated or when he will be tortured or how this will be done. His problem is a crack deep in the interstices of being. He was born into a wealthy, upper middle class English family which had accumulated wealth and political power in Natal. He had gone to the best schools in the land and left school a convinced enemy of race discrimination. While he was not very active in race politics, he had strong views on how black and white should live in South Africa. The colour bar he had always condemned as a stupid monstrosity; merit, and not race or colour should fix the position of the individual in national life.

The African, he argued, had to be given a vested interest in upholding democracy because liberty was the thing any decent person lived for. Shawcross was sometimes angered and sometimes puzzled when the Pentecostalists and other Zionists attacked collaboration across the colour line. He could never understand how they could believe that the white liberal was as dangerous an enemy as de Haas. He finally concluded that fear was at the root of race prejudice; that if the whites could be shown that the man on the other side of the colour line wanted what they had, they could be cured of their fears; that if it could be shown that the black man had evolved a sub-culture based on christian, democratic, Western foundations, ground could be established for a meaningful black-white dialogue on co-existence.

As he sits in his cell, he wonders how he would have fared in a country governed by Mareka or Masilo or Maggie or, even, Chief Yedwa. They would not treat him differently from the way the CNP does. He now and then attacked them in the past, more obliquely than directly, as black racists. He said he had no quarrel with African nationalism, which he regarded as distinct from Black racism. He respected the African nationalists because they were committed to individual liberty, freedom and the brotherhood of Man. He told all with ears to hear that he would regard it a privilege to be a citizen of a country ruled by moderate gentlemen like Bishop Theodosius Ngema or Chief Bulube or Mr. Malenge Mlawu, the African sugar-cane magnate. These men are moderates; they want nothing more and nothing less from the white man than the right to lead useful lives; they are christians; they oppose Zionist racism; they are not bitter against the white man; they are even prepared to guarantee minority rights in the democracy toward which they are striving. In the last fifty years, for example, they have produced no less than three declarations to show where they stood. There first was the Ten-Point Programme, supported by such venerable gentlemen as Z. R. Mahabane. Then came the Freedom Charter to uphold which the great Chief Albert Luthuli was prepared to see the Africans split. Now the leaders of the black administrations in the rural reserves are talking of a Bill of Rights.

What greater proof is needed to demonstrate the commitment of these men to the principles of the Magna Carta and the Declaration of Independence! To liberty and democracy!

Shawcross takes great care not to say a word about the Bloemfontein Conference and its ideal of nationhood; he never mentions its role in the race quarrel. To him the things which matter are the Pass Laws, segregation, equal pay. He never bothers about thinking of the nature of the world which the African wants for himself. Shawcross passes for a great liberal; a great friend of the Africans; a great student of the race problem and of history. But for him, as for most whites, the Africans had no history before the advent of the whites!

Inevitably, people like Mareka, Maggie, Maimane and others figure prominently in his study as contrasts who throw into sharper outlines the importance to white South Africa of leaders like Bishop Ngema or Chief Bulube or Mr. Mlawu. He dismisses the opponents of coalitions across the colour line as extremists. He writes frequently, mourning the fact that a powerful christian leader like Bishop Maimane should accuse the liberals of being committed to white supremacy. How does anybody in his senses dare to say this? To which Maimane often replied:

The answer is simple. The liberal is committed to a values-system developed by the white people to serve the ends of white people. They use these values as criteria by which to determine worth in a black person. Their ideal is to make him a black carbon copy of the white man; to make him see fulfilment for himself and his people in a life defined by the white people to serve white interests. The followers of de Haas are committed to a values-system evolved by the whites to preserve white domination. They use race and colour as weapons for ensuring that the African never becomes a threat to white supremacy. Both the liberals and the followers of de Haas are committed to the white system of values; they quarrel only on the strategies by which to preserve white supremacy.

Nonsense! Nonsense! Nonsense! Shawcross shouts in his cell.

Shawcross is still screaming at the top of his voice when an African sweeper goes past. He casts a quick glance at Shawcross through the hole on the door.

Do you want any help, baas?

I want to get out of here. Call me the guard!

Yes, baas; the guard I shall call! But, baas, the lords around here . . . well, baas . . . you understand. If you shout too much, nobody might come.

Nonsense! Nonsense! Nonsense!

The African talks to himself, and moves a little distance from the hole. Hm! What shall I do with this baas? He does not understand. . . .

He returns to the hole. Shawcross now stands near the hole.

Call me a guard; tell them the white man in this cell has something they might want to hear.

The African walks away, mumbling to himself.

He does not understand; with the Boers, you cease to be a white man the moment you have a conscience; he does not understand . . . the baas does not understand . . . .

* * *

Robert Shawcross sits on a comfortable chair in front of a huge desk behind which sits a giant of a man, with red hair, in a dark

191

grey suit. His looks and voice, like his manners, bespeak a man who is accustomed to commanding. He is Brigadier De Villiers Swanepoel, chief of the assassinations division of the security police in Pretoria. There are very few people, on both sides of the colour line, who want to get anywhere near Brigadier Swanepoel.

Well, professor! I'm sure you've been doing some thinking and I hear you have something to tell me now.

I'd like to get out of here and out of this country.

The choice, as you know, is yours.

I know . . . I know. . . .

Professor, you know I have nothing against you. I'm sure that before Hawthorne came to your house, the police knew nothing about you. But, as you realise, the government has to protect everybody against subversion. The government is merely doing its duty, just as I am doing mine here. That's what I'm paid to do.

I know . . . . Well, Brigadier, I don't know what you want from me.

Hawthorne features in curious ways in your diary. You keep him somewhere in the shadows. We have him on our files and we are watching him. When he went to Durban, we naturally wanted to keep an eye on him. He stayed with you and so we became interested in you. We raided your place, as you know, and some of the papers the police found justified the installation of electronic recording devices. . . .

In my house?

There was nothing illegal in that. The police had reason to believe that a crime against the state was likely to be committed and in terms of the amendments to the Security Act made last year, the police had to install bugging equipment in your house.

You mean, they burgled into my house?

No. You and your family were in the house when they installed the recording equipment. You remember the police raided your house again after the Hawthornes had left? Ja; they removed the equipment. You notice that I am being very frank with you. The recordings revealed that you had the diary and that you were a member of an underground unit to which Hawthorne belonged, the African Freedom Army or AFA. Can you tell me about your role in it?

And if I choose to speak to the magistrate?

Don't fool yourself; you are not likely to get there for years if you prefer to be our guest. See what we offer you! If you give us the information we need to complete the picture your colleagues in AFA have already furnished, you can be a free man in forty-eight hours; if you want to, you can have a permanent exit permit and arrangements could be made to pay for you and your family's air tickets to any place chosen by you in the world. And, that means a better future for your children and peace of mind for you.

A messenger comes in through a side door and hands a piece of paper to Swanepoel and withdraws. He reads it slowly and turns to Shawcross.

This has something to do with your family. You have three kids, all girls?

Yes.

The first is aged five, the second three and the third eight months. The baby fell from her cot and broke her arm. She is at Addington Children's Hospital. Your wife wanted us to let you know this. To speak for myself, let me say how sorry I am that this should happen while you are here. Mind you, we have nothing against you; we are after Hawthorne.

I was a member of the AFA. I joined it because it set out to awaken the whites to the dangers our policies were creating for the whites on the homefront and in the outside world. We were going to use violence to property and avoid personal terrorism . . . .

I can understand that. I understand also, that mistakes could be made.

Well, er . . . yes.

Hawthorne ridiculed the whole idea, as you know.

Yes, he did and got himself into trouble.

We know about that; but he also got you into trouble.

I had nothing to do with his troubles. On the contrary, he let me down very badly. He made me join the AFA and assured me that it would never resort to violence to the person and there, with his own bomb, he killed Jennifer Huggins, one of our closest family friends and the finest ambassador the whites had in the black community. . . .

He pulls a handkerchief from his pocket and buries his head into it, sobbing bitterly, then, his voice shaking: Forgive me, Brigadier. I was present at the funeral and I just don't know how I shall live with the picture of the thousands of little black faces whose future had suddenly been ruined by the insanity of one man. . . .

Contempt is written all over the Brigadier's face. He has no sympathy with and no time for a white person who shows human feelings toward the black people.

These are the things we are trying to stop. You can vindicate Jennifer Huggins, if you want to. We are having a number of trials coming up in Johannesburg, Kroonstad, Bloemfontein, Port Elizabeth, Cape Town and Pietermaritzburg which involve AFA violence. You will not restore Jennifer to life, but as a state witness you can create the conditions in which white young people who speak English can be made to understand that violence does not pay. He smiles.

But I have nothing to do with those cases?

The people involved are mentioned in your Diary.

Why should I be punished so cruelly? Have I not suffered enough?

It's your family I'm thinking about; that little girl in hospital whom you must see . . . that is, if you care. And I think you do.

* * *

The lights never go out in the headquarters of the security police. People are always moving, silently, ominously, followed by their shadows. The police have returned Shawcross to his cell. There is more than usual activity at security police headquarters on this particular night. The clock downtown has just struck eleven. Black and white security police have begun to crowd into the courtyard of the security headquarters. None of them knows what has happened; not even their commanders have been told the purpose of the order to call at the headquarters. The police stand in small groups and chat in subdued tones in the courtyard. As is the custom in all the branches of the South African police, the Africans stand by themselves while the whites keep the distance. Bashise Busengi is about the only policeman who does not mix with any group on the black side. He dare not come anywhere near the whites. As is appropriate, race exclusiveness is adhered to nowhere, more aggressively, than among the guardians of the law. The law forbids a black person from arresting a white man committing a crime. A white policeman, freshly recruited, has precedence over a black sergeant-major—the highest rank attained by a black man in the force—and takes command of the blacks if no senior white officer is present.

Bashise is unpopular with all sections of the black police in the capital. The security section regards him as an upstart who gatecrashed into the aristocracy of the black guardians of the law. Selected security officers are allowed the privilege to carry revolvers. As a rule, these are old and trusted policemen who have served with exemplary loyalty. Bashise is not only young; he was seconded from the uniformed police branch on the recommendation of Paul Kritzinger himself. He had no sooner reached the head office than he was promoted and made a records officer in the African section of the headquarters. He is one of the highest paid officers in the black force and although he works always at the desk, he enjoys a number of seniority privileges.

For example, he carries a revolver and has a brand new police jeep for his exclusive use. Sections of the police force hate Bashise; they accuse him of informing on them. Privately, they say he licks the arse of every gatwyser. The whites like Bashise; there is no humiliation which will evoke an angry response from him. The consensus of opinion is that the education he has has not spoilt him. His immediate superior is considering the creation of a special grade to which to promote Bashise to make security police work more attractive for loyal blacks like him.

The clock strikes twelve. Three white captains emerge from the operations officer's office and lead their men to their respective rooms where they brief them on the mission for the morning.

* * *

A major security raid is always a closely co-ordinated operation; it takes place at the same time in the same way in every city and large town. The police vans pull out of Johannesburg's Marshall Square, their headquarters, precisely at the moment the raid commences in Pretoria and drive toward Parktown where the oldest and some of the wealthiest English and Jews live. The newly rich Afrikaners are moving in slowly. Many of the managers and directors of European firms in South Africa live in Parktown. In the old days this section of the city was a suburb, but now it has been integrated into Johannesburg. In spite of this an element of cosmopolitanism persists around the area which is visibly un-South African. The groceries stock local and foreign foods. One can walk into a Parktown shop and buy a pound of *kishik* (for the wealthy Syrians here are accorded the status of honorary whitemen, like the Japanese and, of course, the black diplomats from Malawi).

The local bottle store sells the headiest brews from all over the world. In Parktown, more than in any South African suburb, the different national groups constitute visible little communities and more or less live out their carefully adjusted lives. As a rule, the Europeans tend to identify themselves with the English. Even the Hollanders, who bequeathed Afrikaans to the Afrikaners, are closer to the English than to the Afrikaners. Nobody says much about this, but in private conversations among themselves or even with their black servants or with the Africans it is the privilege of some of the rich to meet, the Europeans make it known that they find the Afrikaans character a little too abrasive for their comfort. The Americans constitute a tiny, visibly inhibited group. They go about so carefully one would think they feared the earth might cave in under their feet.

Cosmopolitanism characterises Parktown politics as well. The suburb is one of the strongholds of South African liberalism; it is one of those constituencies which the CNP never bothers to contest. In the inner circles of the party, Parktown is dismissed as a *Jewish ghetto*. In one of those rare moments when de Haas relaxes with his friends he tells the story of the *Jew From Parktown*. Sam Cohen, he starts, was a Jewish millionaire campaigning in Parktown for the (English-Jewish-capitalist-oriented) Unionist Party. He read out the ten principles which constituted his plank in the election. Nobody cheered when he sat down. Sam jumped to his feet, and, holding two lists in his hands, shouted:

Ladies and gentlemen, if you don't like this set of principles, I have another!

While the Jews are highly visible in the political life of Parktown, the English are unquestionably the dominant influence in the suburb. Many of them are descended from either the pioneers who came to Johannesburg during the gold rush or the settlers whom Lord Milner brought in to neutralise Afrikaner political influences in the Transvaal. From the moment gold was discovered on the Witwatersrand last century, they have been consistent supporters of union.

They were the power behind the old South African Party of Smuts and are the backbone of the Unionist Party. William Pitcairn is a lawyer, his family is one of the largest manufacturers of small airplanes. Pitcairn Engineering Corporation was founded by his father in the days of Paul Kruger. The elder Pitcairn, now nearing a hundred, spends his time reminiscing about the good old days when the black man knew his place. He has a passionate hatred for the missionaries who spoilt the *native*. His bitterest venom is reserved for the American missionaries who established the largest number of mission stations among the Zulus and corrupted these splendid children of nature. He employed an unspoilt Zulu, nature's own gentleman, to guard his house when the black hooligans from the locations started breaking into white homes by night in the suburbs. He was going to be away from home for a fortnight on a business trip to Durban and called his faithful Zulu to his bedroom.

You are the only man I can trust with the contents of this box, Zulu. Don't let anybody touch it while I am away! Don't open it yourself!

It shall be as you say, master!

Two weeks later, Pitcairn returned and found the faithful Zulu by the box; he had slept on it, sat on it and for fourteen days lived for it. Every one of the thousands of gold sovereigns in the box was still in its place! This is the Zulu gentleman whom the missionaries transformed into a burglar. And, to drive his point home, he has made it a rule that no black man should enter his house by the front door; not even a policeman. This creates no end of problems for his son William and his wife Greta, both of whom are militant liberals. But then, both agree that the old man is not immortal.

It is fifteen minutes after two in the morning. A knock rings on the main door.

Open the door! We are the police!

William jumps out of bed and opens the door.

We are looking for Brigadier De Villiers Swanepoel; here's our search warrant.

What are you talking about?

The man who rescued Theodore Darikwa.

What on earth would he be doing here?

We thought you might want to tell us something about him.

This is preposterous, Captain de Plooy! You know me very well. I'm an officer of the magistrate's court in this city. You're an experienced and respected officer and you know the law. Don't you know where to ask me about a suspected crime? And this Swanepoel you're talking about? What did you say his first name was?

De Villiers, Brigadier Swanepoel.

The only such Swanepoel I know is in Pretoria. And, in any case, what do you want?

To look around for a while.

Please yourselves.

After the search the police return to the sitting-room with piles of papers.

We'd like to ask you one or two things about some of these papers. *Operation Aburri* sounds quite interesting; it refers to armed raids on isolated white farms on the platteland (rural areas).

That's easy to explain. As you know I recently visited Ghana. Aburri is the name of a botanical garden outside of Accra. And one of the things I found was this plan by the Ghanaians for an armed insurrection against white rule in this country. If I were you, I wouldn't touch it. I brought it for Colonel Prinsloo; but if you want to mess around with it, you'll take the responsibility.

Why don't you come along with us—with it?

Look here, Captain du Plooy! If you want this piece of paper, take it. I'm a lawyer; I'm an officer of the magistrate's court. You can't drag me out of bed this way. If you want to ask questions, I'll be at your office at nine o'clock. Here's my passport.

I'll take the plan with me. See you at nine o'clock, Mr. Pitcairn.

O.K.

* * *

The clock strikes the ninth hour; then the half and finally the tenth. Captain de Plooy and two assistants drive to Pitcairn's house.

Mrs. Pitcairn, we'd like to see your husband.

He's in Botswana now. Took his father's private plane. Here's the telegram saying he arrived safely in Mahalapye . . . .

My God!

* * *

Twelve hours have gone by. The excitement and consternation at the headquarters of the security police in Pretoria has not abated. James Hawthorne is being questioned by Captain Jooste van der Horst. Each new fact on his placing of the bomb under the Kruger statue is transmitted to Piet du Toit van der Merwe, who passes it on to the prime minister—in Cape Town. This procedure has been ordered by the prime minister himself. De Haas has sent a telegram to Colonel Prinsloo congratulating him and the police force on the capture of Hawthorne. He adds in the wire that the police are the white man's first line of defence in South Africa. This is not a new view; he has been saying this for the last twenty-five years. Significance is given to it by the fact that Hawthorne is the first white person to disagree so violently with the CNP that he has killed a white person in protest against CNP policies.

In the mind of most Afrikaners, Hawthorne must be made a warning to all whites that the government will tolerate no defection to the side of the black man and that traitors will pay with their lives, their white skin notwithstanding. Nobody expresses this view in so many words, but the consensus is there and the prime minister's telegram reinforces it. Hawthorne's arrest is a moment of supreme triumph for Prinsloo's strategy of white-anting the underground link between the black militants and the white radicals. The relationship works in a complicated manner; one has to understand the triangular conflict involving the African, the Afrikaner and the English and the Jews to appreciate how it works. The tensions piling up in the black community constitute an immediate threat to Afrikaner power.

Few Englishmen and fewer Jews would shed any tears if Afrikaner power collapsed; but it must not go down with their factories. English and Jewish radicals work with the black militants not so much to crush Afrikaner might as to increase their own bargaining power with both sides. English and Jewish conservatives work with the Afrikaner not so much to oppress the African as to increase their bargaining power in dealings with the Afrikaner. Loyalties and treacheries interplay across the colour line to give a peculiar twist to the underground coalition between the black militants and the white radicals. The Africans have no access to white arms; they lack the skill to handle the weapons in the white man's armoury and rely on the white radicals who ration out the know-how to ensure that it does not place the Africans in the position to blow up Afrikaner power and English and Jewish factories.

Solomon Rabinowitz is a Jewish millionaire who owns one of the largest shoe factories in Southern Africa. He lives in Parktown. Like Pitcairn the elder, he does not allow black people to enter his house by the front door; as a matter of fact, he receives no Africans of any sort in his house. He employs Coloured servants. During the raids after the seizure of the Shawcross Diary the police search his house and lay their hands on papers which prove that he is the treasurer of the Communist Party of Southern Africa.

Like most Afrikaners in the capital, Prinsloo regards the peculiar relationship between the black militants and the white radicals as one of the gravest threats to Afrikaner power. Unlike the other Afrikaners, he is not concerned about the prospect of an African-English-Jewish alliance against the Afrikaners which he regards as a pipedream the British killed when they created the Union of South Africa. He regards the relationship as a major obstacle to a meaningful dialogue between the African and the Afrikaner on the definition of spheres of influence in South Africa. An ardent advocate of segregation, he rejects Afrikaner imperialism as another pipedream—which will be blown to pieces by the black people. For him, Hawthorne's arrest is important because it could slit the jugular vein of the underground relationship. For this reason, he tells himself and his officers that it offsets the news of William Pitcairn's escape.

The consternation derives from another disappointment. Dillo Mareka and that mysterious character Sefadi Masilo were not in their houses when the police got there. Their wives said both had gone to Johannesburg and would be returning the following morning. It is two in the afternoon now and the men have not turned up. The police have checked up on their haunts in Johannesburg, where they have been told the two men are in Vereeniging. The station commander in Vereeniging has combed Sharpeville location and says the men are said to have returned to Pretoria! The operations officer in Pretoria is red in the face.

These damned niggers! Liars all of them; born of liars who are descended from generations of liars!

The officer is still raging when a white constable walks in, followed by the loyal Bashise.

Well, what's the news?

Meneer, it would appear that Dillo Mareka and Sefadi Masilo have fled the country.

What?

The constable nudges the African.

Bashise, tell the meneer what you heard in the location.

Sir, I went to my contacts and they told me that Mareka and Masilo had escaped to Swaziland.

How on earth did they know they were going to be arrested?

Sir, I don't know.

That's funny; very funny, don't you think so?

No Sir; not funny if you know what I know, Sir.

And what do you know?

Well, Sir, it is difficult for us black people to understand the ways of the white people. All sorts of stories circulate in the location, Sir. People say, for example, that all a black woman needs to do to get any secret out of a white policeman is to pull down her bloomers!

Sex with African women creates crises of ambivalence in every police officer at headquarters. The police exist to enforce the law but no section of Afrikaner manhood is more ardent in its violation of the law than the police force. The African's comments anger the officer who bursts out:

Nonsense!

Sir, I reported on the case of Constable Viljoen in Swaziland . . . .

Ja, you did and a damned good report it was, too. But I don't want you to be telling me about it every day of my life . . . .

Yes Sir; I understand, Sir.

No police officer wants to be reminded anything about the Viljoen case. Boet Viljoen was a security policeman working secretly in Swaziland to keep an eye on the South African refugees in the black kingdom. He operated a liquor store, which gave him a wide variety of contacts. Returning from a party organised by Manzini town's Coloured community one night, he asked the driver of the overloaded car in which he was driving to stop down an incline to enable him to spill the water, as the Swazis say. Everybody had been drinking heavily and Viljoen was as heavily soaked in the Queen's Tears as his non-white companions in the car.

He was still unbuttoning his trousers when the car started rolling down the hill to stop in the middle of the narrow bridge across a stream. Somebody banged the door shut as Viljoen was entering the car and cut his evidence of masculinity in two. The end piece dropped into the water while the car drove off with the bleeding Viljoen. Taken to hospital later, it was discovered that he had lost his manhood, which was recovered in a shallow pool of water beneath the bridge.

The surgeons in the hospital did an excellent job on Viljoen. The story was brought to Atteridgeville by Viljoen's black girl-friend. The joke about the policeman who lost his manhood still does the rounds in the shebeens (illegal drinking dens) in the locations.

The white constable nudges the African again.

Tell die meneer what you heard about Boreneng.

Sir, two Dutch nuns drove Dillo Mareka and Sefadi Masilo to Swaziland. Mareka and Masilo were dressed like black nuns, Sir.

Meneer, our border post at Oshoek confirms that two white nuns and two black nuns checked with them an hour ago and crossed the frontier into Swaziland.

Those dirty Hollander bitches! They would do a thing like that!

* * *

XVII. Non-men And Non-women

Ingulube inesifuba; okwayinonisa
endlaleni kwaziwa yiyo yodwa.

(Commend the pig for keeping its secret;
nobody knows what keeps it fat even in famine.)

An eerie atmosphere of grief and exultation hangs over the capital city. James Hawthorne was hanged in the Central Prison at dawn and was buried a few hours later. *The Rand Post* has published a special issue describing Hawthorne's last moments. *The Post* does not say this in so many words, but leaves few in doubt about the fact that the special issue is a salute to James Hawthorne. Its reports tell how the police imposed a ban limiting the number of people at the cemetery to his aging father and mother, his frail wife whom the trial has reduced to a wreck and his close friend Bruno Sitwell, aged seventeen. The undertakers were given instructions to deliver the coffin at the cemetery chapel and to leave immediately, as a precaution against a group gathering at the graveside. The only other person present is the Anglican vicar of St. Filibert's parish, who conducts the funeral service. There are, of course, the usual security police, to ensure that things do not get out of control. After the ceremony Bruno walks up to the priest.

Don't worry, Father, if you help me, I'll carry Jimmy on my head.

But there are Africans outside . . . . I mean, the gravediggers. The law doesn't allow them to enter the chapel.

Bruno carries the coffin to the door, down the steps and is moving towards the grave about eight hundred yards away. The leader of the gravediggers whispers to his workers.

Ever seen a thing like this?

The men are standing a respectful distance away from the grave. When they see the procession, they drop their spades. One of them whispers.

Do I see what I really see? I never knew that the white people could hate their own people so bitterly.

Brother, you do not know the Afrikaner. Come, let us go and help the young man.

It is against the law!
Damn the law!

*   *   *

Marietjie walks through the kitchen door to the back verandah where Zandile is pressing clothes on a large table. She carries a copy of the special edition of *The Post*.

Have you seen this, Zandile?

Zandile takes the paper and glances quickly at the pictures and the headlines.

I'm sorry for his wife. She must have been a woman with a beautiful personality to let him do what he did.

I'm not sorry for him, Zandile; the man was a criminal and a dirty coward at that. Why did he kill that innocent old woman who had not done him any harm? I'm glad he's got what he deserved. And, you know what, Zandile, these dirty English are always trying to create the impression that we, Afrikaners, are bad people; that we are oppressors and that they love the black people. All they want from your people and mine is our money. And those gravediggers? Why did they help the young man with the coffin? They should have left him to carry it alone, to the grave. It would have taught him a good lesson. A law should be made against your people touching a white coffin . . . .

You do not understand, nooi. Those men were not staging a show; they were merely demonstrating to themselves that they take themselves seriously. That is what Bhadama did. I would do it too, if I had the courage. Bhadama merely did his duty to human beings; he did the thing which he had been taught a normal human being does to his fellowmen. Dr. James Moroka, one of our leaders, once told my father the story of two white boys in Thaba Nchu who went out with their air rifles to hunt birds. Both were about twelve. They met a little African boy aged about seven and aimed their guns at him. *Moenie dit doen nie*, he screamed. *Julle sal 'n mens seermaak!* (Don't do that; you'll hurt a human being.) The white boys laughed and replied: *Jy is nie 'n mens nie!* (You're not a human being!) and proceeded to fire the pellets into his legs. They had not been taught to take themselves seriously.

Oh, but children are children everywhere, Zandile.

Perhaps . . . .

Why do we bother ourselves about politics, in any case? We are women and should talk about things that matter most to women. I want to ask you to do me a favour and I'm talking to you like a woman and I'd like you to talk to me like a woman. My doctor says I might have difficulty when the baby comes and advises that I should go to hospital until the baby comes. Do you think you could stay here while I am away and look after the kids? Baas Piet is so busy flying between Cape Town and Pretoria; and with so much uncertainty about everything while the Passes For Women Bill is before Parliament, I dread to think of leaving the children in the hands of a stranger. Baas Piet agrees with me that it would help a great deal if you could stay in.

But, nooi, I also have young children.

I know you do; that's why I wanted to talk to you like a woman.

What will the other white people say when they see me around at night when you're in hospital?

I'm concerned with my children, Zandile. And, I trust Baas Piet. He's a fine man and I know he loves me too much to bother you. I know you'll be safe.

Well, nooi, if you talk to me on a woman to woman basis, I shall answer you as a woman; I shall look after your kids until you return.

God bless you, Zandile. You remind me of Bhadama. God bless his soul too. Black people have been so good to me—even the people at the Malawi embassy . . . . I don't believe much of what is said about the black people hating the whites. Don't you agree?

Some Africans hate the white people, but most of us take ourselves too seriously to waste our feelings on the whites. We neither love nor hate them. We respond to individuals in proportion as they present themselves. I certainly do not love white people; love is too personal and too intimate a feeling to be spread out to the beautiful people, the saints, the thieves, the murderers and the rapists in any race. When a white man says he loves the black people, he lies to himself, just as the African does when he says he loves the white people. If I cannot love a whole people, I cannot hate it either. I love persons and I hate persons.

Don't you love your people? We love ours.

I can't love them just because they are my people. I hate a black rapist as I do a white one. My people and I are bound together by the things we love; by the same values, a similar history and a common destiny. We belong together. I do not have to love them to belong to them or to identify with them. I certainly have a duty to them; I have to be responsible and protect their values. But my duty has nothing to do with love. Besides, this word love is overworked by the white people. In my culture, love is a relationship between consenting persons . . . .

Aren't you people wonderful! Bhadama . . . . Sometimes . . . sometimes I wish I had the heart of a black person like you or Bhadama. But I know I can't.

Please, don't make any mistakes about us; we are human like everybody else, with all the good and the wickedness which go with that.

Which white woman would leave her home, her husband and her children to look after my family?

It's just that they don't take themselves seriously enough, nooi! And when people don't take themselves seriously enough they can be very, very ugly . . . .

* * *

That night, Zandile and Pumasilwe sit up until late into the night in their bedroom. The nights are the only time when couples live together in the location. But they also have to share their lives with their neighbours; there is a whole infinity of responsibilities a person has to perform as a member of the community. If there is a death, neighbours have to rally and stand by the bereaved until the painful moment is over. More often than not, this means that for some days people ignore their families in order to support the bereaved until they return to normal life. Then, there are the hundreds of tiny mutual benefit societies which preserve social cohesion. In these, people exchange views and experiences and develop solutions to common problems. The churches constitute another institution which activates life in the location. As a result, the location is a hive of activity after the sun has set; the rhythms which give uniqueness to the location experience suddenly burst into the open and become alive at night.

Outsiders say the location is a place of incredible contrasts. By day, it has the look of a city of the dead. The blinding glare of the sheet metal roofs repel the eye the moment one approaches it. The reflections suggest a massive warehouse, stretching as far as the eye can see. The rows of similar brick houses have the look of thousands upon thousands of mounds of earth in a cemetery. More striking than anything, however, is the massive emptiness of the place. Except for the occasional coal dealer on an ancient cart drawn by a work-weary mule or the bone collector with his tattered hessian bag or the milkman speeding by on a bicycle with incredibly disaligned wheels or the unemployed or the hungry and unwashed kids who grow up on the dusty streets, the location is an empty town; a disembowelled city.

An atmosphere of waste hangs over the place; it strikes the eye wherever one turns. Waste is in the bent back of the white-haired woman who opens the door for you, probably holding her daughter's or son's baby. The wrinkles on her face tell the story of a lifetime of toil; of wasted exertion washing a white woman's underwear. The glow in her eye tells a different story; it describes a woman with a purpose.

Waste is the gulleys which intersect the untarred streets; the monotonous similarity of the houses; the children dressed in rags who have nothing to do because they have nowhere to go. Waste is the thousands upon thousands of kids who crowd the schools.

These people are not regarded as living potentials in the process of becoming; they are labour-power—the private property of the white man. He owns their productive potential; that is why he locks them up in the location when the sun has set. He owns their labour; that is why he sends them to school and gives them an education designed to make them efficient producers of wealth for him and not the intellectual equals of the whites. He owns their skills; that is why they can learn some things and be debarred from learning others. Above all, he owns their lives; that is why he has built the location. They can live in it as long as they produce for him; when they are too old to work, he throws them out of the location and dumps them in the rural reserves where they starve, die and rot as new producers are born in the location, trained in the schools, and regimented accordingly to continue the cycle of production.

The African is born into this cycle; he lives in it and dies in it. The waste is in the massive distortion of a people's whole life; in the feeling of being owned by the white man which the location is intended to develop in the African; in the laws which seek to shatter the inner logic of *umteto wesintu*; in the humiliation intended to crack the African's sense of self-worth. More tragic than these cycles of waste is the realisation that the white man left Europe and came to this part of Africa to waste himself by wasting the African.

Things change when the sun has set. The Africans cease to be the ciphers on the white man's books when they return to the location. They throw off their working clothes and wear what they call home clothes. The most fastidious of them wash themselves before covering their bodies with home clothes. The ritual has more than a symbolic significance; the people change the gears of their personality. The transition defines a fundamental contradiction in South Africa. By day, black and white constitute an integrated society and reject each other when the sun has set.

The change into home clothes and the ablutions are as fundamental a rejection of the white experience as any the African ever makes; he moves from the world of being owned to the world of self-realisation; he asserts the validity of *umteto wesintu*, he enters a world of different meanings. If he is a Zulu, he can switch on the loudspeaker to hear Kingana Masikane, the Zulu broadcaster from Durban, roar out the salutation Z-U-L-U! He wakes up earlier to hear the salutation which precedes the morning news. Each time the salutation is repeated, something swells up within him; he calls it *usinga*—the irresistible urge to become. Each time he hears the ancient salutation, he feels a millimetre taller, spiritually. It is a vital signal, a message spoken in the wind from the land of Zulu, to assure the millions of paths to Blood River that movement continues; that the "cord of destiny" is being woven. To weave the cord, as the ancient poet advised, is the thing to live for; it is the pillar which sustains life.

The Basotho, Xhosa, Shangane and other language groups have their own vital signals which they send out in their own ways. All of them converge at the point of meaning.

It is this point which establishes the final absurdity of the government's contention that tribalism is a fact of African life. The Basotho, the Shangane, the Xhosa, the Zulu and other African groups agree on one fundamental principle: their evaluation of the person. Each person is an idea into which the infinite consciousness behind creation individualises itself; each language group is a cluster of ideas. Each idea is valid and legitimate in its own right and propels itself to fulfilment in terms of a logic which inheres in itself as an individualisation of the infinite consciousness; so is each cluster of ideas. People might speak Xhosa and Sotho—that does not matter; the important fact is that at the level of fundamentals and meanings, they are of one mind and are moving to the same goal.

It is this unity at the bottom which government policy seeks to smash and which the location is designed to corrode. It is this evaluation of the person which the African defends when he changes into home clothes and washes his body. It is this precept which made possible the Bloemfontein decision to weld all the African language groups into a single nation. The African's slogan is: *Jaws Which Belong Together, You Grind Together!* This, he argues, is the logical culmination of the African evaluation of the person and the black people's common experience in history; this, he insists, is the only real answer to the wastefulness of the white man's culture.

* * *

Zandile did not change her working clothes when she came home; not because she was making a declaration of war. It is said in her community that the feminine mind is capable of dealing with a thousand ideas at one and the same time. Pumasilwe knows that the feminine mind sometimes works in an exceedingly complicated way; he grew up taught that it has to do this because woman is the *Big House*. The element of finality in the dictum has frustrating connotations. Sometimes a fellow wants to touch the body of the woman he loves even in the midst of a business conference in the bedroom. But when she is clad in armour, where does he touch her? The limitation is a continuing source of irritation. Things are not improved by the subject under discussion.

And, you tell me you agreed to ignore me and your family to look after that gatwyser's children while he's busy helping to get the Passes For Women Bill into the Statute Book? Don't you have any sense in your head? Where's your pride?

You said I should take the job!

Are you trying to be smart? I don't like it when a woman gives a reply which does not answer the question. Women do that. Every woman thinks she's a genius and her husband a dolt!

I would not be in this house if I thought that way. Only, I find it difficult to understand why you don't understand my position.

What do I not understand? The insensitivity and the sickening sentimentality and the contempt so transparent in everything that woman said about everybody, barring herself, her husband, her children and her people! She thinks we Africans are just a bunch of non-men and non-women; non-people!

I'm grateful for that; she limits her range of thinking and when my enemy makes a fool of herself, I rejoice.

Rejoice .... Rejoice .... Hm! With that Boer male around the house, at night?

An unintended, though inevitable and embarrassing, by-product of the acrimonious public debate on the Passes For Women Bill is that it saturates the atmosphere with thoughts of sex across the colour line and aspects of it have aphrodisiac effects on some white men. Sex between the black woman and the white man has become a subject of heated discussion in homes, churches, private clubs and, inevitably, the English and Afrikaans sections of the press. Every now and then the newspapers come up with scoops on the subject and give them the widest possible publicity—for different reasons.

The English use the Afrikaner male's appetite for the African woman as a stick with which to beat him for political purposes. The Afrikaner is vulnerable on this plane. Most of the males involved in sex crimes are Afrikaners. The Afrikaans papers report on interracial sex to mobilise white support for the Passes For Women Bill. The *Black Peril* has assumed the form of a black woman. Other complications have set in. A prominent Afrikaner politician, an ardent advocate of race separation, has died unexpectedly after taking a drug prescribed by his doctor. The post-mortem reveals a blood allergy which occurs only among a tiny African clan in a remote part of the Okavango swamps in South-West Africa. This creates a muffled crisis in the ranks of Afrikanerdom. Trusted Afrikaner scientists start investigations to determine the percentage of African blood in Afrikaner veins. The de Haas regime is embarrassed by the element of Africanness in the Afrikaners (the people of Afrika).

Sex across the colour line is an old South African practice. For about a hundred years after Jan van Riebeeck had landed at the Cape of Good Hope black and white could intermarry if they were so minded. The Dutch Reformed Church saw nothing wrong in the practice and its clergymen dutifully solemnised the marriages. The famous Simon van der Stel, the Cape governor after whom Stellenbosch University is named, was a Coloured man. Stellenbosch is the oldest and finest centre of higher learning in the Afrikaans community. Not even the ingenuity of *Die Aanslag* and the CNP can obliterate these facts of history. Government propaganda adopts the line that there is a very small amount of African blood in the Afrikaner and takes the strongest exception possible to suggestions that the quantity is large enough, in fact, to make the Afrikaners a people of mixed blood. The figure "conceded" is one percent. The Afrikaner researchers' figures show that whereas fifty years earlier the Afrikaner's blood was thirteen percent black, it is now a little less than eight percent non-white.

Not unexpectedly, the English press finds the new figure not insignificant in view of the Afrikaner's preoccupation with race and colour. English commentators write luridly on the virility of Afrikaner men who smash their careers, commit suicide and fornicate in holy places in homage to the African woman. Coenraad Buys, the Afrikaner who went "African" last century, is an English favourite these days. He successfully serviced no less than forty Xhosa wives and concubines. Some English academics are giving a new and irritating twist to Buys's performance. He was, they charge, motivated by a deep-seated desire to dominate which had its roots in an abiding feeling of inadequacy. The CNP's sensitivity on the colour issue, they conclude, derives also from this lingering weakness.

Sex and politics have become such an explosive mixture and have inflamed passions so violently Afrikaner women, who, as a rule, are a thoroughly domesticated breed, stand in the front line where they campaign militantly against the alleged irresistibility of the African woman. As in all situations where women compete for men, no sensibilities are respected by the ladies. Kritzinger's wife leads the campaign in Pretoria. She discusses the peculiarities of the African woman with such brutal, though honest, candour she is in great demand as a speaker in Afrikaner women's associations all over the country—including women's hostels in Afrikaner universities.

Her main point is that true and loyal Afrikaner daughters must hold their skirts tight to save Afrikaner manhood from the wiles of the black woman. No true and loyal daughter of Afrikanerdom should employ an African nurse for her children. That, in the first place, breeds Afrikaner communist-liberals. More than this, however, no Afrikaner woman, who is proud of her race and seeks to preserve its purity, should ever, ever employ a black nanny for her baby boy. The male baby nursed by an African develops a dangerous indifference to the odours her body emits and, as he grows up, acquires a self-degrading feeling for the black woman.

Campaigns like these are, strictly speaking, not a new development in African-Afrikaner relations. An interesting development is the Afrikaner male's stout and continuing refusal to have his tastes in this regard dictated by women. The smells which the Afrikaner women find so repugnant are just the thing which makes the black woman literally irresistible to the Boer. Besides, the males seem in no mood to allow females, even of their own race, to deny them the freedom to prove their masculinity against any female challenger of any race.

In the locations, the appetite for the African woman is described as the Afrikaner's quest for that part of his umbilical cord which lies in the black community.

Startling in its implications, however, is the new use of sex as a political weapon; as a technique by which to *xina* the Afrikaner. In this atmosphere of confused thinking on sex, Pumasilwe experiences difficulty in drawing the necessary difference between political imperatives and jealousy.

You are mistaken, girl, he continues to fume, if you think that by agreeing that you should work for Piet van der Merwe I was saying you should sell your soul to the Boers in the way you want to do. Imagine what people in the location will think of me! Dillo and Sefadi left the country. I have been chosen to lead the underground and the first thing I do is to allow my wife to look after the children of the private secretary to de Haas!

They might as well ask why I work for these Boers. But my real point, Father of the Children, is that we are at war with the Afrikaner; he uses the gun, we use the mind.

The Boers have buried their teeth into our flesh and we've buried ours into theirs; we're not going to let go; we're in this fight to the finish, even if it takes a thousand years. If there are millions of paths to Blood River; if I am one of these, what does it matter if people call me names? If they call you names? What does it matter if I perish in the bid to bury my teeth deeper into the Afrikaner's flesh? *Indlondlo izendlalela ngabazingeli bayo!* (The deadly ndlondlo snake lines its grave with the corpses of its hunters.)

Pumasilwe is not sure he understands very clearly what is going on in his wife's mind. He is not in doubt about her determination to do something; the Zulu identifies himself with the dreaded ndlondlo only in the moment of decision. For a while he gropes for something to say.

Try and understand, Father of the Children. I am a revolutionary, too; and the revolutionary's function in life is to destroy the evil around him.

Well! Well! What on earth are you going to destroy?

Why don't you wait, friend? You'll see the ruin when the Passes For Women Bill becomes law.

* * *

Akumbethe wamela ilanga.

(The rainbow has pretty colours, but the sun shines forever.)

The debate on the Passes For Women Bill is running into snags in the Senate. It encountered some rough weather in the House of Assembly, where the younger Afrikaner militants dominate. The opposition to it, toward the last stages of the second reading, slowed its movement through the Lower House. If this could happen in the Lower House, where Afrikanerdom's frontline fire-eaters are concentrated, worse might be expected in the Senate where the old stalwarts of the Dutch Reformed Church are a power to reckon with.

The Dutch Reformed Church is committed uncompromisingly to race segregation, but as the custodian of the damaged Afrikaner conscience and the guardian of its morality, the Church finds it difficult to support policies which violate morality in ways everybody can see. Not that the Church can come out with a public criticism of the government; that is unthinkable in Afrikanerdom's present mood. What some churchmen are doing, however, is discreetly to exert pressure on the older and religiously committed senators for the purpose of slowing down the debate.

This, however, is not the prime minister's only headache. The responsibilities of office have awakened some of his interest in international attitudes to his policies. If there is anything he does not want to happen, it is to drag on the debates until the world is awakened sufficiently to the evil of the Bill to make its passage an international issue. He does not think world opinion is so strong against CNP policies as to translate its objections into effective action against Pretoria. He has no doubt in his mind that there still are people in positions of power in Western Europe and the Americas who believe in the inherent superiority of the white man in the world and who will not rush to encourage campaigns to crush CNP rule.

One of these days, he might need military support from the white countries against the black hordes from the free African states; alliances with some of these countries might be Afrikanerdom's only guarantee of survival in Africa. He still rejects van Warmelo's policy of dismantling the republic of South Africa and reverting more or less to

211

the position before Union. Like Churchill, he is not in the mood to preside over the carving up of his own empire.

The prime minister knows that most people in the world find it difficult, almost impossible, to understand the Afrikaner's position. How do the Afrikaners hope to reverse the march of events or to stop the momentum of history? People ask how the Afrikaner can be in his senses when he gives the entire Black World a vested interest in his destruction. How can he survive if he is finally thrown out of Africa, when he has nothing to give? The Jews survived because they had something to give.

The Afrikaners are only a speck of humanity in the world; their language has significance only between Cape Town and the Limpopo; they are producing no great art and are committed to ideals of fulfilment which humiliate the African and degrade Afrikanerdom and disgrace white civilisation in the process. Yes, the Afrikaners have political control over the richest, largest and most powerful country in Africa. But in the final analysis this power is founded on African labour. What will the Afrikaner do when the African withdraws his labour? The questions go on and on and on. In the end the outsiders' minds are wearied by what they regard as the suicidal intransigence of the Afrikaners. Some of them conclude that the Afrikaners are driven by the terrible death-wish which carried the Nazis to catastrophe. The prime minister frowns and gets up from his desk. He glances at his dead predecessor's portrait.

Thus fortified, the prime minister feels consoled by the fact that the world also finds it difficult, almost impossible, to understand how, in view of the cruel humiliations the whites inflict on the Africans, men like Magagu Geja kaBulube can still be friends with any white person at all, let alone dream of a non-racial society. How can a normal human being, spat upon at birth, spat upon through life and spat upon even in death see fulfilment for himself in anything but killing the white people and driving them into the sea? Is it because the African is insensitive to humiliation that he does not murder the whites? So many white people have said that there is a real, if intangible, defect in the African's make-up; perhaps they are right, the outsiders say.

Questions are raised even in Free Africa. Educated black men, leaders, journalists and thinkers are disgusted with the inexplicably stupid patience of their brothers in South Africa. Why do they not rise against oppression; why do they not organise a Mau Mau movement, for example, to kill the whites, burn their factories and farms and homes? For goodness sake, why do they not do something about their humiliation instead of pinning their backsides to the ground? De Haas looks at his wife's silver-framed, tinted photo on his desk.

The prime minister is delighted when black people attack the "stupid" patience of the blacks in South Africa; they confirm some of his pet theories. In arguments he starts by saying that the Afrikaners are a God-fearing people; that while they are a severely disciplined people, they treat the black man with the justice he understands. His acquiescence to white domination is proof. The Africans, he continues, are a child race; it is a crime against them to force them to see fulfilment for themselves in terms of white criteria. If they are segregated from the white men who put wrong ideas into their heads and are allowed to have as many wives as they desire and all the beer they need, these children of nature feel fulfilled. This is what contentment means to them.

In the best of worlds, the ideal would be to leave them alone and to let them enjoy the primitive simplicity of their life. But witchcraft is no answer to disease and disease knows no colour. To save them from their ignorance, the white man has to provide health services; he has to establish schools, where they can learn the habits of hygiene. To provide these is the burden of the white man; to save the African from ignorance is his mission in South Africa. But why should the white man pay for the services he gives, while the black male runs around with women and wastes his time drinking?

The Pass Laws are designed to control African movement in ways that will produce the best results for the bearers of civilisation on the one hand and their wards, on the other. Here he grunts. Segregation is designed to protect the blacks against the greed and avarice of irresponsible whites who introduce the evils of white civilisation into the black community to advance their own selfish ends and would not mind if the black race was wiped off the face of the earth.

The Americans virtually exterminated the Red Indians with their "kindness." The Afrikaner's way is not only a guarantee of African survival; it has enabled the black people to breed at such a rapid rate they to-day stand in the ratio of 4 to 1 to the white man. The outsiders see no reason why, in these conditions, four million Africans cannot sacrifice their lives to kill four million whites; there could still be twelve million Africans left who would still constitute a black nation which would be larger than the populations of some African countries. The questions go on and on. In the end men conclude that the Africans in South Africa have either been so crushed they have lost their feeling for freedom or become insensitive to oppression.

De Haas attaches the greatest importance to the mood reflected in the questions. If the international community is still asking questions, it is still trying to define the problem. His belief is that a problem understood is a problem solved. If the outside world is still struggling to understand, it is not yet ready to act against the humiliation of the black man.

But time, de Haas insists, is not on the side of the Afrikaner; history too is against him. The Afrikaner must consolidate his position now while the world still struggles to understand; he must act boldly and swiftly now while Free Africa is still weak and while the black people in South Africa are still struggling with their own problems of unification. Time after time he makes it clear that speedy action, decisive action, motivated action are the Afrikaner's only guarantee of survival in Africa. The Passes For Women Bill is conceived in the will to act.

The prime minister is impatient with those among his followers who do not feel driven by the sense of urgency which gives him no reason to be complacent. He handles his cabinet in the true style of the Voortrekker patriarch; he is the elected leader of Afrikanerdom and, for the time being, the guardian of its destiny. He wants to be involved as directly as possible in the decisions of everyone of his ministers, to accelerate movement in establishing permanent guarantees of security.

The debate in the Lower House on the Passes For Women Bill is not making the progress he would like. The stumbling block is not the English-oriented Unionist South African Party, whose hypocritical fulminations he can afford to ignore; it is the low rumblings in sections of the powerful Dutch Reformed Church and in the influential universities. Some academics question the desirability of rejecting morality in formulating racial policy. The most powerful of these are, of course, in UBRA. They have won over to their side half a dozen theologians who use devastating arguments on the morality of the Bill before parliament. Pierre van der Spuy is a theological giant at Stellenbosch, a power to reckon with in the Dutch Reformed Church, and an ardent advocate of segregation, like his friend, Dominie de Villiers of the Groot Kerk. He recognises the Bill as an index of Afrikaner decadence; as the sort of law a people losing faith in the God of its fathers will resort to, in the mistaken belief that they are building for security. Nobody ever dreams that Dr. van der Spuy might split the CNP or walk out of it. The greater the eminence attained by an Afrikaner in his community, the more difficult it becomes for him to act independently. Unlike the English or the Jew, he has no choice of worlds. And if he splits the CNP he might be punished harshly; Afrikanerdom does not treat dissent with much tolerance.

Dr. Sarel Badenhorst created a South African sensation when he wrote a book in Afrikaans to prove that segregation has no foundations in the scriptures.

He lost his job as a professor of divinity, was defrocked as an ordained minister of the Dutch Reformed Church and was eventually hounded out of the church. His bank, the *Vereenigde Volksbank* (the United People's Bank), suddenly found faults with the mortgage on his house and he ended up a broken man, economically and socially. He could not cross over to the English or Jewish side; he did not want to. He died in oblivion and liked it that way. It requires a courage which is almost superhuman for an Afrikaner to stand up against the tribe and few men in any race have that courage. If van der Spuy dares not split the CNP and therefore gives no press interviews, he can mobilise Afrikaner opinion in ways which could topple the leadership of de Haas. He has enough authority in the church and the universities to do this.

But this is not the prime minister's only headache. There are indications that the police are developing a political philosophy of their own. De Haas is convinced that Prinsloo's strategy in disarming the Valley Of A Thousand Hills and other Zulu reserves was dictated by weakness. The Afrikaner cannot afford to be caught or seen in any situation of weakness. Like all young societies, Afrikanerdom lacks self-confidence and is sensitive about its identity, security and everything which concerns the Afrikaner.

South Africa does not have television because this medium will show the Afrikaner naked before the Africans and expose the boils and chancres in wrong places. To conceal Afrikaner weaknesses and project the Afrikaner in the image of a hero and a conqueror is one of the guarantees of security which TV would smash. Prinsloo bungled things at this level. But then, Prinsloo is in a strong position; he enjoys the confidence of the minister in charge of the police while the minister is too valuable a member of the cabinet to be upset with demands for the transference of the Commissioner of Police to another department. De Haas once toyed with the idea of sending Prinsloo as South Africa's ambassador to Holland. The Minister of Justice would not hear a word about it. Well, he will think about it. Prinsloo is not to be trusted.

Problems for the prime minister do not come from his Afrikaners only. The Zulus have begun making ominous noises against the Bill. Both the police and the district commissioners in Natal had reported that the Zulus were not likely to be too deeply involved in campaigns against the Passes For Women Bill. Eager to please Prinsloo, the Natal police argued that the Zulus had not recovered from the shock they received when their guns were seized by the police. The white police in Natal, like the police everywhere in the land, relied on reports they received from the African police under them. Now, the press reports a rash of strikes in Natal. This is a bad sign.

The prime minister, like most Afrikaners, regards the Zulus as the curse God inflicted on South Africa. If there is one mistake which God ever made, it was to create the Zulus. Van Warmelo once called, he remembers, a conference of black leaders to discuss independence for the black reserves. The Zulus staged strikes which wrecked the conference; the black leaders said they did not want the "balkanised independence" offered by the prime minister.

So, if the Zulus withdraw their labour now, they can transform the Bill into an international issue; their example can produce strikes on the Witwatersrand. With a weak man at the top in the police force, it does not surprise the prime minister that the Zulus

215

have, as they say, begun walking barefooted against the Bill. The prime minister does not trust the Zulus even when they profess loyalty and he thinks those reports about Zulu non-involvement in demonstrations were fed by the Zulu police to their gullible English seniors; he dismisses the reports as part of the continuing treachery which the Zulus inherited from their ancestor, Dingane.

A miracle has taken place in the prime minister's health. The cardiac complaint which once worried him has cleared! His explanation for it is that God cured him so that he might lead Afrikanerdom through the dark valley into which it has been thrown by those powers which have abandoned the white supremacy philosophy. But his doctors quietly say that de Haas enjoys the exercise of authority and that this could explain the improvement in his health. For his part, the prime minister, always a demon for work, now works harder than he has ever done. To keep events under control he spends half of each week in Cape Town, piloting the Bill through parliament and half of it in Pretoria. He flies to the capital with his Minister of Justice, whom he has ordered to instruct the police to be on the look-out for strikes and strike-organisers.

*   *   *

Race and politics aside, the Dutch Reformed Church has an interest all its own in measures which do violence to morality. A revolt by the black people in the white-led churches is developing which threatens to crack the foundations of christian dogma and theology in South Africa. The Dutch Reformed Church supported the government's policy of corroding the influence of American, British, German, Hollander and Scandinavian missionaries in the black community. These upheld a theology which encouraged liberal attitudes to the race issue on both sides of the colour line and extended the area of the Afrikaner's isolation.

But the DRC was so determined to eradicate Western democratic teachings on the sovereignty of the person and the humanism which these emphasised in theology, it actively encouraged the government to give all possible latitude to the black separatist churches. The latter are interested in the church mainly as an instrument for social reform in the African community; they avoid political commitments and are not adequately equipped for active involvement in the polemics of race. Most of the African clergymen in white-led churches hold university degrees in theology or divinity.

Separatism has imparted a momentum to events which limits the appeal of white theology to the rank and file of the African people. In the old days, the largest black congregations in the urban areas were the Wesleyan Methodists and the Anglicans, both of which were of

216

British origin. The Anglicans, in particular, had produced a brilliant galaxy of black and white opponents of the government's racial policies and had given the world such famous white names as Arthur Blaxall, Trevor Huddleston, Ambrose Reeves and Michael Scott. Blaxall was a frail man with the courage of a whole pride of lions. Caught distributing funds among the dependents of the underground, Blaxall, then in his seventies, admitted openly that he had committed the crime, which is almost indistinguishable from aiding and abetting treason in South African law, and readied himself for a long jail sentence. His simple defence was that he had done what he believed Christ would have done had he lived in South Africa at the time.

The old fighter was ready to go to prison for the rest of his life if it pleased the rulers to do that and, in view of his age, even to die there if the government of the time wanted that. The government was not going to transform old Father Blaxall into a martyr; they freed him and allowed him to return to Britain where he subsequently died, mourned by thousands of African friends who admired his quiet determination to see that justice was done to all human beings, regardless of race.

In the situation which prevailed at the time, it was possible for the like-minded on both sides of the colour line to develop a communion of minds moving events toward an open society in which no person would be punished for being the child of his parents. The black theologians were involved in the massive black effort at the time to persuade white South Africa to accept the African's ideal of nationhood. This was the age of bridge-building across racial lines. As a result of government policy, these black bridge-builders are isolated from their white allies and, in the atmosphere which exists in the locations, feel free to address themselves to the fundamentals of the christian experience. They have evolved what they call Black Theology.

Father Mlawu Zama speaks for one of the most militant schools in the Black Theology movement. The Black Theologians are agreed on one basic premise: they are committed to a christianity that will have valid and relevant meaning in the African experience. Father Zama, an Anglican, takes the position that the dissection of God into the father, son and holy ghost categories leads to the use of race as a determinant of human categories and does violence to the sacredness of the person.

The *buntu* evaluation of the person has its roots in antiquity, Father Zama teaches; it is the larger truth which the Africans have been translating into experience down the millenia. In the eighteenth century among the Zulus, the Court Poet to Senzangakhona said the nation is a cluster of ideals in the process of becoming a larger ideal.

Shaka founded a nation on the *buntu* ideal, just as Mshweshwe did or as Palo had done before them. Shaka taught that to be a Zulu was a matter of commitment and had nothing to do with blood or parents; the Zulu was the person committed to weaving the cord of destiny, no matter what his sex or race or colour was. John Dunn had been an Englishman; Cetshwayo elevated him to the position of a provincial governor. If Dunn betrayed the trust, it was because the values of his culture did not give him much of a choice. The treachery was one more powerful argument why *buntu* missionaries should be trained in Africa and sent to Europe and America to civilise the white people and save them from self-defilement!

The Dutch Reformed Church adopts a hostile attitude to black theologians like Father Zama who, it says, are giving ideological symmetry to heathenism. By regarding the person as the source of all authority, some Afrikaner theologians charge, Father Zama and the black theologians who follow him are mortgaging mankind to sin. Theology and politics are so mixed up in South Africa there also are many Afrikaner students of divinity who are alarmed at the consensus of opinion at the level of fundamentals which has emerged in the black community in spite of the government's use of tribalism to separate the black people. The Africans insist that the race quarrel is a war of minds; a collision of ideals of fulfilment; they are evolving methods of struggle based on this evaluation of the race problem. Their attitudes to themselves and the white man are determined by this evaluation; so also, their goals, strategies and priorities.

The outside world does not understand all this; most people in Free Africa do not understand it either. This is not surprising. Black and white have been in contact for the longest time in Southern Africa. In that time the Africans have evolved a synthesis of cultural experiences which is not like anything black-white contact produced anywhere on the continent; the synthesis beats in terms of its own pulse and when it beats, it leaves most outsiders mystified; it leaves some saying the African has lost his feeling for freedom while others charge that he is stupidly patient. Some free Africans are so angry with the black South Africans they take it out on the refugees in their lands.

But the black South Africans insist that they are building for eternity; that they are laying the foundations for a nation which will one day make it impossible for any white man anywhere to punish any African for being the child of his parents. It is this insistence, whose implications create consternation in the Dutch Reformed Church, which convinces the Church and the government that black theology is subversive. Not one voice is raised in the DRC when the government bans Father Mlawu Zama . . . as a communist!

*   *   *

A war of minds involving black and white christians is an exceedingly complicated matter; everything is complicated where one side uses the *xina* principle while the other relies on the gun.

218

An idea cannot be killed with a bullet while there are physical limitations to the use of the gun. A balance in African-Afrikaner relations has developed which the government preserves by taking away with the left hand what it gives to the African with the right. Kritzinger calls it giving the illusion of freedom. Pretoria is beginning to be aware that the policy of encouraging tribalism defeats its own ends by stressing the universally valid principles of the *buntu* way of life. If this is producing a consensus of opinion in the black community which evokes identical responses to similar challenges, it enables the African not only to launch a frontal attack on the Afrikaner mind but also to confront the white people with an alternative to the status quo which depends, for its translation into reality, not on white support but on African initiatives.

At the roots of the black experience the differences which used to divide the rural people from the urban, the "tribal" communities from the locations, the educated from the unschooled, the christian from the pagan, the chiefs from the elected political leaders and the Basotho, Xhosa and Zulu from each other have begun to be blurred.

In each language group emphasis is on the jaws which belong together grinding together. Zamaism is bridging the gulfs which keep the separatist churches and the white-led apart. Church rallies organised across denominational lines attract thousands because they speak a language every African understands. *Ubuntu* and *umteto wesintu* have the same meaning in every language. At these gatherings, politics is avoided while emphasis is laid on *ubuntu* or *umteto wesintu* or the eternal person.

The Africans charge that when they stress the values of their own culture, they are doing precisely what the government has been saying they must do all these years; when they incorporate these in the christian experience, they are doing no more than the reformers in Europe did. The Dutch Reformed Church, they say, came into being because the christianity taught by Rome did not serve the best interests of some European peoples. This argument creates difficulties as much for the DRC as for the security police. Largely as a result, policy is not to declare war on the transformations taking place in the black christian community; it is to leave them free to release steam in the rallies and to act only when sedition or conspiracy or treason is established.

In the African community, self-defilement is almost indistinguishable from unforgivable sin. Even the vocally anti-white militants deny that they are racists and, to demonstrate that they have not been contaminated by the poison from the white side, have formed a united front with the Coloureds and the Indians. They argue that they use race as a vehicle for isolating the whites. However, something happens at a conference of Southern African students which gives the white community a traumatic shock. The African students first refused to sit in the same dining room with the whites and eventually pass a motion expelling the white delegations from the assembly. The black people have never treated the white people like this before.

This humiliation of the whites is noted by *Die Aanslag* which is alarmed to see the blacks put the white man in his place but tells the white students in so many words that the blacks served them right by kicking them in the teeth. Nobody is more concerned over the incident than Colonel Prinsloo, whose feared security police have collected enough information to convince him that the communists have nothing to do with the ferment in the black community; that what the white people are up against is a process of history. He flies to Durban and from there drives to Mkambati Reserve where Magagu Geja ka Bulube lives.

Chief Bulube, I have come to talk to you about the problems of our country; your country and mine. I have come as a concerned Afrikaner and not as a policeman. Some people in Pretoria, men highly placed in government, say the crisis in black-white relations is approaching the moment of decision. In the past, the gun settled everything for black and white. Some say this approach worked in the past, it would work now. Some say, like me, that you and the prime minister should meet and exchange views on a man to man basis. Nobody has given me any mandate to approach you. As chief of the police, I am free to investigate every aspect of security. I have children and I do not want them and yours to grow up looking to an appointment on the battlefield.

Don't you think the meeting would be a little premature?

Premature? After all the blood my people and yours have been shedding in the sixty years from Union? We had our Queenstown, Sharpeville and other shootings; but you also had your Cator Manor, Bashee Bridge and Paarl killings of whites.

Yes; premature. Your people are not as yet ready for a meaningful dialogue.

I could not agree more; but somebody, somewhere has got to start the process moving! Would you believe it if I told you that not one cabinet minister has ever spoken to an educated African? That not one Afrikaner member of parliament has ever heard of Dr. Seme? That very, very few Afrikaner academics have ever read any book or newspaper article written by an African? I admit, we do not know you. I think we should start knowing each other in order to talk to a mutually acceptable point. Please, do not misunderstand me, Chief; I'm not a liberal; I think those people are just a bunch of hypocritical sentimentalists. I love my people and I'm concerned with their future.

After a deep breath Bulube answers: In the sixty years since Union we have been developing an ideal of nationhood, acquiring an experience of nation-building and building a momentum for moving to our goal which your people do not possess.

We want to build a larger nation on the basis of our larger truth; you want a smaller nation founded on a smaller truth. I do not think there is much common ground for us there. We pleaded with the white man to accept our broader definition of nationhood for fifty years, to no avail. We have decided to proceed to our goal of a larger nation based on the larger truth by ourselves. We think the white man is not important for the purpose of establishing a union of the black peoples of Southern Africa. The only people who matter now are the Africans. If they agree to unite with us, we shall solve the race problem on our terms—in this country, in Rhodesia, in Mozambique and in Angola. Only when we have created the nation after our design would a dialogue be worthwhile.

But, don't you see where you are driving the whites? You force them to close their ranks; you drive them into the laager! Prinsloo is insistent.

Now, now! Colonel! They've never been out of the laager; the whites have always closed their ranks. When we were weak and divided, white unity bothered us; we stood alone then. Things have since changed. At last we speak one political language and have one alternative to the white man's closed society. Our priorities are fixed, no longer by what the whites do to us but by the changes taking place in the world.

We want to establish a satisfying place for ourselves in that world and we do not think the white people can or are able to do anything to help us reach our goal. But this does not mean that I would not want to meet the prime minister. There are things I would like to tell him about his administration which he probably does not know . . . .

*　*　*

The prime minister is in Pretoria these days. He exercises such control now that the Minister of Justice had to get his personal approval of the permit for the rally which African christians from many parts of the country plan to hold in Atteridgeville. The granting of the permit is a cosmetic designed to placate people like Dominie de Villiers and his friends. On this particular morning, the prime minister is at his desk. The clock has just struck nine.

People are always on their toes when the prime minister is in Pretoria; he demands hard work from everybody and sets the example. There are times when he starts work at seven in the morning. Most of his cabinet colleagues do not get to their desks before ten o'clock. They have too much time to waste, he says of them.

Piet van der Merwe, that model, always sees to it that he gets to the office at least half an hour before the prime minister's arrival. He enjoys doing this; he feels he is doing his duty in creating the desirable destiny for the Afrikaner. The prime minister is fond of Piet; a relationship almost like that between a father and his son exists

221

between the two men. In Cape Town, just before flying to Pretoria, he called Piet to his office.

Piet, you get on well with the diplomats from Malawi. Your head is in the right place and the stuff inside is good Afrikaner brains and not mud. I know; I can tell when there's mud in a young person's head. You have a future; one day, you could sit on my chair here. You have the heart and the brains to do it. But, by that time a new generation will be in charge in the black states. I often wonder if it would not be helpful to you to have a stint as our ambassador in Malawi. That place, you know, can be developed into our window on Africa! Only, I need you here, too. What would you do if you were in my position?

Meneer, all I live for is to serve my country and my people.

Well, you'll stay here for awhile yet, but someday you must go to the black states.

*   *   *

The church rally has attracted thousands of delegates from many parts of the country and the traders in Atteridgeville have never had it so good. Even the women who brave the winds, the heat and the cold of the plateau around the capital city grilling mealie cobs or sheeps' trotters on coal braziers on street corners are doing brisk business. In front of every family with children cold drinks are sold. The women's rally has been going on for three days and the police see nothing wrong with it. The third day is the last the delegates will be in the capital. The first item on the programme is a sunrise prayer meeting on a hill behind Union Buildings. About twenty thousand women join the procession to the meeting place and, after the prayers, the river of womanhood flows, not to Atteridgeville but straight to Union Buildings. Before police in sufficient numbers arrive, the women have surrounded the seat of government and are holding up posters demanding an interview with the prime minister, to whom they say they want to present a petition against the Passes For Women Bill.

Piet's uppermost thought is of the safety of de Haas. He races to the prime minister's office as the women's representatives enter the courtyard.

Meneer, the women have surrounded the place; what do you advise?

Tell them to get out of here and keep that damned door locked! Hear?

Piet hesitates for a while; he is not sure that twenty thousand angry black women can be told to clear out of Union Buildings and be obliging.

Did you hear what I said? I want no damned incidents here! Where's Kritzinger? Where's Prinsloo? Tell them to deal with those hordes and, for God's sake, lock that damned door!

222

That night the prime minister has a conference with the Minister of Justice, the Police Commissioner and Paul Kritzinger, who is in charge of the Pretoria police district. The temper of the phenomenon is in flames.

What I want to know, he bawls out, is how the women travelled from every part of the country, passed through the Witwatersrand to converge on Union Buildings without any policeman realising what they were up to!

With this, he bangs his hand on his desk, scattering the pages of the memorandum the Minister of Justice submitted earlier in the day and in which he gave a detailed report on the women's demonstration.

Prinsloo, I demand an explanation from you. I hear you have explanations.

Meneer, the problem has more fundamental origins than what appears to be police incompetence; it is part of the world-wide movement in which the black, brown and yellow races are coming into their own . . . .

I don't want to hear any more of that nonsense about fundamental contradictions in the white experience. I've heard enough of it from other people and what I've heard makes me sick!

The prime minister is too angry to want to listen to Prinsloo, whom he does not trust much, in any case, and whom he regards as a dangerous capitulationist.

Isn't there anybody in police headquarters with the brains to do one simple thing, in a simple way: to keep law and order?

That is being done, meneer; but we do not have enough police to watch every black man.

Why should you want to do that?

In their segregated areas the black people have evolved their own principle of unity. We told them to develop along their own lines. They are doing this to its logical extreme and have united themselves on what they call the *Buntu Ideal*.

Why did you allow them to do that?

That is a political question which calls for a political answer. Neither the police nor the army can shoot the *Buntu Ideal* out of existence. This is where christianity served our best interests; it corroded the *Buntu* philosophy. As I have had to point out to the prime minister on another occasion, the liberals and the communists are the putative and not the actual enemies of white civilisation. Like us, they are the products of the culture we inherited from the Greeks, the Romans and the Jews. Like christianity, they helped to corrode the *Buntu Ideal*. As long as the whites attacked the black philosophy from different angles, the blacks were not free to evolve strategies based on their own philosophy or to develop their own weapons. They fought on ground dictated by the white people, formed controllable coalitions with the whites and used weapons borrowed from us. It was always easier for us to deal with their continuing revolt then. Things have since changed. By separating them from the whites, we gave them the freedom to stand on their own feet and to attack from positions we did not know, using weapons we could not control. This circumstance leaves the police in situations of obvious weakness. Every black man has become either a rebel or a potential rebel and we need a policeman to keep an eye on every black person. With the disparity in black and white numbers, it can be seen that the police are being saddled with a task that is, strickly speaking, not theirs.

Capitulating! Is that what you are advising? That we give up?

No, Mr. Prime Minister. We are caught in what has become a war of minds. The question is whether or not old policies can cope with this development.

When the prime minister mentions the word capitulate, everybody knows that he has reached the limit of provocation. In his view, there is not an uglier crime which a white person can commit than to capitulate to the black or brown or yellow man. But Prinsloo is not the type of Afrikaner whose knees will quake when the phenomenon goes into tantrums. There are Africans, English and Coloureds who regard Prinsloo as an honest man who can be respected in his own right even when people disagree violently with his views. Like most Afrikaners, he certainly thinks in a rut; he sees men and events from the narrow horizons fashionable in his community. He differs from most Afrikaners, however, in that he is not averse to the idea of considering alternative guarantees of Afrikaner survival. If the Afrikaner cannot think in these terms, he argues, he is going to create for himself the type of situation in which the Jews are now caught in the Middle East; he will tie his resources to the demands of perpetual war in a hostile continent.

Kritzinger speaks after Prinsloo. While he agrees with Prinsloo on the value of christianity as an instrument for destroying the *Buntu Ideal*, he urges that the police should develop a programme for defusing the strikes. The prime minister nods approval although he is not sure in his mind if he understands everything implied in Kritzinger's proposal. When the meeting is over the phenomenon walks over to Kritzinger and asks him to stay when the others are gone.

What did you mean by the words "defusing the strikes?"

The strikers are putting us on the defensive in the eyes of the outside world. More police vigilance, I believe, would unearth crimes that would put the strikers on the defensive.

But nobody wants to hear anything in favour of the police . . . nobody in the outside world.

It depends on how things are done, Meneer. The world is crazy about the word freedom just now. The white man must consider the prospect of appearing to bend to the wind; he must go through the motions of freeing the black people without surrendering anything substantive.

Somebody in the United Nations will start screaming about fraud.

It depends on how the strikes are handled. If independence is offered as a response to the strikes, the United Nations will be forced to consider alternatives. The world could then be told that we are doing our best; the strikes would be seen to be a stumbling bloc to progress.

Smuts tried something like that and failed. Why can't the police do their work without going through the motions of capitulating?

Can you shoot the *Buntu Ideal* out of existence or otherwise destroy it without the help of the white missionaries, the liberals and the communists?

Why not? You can't shoot an idea, of course; but to kill it, you don't have to send the missionaries and the communists back into the reserves and the locations.

You can't stop the kaffers from breeding?

No. But what are you driving at?

Then, where do we go from where we are?

Why go anywhere at all? Stand firm where we are and keep our powder dry. That's what our ancestors did and that's what I propose to do. I never think of alternatives, for I know and want none. We have to be frank about these things. We have nothing to hide . . . .

The phenomenon stresses the last two words with the confidence of a man with no skeletons in any cupboards. He has lived for Afrikanerdom; the only thing he dreads in life is the humiliation of Afrikanerdom. His whole life has been devoted to the glorification of the Afrikaner and when he sees his people at the height of their power he is assured that everything he did and everything his people did was right because they could not be wrong; not with the destiny especially cast in heaven for them. Kritzinger lacks the assurance of the prime minister; he has many things to hide.

But, meneer, how long can we stand where we are? We have the gun to-day; what if the kaffers have it to-morrow? Angola and Mozambique are now free. What if the black people pool their uranium resources and get some crazy communist to teach them how to manufacture a portable nuclear bomb with a limited explosive capability? Such a weapon could blow a whole factory, a whole block of buildings out of existence . . . .

Kritzinger, you worry too much about dangers which do not exist.

The black people, in common with the brown and the yellow races, are in the majority in the world and control most of its natural resources. One day they might become better trading partners of the West than we are.

So what?

It's something to think over, meneer.

Well, Kritzinger, if you want to know how I feel about these things . . . . Let me tell you again, as I have done on many other occasions. I keep my guns oiled. I'll shoot for as long as I am able. If God created us for final destruction, I want to see the Afrikaner go down fighting; every Afrikaner! Capitulate? Never!

I'm not for capitulation, meneer; I would create an illusion of freedom and offer it as a reality and justify the offer and then oil my guns.

He looks at his watch, then says quietly, Meneer, the old girl at the house will start worrying.

Alright, friend, you may go. . . .

The prime minister stretches out his right hand to Kritzinger. He is not sure if he understands fully what the chief of the Pretoria police district was trying to tell him. *Offer an illusion and justify it?* What does that mean in concrete terms, he is asking himself. It sounds like a statement of a fundamental truth; it is so pregnant with meaning it has to be turned over a thousand times in one's mind before its implications are clear. But that is the beauty of having a policeman with an expansive mind. If the phenomenon does not understand the signals Kritzinger has been sending, he is happy there is at least one policeman with the mind which can cope with anything from the English, the Jews, the liberals and, of course, the communists. If these groups could be cut off from all contact with the African people, the strikes could sooner or later be controlled.

* * *

XIX. Memorandum To Free Africa

Amanga neqiniso kawahlangani.

(Lies and the truth do not go well together.)

If de Haas dislikes the Hollanders intensely, a fact he never tires of emphasising in conversations with his friend and confidante, Paul Kritzinger, he has an incurable distrust for the Americans. Not exactly without reason, some of the wealthy English in Parktown quietly say. De Haas provides all the inflated investments from South Africa and all the thanks he receives from the Americans are kicks in the teeth for disciplining a few million niggers. De Haas confesses to Kritzinger that he never knows what the Americans are up to when they visit his country; they have been corrupted by liberalism and lost their sense of racial pride. A white American will not hesitate to enter South Africa to spy on the whites for the black people. De Haas tells his friend that he has his own views on what goes on in the American embassy.

As a rule, foreign diplomats are not allowed to enter an African location or a rural reserve without a permit. It is a crime for any non-African to enter any African area without a permit. In spite of these precautions, the American diplomats move in and out of African areas whenever they want to. Not without reason, the Africans quietly say. They want to see the conditions in which their investments operate. Everybody knows the Americans do these things; what galls de Haas is that they do it in such a way that it is impossible to catch them in the act. The smart boys in the security police have produced the theory that after sunset the American diplomats paint their faces black and enter the locations in the dark. De Haas is inclined to believe anything against the Americans and worse against the Hollanders. Kritzinger dismisses the security police theory as palpable nonsense.

At no time has the prime minister been annoyed more intensely by the nose-poking of the Americans than at present. Jona Masondo was a policeman in Benoni. He was a little less than thirty years of age with a young wife and a month-old baby. The three lived in Benoni location. One night the police raided the location; a young African shoved an *intshumentshu* between Masondo's ribs near the spinal column. Masondo did not die; his right side was paralysed and he spent months in hospital. His condition did not improve and shortly after being discharged from hospital he was endorsed out of the location because he had lost his productive potential. Like his late father, Masondo had been born in a location; endorsement meant that he had to be sent to a rural reserve in Natal which he did not know, and to live among total strangers.

The white experts of the Native Affairs Department discovered that the name Masondo belonged to the Nyambose clan. Jona was transported to the Nyambose reserve where his condition deteriorated until he died. That brought the pittance called a pension to an end. The amount had barely been enough to keep body and soul together among the three members of the Masondo family. The child's health broke down. Hunger dried up its mother's breasts. Day after day the baby would cry until it was hoarse, as its flesh shrank and the bones protruded. The one thing Masondo's wife could not survive was the vacant, hungry and accusing stare in the baby's eyes. She prayed hard, shed scalding tears and made herself a nuisance at the local police station or the native commissioner's office asking for assistance. Nothing availed. One night she sprayed her blankets with paraffin, wrapped herself and her baby in them and set them on fire.

The tiny mound which marks the grave of the woman and her baby has become something very much like a shrine. Students from different parts of the Natal province visit the grave. Magagu Geja kaBulube has visited it, too. Talking to an American journalist one day, he explains the pilgrimage in these terms:

I have never known a more powerful demonstration against race oppression. With people like these, the white man cannot say he has conquered the African . . . .

The American looks puzzled.

But Chief, the woman is dead? Who's the winner?

The protester. The world did not understand why we in the rural reserves rejected the independence offered us by the government. Masondo's wife spoke for us with an eloquence nobody can mistake.

Subsequently, the journalist sneaked quietly into the Nyambose reserve, took photographs and made a film which he later showed to his people in the United States. The American papers are full of the Nyambose pictures and the film has become a TV hit. If faces are red every day in the Department of the Interior, which grants visas, the Masondo protest is taken deeply to heart in Free Africa where a new generation of leaders is leaving the universities.

Unlike the first generation of liberators, these young men and women are hostile to the old guard's acceptance of white definitions of the race problem in South Africa and reject the strategies adopted in the last twenty-five years to corrode race humiliation. The old guard which leads Free Africa regarded democracy, one-man-one-vote, race equality, equal pay for equal work and the abolition of the pass laws as the solution to South Africa's race problem. The underlying assumption was that the integration of the African in a white-oriented society was something to live for. The old leaders ran around the world and shouted themselves hoarse in the United Nations in campaigns to smash race oppression with the might of the conference resolution!

Year in and year out the halls of the United Nations and every other international assembly reverberated with their denunciations of white domination. The humiliating defeats suffered have exhausted the energies of the old guard and soured some of its attitudes to the black people of South Africa, whom it accuses of not fighting with the determination which events demand. It is not unusual for the old guard in the press, the universities, and in politics, to declaim against the black South Africans for what is believed to be their failure to fight white domination the right way. It is not unusual to find these people releasing their frustrations on the refugees from South Africa whom they now attack as parasites who will sponge on Free Africa and fight for liberty with their arses on swivel chairs in the capitals of Free Africa.

The refugees, in most cases, complicate their own position when they attack the new leaders of their people who have accepted the white challenge, redefined the race problem and are establishing a dual authority situation right under the nose of the CNP. There is intense anger among the leaders on the homefront who regard themselves as being in the front line; they resent the attacks made on them by some refugees who lecture them on how to fight white domination from the safe positions guaranteed by foreign flags. The leaders inside South Africa charge that the present generation of their people has given them the mandate to redefine the race problem and evolve appropriate strategies to crush white domination. They are not inclined to pay much attention to refugees whom they regard as having diminishing mandates—that is, mandates valid before Sharpeville.

The rising generation of Free Africans is concerned about these quarrels, which it regards as expressions of the frustration caused by unresearched definitions of South Africa's crisis of colour. It acknowledges that to fight for borrowed ideals, using borrowed weapons on ground chosen by the enemy is a sure invitation to defeat. The young leaders argue that the failure of Free African campaigns against white domination in Southern Africa in general and in South Africa in particular springs from inadequate clarity on the black people's real goals. In 1912 they rejected the ideal of nationhood adopted by the whites and did the same at the Umtata Conference in 1973. Free Africa, the argument continues, should pause and make itself better informed on the real goals of the African people in South Africa.

The young leaders in Free Africa proceed to demand that the black people in South Africa should be taken as they are and not as they should be; that while the urges which motivate thought and action among them are the same as those in Free Africa, their experience has about it a uniqueness which makes the war of minds a conflict with no parallels in the rest of the continent. Some, in particular those who had their education in South Africa, demand that the Committee for the Co-ordination of Resistance in Southern Africa, which has its offices somewhere in Central Africa, should recast its whole strategy against white domination.

They urge the establishment of direct contact with the Africans in the front line in Southern Africa. The Committee eventually contacts Magagu Geja kaBulube with the request that he should furnish it with information on why the Africans reject the "independence" offered them and why de Haas regards the passing of the women's Pass Bill as a moment of fulfilment for himself and why the Africans oppose it. Further, the Committee requests Magagu to advise it on how it might best help the Africans on the homefront in their struggle against white domination.

This is a new and welcome departure in the attitude of the Committee. In the past, it had adopted the agitatorial approach to the race question in Southern Africa and had defined freedom in terms of slogans borrowed from the white side; it had spoken of African social-ism, African humanism and the like. The weapons used to move events to these goals had been borrowed from the whites. Political parties had been formed and resistance movements organised along white lines and strikes and boycotts launched on white bases to make white supremacy expensive to maintain. When the Africans in South Africa showed little enthusiasm for these methods, they were told that these strategies had brought independence to Free Africa and would work in South Africa. The victims of white domination had turned inward to themselves and proceeded to evolve their own strategies and to define their own goals. While the African states gave to freedom a meaning taken over from the white side, they almost went on their knees every year begging the white nations to act against the white minorities in Southern Africa.

The Committee could not help using borrowed weapons against white domination in Southern Africa. The countries which supported it had given to freedom a meaning which split their peoples into capitalists, communists, social democrats, liberals, christians and atheists precisely in the way the white peoples had divided themselves in Europe and the Americas. At this point, the old guard had not given to freedom a meaning that would satisfy in African conditions; they wanted to have what the white man had; he was their exemplar, their paragon of excellence. How could they hope to win against him if he still did the thinking for them, the new generation asked.

The new Africans attached importance to Seme's theory of civilisations in collision. They took note of Bulube's view that while the dominant conflicts between capitalism and communism took place within the framework defined by the Graeco-Romano-Hebraic evaluation of the person, the main ideological quarrels of the twenty-first century would be between the *Buntu* evaluation of the person and the one evolved by the Greeks, the Romans and the Hebrews.

The crisis of colour in Southern Africa, the new leaders continue, is a decisive climacteric in the global revolution which will determine the relations between black and white in the twenty-first century.

Because of its importance in this regard, the race quarrel in Southern Africa has begun to be seen in different light by some people in Free Africa. Importance is attached, no longer to the exertion of pressures to force the whites to make more concessions, but to African definitions of the race problem, to African alternatives to the status quo in Southern Africa and to agreement by the black people on final goals. This change in the mood of the young people finds expression in the request from the Committee for a statement of the African's case by people in the front line against white domination.

Bulube prepares a long memorandum which, he hopes, will enable the peoples of Africa to see the race quarrel in South Africa from an altogether different perspective. He prefaces his remarks with the statement that race discrimination, colour prejudice or segregation are the by-products of the effort men have been making in the last six or seven hundred years to find a way by which black and white could live together on the basis of the Graeco-Romano-Hebraic ideal of fulfilment. The effort failed because it rejected the validity of the African's evaluation of the person and denied its legitimacy. Because the whites had the gun, they sought to impose the Graeco-Romano-Hebraic outlook on the Africans.

Slavery, colonialism, segregation and South Africa's racial policies have all been attempts to establish the permanence of the imposition while the slave revolts, African nationalism and the attacks on white policies in Southern Africa are vindications of the unifying *Buntu Ideal* which gives meaning to life in Sub-Saharan Africa.

If the race quarrel is seen as a collision of conflicting philosophies, the obvious way out is for wise men on both sides of the colour line to reconcile the conflicting perspectives. Then, and then only, can black and white work together to evolve programmes which will give to life and freedom a meaning that will satisfy on both sides in the conditions which exist in South Africa, Free Africa and the rest of the world.

Bulube warns Free Africa to take note of the inner dynamics of race conflict. There has been a fundamental switch in government strategy for the perpetuation of white domination. Where, before, emphasis was on the white man remaining master, stress is now laid on independence for the black reserves. The change has come about because of the African's continuing revolt on the one hand and, on the other, Free African and other pressures. Pretoria has decided to react to these pressures by offering the Africans the shadow of freedom and not its substance. When the Africans reject the offered independence, they refuse to accept the shadow.

Some Afrikaners are concerned about the state of black-white relations, just as some white liberals are. But both have one fatal weakness: they have illusory power and not the real power that the CNP and de Haas have. To form alliances with them or to strike deals with them might have immediate tactical advantages only where there is agreement on the African definition of nationhood. The liberals, like the communists and UBRA, reject this definition. In this setting, the African does not have much of a choice; as Sobukwe often put it, he has to learn the habit of "going it alone" on the homefront.

The change in government strategy calls for corresponding changes in Free African strategies. Where, before, stress was on race equality, emphasis should now be laid on a geopolitical alternative; Free African resources should be mobilised to confront Pretoria with this alternative. The CNP government should be put under pressure in the Organisation of African Unity, the United Nations and everywhere else in the world, to define the term *independence*; to state in the clearest terms possible the type of freedom it offers the victims of its policies. Among other advantages, this approach will reinforce the black people's demands in South Africa. It would also lay the foundations for a co-ordinated strategy involving the segregated administrations, the OAU and the United Nations.

Bulube makes it clear that the Afrikaner has demonstrated that he is incapable of providing the quality of leadership which will give a satisfying meaning to life among the blacks and the whites. It is the business of the African to assume leadership, which he has done, to create the situations to which the Afrikaner will be forced to respond and to seize the initiative to influence events to goals chosen and determined by the historical owners of the land: the black people. If the Afrikaner does not want to live in societies where perspectives have been reconciled, he is always free to clear out of Africa and go to white countries to live among people who have his skin colour. But if he wants to live in Africa, he must do the things that are done in Africa. Otherwise he is going to create a climate of thinking which will force the black peoples to gang-up against him and work for his ultimate expulsion from Africa.

The white skin alone will not help him much in the final analysis because while Europe and America are white countries, they are more interested in the metals, the oil and other resources owned by the black, brown and yellow races. They will support the Afrikaner only as long as it serves their interests to do this and when their economies necessitate the accommodation of the African, Europe and America will come to terms with the African. Free African policy would be helpful if it developed a way of controlling African resources which will respond to this prospect on the one hand and, on the other, take advantage of the peculiar relationship into which history threw Africa, the Americas and Western Europe.

Bulube points out that where the race quarrel was seen no longer as a mere collision between biological incompatibles and where it was seen as a clash between conflicting evaluations of the person, emphasis would no longer be on reforms; it would be on building up the African's control of his resources inside South Africa, on co-ordinating his strategies with Free Africa and other forces working for freedom in the world. It would be necessary for Free Africa to create new polarisations in the United Nations on the race quarrel and to confront the Security Council with alternatives it cannot ignore. He warns against the assumption which has gained ground in Free Africa that South Africa's black people will be freed by Free Africa.

As the history of the blacks shows, it is they and they alone who will free themselves; their allies, supporters and friends can only help create the conditions in which victory can come sooner, on terms dictated by the African. Free Africa is not doing the black South Africans a favour when she fights race domination; she is defending the honour of the black race as a whole, where every person of African descent is punished simply because there is African blood in his veins. This is the insult Free Africa must wipe off the face of the continent, regardless of whether or not the Africans in South Africa are free.

If the race problem is seen from the perspectives just outlined, Bulube continues, Free Africa will reinforce the leadership initiatives now being asserted in South Africa instead of asking the white powers to help the United Nations bring about change in South Africa. This background, Bulube explains, provides the setting in which the Passes For Women Bill must be seen. The measure is important, not so much because it limits the freedom of movement for the African woman but because it shows how African labour-power, Afrikaner political dominance and English control of the economy are manipulated to preserve white domination and provide the inflated profits for foreign investors in America, Western Europe and Japan.

The manipulation has created a peculiarly revolutionary situation in the labour-political-financial balance. African policy and diplomacy seek to smash the balance while white policy and diplomacy set out to preserve it. Contradictions have arisen in the conflict which move events to a head-on collision between the united black administrations and the white government.

The white attempt to expel increasing numbers of Africans from the "white" areas into the rural reserves (which can no longer carry their present populations and which are so overcrowded they do not have enough land to produce their own food) is the dynamite which is sure to explode into a conflagration that might hurl black and white into a bloody fight.

The rural administrations are preparing themselves for the

moment of decision; they have formed themselves into a united front and have decided to co-ordinate their policies and actions. When the collision comes, they want to withdraw their labour simultaneously from white industries and paralyse the South African economy; they want to act jointly in refusing to accommodate any more expellees from the white areas; they want, in short, to keep the Afrikaner in the cleft stick he has created for himself.

This sets the Pass Bill in perspective. In the old days, it was beneath the dignity of a self-respecting Afrikaner son of his father to humiliate himself and venture into industry and commerce, which, besides, were dominated by the English and the Jews. Agriculture was the Afrikaner's traditional field. So much importance was attached to it, it continues to this day to be the main determinant of white policy in many walks of life. For example, the parliamentary voting system for members of South Africa's all-white parliament is a case in point. It operates in ways which ensure that the legislature is dominated by the rural, mainly agricultural, areas.

After the Anglo-Boer war of 1899-1901 the influx of the Afrikaners into the cities began in earnest. A new class of worker emerged who saw fulfilment in narrowly racial terms but who belonged no longer to rural society but to the cities. He was followed by the Afrikaner entrepreneur, who first pursued aggressively nationalistic economic policies because gold placed him in the position of a seller to the world. Since then, leading economists have been warning that gold should no longer be regarded as the backbone of the country's economy. These warnings have produced changes which cast African-Afrikaner relations in an altogether new mold.

On the one hand there is growing uncertainty about gold continuing to be a vehicle of international monetary exchange. If the nations finally reject gold, South Africa would lose some of the political pressure the production of the precious metal gives her. On the other hand the mineral's depletion in the not-so-distant future constitutes a problem which calls for immediate action.

Government policy now emphasises the development of manufacturing as the new backbone of the economy. This throws the Afrikaner out of his traditional isolationism, right into the maelstrom of international commerce; he finds himself exposed to international pressures against which agriculture and gold protected him. He finds himself increasingly dependent on foreign lands for investment capital, expertise and markets. At the same time a new balance of power is emerging in the world. The whites have lost their dominance; the centre of gravity in international affairs has shifted from the North Atlantic to the Indian Ocean, which is the centre of the non-white world.

Different trading blocs have emerged and each of them sees fulfilment in terms of its own interests. The Western Europeans have joined forces in the European Economic Community while the socialist lands of Eastern Europe have established their own trading club. China and Japan are exploring the possibilities of a Far Eastern bloc. The Americans are kicking Japan so violently in the teeth each time they are in trouble they leave Tokyo with no alternative other than to establish an independent economic and political position of her own in the world. This has profound implications for black-white relations. It means that Japan might eventually change her attitude to nuclear weapons and decide to become a nuclear power. The world would then have three non-white nuclear states which have a vested interest in the destruction of white arrogance in the conduct of international affairs. But this is not the only red light history is flashing before the Afrikaner.

The Arabs have decided to use their oil as a political weapon against the Jews and in doing this have shown that for the time being at least they possess and control a weapon more powerful in its effects on the international community than the combined nuclear arsenals of all the super-powers. The Afrikaners are particularly uneasy about the growth of Arab unity and power. If they can turn the whole world upside down by withholding their oil what would stop the Free Africans from developing a similar unity and one day using their metal and other mineral resources as political weapons against South Africa's racial policies? What would stop the Arabs transforming themselves into a nuclear power, now that they have enough money from their oil?

Nobody can stop the proliferation of nuclear powers. Who, for example, would blame the Japanese if they agreed to build up Arab nuclear power in return for oil? What would stop the Africans from developing nuclear weapons or buying these with their metals? A combination of non-white trading blocs, the emergence of China and Japan as nuclear powers, the Arab use of oil and the Africans' employment of metals and minerals as political weapons—all these would create a balance of power in the Indian Ocean which would place the Afrikaner in a weak bargaining position with Europe and the Americas.

Whatever the Afrikaner did, for example, he could, because of his numbers alone, never be a very significant factor in American and West European trade. His next bargaining point is the strategic importance of Cape Town on the sea route between the East and Western Europe and North America. If the Africans could create a state that would straddle the southern part of the continent they would reduce Cape Town's strategic value. Bulube stresses this factor in formulating Free African policies.

For the Afrikaner, these changes mean that each year sees his power to bargain with the powers of the West decline; this weakness leaves him with cruelly limited options. To count on continuing Western support he has to transform South Africa into an attractive investment field. He can do this only by tightening his already rigid control of every department of the African's life and this is where the passes for women come in. In the old days, when gold was the backbone of the economy and agriculture the pillar of racial politics, the white man needed to control the labour of the males and only African men carried the passes. First introduced in the Cape by the British to control cheap African labour which was to substitute slave labour after the emancipation of the slaves originally imported from the Dutch East Indies, the pass to-day determines the position of the African in every walk of life from birth to the grave.

The laws presume him to be a criminal until he produces his pass to prove he is not. The document has transformed the Africans into a caste which lives only to serve the interests of the white man. Race and colour fix the membership of this class and establish the position of the African in South African society. This position is always at the bottom. Its permanence is guaranteed by the race laws, the police and the army. The pass is important because it translates a given philosophy into action. The African's creative and productive potentials are presumed to be the private property of the white man.

The African does not sell his labour, which he does not own; he exchanges it for a wage determined by those who own it. This wage is designed to keep him productive for the longest time possible. To extort maximum advantage from this possession, the white man must control its supply, distribution, use and disposal. The pass, like the law, the police and the army, is an instrument of control; it prescribes the place where the African shall be born, live or die to serve white interests.

If he is to be employed in agriculture and the mines, he must, as a rule, be born in the rural reserves where white policy deliberately keeps the population density at an average of about 117.2 per square mile in order to create the extremes of overcrowding, hunger and deprivation which will force the African to leave the reserve and work for the whites for wages designed to inflate profits for investors in agriculture and mining.

If he is to serve industry, commerce and in domestic service, he must be born in a location which is laid out in a convenient place outside every white city. As in the rural reserve, conditions of extreme poverty, hunger and deprivation are created to force the African to leave the location by day in order to produce wealth for the white man. As in the rural reserves, the pass regulates his movements in such a way that every white city is provided with adequate supplies of cheap labour. The pass determines his movements between where he is born or where he lives and where he works. It is a crime for him to be outside of the area where the pass says he should be at any given moment of his life. If one of his parents dies in Johannesburg where they live, which is about forty or fifty miles from Pretoria where he might be living himself, and he attends the funeral, any policeman might stop him, demand his pass and arrest him if he does not have it on his person.

He must not and cannot be free; it is a crime for him to be free from the pass.

Once the child of his parents reaches the age of 18 and becomes productive in the eyes of the law, it becomes a crime for him to live with his parents in their home without the permission of the location superintendent. It is a crime for an African from outside to enter a location without a permit or to remain in it for longer than 72 hours without the permission of the white authority. Any African can be "endorsed" out of any location, that is, he can be expelled from it if he is not employed. This means that an African's elderly parents may not live with him unless he has the permission to have them in his house. Sometimes children under 18 are endorsed out of the location because the law says they are not productive and have no right to be in a location, even when their parents live there. The expulsion is intended to reduce the costs of maintaining the location, although a substantial proportion of these is borne by the African in the form of rents, taxation and the fines paid for the infringement of the many Pass Laws.

The African who carries a pass may not be paid the same wage as the whites, the Coloureds or the Indians who, in turn, are paid according to different rates. He may not organise trade unions of his own or join those organised by the whites. If he has to negotiate with his employers he has to form staff associations or organisations according to firms. This enables him to negotiate with his immediate employer and not with the industry. Different employers in the same industry, in the same city, sign different agreements with different staff associations. In this way, the managers can easily weed out the agitators whom the police readily endorse out of the city. The system enables the managers to pay the wages they like and to collect inflated profits. The same principle applies in agriculture, where the African is obliged by law to work for six months every year for the white farmer on whose land his family resides to cover rent, grazing and tilling rights. During the next six months he might seek employment in an urban area. The pass enables the farmer to keep track of his movements in the city and tells the police when the period for his employment in the city has expired, when he must be endorsed out of the urban area.

The conditions created by the pass system call for the continuous tightening of race segregation in order to preserve the caste system and ensure that the whites enjoy their high standard of living and have enough to pay the high profits with which to bribe American, West European and Japanese investors into conniving at the violence white policies do to the person of the African. It is a condition of Afrikaner dominance that these profits should be as high as possible in order to buy the conscience of foreign investors who, in turn, exert leverage on their governments against decisive world action against race discrimination.

This circumstance, however, leaves the Afrikaner in the grip of a tragic and cruel vice. In order to be able to purchase the conscience of the foreign investors who subsidise his political dominance and placate the English who control the economy on the homefront he has forever to damage his personality by imposing a brutally inhuman tyranny on the African. As the Africans say, he has to fulfil himself in self-defilement. This leaves him a prisoner of those who protect him against attacks in the United Nations, for example.

African policy, Bulube points out, also has to take into account this weakness of the unliberated Afrikaner. In this setting the Afrikaner is only a political manager of an estate he does not own. Historically, the land belongs to the African while capital is owned by the English and foreigners; the Afrikaner owns nothing, other than that which he holds by the sheer force of arms.

But there is no guarantee that what he holds will be his forever. The day is not far when the Africans will have the guns and when they will restore to themselves what was seized from them at the point of the gun. If the Afrikaner can yield no ground, it is because he has none to concede; if he cannot give anything, it is because he owns nothing; he has nothing to give. Thus, when he tries to give freedom to the Africans in the reserves, they turn their backs on him and reject it because whatever he gives cannot be other than hollow, meaningless and of no value. The dilemma creates cataclysmic frustrations in the Afrikaner psyche. It is these which make de Haas a phenomenon and go a long way to explain the Afrikaner's peculiar preoccupation with race and his anger with the outside world. It galls the Afrikaner to find himself treated as the polecat of international affairs and attacked by those very countries whose system of economy he upholds and to provide profits for whom he commits himself to perpetual self-defilement.

The switch to manufacturing creates additional headaches for the Afrikaner. Agriculture and mining swallow up so much cheap African labour the commodity is, strictly speaking, scarce in South Africa. Without it, however, there can be no inflated profits and virtually no bargaining power for the Afrikaner. One solution, taken from the days of British rule, like the pass, is the importation of workers willing to accept low wages. These come from Botswana, Lesotho, Malawi, Mozambique and Swaziland. In the old days they were imported from as far afield, sometimes, as Angola, Zambia and Rhodesia. As a result the African population in the major industrial areas often has communities from as far afield as Angola, Botswana, Lesotho, Malawi, Mozambique, Namibia, Rhodesia, Swaziland and Zambia. The poverty of countries like Botswana, Lesotho, Malawi and Swaziland is still so great thousands of their black citizens are allowed to enter South Africa every year where they prefer to suffer all the humiliations that go with the black skin only to eke out a living.

This practice reduces the black states of Southern Africa to the status of human stud farms where, as in the locations and the reserves, cheap labour is produced and bred to serve South African mines, industries and farms. In this setting, the governments of the labour-exporting countries function as the business managers of the stud farms. This creates endless debates and serious conflicts in the assemblies of the Free Africans where collaboration with South Africa is assumed to be almost indistinguishable from treason to Africa.

The Afrikaner's weaknesses force him to take advantage of the conflicts both to neutralise Free African hostility to Pretoria's racial policies and to create the goodwill South Africa must have in order to sell her products freely in African markets. She has come out with a brand-new foreign policy for Africa. In the locations it is known derisively as the *New-Look Policy*. South Africa tells all with ears to hear that she wants to make friends with the black states of Africa; that she has plenty of money for aid and to reinforce the New-Look Policy and give it additional appeal she beams especial broadcasts to East, Central and West Africa. The line taken in these is that South Africa is moving her black peoples toward freedom in separate states; that she needs time in which to do this and that she would like the opportunity to have a dialogue with the Free Africans for the purpose of co-ordinating action against common problems. The broadcasts create a type of confusion in Free Africa which encourages splits in the black ranks on how to destroy white domination. The geopolitical alternative, Bulube points out, is designed, not only to unify and consolidate the revolt against white domination in Southern Africa, but also to bridge the gulfs which the New-Look Policy has created.

South Africa devotes a lot of time and energy and spends a lot of money on propaganda in Free Africa not only for political reasons but because she genuinely needs the goodwill of the Free Africans who could be her best customers. At one time she almost succeeded in persuading Tsiranana, a former president of Malagasy, to establish a diplomatic mission in Pretoria and to allow South African investors to build factories in Malagasy and manufacture goods they could sell to Free Africa. Tsiranana received large sums of money for development purposes. The students got wind of the plan, stirred up the workers and the two blew Tsiranana's plan to pieces. As if to rub salt into the wounds, the regime which succeeded Tsiranana's borrowed money from Peking to repay the loan Tsiranana had raised from South Africa! Pretoria regards Free Africa as South Africa's natural market. Every Free African capital south of the Sahara is within a day's flight from Johannesburg. Distance alone would give South Africa a virtual monopoly in the markets of Africa. The Free Africans, however, tend to be fastidious customers; they insist on the abandonment of South Africa's racial policies before they can do real business with Pretoria.

Van Warmelo tried to solve this problem by offering the reserves independence. The Free Africans seemed impressed by the New-Look Policy at the time it was formulated; they even told South Africa that before coming to them for exchanges of views on common problems, she should have a dialogue with her own black people. Van Warmelo was delighted; he started consolidating some of the reserves into larger blocs, when the Africans blew his policy to pieces by rejecting the independence he offered them. Since then, the New-Look Policy has been encountering heavy weather in parts of Free Africa.

Bulube tells the Committee that the deadlock on "balkanised independence" cannot be broken or the race problem solved by agitating for reforms in the present power-structure. The white man set up this structure for his convenience and not to serve the African. For the black people to see fulfilment in integration in the power-structure is to define the African's destiny in terms dictated by the white minority. And, in any case, the Afrikaner, who is the majority group among the whites, is psychologically not as yet ready for a major readjustment of attitudes on the race question.

In this setting, the answer to the challenge of colour is to confront him with a geopolitical alternative and unite the black peoples of a partitioned South Africa with the Africans of Angola, Botswana, Lesotho, Malawi, Mozambique, Namibia, Swaziland, Zambia and Zimbabwe. Together, these people, who number about 60,000,000 blacks and who are bound together by bonds of race, culture and marriage, would together form the largest, wealthiest and most powerful nation in Africa. By straddling the continent from the Indian Ocean and the Atlantic, they would control the approaches to Cape Town and reduce its strategic value. Powers like America and the Western European countries would take note of that. A balance of black-white power would be created in which no white man would ever again punish an African for being the child of his parents; no crazy white would dare to bomb unarmed Zambian villages, either.

In a world of proliferating giant-nations, the Africans should see their future from the perspective of giant-nations. The beauty of the geopolitical alternative, Bulube adds, is that it needs acceptance only by the Africans in order to become a political reality; no white man need be asked to change his views or to make concessions or to integrate any African in his society or to give freedom.

Bulube's critics charge that his solution is too idealistic for Africa where tribalism continues to be a fact of black life. Bulube concedes that tribalism is an African problem but points out that it has become a divisive factor largely under the impact of white influences which split men into categories. Christianity, capitalism and the white man's schools transformed human groups into separate islands and stressed individualism. With his sense of community disintegrating, the African clung to every straw which he believed could save him. Tribalism assumed an importance it rarely ever had as a creed of black salvation. The whites used it to set the African lingual groups against each other; the stratagem worked. It made possible the carving up of

Africa into colonies owned by the whites. After independence it brought to power men who saw little beyond the narrow goals the lingual groups set themselves. The same trick is being tried out in South Africa.

This, Bulube continues, calls for co-ordinated action. Africa is only at the beginning of the rebirth into a new destiny. The lingering stress on tribalism weakens Free Africa for effective involvement in Southern Africa or in the solution of problems like the Sahel tragedy or in the exploitation of Africa's resources in ways which will benefit the peoples of Africa. The answer to these problems is for Africa to turn inward, to the essence of *ubuntu* and explore herself ruthlessly in the bid to attain clarity on the truths which have enabled her children to endure so much for so long.

When these truths are known, the synthesis of ideas produced by contact with the white man will project *ubuntu* as the durable ideal which enabled the Africans to survive slavery, colonialism and negrophobia; *ubuntu* will be seen as the basis of unity for which Africa has searched in the last thousand years. People might then speak Woloff or Hausa or Yoruba or Swahili or Shona or Zulu; they might have different customs—all these differences will no longer matter. The important thing will be the fact that the experiences of the Woloff, the Hausa, the Yoruba, the Kikuyu, the Shona or the Zulu will each be seen as a translation of the *Buntu Ideal* into satisfying social action in different environments. When the peoples of Sub-Saharan Africa see themselves from the *ubuntu* perspective, they will be ready for the unity they desire. When the *Buntu Ideal* comes into its own, tribalism will wilt away and cease to be a factor of political significance.

Africa needs this unity in order to give effective reinforcement to the black people in Southern Africa where the Africans realise that freedom, like power, is seized and never given. To press for mere reforms is to legalise the thievery by which the Africans lost what belonged to them. That is why they reject the independence offered them in the reserves. But their power to resist is limited by Free Africa's inability to give decisive support on the international plane.

There would, Bulube warns, be no point in Free Africa committing herself to the liberation of the South when the people in the African states were not free. The people who must help Southern Africa must themselves be truly free. The freedom which Free Africa has still has meaning in the lives of the privileged. The tumultuous upheavals going on in parts of the continent are attempts to extend the area of freedom for the deprived in Africa. The extension will take place in two stages. There first must be the period of sloughing off the habits of living and thinking acquired in the house of bondage. The habits were drilled into the generation of the liberators by the schools they attended. The rhetoric of independence still lays stress on freedom

241

as the thing to live for. Africa has less need for the emphasis on freedom and for more on social responsibility.

The African revolution has not as yet reached its real goals; most of the leaders of Free Africa still see nothing wrong in being the black carbon copies of their former masters. Most of them regard Britain or France or America as their models of perfection. Most of them again are, like their civil servants, christian preachers and ardent churchmen; they see no contradiction in the fact that by urging their people to worship at the altars of the white men's gods they lead them straight to the socio-economic blunders which produced slavery, colonialism and negrophobia.

The black carbon copy leaders will fall into the error of the whites whom they emulate. For some time, they will rule their people in the way the white man lorded it over them. They cannot help doing this because they see freedom and sovereignty from perspectives borrowed from the white side. For them, self-determination means the assumption of the positions held by the former white colonialists.

The abuses their type of freedom is producing creates conflicts and tensions which are alien to the African way of life. A cry is rising from the deprived in Free Africa; it is a cry from the heart of those for whom black carbon copy freedom has no meaning; those whom it crushes precisely in the way the colonialist did. These people feel cheated by the black carbon copy leaders; they want their own type of freedom; the freedom to make the best possible use of their lives and in that way to realise the glory and the promise of being human. They have begun to roll up their sleeves for a massive heave by which they will push the *Buntu* revolution into its next phase, when no person shall be denied the right to make the best possible use of his life. Free Africa is going to go through a protracted period of violent upheaval and the only way to narrow down the area of conflict and dislocations is to stress the unifying power of *ubuntu*. South Africa is already involved in the collision of clashing evaluations of the person and the black people want the final outcome to be determined by themselves, no matter what the cost is. That is why they are rejecting the independence offered them in the reserves.

Against this vast background, Bulube points out, what the white man does in South Africa is relatively unimportant; what matters now is the destiny which the peoples of Southern Africa choose for themselves. Ugly as the future will be into which the Pass Law for women has thrown the African, the enactment of the law is a peripheral issue; the humiliations and the suffering through which the Africans have to go are the blows a people determined to be free must be ready for. The ugly mind which will hurt the African is something which the whites ·cannot escape; they no longer can help fulfilling themselves by defiling their personality. The African must avoid falling into their error. To agitate for reforms, for race equality in a white-oriented society, is to expose the African to continuing contamination by the white man's bias for self-defilement. The geopolitical alternative is a precaution against this danger.

The switch to manufacturing, Bulube again warns the Committee, has intensified the shortage of labour and, by doing this, has changed the position of the African woman and changed the whole character of the race quarrel. The transformation calls for corresponding adjustments in Free Africa's policies for Southern Africa.

In the past, the African woman could either be a domestic servant or a professional. The proliferation of factories has changed her into an industrial worker. Already, she has established herself in the plastics, weaving, clothing, canning and many other industries. When the Africans enter a field of employment they do so in large numbers. This leaves them free either to swamp the field or to be in the position one day to withdraw their labour and paralyse industry by themselves, without the support of the Coloureds, the Indians or the white liberals. The pass system was developed to prevent them using their labour as a political weapon.

The women differ from the men in one major respect: the law does not yet require them to carry passes. They are thus free not only to move in and out of urban areas and therefore sell their labour to the highest bidder but also to transform themselves into a new class of black workers which, because it does not carry the passes, is able to sell its labour to the highest bidder, organise itself into trade unions, go on strike and force the employers to sign industrial agreements with it. The prospect strikes at the foundations of white privilege and economic advantage and by doing this cracks or threatens the pillars on which the superstructure of Afrikaner political dominance is built.

Bulube urges the Committee to consider this weakness in the Afrikaner as the condition on which to base strategy. It is a waste of time, he insists, to concentrate on collecting statistics which show how wicked apartheid is. Tomes were written in Germany exposing the evils Nazism perpetrated against the Jews and what good were they? What is happening in South Africa is a power conflict which is not altogether unrelated to the functioning of Nazism. The power of the Nazis was only smashed when a new alignment of forces emerged in the world. Race discrimination will be crushed when the Africans have created an altogether new balance in black-white relations not only in South Africa, but in the whole of Southern Africa. To help establish this balance is what events call for in Africa.

Bulube warns against people getting excited over events in Southern Africa and losing their sense of judgment. War, whether it be of minds or of peoples, is an ugly thing. Men involve themselves in such a clash not to pay each other compliments, but to destroy those who oppose them or their ideas. The war of minds, which is steadily becoming a shooting war in Southern Africa, is an ugly development and will continue to be ugly for many years to come, as long as people see it as a simple clash of colour.

The collision between the African and the Afrikaner, he repeats, involves ideology, fear, human greed and uncertainty about the future. When the Afrikaner's security in the Cape called for non-discrimination, the white people married African and Malay women. When security needs called for a change of attitude, the Afrikaner committed himself to a self-defiling and self-mutilating form of race prejudice. Bulube sees no reason why the Afrikaner will not be forced to change his attitude when a new balance of forces is created by the black people.

He makes it clear that this does not mean that people should waste time talking about non-violence. History has developed a situation in which violence has become an issue of practical politics in Southern Africa. Those in the position to use force should strike as hard as they can. At the same time those who are not in the position to have the guns should crack the balance based on African labour, Afrikaner economic dominance and English finance-power.

The acid test for the quality of African diplomacy is not the choice between violence and non-violence; it is the acceptance of both as inseparable complements in the crisis which has developed in Southern Africa. This situation must always be seen in the light of the multiple weaknesses on the side of the Afrikaner and calls for confronting the Afrikaners with an alternative or disaster.

The answer to the problems outlined above, Bulube sums up his memorandum, is a geopolitical alternative to the type of independence which is offered by the whites and which Magasela seems prepared to accept; it is the independence which the African chose for himself in 1912. Magasela's attitude is a reaction to the cruel conflict between the African and white ideals of nationhood. The police murdered Magasela's son not so much to stop the manufacture of a portable nuclear bomb, important as that was, as to force the professor to get out of the white man's asphyxiating society at any price and as quickly as possible. With the balkanised reserves out of the way, Pretoria reckons, it might be easier to persuade the Americans to form a naval or even military alliance with the whites. The murder was the type of ugly pressure which the ugly war of minds is producing; it was a deliberate move to stampede Magasela and those Zulus who follow him into legitimising larceny, Bulube says.

Such independence will be a leap to disaster, the chief warns. The overcrowding in the reserves is so acute it will be impossible for them to develop into viable states. To survive at all, they would have to adopt a communist system of economy; if this is what Pretoria is driving the Africans to, it must be warned that it is freeing them only to prepare for war against the whites. To free them and give them a sense of grievance is an invitation to disaster; to offer them the illusion of freedom and withhold its substance is a provocative act. And Pretoria is not stupid; de Haas's government knows what it is doing. Crowd up the

Africans in the reserves, starve them and force them to embrace communism and then ask Washington to line up with the whites against the Africans; make the mess and then ask the Americans to come and clean it up.

Bulube always argues that the Americans are not all so dumb as not to see what Pretoria is up to. For them to gang up with Pretoria could produce an Indian-Chinese-Japanese nuclear club which would join hands with the Africans and possibly the Russians, to keep the Americans out of the Indian Ocean. Alternatively, an American alliance with South Africa would bring about the proliferation of nuclear weapons in the Indian Ocean, which would threaten the sea routes to the oil fields of the Middle East. Besides, Bulube notes, America and South Africa are geographic rivals for the markets of Free Africa. The day is not far when Free Africa might become a better investment field for America than South Africa. In the final analysis, Free Africa has more resources to offer America than South Africa.

Bulube condenses his ideas on the geopolitical alternative into the following programme:

i. Independence for all the African people of South Africa on the following bases:
   a. Partition based on the equitable distribution of the land, the mines, railways, seaports, industries and other resources;
   b. The payment by the whites of reparations for the violence and the deprivation inflicted on the African people;
ii. The unification into a new nation or union of all the black peoples of Southern Africa;
iii. The creation of a viable balance of violence in Southern Africa. The present balance, which is founded on exclusive white possession of the gun must be substituted with a balance based on the portable nuclear bomb. Africa has all the uranium she can ever need to produce the plutonium from which to make the bomb. China and India have the know-how for training the Africans in the manufacture of a portable nuclear bomb; both have a vested interest in seeing white domination blown to pieces not only in Africa but in the Indian Ocean. But race arrogance hurts the man of colour not only in Southern Africa; it hurts him in different parts of the western hemisphere. Free Africa must create the conditions in which her struggle against white domination must have a powerful pull on the thinking of the young black Americans;
iv. The convention of a conference of the black and white states of Africa to fix a permanent place for the Afrikaner in the African sun;
v. The rejection of the sham independence now offered by Pretoria and the enlistment of United Nations and Organisation of African

245

Unity support for the African's Geopolitical Alternative. The time has come when the industrial nations must be confronted with a clear choice in South Africa; this must be done to the Security Council of the United Nations as well;

vi. The establishment of an Indian Ocean Consensus. While the whites established a hurting and often humiliating relationship between Africa and the white nations of Europe and the western hemisphere, the Africans and the Asians are linked by a common historical experience. The American-Russian power build-up in the Indian Ocean seeks to entrench this experience. By creating the conditions which will bring nuclear war into the Indian Ocean, America and Russia forced India to become a nuclear power. South Africa will use this as an excuse for exploding her own atomic bomb and if she does this, Zambia, Tanzania, Zaire and Nigeria will have no business to sit down and not develop nuclear arms. And when Africa has her own nuclear bomb, who will stop its use against South Africa? America is most likely to gang up with white South Africa; some of her NATO allies are already pushing her in this direction. The South Africans are putting all possible pressure to tie America to an alliance with Pretoria. In this setting, it is wisdom for Africa and Asia to put their heads together and develop an Indian Ocean Consensus to:

a. develop an African-Asian defence policy for the Indian Ocean;
b. create machinery for the use of African and Asian resources for the good of the peoples of Africa and Asia;
c. promote trade between Africa and Asia;
d. co-ordinate development and mutual co-operation policies;
e. transform the Indian Ocean into an African-Asian lake;
f. evolve a plan for the development of the Transkei as the southern sentinel guarding the western approaches to the Indian Ocean, while the Red Sea performs a similar role in the north. The islands between China and Australia would be recognised as the eastern gateway to the Indian Ocean.

Bulube points out that the ideal for Africa in an ideal world would be to serve as a halfway house between Asia and the white lands. But the troubles facing the western democracies, which issue largely from the collapse of colonialism, make it necessary for Africa to turn her eyes to the east. One day, leaders might arise in China and Russia who will see no point in a fratricidal war among ideological allies. Then, a new balance will emerge in world power dispositions; the Africans must be ready for this prospect. Pretoria is forcing independence on the Africans to anticipate events in this regard. Once the Africans are "free" Pretoria will be free to have the military alliance with America. The Africans and the Asians should be ready for this.

Bulube explains in a footnote that the formation of a larger nation or union is but a translation of the *Buntu* principle of agmination into political action; an extension to Southern Africa of the ideal of nationhood adopted in 1912. Urgency is given to the need to form the union by developments in Southern Africa. The collapse of the Portuguese dictatorship has cracked the white united front in Southern Africa. The security vacuum which this has produced forces Pretoria to move at two levels to preserve white domination. On the one hand it is doing everything in its power to persuade the Americans to sign a defence treaty with South Africa. The bait held out is that it is in the interest of the United States to protect white domination and in that way guarantee the safety of the sea route between America and the oil fields of the Middle East. If America makes a deal with Pretoria, Free Africa might have to consider a deal with China or Russia or with both. Free Africa also has to work out a formula for the involvement of the Black Americans in the shaping of United States policy in Southern Africa.

On the other hand, Pretoria is quietly encouraging the white supremacists in Angola and Mozambique to break away from black rule and to declare independence and then to join a Pretoria-oriented white united front. In the old front, Pretoria always had to consider Lisbon's sensibilities. In the new front, the whites will gang up to defend the white skin. With the lines being drawn so clearly in terms of black and white, the Africans of Southern Africa do not have much of a choice; they have to form their own united front, seek their own allies and manufacture their own weapons. The creation of the black united front calls for the rejection of the type of independence the whites are offering in South Africa and which the Portuguese offered after the revolution in Portugal.

The formation of the larger nation on the basis of the Larger Truth will restore to the Africans their land and enable them to control the gold, the oil, the diamonds, the copper, the chrome, the uranium, the iron, the coal and other minerals and enable the Africans to use these precisely in the way the Arabs have used oil as a political weapon. Bulube warns that the whites will fight bitterly for the control of Africa's wealth and realism requires that African policy should be based on this probability.

Bulube asks the Committee to bear another unpleasant fact in mind.

The presence of the Afrikaner in Africa creates a problem to which Africa must address itself directly. On the one hand, the *Buntu Ideal* rejects the punishment of the person for being the child of his particular parents. One day, the Africans will crush the power of the Afrikaner, just as Hitler's power was crushed. It is possible that after victory, some Afrikaners will still want to belong to Africa, their white skin notwithstanding. *Buntu* statesmanship requires that the right of those people to a place in the African sun should be recognised.

Bulube gets into serious trouble each time he speaks of a place for the Afrikaner in the African sun. He is attacked for this as much on the homefront as he is abroad. At the La Guardia airport in New York, while on a trip to America, a black reporter confronted him with the same problem.

Chief Bulube, you have gone on record as saying that you do not hate the white people. Does that not sound strange in a man who has suffered so much and has lost so much? The whites despise the very soil on which you tread!

Yes, they do. But I can't afford to be like the white people. I am different; I am an African. If the whites prefer group hatred, that's their business. My system of values rejects the white man's approach. That is why we fight him.

You don't hate the Afrikaner either?

No. I have more important things to do.

You mean ... you don't mind what he has done to you and your people?

I am deeply concerned about everything evil he has done to my people and I want him to pay for it and I will see to it that he does pay ... even if I have to meet him on the battlefield one day. But while I do not have the gun, I will not stop fighting; I shall use my brains.

Why don't you support the militants' demand that your goal should be the expulsion of the Afrikaner from Africa?

I draw the distinction between the person and the values which determine human behaviour; wrong values distort the psyche of a people. Wrong values have damaged the Afrikaner's psyche; that is why he is so obsessed with race and colour. He is a man with a sick soul. His sickness, however, is a challenge to the *Buntu Ideal*. In the childhood days of the human race, the leper was rejected by society; to-day, we know better; we do not throw him onto the streets. We know that one sick man can infect a whole community. We treat the leper . . . .

Chief, do you really think you can change the Afrikaner?

No! Do not get me wrong. Firstly, I am not concerned with changing him; I want my land. If I do not have the guns to create the situations to which I must force him to respond, I must use my brains.

I do not know if I understand you . . . .

We have to clear our minds on three things: the basic weaknesses in the white man's civilisation, preparing ourselves for a decisive confrontation and guaranteeing viability for the type of society we shall create when we have destroyed white power. The commitment to conflict is the basic weakness; it is the dynamic which stimulates the white man's civilisation. Conflict between good and evil, between the person and his neighbour, man and woman, the citizen and society, man and nature . . . . Conflict everywhere, in every direction. In the process, wealth is wasted, the environment is polluted and the white man bleeds himself slowly to death. Britain and France bled themselves out of being the great powers of the world. America bled herself in

South Vietnam until she had to get out of the war via the backdoor. The Portuguese bled themselves in Africa until whatever wealth they had was nearly burnt up. The Afrikaner is committing the same mistake in South Africa. Every year now he burns up millions of rand in defence and related budgets. The bleeding is on in earnest; our business is to see to it that it continues until he goes the way of the British, the French and the Portuguese. Help the Afrikaner to bleed himself . . . that is our secret weapon.

But that might take you another thousand years!

That brings me to preparing for the confrontation. And if all of us in the Black World use our brains, we do not need to wait even for a thousand days! We are forging the weapons by which to hit where the white man is weakest. We are organising our labour and building an internal power-structure with which to challenge the white power-structure. But we have to control enough force to keep the confrontation crisis always moving at our pace and in directions determined by us. And here, we need the help of Free Africa. Instead of spending money flying refugee leaders all over the world should Free Africa not consider sending some of our refugees to school, to study the manufacture of small, portable nuclear bombs to meet the white man's guns with these bombs? We have so much uranium in Africa which is controlled by our own people . . . Niger, Gabon. The French, the Germans and the Japanese are already involved in processing our uranium . . . . Why not give us a little of it to blow up white domination in the south of the continent?

Isn't that something?

When everything is over, we shall establish a society in which it will never again be a crime for a person to be the child of his parents. We started in 1912 to lay the foundations for this society; we are building it as I talk to you.

Chief, do you have any message for black youth in America? There are so many of us who want to do something about the position of our people in Southern Africa . . . .

Tell them to study as they have never studied before. Where the white man spends one hour, the young blacks must spend ten hours studying. Where the white man reads one book, the young black must read twenty books. Our aim must be better black brains. Next, please tell the young blacks that if they seriously want to help us, let them go to school and study physics and the chemistry of uranium and then go to Niger, Gabon and elsewhere to work on African uranium for the purpose of enabling us to create a balance of violence which will serve our interests in Southern Africa. Above all, tell them not to be afraid of the white American; he is divided too deeply on the race issue to decide the course of events in Africa.

In his memorandum, Bulube describes some of the strategies already developed by the black South Africans for translating their programme into action. Segregated institutions are exploited to build up machinery by which to assert African leadership initiatives which are otherwise forbidden by law. The goal is a national strike to paralyse the economy from within. If, one day, the Portuguese in Angola and Mozambique declare unilateral independence and form a new united white front with South Africa and Rhodesia and eventually declare war on the black peoples of Southern Africa, the Africans in South Africa want to be ready to paralyse South Africa's war effort with a strike. People outside South Africa should realise that people on the homefront are not free agents; they have to develop weapons on the basis of the resources at their disposal.

Bulube repeats that the Africans in Angola, Botswana, Malawi, Mozambique, Lesotho, Namibia, Rhodesia, Swaziland, and Zambia should together form themselves into a union which will create an altogether new economic balance in Southern Africa. The 60,000,000 blacks in this part of the continent would form a trading bloc which would unite with those being discussed in West and East Africa. A union of 60,000,000 Africans surrounding South Africa would be an attractive market and would be a powerful economic level with which to smash the laager mentality and crack the balance founded on black labour, English capital and Afrikaner political power. Some of the reserve administrations have taken the first steps to lay the foundations for the union and are on preparations for joining the Africans listed above if and when they accept the principle of an effective black united front.

In his speeches, Bulube finally lays increasing stress on forging an economic weapon controlled by the 60,000,000 Africans to crack the obnoxious balance. But this weapon must complement political offensives against white domination. The geopolitical union he has in mind will form a pincers surrounding South Africa from the east through the north to the west. The pincers will create a political setting in which white political power could eventually be cracked.

He tells the Committee that he and his people have evolved a strategy which works at two levels. Externally the markets and the pincers are the weapons with which to crack the white united front. Internally, black policy exploits the governmental institutions set up by the government in Pretoria to create a dual authority situation in which white power will be opposed by legal black authority.

The segregated administrations are forming a united front of their own and will one day use their legal powers to withdraw African labour on a national scale from the white power-structure to crack the balance and smash white domination. The chief merit of this strategy lies in the facts that it makes non-violence effective and enables the Africans to fight on ground chosen by themselves, using tools controlled by themselves in and outside South Africa. Bulube implores the Committee to study this strategy. The strikes which have become an almost endemic feature of life in Natal are political exercises by which the Zulus create the dual power situation. The point to note about them is that there is no political party which leads them; no co-ordinating trade union organisation. In this regard, he points out, they might be described as spontaneous. But there is methodical organisation behind these demonstrations. The white authority smashed the political movements which stressed ideological loyalties that split the Africans. The black people were told to develop along their own lines; government policy destroyed the ideological leaders who were based, as a rule, in the urban areas and shifted the centre of gravity in the leadership to the rural areas where the new leaders were free to change their tactics. They abandoned the use of Western-type political organisations and used the government's stress on "tribalism" to stimulate loyalty to the *Buntu Ideal*.

A unity at the level of fundamentals emerged which involves every African and which has now become the driving power behind the strikes in Natal. Where the African has been freed from divisive coalitions with the other races and where he defines the race problem in his own terms, consciousness of *ubuntu* evokes identical responses to similar challenges.

Bulube assures the Committee that after three hundred years of contact with the whites, the Africans in South Africa now have an answer to tribalism. The Zulu, the Xhosa and the Swazi are committed as powerfully to *ubuntu* as the Bapedi, Batswana and the Basotho are to *botho*, their version of *ubuntu*. Bulube adds that he looks forward to the day when the Bapedi, Basotho, Batswana, Swazi, Venda-Tonga-Shanganc, Xhosa and Zulu will each march along "their" lines in a co-ordinated national strike to defend the *Buntu Ideal*. To get to that point, he concludes, he needs no political parties, no guns, no armies; all he needs are clarity on the *ubuntu* ideal in every African, understanding on the part of the world and moral support from Africa.

He admits, finally, that whether or not he likes it he has to move by stages to the moment of final confrontation. There first has to be the unification of the segregated rural administrations on the basis of which to build the dual authority situation. This will be followed by the use of African labour as a political weapon. The last step will be a national strike. The excitement over the passes issue, he warns, is important only as an instrument for the politicisation of the masses of the black people.

* * *

XX. Moment Of Confrontation

Isinamuva liyabukwa.

(The last to dance receives the most cheers.)

The Passes For Women Bill has at last been approved by the Senate. The state president has signed it and it is now the law of the land. Although the CNP fought bitterly for the Bill, most Afrikaners are restrained in their joy over their victory. The debate brought to the surface a number of weaknesses in the Afrikaner's position. It demonstrated that the Afrikaner is not the master of his destiny, the turgid rhetoric stressing this notwithstanding.

Bulube exploited it skilfully not only to tear the chiefs away from supporting the government, but also to alienate the black police and to transform tribalism into an instrument working for the unification of the African people. In the old days, the clan chiefs were a more powerful instrument of control in the hands of the government than, in some cases, the police. In the rural reserves, the chiefs controlled land tenure and their duty was to use this power to ensure African conformity with government policy. Recalcitrance was punished with the loss of residence rights, a period on the roads in winter and the prospect of finding no place to live or grow food. Ambitious chiefs used the weapon both to line their pockets and to build their power in the reserves. Those who lacked enthusiasm for their functions lost their jobs. Such was the policy of the CNP. And any challenge to the authority of the chiefs brought in the armoured section of the white police force. Armoured cars and Saracen tanks rolled into situations of trouble in both the rural areas and the urban locations. And when the segregated administrations were set up, they were given power to regulate the flow of cheap labour from the reserves to the urban areas.

The intention was to strengthen the position of the chiefs on one hand and, at the same time ensure that they exerted pressure on their people to accept the position where the whites regarded their productive potential as white property. The stress on the Africans developing along their own lines provided Bulube with the opportunity of a lifetime. A clan chief himself, he promptly stepped forth and,

253

adhering to the strict letter of the law, confronted the CNP with the ruthless logic of its policy. At first, some people called him a collaborationist, which is a hideous political swearword in the African community. But two things happened as he pursued the logic of the government's laws. The policy cracked and as this happened, a leadership vacuum developed on the white side which Bulube did not hesitate to fill. Pressed to demonstrate that CNP racial policy was not a variant of Nazism, de Haas, like van Warmelo, offered the Africans another shadow of independence in the reserves. These offers had never been made in South African history. To everybody's surprise, the Africans again rejected the independence.

The resulting deadlock brought the white government face to face with the unworkability of its racial policy. Bulube came out with an alternative which promised to give the Africans an incomparably more rewarding type of freedom than any the government could offer in the reserves. The alternative did not stop there; the prospect of Free African markets for South African manufactures threatened to crack the alliance between Afrikaner political power and English capital and also threatened to split the Afrikaans community itself.

The economics minister in the de Haas cabinet resigned to form a political party committed to race equality. Behind him, of course, there was English finance. He started negotiating secretly with Bulube for a new alliance between African labour and English capital. That alarmed the young entrepreneur class in the Afrikaans community who also approached Bulube secretly and offered him the whole of the Natal province, including the key port city of Durban in return for an alliance which would allow Afrikaner capital access to the markets of Free Africa and a mutual defence treaty by which the Zulu army of the future would rally to the support of the Afrikaner in situations of emergency.

These developments impressed the chiefs and they saw themselves leading their people, behind Bulube, to the freedom which the white man's gun had destroyed. The black police, too, were impressed. Bulube demanded that they should be promoted to positions of authority in the force and assured them that the geopolitical alternative he proposed offered them the opportunity to be better human beings than the despised traitors who arrested their own people to entrench their humiliation. He made public a plan by an underground movement in the locations to compile a list of policemen who would have to be murdered for collaboration. This had shaken the police force and, in Natal in particular, the police developed an incredible reluctance to shoot the Africans during strikes.

All these things had taken place while most whites were busy on the Passes For Women Bill. Some Afrikaners like Prinsloo had watched these developments with increasing concern. With the chiefs hostile to the government and the black police dreading the advent of the day of judgment, the pillars of white power in the black community began to crack. What was galling was that Bulube had not broken any law; he had merely pursued government policy to its logical conclusion and in doing that had shaken the obnoxious balance and threatened to split Afrikanerdom itself. He had not stopped there; he had seized the initiative to influence events and transferred leadership in thinking about the future of South Africa from the white side to the African. While the whites quarrelled publicly on the smell of the African woman, the size of her breasts and the shape of her legs Bulube had quietly shifted the centres of power from the white side to the African.

The change was fundamental; South Africa would never again be what it had been before. The freedom with which the Africans staged strikes whenever they wanted in Natal was evidence. They had placed themselves in the position where they could seriously work on a timetable to the moment of confrontation. Thoughtful Afrikaners are aware of these changes; they are aware also of their implications for the future of the Afrikaner in Africa. What they do not know is what to do and, in their indecision, they cling to the gun. But the gun is no longer their guarantee of survival. They enacted the laws which the Africans now use to create the dual authority situation; they created the situation in which they are now caught. How can they shoot the African who carries out their own laws?

This is the question Colonel Prinsloo asks when government leaders ask him why the police do not shoot African strikers into submission. The Africans, he tells some of his critics, are now aware of their power and nobody is going to make them forget about it. Only, they have not as yet consolidated it; now, he urges the Minister of Justice, is the time to negotiate seriously with them. They are still weak enough to accept white terms. To-morrow they will be strong enough to dictate their terms; this, he says, is the message of their rejection of the prime minister's independence offer.

* * *

The African women's invasion of Union Buildings cut a gaping wound in the prime minister's personality. He has not as yet begun to understand how such a thing could take place in Afrikanerdom's own city. He still sees himself isolated and beleaguered in his own seat of power. The humiliation wounds him every moment of his life and keeps his temper always in flames. His doctors are concerned about this; they warn him that too much worry over the event might weaken his heart. But if there is one thing that de Haas does not care about when he is on the warpath against the black people is his own personal safety or health. For Afrikanerdom, he would not hesitate to sacrifice his life at any time. If thinking and worrying about the women's demonstration of power will cost him his life, well, he tells Piet van der Merwe when things go wrong, let him die. In so far as he is concerned, he will know no rest until the kaffer is back in his place. The phenomenon in him has been awakened and friends and foes tremble when he opens his mouth, for he has revived his old style of talking. Whenever he opens his mouth, he talks in tones of thunder. The temperature of the cabinet room rises each time he walks into it, followed by the faithful Piet.

The fires which rage in the prime minister's bosom are stoked by the strikes in Natal, which have spread to the Witwatersrand, the industrial heart of South Africa. He explodes promptly each time anybody associates them with the economic position of the African. This does not arise out of any insensitivity. De Haas believes honestly that the Afrikaners are God's chosen people; that God brought them to South Africa as a reward for their loyalty to him and that he created the black people specifically to hew wood and draw water for the Afrikaners. The productive potential of every African is the God-given property of the white man. The latter has the right to use it as he thinks best. If he does not exploit it fully, he sins against God, like the man who did not develop his talents. The more the Afrikaner squeezes out of the African, the more he does God's will. If there is anything wrong with this, he advises, people must blame God and not the Afrikaner.

In this mood, the prime minister regards the strikes as sin and treason and ungratefulness all rolled into one. The white man brought civilisation to South Africa and all he gets from the ungrateful black people are kicks in the teeth. But what can one expect, with a Police Commissioner like Prinsloo entrusted with the protection of the whites from the black hordes? When alone, the prime minister catches himself wondering sometimes if Prinsloo is not motivated by treason. Not even the phenomenon, however, can take this to the cabinet. He once sounded Kritzinger on the doubt. While the Pretoria district police chief neither confirmed nor removed the prime minister's suspicion, he reacted in a way which left the question unresolved in the mind of de Haas. On another occasion the prime minister sounded faithful and loyal Piet who reacted strongly against the thought that Colonel Prinsloo could be disloyal. The prime minister, however, took Piet's views with a grain of salt; Piet would not do anything that would open the way to Kritzinger's promotion to the post of Police Commissioner.

De Haas is a man of action and prefers to act decisively. But with the most powerful members of the cabinet behind Prinsloo's continuing to be Police Commissioner, the prime minister has to move carefully. Besides, the strikes are beginning to attract international attention. While some commentators attach importance to their political implications, others argue that the demonstrations corrode South Africa's reputation as an investment field. Both sides blame the government for the strikes. The government's economic advisers warn that foreign investments continue to flow out and that new capital from abroad is not coming in in encouraging volumes. This annoys de Haas; Afrikanerdom, he always tells his cabinet, works so hard to ensure that foreign investments produce high profits and the people who are loudest in attacking the government are in those countries which have investments in South Africa. They punish the Afrikaner for looking well after their property.

* * *

A new factor is emerging in the strikes. Arson is cõming again to be used over a widening area. In the sixty years since the formation of the Union of South Africa, the Africans have rarely used fire as an instrument of protest in industrial disputes. They used it extensively against Natal's sugar-cane fields during the stormy fifties; they used it also to burn down forests in the Harding district. But not even in those times did they burn down factories. As a matter of fact, now, a factory does not have to be involved in a dispute with the Africans before it goes up in flames if it is owned by the wrong people.

After the fire which destroys the Buitendyk plastics factory just outside Pretoria, Kritzinger calls in Bashise and, to the African's surprise, asks him to sit on the chair on the other side of his desk. The African, who is beholden to Kritzinger for many favours, hesitates to jeopardise the position of his benefactor. It is true that Kritzinger is chief of the Pretoria police district, but that does not mean that he should commit treason against Afrikanerdom and treat an African as his equal in his office. A hostile white constable might enter, note the equality and report that to higher authorities. Bashise has a vested interest in Kritzinger's security and wants to show that he is concerned about the safety of his benefactor. Kritzinger recommended him for promotion to the headquarters of the security police.

Sit down Bashise, he says in Zulu. I want to talk to you like a man and I want you to answer me like a man.

If you insist, Sir, I shall sit down for, as we say, to stand up when discussing serious matters complicates them.

Bashise, you are a Zulu. . . .

The remark is deliberately a rhetorical question. Kritzinger knows Bashise is a Zulu; he speaks to him in Zulu. An Afrikaner's emphasis on one being a Zulu can be ominous, particularly in Pretoria. Bashise does not answer.

It is a bad sign when the Zulus play with lightning. . . .

The African is still uncertain about the white man's intentions. In his culture, there is a formal way for presenting a problem and tradition and usage require that it should be introduced, the theme developed, the central point established, explanations made and the presentation concluded. But then, Bashise is saying to himself, the

257

white people are not cultured; they do not know how to carry on a conversation; they exchange sounds and noises and do not converse.

Playing with lightning . . . you know what I mean?

I don't know if I understand you, Sir.

Come off it, Bashise! You know what I'm talking about! Those strikes. You Zulus like to make everybody believe that you are stupid. . . .

Sir, everybody says we are.

Telling me! But what are you trying to tell the white man in the strikes? Don't speak to me like a policeman, for the question would not be fair to you; answer me like a man.

Sir, the people are saying they want value for their labour.

You know I know that. But why is it that each time the government wants to talk to your leaders, you Zulus go out on strikes? Why do you play with lightning, as you say in your language? Some time back the late prime minister called your leaders to Cape Town to offer them independence. Before your leaders left for Cape Town, you people started playing with the lightning. Baas de Haas consolidated some of the reserves scattered all over Natal into five or six areas and asked your people to consider the consolidation as a basis on which to discuss independence. Before your leaders replied, you people started playing with the lightning. You are doing the same thing now . . . why?

I think the people want the prime minister to offer real independence; Sir, they don't want to be free to come and beg for jobs as the black people do from some of the independent states of Southern Africa.

Now, you are talking like a man. Is that why your people are now burning factories?

Sir, I don't know who are burning factories.

It could be Zulus or Xhosas or Basotho or all of them; you're right. But what are they up to?

Well, Sir, you said I should talk to you like a man. . . .

That is what I want you to do.

The government made a mistake when it forced Dillo Mareka to flee the country. He talked a lot, made blood-curdling threats but was slow to translate his words into deeds. Other leaders have emerged in the underground who act first and talk afterwards. They are angry, Sir, very angry with Britain, America, France, West Germany, Italy and Japan who build factories in this country and suck their blood in profits, Sir.

But these factories give them jobs?

And little money, Sir. They say the white people, together with their Japanese hangers-on, are ganging up against the black people.

But if they use fire, the police will shoot them.

They will still burn the factories, Sir.

And be shot. . . .

And burn. . . .

Come on, Bashise, you people have better sense than that? Do you know the people who organise the arson?

These things are in the wind, Sir.

Rumours help in unsettled times.

Yes, Sir.

You realise, of course, that if your people burn down the factories and the police shoot, the whole country can in the end go up in smoke. You don't want that to happen, I know. What would you do if you were in the prime minister's position?

Sir, I would ask Chief Bulube to come to Pretoria and I would start negotiations with him. The problems between us and the white people are complicated, Sir. The negotiations would take a long time, I know. But I would start to negotiate, Sir.

But, playing with lightning creates too much noise for negotiators to hear each other when talking.

I would negotiate a call-off of the play with lightning, Sir.

I'm going to mention some of the things you told me to the Commissioner of Police. I'll recommend you for the highest post the Commissioner is planning for a black man; a special political adviser to the Commissioner on black politics. Then, you will help shape police policy. I know you can do it; I'll speak to him about it. Alright, you can go now, Bashise.

The African rises and as he walks to the door, Kritzinger calls out.

Bashise! Before you go .... Did you know that the prime minister had invited Bulube to come to Pretoria to discuss the consolidation of the black areas? And Bulube said he was too busy? What are things coming to when a black man can say that to the prime minister?

Hm! That's serious, Sir.

And, the Minister of Bantoe Affairs told the chairmen of the Bantoe administrations not to meet in conference to create a black united front. As you know, they met and did precisely what they were ordered not to do. How do you negotiate with people like that?

That's bad, Sir; very bad.

The African is shaking his head vigorously. Kritzinger is impressed by the vigour. In the government he is known as the top police expert on the mind of the black man. In the anthropology classes he has been told that the Africans do not shake their heads vigorously, unless when disturbed to the roots of their personality. When he sees the African shake his head, his anthropology is vindicated. He tells the white officers under him that they must never make the mistake of judging the African by white criteria only; they should understand reality from the African's perspectives as well, in order to be efficient arms of the law. In his lectures, for example, he tells the police that it is bad manners in the African community to look the next person in the eyes. Friends do not look each other in the eyes; that is done to enemies. When an African does not look a policeman in the eyes, it does not mean that he is a crook or that he feels guilty; he just does not want to commit an act considered hostile in his community. When he starts looking the police in the eyes, he tells his men, they should regard that as a declaration of war. Bashise takes his time shaking his head, to impress his benefactor. And when he thinks he has done a good job, he pulls himself together. Kritzinger drives his point home:

You see now, why we need a black political adviser to the Police Commissioner? A responsible person ... with his roots in the black community?

Yes sir. . . .

You don't have to worry about the pay. This will be a special job with a special salary, a house and a car.

That would be a major assignment for me, Sir . . . .

For some moments the two men are silent; neither looks the other in the eyes. Both of them know that they are blood enemies; that the only link which forces them to co-operate is the gun. As long as the white man has the gun he is able to create the conditions which will force the black man to co-operate on white terms; he can corrupt the African and throw breadcrumbs for him to pick on terms dictated by the whites. Every moment of his life the African is probing the white man's positions in the endless search for points of weakness. This goes on in every situation of black-white contact. In time, a balance of weaknesses develops which takes on the form of a habit of thinking and congeals finally into a mode of behaviour. The balance creates its own peculiar forms of discipline on either side of the colour line; it leaves the Afrikaner knowing very clearly how far to go in provoking or placating the African and regulates the latter's behaviour toward the whites in the same way. The contradictions which arise from all this are given the generic name of the South African way of life. The white policeman continues:

A major assignment indeed, Bashise. You deserve it. When is your leave due? You might need a little rest to make your plans before you take on the new job. But, don't worry about the leave; that can be fixed at any time.

Thank you, Sir! Good Morning, Sir!

* * *

The police are concerned about the spread of the strikes from Natal to the Witwatersrand industrial complex. Their problem is that the government regards the demonstrations as a political protest and not merely a reaction to economic disadvantage. The task of the police is complicated by the bans which make the organisation of African political organisations and trade unions illegal. In the old days, when these were legal, the police knew each and every African leader holding office at any time in every part of the country. In emergencies the police swooped on the leaders, arrested all of them and paralysed African action. An altogether different situation has developed since the Sharpeville shootings. In so far as the whites are concerned, there should be perfect peace and order in South Africa because there are no agitators and no subversive organisations to stir up strife in the black community. Those whom the government calls the communists have been stamped out of existence. Here and there a tame and often frightened workers' group might exist by mutual agreement between the white employer and his black workers. The association functions more to keep the actual and potential agitators visible than to effect real improvements in the workers' conditions of employment. In situations of confrontation, these staff associations, as they are called, are careful to keep as much out of trouble as they can.

The inexplicable situation has developed in which the workers in a given industry will stage a strike which is not led by any visible leader or group. Nothing angers the prime minister more than this circumstance. And, when he is in this mood, the cause of all the trouble is Prinsloo, whom the prime minister regards as a weak constable. But Prinsloo is not the type of man who takes blows lying on his stomach. His counter-attacks threaten to split the cabinet from top to bottom. He argues, for example, that the white man's ideal of fulfilment is cracking under the strain of conditions which exist in South Africa and that the crack shows itself in the morale of the police force, in particular, its black section.

The point has been reached where Afrikanerdom has to offer the police concessions which will keep the loyalty of the black police, who are coming under increasing pressure from the violence in the locations. More and more police are killed in mysterious circumstances; the position is so serious police policy has had to be changed drastically; black officers now command police stations in the locations where, before, the whites held these positions. The government has to make it worthwhile for the black police to continue to make these sacrifices. Urgency is given to the need by the corruption which, Prinsloo points out carefully, has developed in the police force. He quotes cases of policemen committing every conceivable crime. Two were caught burgling a departmental store . . . in uniform! Black police make easy money on the streets where their orders are to search every black person for arms. A policeman will search and arrest an African and release him on the payment of fifty cents. This has not only reduced the searches to a farce; they have made the law ridiculous and thrown the police force into disrepute. The white man, Prinsloo continues, cannot afford to see the police force turned into a laughing stock among the black people. The position has been reached where the Africans boast that every policeman has his price; if he is white, there always are the legs of a black woman; if he is black, well, the sky is the limit.

Prinsloo never mentions the word revolution in his reports. The word has earth-shaking implications in South Africa and no decent white person ever refers to it. But among his trusted friends, Prinsloo confesses freely that extensive corruption in any police force is an important indication of a revolutionary situation developing.

Day after day the police arrest the agitators and bring them before the courts of law in every major city of South Africa; more often than not the men are acquitted; the laws designed to preserve freedom for the white man fail to serve this end when the black man demands equal treatment before the law. When the law is embarrassed, corruption sets in; men entrusted with the responsibility of maintaining law and order commit incredible crimes in the name of the law. This, Prinsloo argues, is a challenge which Afrikanerdom has to face.

The spread of the strikes brings the police under increasing criticism; all the whites feel that their privileged position is threatened. The English press blames de Haas and the CNP for this state of affairs. The government blames the white liberals, churchmen, radicals, communists and other agitators. In the latter group are white students who attack the white power-structure. There are some brave white students who stand out to be counted and pay the consequences; these are mainly Jewish and English-speaking. In the Afrikaner universities, the students are angry, frustrated and paralysed for action. Many are too frightened to act against their government and their people. As a result they watch apprehensively as the CNP grapples with a crisis which gets out of control with each year that goes by.

In these conditions, Dr. Robert Shawcross's African diary has become a priceless source of information on actual and potential African agitators and, of course, their white allies. The police have seized the passports of Dr. and Mrs. Shawcross; they have put enough pressure on the historian to force him to travel from city to city all over South Africa testifying for the government against men and women of all races charged for conspiring against Afrikaner domination. Some of the people arrested were his best friends; people who trusted him and told him things they did not want known to the government. Others were his colleagues while the overwhelming majority of them were men and women for whom he had the highest respect and admiration. Wherever he goes he finds himself witnessing against people who uphold the truths by which he gives meaning to life. In the English press he is attacked savagely as a moral coward, a turncoat, a traitor. And when Englishmen swear, they put Lucifer himself to shame. Some English and Jews are so angry with him they advise him to commit suicide. Some whites come secretly to Bulube and ask him to raise his voice in protest against Shawcross's treachery. The African declines to do this.

Don't you see what is happening? When we Africans say the white man's system of values cannot cope with the problems of a racially mixed society, we mean that it debases the person and creates situations of corruption in which an honourable man is drowned in dishonour and forced to be a traitor for once having tried to do the honourable thing. The original crime was in the creation of such situations and in the use of power to destroy every white man's conscience. Tyranny is encouraged, not by the fall of those whom it crushes, but by the continued silence of good white men.

A wave of intense hatred for the white liberals sweeps the country as Shawcross moves from one city to another to witness against the black people fighting for their freedom. In the locations Shawcross has become the embodiment of everything wicked in the white bosom. The CNP is delighted with this; it widens the gulf between black and white and forces the English to co-operate with the Afrikaner in maintaining the obnoxious African-Afrikaner-English balance on terms dictated by the Afrikaner.

In the junction city of Ladysmith in northern Natal, Jabulani Kumalo is in the dock on charges of treason and conspiracy. Jabulani has become an underground hero; he co-ordinates plans for striking in the Zulu community. Shawcross used a code in making some of his recordings which the police have cracked; that is how they discovered Jabulani's role in the underground. In ordinary life, Jabulani was a respectable principal of an African high school in the city. His only interest, other than his work and the Wesleyan Methodist Church, whose steward he was, was football. A prominent leader in the football world, he travelled extensively over South Africa. When black American sportsmen visited the country, the government saw to it that they stopped in Ladysmith to talk to a responsible African who was objective in his assessment of black-white relations. Government agents were always at pains to make it clear that Jabulani Kumalo was not an advocate of the CNP's racial policy. Their only interest in him was that he was not influenced by the thinking of the agitators.

A deep friendship developed between Kumalo and Shawcross. The two men seemed shaped for such a friendship. Both were men of integrity; both were moderate and both could listen to a different viewpoint. As a matter of fact it was Shawcross's admiration of men like Kumalo that reinforced Hawthorne's case for Shawcross's involvement in the underground. In one of the conversations between Kumalo and Shawcross the African had told the historian how the black people neutralise police dogs. Sprinkle ground hot chillies wherever the dogs might pick up an incriminating trail and they will promptly go on strike. One of the qualities the two men had in common was their sense of humour. They agreed that the race quarrel was tragic and that in spite of this there was an element of humour in it which showed that in the final analysis, black and white were human.

Kumalo told Shawcross that the broadcasting of hot ground chillies in a riot can have obvious dangers for the Africans who never are masked. What the Africans do is to carry rubber syringes filled with water in which ground chillies have been boiled and which has been cooled. This is squirted into the dogs' eyes. Kumalo told Shawcross that the police had not as yet invented protective goggles for the dogs.

The prosecutor is the dreaded Dr. Amherst Kriel, a former professor of political science at the University of the Free State. Kriel is Afrikanerdom's top authority on communism and the sabotage tactics it uses. He obtained his law degrees in Germany in the 1930s and has an abiding hatred for "Zionist" communism. Kriel boasts that he has never spoken to an educated African; they are all communists.

Kumalo is in the dock when the prosecution calls in Dr. Shawcross as a state witness. As he enters the court by the side door, his eyes meet Kumalo's. Shawcross turns his face speedily away from the African's and drags himself into the witness-box. The case goes on for three days. The judge finds Kumalo guilty and sentences him to death but points out that he would allow Kumalo to send his case on appeal.

Trials are going on all over South Africa, in the largest cities and in tiny rural villages. Lusikisiki is a small town in the Transkei. For years the police have been waging a private war with the Africans who resisted the government's policy of crowding the Transkei in order to create the conditions of poverty and starvation which would force hundreds of thousands of able-bodied Xhosas to leave their homes and sell their labour at the lowest rates possible to the whites in the mines of South Africa. In the dock is Booi Makaluza, one of the leaders of the army on the hill, as the Transkeian resisters are known. The prosecutor on this occasion is the local police station commander, a crusty Orange Free Stater whose Afrikaans is remarkable for the way he pronounces his gutturals; each time he pronounces the letter "g" it is as though he is scraping the bottom of a Dutch oven.

Makaluza is defended by a brilliant Jewish lawyer, Abe Baumhaus. The station commander holds the rank of sergeant. He is in his fifties and the fact that at this age he is still only a sergeant in a tiny police station in a small rural village in a black reserve is something about which he is very bitter. Once the Afrikaners rise to positions of power, the sergeant always complains, they become like the English; if a fellow Afrikaner has not gone to school, they despise him. He hates the men in Pretoria because they punish him for the fact that he left school in the sixth grade because his parents were too poor to give him a good education. But if he hates the Afrikaners on top, he hates more the English, the Jews and the Africans, in that order.

Abe Baumhaus always refers professionally to the prosecutor as "My learned friend." The prosecutor goes into a rage each time he is referred to in these terms by the Jew from far-away Durban. One other point which angers the prosecutor is the fact that a white man has travelled more than a hundred miles to defend unruly Africans in a remote reserve. That makes Baumhaus, in the prosecutor's view, a communist; to the prosecutor, all Jews are communists. He squirms uneasily in his chair on the first day of the trial when Baumhaus refers to him again and again as his "learned friend." On the second day he rises up in court:

Your Vorship, I rise to protest. The lawyer for the prisoner refers to me as his lear-r-r-r-ned fr-r-r-ient. Your Vorship, I am not his fr-r-r-ient and I am not lear-r-r-r-ned neither!

The trials are proceeding while the strikes continue to be organized. While scores of African leaders are jailed as a result of the Shawcross diary's revelations, their elimination does not bring any abatement in the spread of the strikes. The situation has arisen when the disciplined anger of the black workers has developed a momentum of its own which needs no leaders in determining its directions.

The government finds this puzzling. In white societies, the organisation is the instrument for concerted action. When the Africans launch successful strikes without leaders, even the police are puzzled. Prinsloo is about the only one who has a rough idea of what is happening. The segregation of the African into overcrowded locations and reserves has brought what he calls "tribal" forms of discipline into action once more and it is these disciplines which make possible the organisation of strikes without trade unions, political parties or visible leaders.

Added to this is a pattern of arson which threatens to assume dangerous forms. The factories set on fire are generally those known to be owned by the members of the CNP and other supporters of the government. This intelligence creates a cabinet crisis. Some ministers accuse the Jews of supporting the African revolt. The motive is said to be the subversion of Afrikaner authority for the purpose of establishing Zionist communism in the world. Other ministers regard the English as the nigger in the woodpile. The encouragement given to the strikers by the slanted reports in the English press, it is said, stems from the desire to smash the power of the rising entrepreneur class in the Afrikaans community. The prime minister himself thinks the trouble has its roots in the weak quality of the leadership which Prinsloo gives the police force. But in the bitter quarrels which have developed in the cabinet, whose sessions are now invariably stormy, the phenomenon does not feel free to act as his instincts tell him. He wants Prinsloo replaced as Commissioner of the Police while the Justice Minister, as usual, and supported by half the cabinet, opposes de Haas. In the old days, the phenomenon would have stormed out of the cabinet, tendered his resignation to the State President and formed a brand-new cabinet. Not so now; he would be accused of splitting Afrikanerdom and deserting his people in a crisis. The English press would be delighted because the English would not have had anything to do with the crisis; the explosion would be a squabble inside the "united" Afrikaner community. De Haas retreats and averts a disastrous clash with the police chief.

265

Not knowing whom to arraign, the police arrest every striker. The arrests, in turn, spark off more strikes until there is no room in South Africa's vast prisons. Concentration camps are established in the rural areas where the strikers are locked. But with thousands of young whites tied down in unproductive military employment in Rhodesia, the South African economy is crippled by the jailing of thousands of black workers. The Afrikaner entrepreneurs, supported by sections of the Dutch Reformed Church and some of the universities, start a campaign to get rid of de Haas. In the excitement of the moment,one night, a fire breaks out in the petroleum refinery owned by an all-Afrikaans corporation outside Pretoria. The explosions spread the flames to the factories near the refinery's storage tanks and for a while it seems the fire might spread to nearby Boreneng and on to Atteridgeville. Fire engines, police ambulances for black and white, doctors and nurses are rushed to the industrial site.

In the chaos, the roads are crowded with vehicles and people. Paul Kritzinger is racing through Atteridgeville, which is the shortest route to the petroleum refinery, when he recognises Sister Anastasia t'Hooft's car coming in the opposite direction. He stops it and rushes to her. He looks at his watch and almost shouts to her:

What on earth are you doing here, at this time, on a day like this, Sister?

I am driving Nurse Mampa home.

For goodness' sake, Sister t'Hooft, take her home as quickly as you can and drive back to the convent as fast as you can!

I'll do that, Captain.

Hurry up, Sister; this is not the place where a white woman should be alone at night.

What could a nun be doing in a black location at night, Kritzinger asks himself. He has often been told that she rides into the location, bringing in the Africans who attend night school at Boreneng. Why on earth should Boreneng run night classes for black people in the first place? The more educated the African becomes, the more trouble he gives the white man; the more he demands race equality; the more he wants white women; the more he turns to communism. At police headquarters, the nuns have an ugly name. The story about them which hurts Kritzinger most is that they have affairs with the Africans. The lie is told with so many variations the white police have made themselves believe that it is true.

The enemies of the Afrikaner are Kritzinger's personal enemies. The friends of his enemies are his own personal foes. All he needs to regard a person as an enemy is to be told that that person associates with the enemies of the Afrikaner. Sister Anastasia t'Hooft is not the politically-conscious type of nun, but is known as a passionate advocate of increased health services for African mothers and their babies. That makes her an enemy; a communist aiding the movement to

266

Blood River. Well, Kritzinger tells himself, enemies exist to be fought and if the nun is going to run around the location on a turbulent night, she is asking for trouble; she must get it; get it soon, in a way which will teach all the white girls in the world to think twice about coming to do missionary work in South Africa.

Kritzinger moves swiftly to his car. He has made up his mind. Rarely does an Afrikaner get such an opportunity to strike and strike hard at his enemies. He walks like a man determined to strike. He jumps into his car, without turning round to see if anybody recognises him and drives up the location street to the headquarters of the location police where he parks his car and goes in for a chat with the station commander, Sergeant-Major Pitso.

Bashise's cottage is about three houses from the police station. The evening is warm and Bashise sits in the unlit verandah of his house, cooling himself. From where he is, he can see what is going on in the front yard of the police station. He sees Kritzinger's car drive in.

That white man, he tells himself, well, there's something wrong in his head. To be out here, on a day like this in a location? He knows people don't like him here.

After a while, Kritzinger emerges from the police station and, instead of getting into his car, leaves it in the yard and walks up the poorly lit street past Bashise's cottage. The African thinks this unusual even for a student of anthropology. Whatever the motive, he is certain it is not in his interest for the chief of the Pretoria police district to know developments in the location which Bashise himself is not aware of. He rushes into his house, puts on his blue denim petrol-pump attendant's overall and cap and dashes through the back door to the land between the rows of houses used by night-soil collectors when the location is asleep.

In the older locations, these lanes are narrow; there is room in them only for wagons, drawn by oxen, on which the night-soil buckets are loaded. As they run parallel with the streets, it is possible for a person to move down a lane without being seen by the people on the street even on a partially moonlit night like the one on which Kritzinger visits the location. The lanes are not cleaned; dead cats and dogs and rats are sometimes thrown there. The night-soil collectors are the poorest paid workers in the location and, as a class, are treated with as much regard as the human bone-breakers of Tibet. They are always in a bad temper, eager to avenge themselves on a society against which they are bitter and when the contents of the buckets spill on to the lanes, they leave them there, as their own especial type of commentary on life in the location. Bashise is adept at stepping on the right spots even on the darkest of dark nights. The sky is partially overcast, but the moon shines powerfully enough behind the clouds to enable him to keep track of the police chief without being seen. All sorts of ideas pass through the African's mind. Could it be that Kritzinger has an affair with an African woman? That would be stupidity of the dumbest type in a man occupying his position. He cannot sit on a thing like that forever. And, if the girl was in the location he is as good as a dead man already. The boys with the *intshumentshu* would not miss their opportunity. People like Maggie would not hesitate to trap him; it is fun to smash the pillars of Afrikanerdom between the legs of an African woman.

The Afrikaners know that sex with the African will destroy them; but no section of whites shows greater determination to sacrifice almost everything for the opportunity to get between black legs. The joke in the locations is that no matter how highly placed a Boer is, he cannot resist the legs of an African woman. But then, that is one of the stories told in the locations. Bashise cannot imagine Kritzinger being so foolish as to take these risks. He remembers the woman he met in Swaziland with her two Coloured sons. She had a lot to say about Kritzinger. But this is dynamite, Bashise tells himself, and he quickly forces the thought out of his mind. Failing to find an answer for Kritzinger's curious behaviour, Bashise decides to follow the instincts of a policeman—and to stalk his chief.

Kritzinger walks through the smaller gate of the location. The main street in Atteridgeville, unlike the others, is tarred, to facilitate the movement of police vans during Pass raids over week-ends or riots. The road is part of the highway to the refinery. Beyond the gate, a dirt track branches from the road and leads to the Roman Catholic mission station at Boreneng, on a hillock outside the location. To Bashise's surprise, Kritzinger follows the road to Boreneng. There has been a lot of ugly talk at police headquarters against the Dutch nuns, where some officers swear that the nuns are communist spies in the habit of the religious. Nobody in the police force doubts that the two nuns who drove Mareka and Masilo to Swaziland were "communists." As is always the case when women are involved in the clash of colour, sex moves in. A rumour, in which the security police are particularly interested, runs to the effect that some of the Dutch nuns have affairs with black men. That, Bashise tells himself, might explain Kritzinger's peculiar movements. The African keeps his nose on the white man's trail. If the police wanted to make any arrests, though, the chief of the uniformed section in Pretoria would hardly be the man for the job. But, Bashise tells himself, Kritzinger is an ambitious man who will do anything to push himself to the top.

Half a mile beyond, the road is hidden from view by a slight incline. A small cluster of tall gum trees stands between Kritzinger and the African trailing him. Bashise climbs one of the trees to see what Kritzinger is up to. The police chief is walking down the dirt road to a drift at the bottom of the little valley when Sister Anastasia t'Hooft's car drives past Bashise's perch, down the incline. The African gasps in disbelief. His first reaction is that the rendezvous has been arranged;

that Kritzinger and the nun have an affair. She is alone in the car. That, in itself, is not unusual; she often drives groups of African Roman Catholics into the location after meetings at the mission and returns alone. She has done that for years and nothing has happened to her. She is well-known in the location and nobody imagines she would be in danger at night. The lights now shine on Kritzinger, who raises his hands to stop the car. The African gasps again when the car stops. Kritzinger climbs into the car which quickly moves off and rounds a nearby curve. Bashise is certain he hears the sound of a gunshot. A few minutes later, the car turns round and comes toward the cluster of trees.

The car moves off the narrow road. Bashise can see from his perch that Kritzinger is behind the driver's wheel. The nun slouches in a curious position by his side. The police chief parks the car among the trees, away from the dirt track. Kritzinger opens the door, and Bashise sees that the nun is dead. Kritzinger seems to be cutting something from her body. The African holds his breath and asks all his ancestors to prevent him coughing or sneezing. He is sure now that Kritzinger had ambushed the woman. The stories at security police headquarters about the nuns now begin to make sense; ugly sense; the sort of sense which the insensate hatreds between black and white are developing and now are spilling everywhere. For a moment, Bashise is seized with fear for his own life; if he were to make a sound—or a sudden movement, Kritzinger would shoot him on the spot to wipe out the evidence. After a while, Kritzinger straightens himself, wipes his hands with a handkerchief, shuts the car door and walks back to the location.

Bashise keeps his perch until he is sure the police chief is well out of sight. Then he climbs down and moves cautiously to the car, still puzzled. The moon shines brilliantly now. Bashise looks through the window of the car and sees the nun sprawled on the front seat of her car.

So, this is what happens? When the culture of the white man cracks it goes to these extremes of ugliness? It destroys itself . . . and those who uphold it.

He walks away, shaking his head. It is not until he reaches the main road that he remembers the police dogs might pick up his trail. But so far he has not encountered anyone. Good. It is not his murder! He quickly moves to the centre of the tarred road and keeps to the tire track until he enters the location. Let the dogs run. His track is dead.

Among the Zulus, it is said that the woman has one very clearly defined attitude to a secret; if it is too small, she sees no reason why she should keep it in her bosom. If it is a great secret, she regards it as a crime against humanity to keep it to herself. Bashise realises he has stumbled on a secret of the times, as the English press would say; he walks on, not knowing what to do with it at that moment.

XXI. A Deity With Clay Feet

Impangele enhle ekhala igijima.

(The wise guinea fowl keeps running as it sounds the alarm.)

The days go by painfully for Bashise. A heavy downpour had fallen toward dawn on the day of Sister Anastasia t'Hooft's murder. That solved one of his problems. The absolute erasure of his trail, however, did nothing to remove the fears which develop in him as he considers the implications of the murder, for, he tells himself, he has witnessed a dimension of ugliness in the white man which he had not thought possible. The white people are held before everybody as God's own chosen people and the nuns are projected as the cream of white womanhood—even by the Calvinist Afrikaners. This does not mean that they love the nuns; they are repulsed by the Roman Catholics. But the nuns are virgins, a strange virtue by which the white man sets the greatest store. By choosing freely to allow no man between their legs they embody the noblest notions of purity known in the white experience. This, even the most rabid Afrikaner enemy of the Catholics will concede. What urge then would be so powerful as to drive Kritzinger to the extreme of killing a nun and cutting out her organs of procreation? For, when the police got to the scene of the murder they found that the nun's body had been terribly mutilated and her private parts cut out. Why would a white man in a responsible position do this sort of thing? The answer is quick.

The press, churchmen and government spokesmen on the white side are unanimous in saying that the murder was a ritual killing. Everybody knows that ritual murder has always been attributed to the African peoples. The story is given wide publicity around the world; a chorus of abuse, lectures, sermons and excoriations has immediately arisen from the African's "friends" and his foes, on the homefront and abroad. A point which is particularly gratifying to the government is that even at the United Nations, those governments which attacked Pretoria with the greatest bitterness do not think to deny that the crime has been committed by an African; in their defence of him, they weakly argue that he has just been provoked too much.

The Dutch people are shocked by the crime and are divided in their reactions to it. Most complain that the African makes the task of

271

his friends difficult if he resorts to actions which strengthen the hand of the government in Pretoria. Some urge that it might be wise to withdraw Dutch nuns from South Africa before African anger against the whites explodes into an uncontrollable conflagration. A very small section of the press in Holland, recalling Nazi tricks, warns against seeing events in South Africa too simply through the eyes of the ruling white minority. Is there not the possibility that agents-provocateurs might have been at work in the Boreneng murder?

Afrikanerdom is hysterically beside itself with rage. The government press extorts maximum advantage from the murder, which it represents as a cast-iron case for the segregation of the races. Loudest in demanding action is Kritzinger's wife who stops almost at nothing in her clamours for the defence of white womanhood. One night, an African is caught by the police sticking a bill-poster to the side of the Kruger memorial with these words:

IF THE WHITE WOMEN ARE THAT BRITTLE, WHY DON'T THEY AND THEIR FAMILIES RE- TURN TO EUROPE? DOWN WITH THE PASSES FOR WOMEN!

De Haas has long since been transformed into a phenomenon in Afrikaner politics by his strong doomsday premonitions of coming disaster. He tells his closest friends with fierce joy that he knew something would one day happen to those pretty Hollander girls at Boreneng who would not listen when told by those who know the kaffer to have nothing to do with the blacks.

His foreign minister calls in the Dutch ambassador, Jonkheer Frykenius van Imhoff. The relationship between the ambassador and the foreign minister is characterised by a warmth which goes beyond the requirements of protocol. The link between them is the love they share for ancient Greek literature. The foreign minister, Brand van Zyl, is the son of a former Greek professor at the university of Pretoria who translated Sappho's poetry into Afrikaans. His son is writing a critical assessment of the great Greek lesbian's compositions. In matters of culture, van Zyl is regarded in the CNP as something of a maverick whose cosmopolitanism serves the very useful purpose of smoothing feelings when Pretoria and some Western capitals start calling each other diplomatic names. As for the ambassador, he was formerly a professor of Greek at Utrecht. By a happy coincidence, he also is an authority on the poetry of Sappho.

Your Excellency, the government of the Republic of South Africa requests you to transmit to the government of the Netherlands and, through it, to the Queen, the royal family and the people of Holland the condolences of the people of South Africa on their recent bereavement. The forces of barbarism have struck at the innocent who left the security and safety of their land and crossed the seas to save the primitives from their savage ignorance. On this sad occasion the government of South Africa cannot help drawing the parallels between the murder and the arson which seeks to destroy the achievements of white civilisation in the southern part of the dark continent. Needless to say, the government of South Africa is under the obligation to protect life within its frontiers. But our ability to do this is limited by the disparity in black and white numbers. My government would request the co-operation of the Dutch government in making it known to Dutch Christians that the services of foreign nuns are not appreciated in the black community. If the black people do not appreciate what the Netherlands are doing for them, it would help all concerned if they were left to themselves.

The ambassador expresses his and his government's appreciation of the message of condolence and assures the foreign minister that he will transmit the suggestion on the possible withdrawal of Netherlands nuns from Boreneng to the appropriate authorities in Holland.

The minister rises to see the ambassador to his car. Outside, the ambassador suddenly stops walking as he approaches his car. He is a pedant even in this moment.

You know, I sometimes have the feeling that we live in momentous times, when history is taking a new turn. We are coming to the end of a great literary era and are on the threshold of entering a new age. In the last twenty-five hundred years the best European literature has focused on the mind. The revolution which is now freeing millions of peoples in Africa, Asia and elsewhere is laying the foundations for a literature which will focus on the essence of being human. The prospect has frightening implications . . . . For these people the mind is not everything.

Well? At least I'm glad I shall long be dead when the change gets into its stride, the minister smiles amiably.

I'm glad, too, I won't be around . . . . At least, they'll have larger planes and bigger and faster ships then . . . minds or no minds! And the ambassador jumps into his car.

* * *

Bashise is a worried man these days. The evenings under his verandah are no longer the moments of peace which meant so much to him in bygone days. No matter how hard he tries to forget the secret history has knocked into his future, it comes up every moment of his waking life; it comes up even in his dreams. He screams and wakes up

273

and sits up, breathing heavily as though he has been chased by terrible forms. He cannot tell it to his wife; he cannot tell it to anybody because, in the final analysis, to keep it to himself is his only guarantee of remaining alive. But keeping it is giving it the dimensions of a perpetual and cruel lie in his soul; furthermore, keeping it makes him a collaborator in the calumniation of his people; it makes him the slave who will drink the saliva of his oppressor in order to survive. If he lets the secret out, in order to let the world know the truth about the innocence of his people, his wife and his family will be punished cruelly every moment of their lives to their death. He never forgets what happened to an old friend of his, Samuel Baloyi. Such is the vindictiveness of the Afrikaner when he hates.

What sort of people are these, he asks himself when alone on his verandah, who fulfil themselves by burdening the conscience of others with impossible choices? What on earth would drive a respectable officer like Kritzinger to murder an innocent woman in order to give the Africans a bad name for the purpose of establishing the Afrikaner's case before mankind? To take on such a putrescent task?

In the old days Bashise spent some of his time under the verandah roof reading history; that helped him fix his position in the momentum of events. He saw the Afrikaners as an embattled people and himself as one of the executioners slowly tightening the noose around the white people's necks. "Slowly" was the operative word; it meant that he could strike when no white man saw him. But now a situation has arisen with which he cannot live; if he continues to fight in the shadows, he might crack; he might end up in a mental hospital. He never knew precisely what happened to Dr. Robert Shawcross when he finally broke down and agreed to be a government witness to send scores of his own friends and brave men and women to the gallows, to jail, or into exile. He tells himself that he knows only too well what tortures there are! He grits his teeth.

Deep wounds are cut into his remaining pride by the barrage of attacks and taunts, the anger, the feeling of outrage and frustration in the columns of government papers against his people. Nobody is in doubt about what is in the minds of *Die Aanslag's* editors, for example. If they had their way, the armoured division of the police force would roll into Atteridgeville to shoot every African male as a lesson to the black people that they must never again touch a white woman. Bokkie, the paper's political analyst, is frustrated by the fact that the Afrikaner has "gone soft" in a world dominated by niggers, kaffers and Asian coolies. As a result savages feel bold enough to mess around with white womanhood. The paper itself is frustrated over the fact that the government does not act firmly enough in finding out the murderer, while it notes with approval that Paul Kritzinger, the chief of police in the Pretoria district, is personally in charge of the case.

Kritzinger's wife, always a crusader for the protection of the white woman, has been transformed by events into a heroine. Every other day, *Die Aanslag* gives front-page prominence to her denunciations of the Africans and their rank-smelling women. De Haas is particularly pleased with the reactions the murder produces in the English and Jewish communities. Leading personalities in these white groups make threatening noises against the African people and warn against provoking the whites beyond a certain point. The white liberals, who are embarrassed by the tragedy, are quick to point out that there are responsible, law-abiding and civilised Africans who abhor ritual murder and who want to co-operate with the whites in eliminating the conditions which led to the Boreneng murder. They urge these "responsible" Africans to raise their voice against the murder and to co-operate with the police in the search for the murderer. This, they advise, would be a valuable contribution to better race relations. De Haas is increasingly delighted with the dilemma of the white liberals who find themselves forced to come out so clearly to support white cultural supremacy. The passions aroused by the murder have at last given him the opportunity to purge the police force of Prinsloo influences. He calls in his Minister of Justice.

If you were in my position, what would you do? First, it was the cowardly placation of the kaffers in the Valley Of A Thousand Hills in Natal; then came the strikes, the invasion of Union Buildings, the arson and, now, the murder of a white woman to serve ritual ends. If these things happened in the full view of the police, what would you do if you were in my position?

Meneer, the situation is not one which can be controlled by the police any longer . . . .

I've heard that before . . . .

Yes, you have, meneer, but what have you done about it? This is a political problem which requires a political solution.

Now is the time for me to do something about it; I instruct you to remove Prinsloo from the post of Commissioner of Police.

Mr. Prime Minister, you know this is no answer to the problem.

The choice is yours to obey or not. The interview is over.

* * *

Paul Kritzinger has been promoted to the rank of colonel and is the new Police Commissioner. He has persuaded the new Minister of Justice, Wessels Bierbuyck, to create the post of special political adviser to the Commissioner and has appointed Bashise to the post. Bashise walks into the Commissioner's office.

Sir, I have come to see you about the Boreneng murder.

Well?

It was a bad thing to happen, Sir; very bad, very dirty and very ugly, Sir. And very dangerous, Sir.

What would be going on in the mind of a black man who would do a thing like that? Kritzinger's voice is guarded.

I don't know, Sir. But in the old days, when we lived in darkness, we believed that the person was the incarnation of the power which activates creation. Every part of his body was charged with this unique power. Our ancestors believed this power was concentrated at its best in the private parts of a woman . . . .

That explains the mutilation!

Sir, the power in the woman can stop the sun in the heavens.

Have you come to make me a holy man?

No, Sir; I have been thinking about your suggestion that Chief Bulube and the prime minister should meet.

Say: The Prime Minister and Chief Bulube; he paused heavily, then said, I don't think the prime minister would like to talk to Bulube any more; Bulube missed his chance. If Bulube has changed his mind and wants to speak to the prime minister, he had better tell the strikers to go back to work before the white people get fed up; he has better tell the arsonists to stop being silly. The whites are a patient people, but they will not allow themselves to be provoked beyond a certain point.

The African, to whom Kritzinger does not offer a seat, turns his head quickly to the wall behind him, as if to see if the door is still shut. He moves a little closer to the Commissioner's desk.

You see, Sir, you are no longer the master of your life and I am not the master of mine. You are the prisoner of your power and I am the prisoner of my anger. That is true of your people, Sir; it is true of mine, too. We are caught in a trap set by history, Sir. A cruel force drives us relentlessly to destruction; it moves events slowly, inevitably, to a catastrophe we cannot escape. Your people and my people hold each other in the grip of death; you will not let go, we will not let go.

You will shoot us, Sir, he continues, but we shall burn your factories; you will shoot us, Sir, and we shall burn your farms; you will shoot us, Sir, and we shall burn your houses; you will shoot us, Sir, and one day white men will kill black women. And when that happens, shall I tell you what will follow, Sir? The Africans, the Arabs, the Chinese and the Japanese will put their heads together somewhere in Central Africa to produce cheap, portable nuclear bombs with a limited explosive potential to blow up the Vaal Dam in the Transvaal and blow up the gold mines of South Africa. And when that day comes, Sir, there will not be enough tears in the world to extinguish the conflagration.

Kritzinger reddened. What are you jabbering about?

You and I are not the people to understand events, Sir, for we are only instruments of the cruel force; you do things you do not want to do, Sir; I, too, do them against my wish. Chief Bulube and the prime minister are the people to understand.

I never thought philosophy was one of your strong points.

I am not a philosopher, Sir . . . .

Well, then, you're a seer; you see into the future which I don't see.

I am a worried man, Sir. This cruel force I have just spoken about—we call it *ushaba* in my language—will not stop before it has destroyed everything beautiful in this land (and ugly, too, he thought).

I'm not sure I know what you want me to do . . . .

Persuade the prime minister to see Chief Bulube, Sir. The two men will put their heads together. If they do, they could drive this land back to sanity; they might; who knows? When you know the things I have seen, Sir. Our leaders must meet.

Come on, Bashise! What's happening to you? What have you seen? What are you talking about? What do you know!

I am a policeman, Sir, and a policeman deals with people at levels where they are at their ugliest. I have seen ugliness, Sir. Do you think there is anything beautiful about the campaigns against us in the papers and in parliament, Sir? The mess we are in over that ritual murder near Boreneng?

You move among the people in the location. I am personally responsible for the case and, if you give me the clues, nobody will know about it. But we've got to get to the root of the murder. Things like these provoke the whites everywhere. . . . Kritzinger seemed out of breath.

You're right, Sir; they do. But, if Chief Bulube comes to Pretoria, he might clear up many things we do not know. If you will arrange my leave, I would be glad to travel to Natal. I am certain, Sir, I shall persuade him to meet the prime minister.

If you insist, I shall pass the recommendation through the proper channels to the prime minister.

Thank you, Sir.

And, you'll go on leave as from to-morrow. I know the tremendous responsibility you carry on your shoulders now; you need a little time to be alone and to plan your course. I agree with you at least on one thing: We live in terrible times.

Yes, Sir. Good morning, Sir!

* * *

Bulube and some of his followers believe that deep in his heart, the Afrikaner does not want to go to Blood River. Spiritually, he might not return from the appointment on the battlefield; there is no possible guarantee that he would. Physically, the appointment could very well be the beginning of the end of his stay in Africa. The prospect of a diaspora has frightening implications; the scattering would destroy Afrikanerdom because, in the final analysis, the Afrikaners have nothing to give to enrich the human experience, culturally, or materially.

277

In a world of proliferating power groups a people has to give in order to guarantee its own survival. Culturally, the Afrikaner has nothing to offer the Africans whose culture is rooted so much in antiquity it can swallow the Afrikaner's if need arises. Economically, the advantages the Afrikaner offers the English, the Jews and foreign investors are guaranteed, ultimately, by the African's goodwill. As long as the Africans are docile, South Africa will remain a good investment field. But the Africans are now making it clear that they want to be masters of their destiny; they realise that they have power and that the white man cannot stop them when they use this power to create the conditions they want in South Africa.

History is telling the white nations to come to terms with the black, brown and yellow nations on the basis of agreement on ultimate objectives. The Afrikaners are an integral part of the white world; history is telling them to come to terms with the Africans; that Afrikanerdom defiles itself when it makes self-mutilating attempts to stop an historical process which is now shaping the course of events in the world. History is saying to the Afrikaner that it will not do him much good to base his policy on the bribing of the West with high profits on investments. One day, the economies of Africa will create world conditions which will hurt the Afrikaner and threaten his survival in Africa. In the final analysis Kritzinger was trying to change the course of history when he murdered the nun; he was trying to stop the frightening process.

The Africans insist that in a situation of challenge with which Afrikaner culture cannot cope, its values are cracking; that this culture cannot cope with the demands of black-white co-existence. A climate of thinking has developed in which the more the Afrikaner dirties himself to please foreign investors the more they kick him in the teeth, while pocketing the profits. The Afrikaner has become a prisoner and not an ally of these people. Some Afrikaners have begun to revolt against this; they say that their people are caught in a vicious trap set for them by the British when they formed the Union of South Africa to channel South Africa's gold and diamonds to the City of London. These Afrikaners—they are a small minority which talks in whispers— say the real demands of Afrikaner survival call for an African-Afrikaner alliance to smash the trap and lay the foundations for an African-Afrikaner solution to the race problem.

Some Afrikaners are tired of living under a perpetual cloud of uncertainty about the future; of determining their lives, ultimately, by the grace of the British, the Jews, the Coloureds and, which is most frightening, the grace of the African. These people have begun to question the value for the Afrikaner of the obnoxious African-Afrikaner-English balance. The pressures they exert quietly combine with events in the outside world and the strikes to persuade de Haas that a meeting with Bulube is in the interests of the Afrikaner.

Irony, long an ingredient in black-white relations, creeps into the new situation developing. When de Haas decides to meet the African, his heart is at war with his mind; it tells him that the meeting with the African will in effect be the moment of capitulation. But Bulube's heart, too, is at war with his head. In the conditions created by the Passes For Women Bill and the Boreneng murder, his heart tells him that meeting de Haas is a moment of capitulation. But like the Afrikaner, the African does not want to be on the banks of the Blood River at this moment, not yet; he does not have the arms to settle accounts. As a result, a balance of forces has emerged; an equilibrium determined by strength and weakness on both sides which gives Bulube and de Haas no choice other than to meet.

* * *

The prime minister has never met a black man on terms of equality before; he has never even come to believe that there are such creatures as black leaders. The English, ever on the alert for situations which make de Haas ridiculous, depict him in cartoons as the Irishman who swore that there was no such a thing on earth as a red fish. When confronted with one, he burst out: "The fellow who caught this fish is a liar!" Throughout his life, the prime minister has regarded every black a prey to communism and every educated African as an agitator. He did not want any contact whatsoever with these people whom he openly denounced as the scum of the earth.

But then, the law, written into the Statute Book by his own CNP, recognises certain types of black people as the leaders of the Africans. His own law requires that as prime minister he should meet these people and to demonstrate to the sceptical at home and abroad that his policy works. Besides, he has come under increasing pressure from the growing Afrikaner entrepreneurial class, whose mouths water when the markets of Free Africa are mentioned, to strike a deal with the Africans instead of allowing them to move to a position of confrontation. *Above all, even the conservative race-haters in the Dutch Reformed Church admit that being the polecat of international affairs hurts the Afrikaner.* They resent intensely, of course, the way the quality of Afrikaner leadership is laughed at and ridiculed in the English press, where the line taken is indistinguishable from the assertion that the Afrikaner is incapable of evolving the type of diplomacy that will enable him to solve the race problem. In the complicated contradictions of the clash of colour one sometimes does not have to read between the lines of press reports to realise that the English are not altogether hostile to the use of strikes by the Africans to embarrass Pretoria. It is in these conditions that the prime minister feels constrained to meet Bulube.

Chief Bulube walks into the prime minister's office in the traditional attire of a Zulu gentleman. This creates a somewhat embarrassing situation; the black leader's costume could be a declaration of political positions or an index of commitment to African traditions. CNP policy preaches that the Africans should develop along their own lines. If the traditional attire is a declaration of political war, there is no point in the discussions; if, on the other hand, the attire signifies acceptance of the government's line, the interview marks a major breakthrough in African-Afrikaner relations.

Bulube, too, has his reservations. If the interview is going to be one more monologue in which the white man will lay down the law for the African, there seems no real point in wasting much time with de Haas. On the other hand, the coming-together might be the beginning of a long and difficult dialogue at the end of which the Africans and the Afrikaners might agree on a treaty to ensure the redistribution of the land and other resources in response to the Africans' demands to guarantee the Afrikaner a permanent place in the African sun.

The two men face and size each other up like two bulls taking up positions for a clash about whose outcome neither is certain. The encounter is momentous; the black world and the white meet either to part forever or to start the painful process which could one day enable the whites to co-exist with peoples from different racial or cultural backgrounds. History stares both men in the eyes.

I am glad, Chief, you found it possible for us to meet.

I am glad you made it possible.

Chief, as an officer appointed by the government, you are no doubt concerned about the lawlessness in Natal which has now spread to the Transvaal. It's the sort of development which does not do anybody any good.

I certainly am concerned . . . .

Just the other day some silly native killed a nun who had given her life to serve his own people. Things like that must come to a stop and I know that, as a chief, you agree with the government that they must stop. Now, I know that you people have difficulties with the rough elements in your community. But we have tried to help; we have destroyed the organisations run by the communists to undermine the authority of the chiefs among your people. We've given the chiefs the power to lay the foundations for responsible government in the reserves and, when your people are ready, you know we shall give you the independence we want you to have. But the strikes and the arson provoke the whites; they make it difficult for the government to do the things it would like to do for your people. I called you to give you the chance to tell me what we, as a government, can do to help you stop the strikes and return things to normal in your province and, of course, the Transvaal. As you know, our power as a government is limited by the mandate we receive from our voters and what we must do must be approved by them.

Mr. Prime Minister, allow me to say that your perception of the quarrel between black and white is determined naturally by the perspectives accepted in your community, just as your mandate is. You will allow me to say I am similarly handicapped, though from different perspectives.

No, Chief, you hold your office for life; you inherited it from your ancestors. Every five years I have to go to the electorate for the endorsement of my mandate.

That makes things easier . . . . I mean . . . using the vote to decide issues. But that system would not work in my community where we attach importance to the essence of being human and not the cash value of the person. We have to move inch by inch and our decisions are based on the consensus principle. That is how the black race has survived the calamities brought on it by contact with the whites in the last six or seven hundred years.

Chief, we have not been here for six hundred years!

You were not the first whites to set their feet on African soil.

I see what you mean. But calamities is not the right word, Chief. Contact with you has not been one disastrous trail all along the line. The white man introduced a number of useful things to make life better for you.

I do not deny that in some respects contact between black and white was helpful, but the overall experience has been disastrous.

The phenomenon strokes his lips; he does that when he is warming up for an explosion. His hands rub his knees now.

What do you mean by that, Chief?

Your system of values makes a mockery of conscience. You confront the person with inhuman choices. In doing that, your system reduces the person to an animal . . . . If I see a white man, a businessman, a scholar or even a saint, I never know whether or not he is an animal . . . until I have had dealings with him and have realised that he attaches importance to the essence of being human.

That's life, Chief.

I'd like to think in terms of alternatives.

Why alternatives?

So that we can attain clarity on what black and white are quarrelling about.

Let me ask you one straight question and I want a straight answer: What is the alternative to life? Tell me.

If you put the question that way, I'm afraid we will have to go back and define terms. Obviously you mean something different when you talk of life. I am life; you are life; both of us are life; creation is life . . . .

Oh! Come off it .... All that talk of alternatives .... It means nothing to me.

The prime minister is visibly uncomfortable. He is used to talking to black people in imperatives and Bulube does not allow him to do this; he forces him to concentrate on principles; to think hard and to deal with the African as an intellectual equal. The phenomenon resents being treated this way by a black man. Tension is rising in the room. The two men do not have a common basis on which to conduct a meaningful exchange of views; their interview deteriorates into an almost repetitious statement of the positions they have taken in public.

Alternatives are crucial, Mr. Prime Minister; crucial for the Afrikaner and crucial for us. See what is happening all around you; in Mozambique and Angola. The world is becoming a very dangerous place for the Afrikaner to live in ... if he does not adapt to the demands of change.

Why do you bother yourself so much about the Afrikaner? Why don't you mind your own business and leave him alone?

Because he has involved himself so tragically in my business. See the problem this way, Mr. Prime Minister: the Afrikaner is caught in a trap laid for him by the British and Lord Milner. The British fought a cruel war with your people ... in order to force you into the Union of South Africa, where they wanted you to become the managers of their financial empire. And that is what you have become. The British are the largest single group of foreign investors. In order to guarantee their profits you have had to impose a tyranny on us which gives you an ugly name in the world. See what they do to you? They call you names in international assemblies, attack you and kick you in the teeth while pocketing the profits you guarantee by oppressing us. This is bad for you and tragic for us; that's the trap I'm talking about. You cannot free yourselves from it; we have to free you ....

The phenomenon is surprised and angry at one and the same time. He is surprised to hear the African refer with some understanding to the way the British treated the Afrikaner. He is angered by the suggestion that the black man can think of freeing the Afrikaner.

Let me say something about the dangers which face the Afrikaner because, if he goes down, we do not want to go down with him. He is isolated in the English-speaking world; he stands virtually alone in the international community. Power is shifting from the white nations to the peoples of colour in the world and this destroys the value of the white skin as a bond of unity among the white people. Resources are going to be the new bond which will tie peoples together and most of these are controlled by the black, brown and yellow peoples of the world. Trouble is developing for the Afrikaner inside Africa. The white united front he tried to create is collapsing. One of these days the Portuguese are going to open negotiations with the Free Africans and strike a deal with them on resources and, when that happens, they are not likely to need the Afrikaner as an ally.

We shall support the Portuguese in Angola and Mozambique—if they break away and declare themselves independent. That will make them African nations; they'll be in our position and might need us then.

Possibly. But without the Portuguese army, how far would they go?

We have maintained our position against you for some time . . . .

You had the gun; we did not. But all that is changing, Mr. Prime Minister. Just as the gun destroyed the power of the spear as a guarantee of dominance among us, the portable nuclear bomb with a limited explosive potential is destroying the power of the gun as a guarantee of Afrikaner dominance in South Africa. One of these days an African government will produce the portable nuclear bomb and pass it on to us to enable us to settle accounts with the Afrikaner. Imagine, Mr. Prime Minister, the humble African sweeper in your office depositing the bomb here to raze Union Buildings to the ground! Nothing would be safe. Imagine sweepers everywhere destroying your factories, your churches, your homes and your mines. We have the uranium here, in Africa. Our young people are studying in America, Britain, China, India, France and Russia; they are mastering the technique of turning Africa's uranium into a nuclear bomb. And when they are ready, well, Mr. Prime Minister, you will see what you will see. Why do you think we rejected the former prime minister's offer of independence in the reserves?

That's no problem; why do you think we endorse so many of your people out of our cities? At the right time, we shall force you to be free. Do you ever pause to think that we can free you against your wish . . . on our terms?

We live in exciting times . . . your people and mine. If you are preparing for what we want to do, we, too, have already taken precautions. We are laying the foundations for a larger nation which will bring together the black people in this country, in Angola, Botswana, Lesotho, Malawi, Mozambique, Namibia, Rhodesia, Swaziland and Zambia . . . . That will give us a black nation of 60,000,000 people, to start with . . . .

And, you think the white people will allow you to do that?

No! But the white man is no longer our problem; he is not important for the purpose of establishing the larger nation. We no longer bother ourselves much about the white man. We have taken him out of our minds; we think as though he does not exist. The people who matter now are the Africans with whom we want to unite. If the white man wants to join us in our great experiment, let him take his place in the queue . . . right at the back. If he cannot stomach that and chooses to stand in the way . . . to oppose a process of history, well, that is his headache, not ours.

That will be the day, when the black people will unite . . . .

We are only at the beginning of things. First there must be an ideal . . . a vision. We do not have to borrow one from the white man; we have had one for thousands of years; we call it *uBuntu*. Every black African knows precisely what you mean when you mention the *uBuntu* concept. Then, there must be the translation of the ideal into action. Look at the map of Africa to-day and remember what it looked like yesterday. See what we have done . . . with these bare hands!

What do you want from the white man then?

He has nothing to give us which we can't get on our own if we persevere in the struggle. So . . . we ultimately want nothing from him. Once people are out of your mind, what can you want from them? Nothing. We want something from ourselves, from our own people, from Africa.

Chief, I don't care for high falutin talk. I want you to tell me about the grievances of your tribe . . . . I want you to tell me how to stop the strikes . . . .

We have only one grievance, Mr. Prime Minister: the violence you do to our ideal of nationhood.

Ideal of nationhood? What are you talking about? Your tribe is your nation. Don't tell me about what the white man taught you in his schools. The political reality in Africa is the tribe; not the nation.

Both of us do not get together to know each other at close range. For this reason, allow me to go back a little in our history . . . Zulu history. Way back in the eighteenth century an African prince ruled over a small clan in Natal. His name was Senzangakhona ka Jama. His clan, like all the peoples of Southern Africa at the time, was committed to the *Buntu* philosophy. His court poet defined the political ideal of nationhood for the Africans in these terms:

> A cord of destiny let us weave
> O Menzi, scion of Jama,
> That
> To heavens beyond the reach of spirit-forms
> We may climb.
> (So long must the cord be)
> The spirit-forms themselves
> Will break their tiny toes
> If they dare to climb.

There was no white man in the land of the Zulus when the poet gave us this ideal of nationhood; there were no white man's schools either. The poet was speaking to the ages; to future generations. Shaka the Great built the Zulu nation on the ideal; so did Mshweshwe in Lesotho, Mzilikazi and many others. In 1912, Dr. Pixley ka Isaka Seme united the black peoples of South Africa on the basis of the ideal. We are building a larger black nation of Southern Africa on the basis of this ideal; the ideal translates the *Buntu* philosophy into political action. Both the philosophy and the ideal have not been given to us by the white people; they belong to us; they are the lasting bond which ties together the peoples of Sub-Saharan Africa.

I can tell you one thing, Chief: every Afrikaner will be dead before your dream comes true.

Oh no, Mr. Prime Minister! You don't have to die. The white man rejected us when it suited him; it suits us to reject him now. But we reject him differently; we offer the Afrikaner an alternative. We want a peace treaty; we want a conference of the black and white nations of Southern Africa at which we shall restore to ourselves that which belongs to us and guarantee the Afrikaner a permanent place in the African sun. We offer the Afrikaner an alternative to being the political polecat of international affairs. Our alternative is better than what Dr. van Warmelo offered us. He offered us the shadow of freedom; not its substance. He wanted to make us the vassals of the white man; this is the position to which the Afrikaner is trying to reduce Botswana, Lesotho, Malawi and Swaziland. He calls that freedom; we reject it. With the poverty and overcrowding in the reserves, he forces us to be communist carbon copies against our best interests. We don't want that.

The prime minister is now visibly angry with the African; he cuts him short thus:

Well, I'm a pessimist. Life is a challenge, a struggle . . . .

I can understand that. Young people everywhere are pessimistic. They are obsessed with the imminence of catastrophe; they would destroy society itself, in the endeavour to guarantee its survival. We, Africans, have been around for too long to think of an end to life. The whites are a young race; they are still concerned with ideas when we concentrate on the essence of personhood; on the person as the source of all ideas.

I don't see what all this has to do with the strikes!

Pessimism predicates fulfilment for the Afrikaner on the destruction of the African people . . . .

The phenomenon cannot take this, as he believes, lying on his stomach. He bangs his palm on his desk.

Chief! I will not allow you to say that!

My mandate is to tell you this.

The phenomenon feels like terminating the interview; he has never been spoken to like this by a black man. But then, there always is the English press which will read all sorts of evils into the abrupt stoppage of the conversation with the African. The eyes of the world are on this interview and the world sees the prime minister through the eyes of the English press.

If you talk of destruction, your people tried it on mine. They failed and that is why I sit on this chair.

You define the race quarrel in terms which cannot be reconciled.

So what?

You don't give me an alternative . . . .

To do what? To destroy the Afrikaner? You can try your luck if you are so minded.

I'll tell you one thing, Mr. Prime Minister. There was a time when we Zulus thought iron was the guarantee of continuance for our power. When the white man came with the gun we bit the dust, as people say. One day . . . .

We know what we are doing. You do what you know; we shall do what we know. You are black; we are white. You go your own way and we shall go ours. That is good for you and for us.

I would still want you to consider alternatives. Mr. Prime Minister. Would you consider the suspension of the colour bar and the pass laws as an argument to dissuade the Africans from continuing the strikes? They are gaining a momentum which nobody might eventually control . . . .

I told you that I am a pessimist. If the worst comes to the very worst . . . the white people know what to do . . . we can look after ourselves. The phenomenon has stopped rubbing his legs. He speaks in sharp, brittle tones which sound like short peals of thunder in the distance.

You asked me for proposals to end the strikes. I would not have come to Pretoria if you had not asked me. I think it would help, Mr. Prime Minister, if you appointed a commission of inquiry presided over by a judge of the Appellate Division to determine the truth behind the Boreneng murder.

Impossible! Impossible! If a commission is set up, the agitators, the liberals, and all the communists, will gang-up and use the commission as a platform from which to attack or discredit the police. I'm not prime minister of this country in order to preside over the calumniation of the police by the enemies of the state.

You appreciate that we have been given a bad name by the incident and owe ourselves the duty to defend our good name.

Let me tell you this: No Afrikaner prime minister can ever accede to your request.

How do you expect the chiefs to maintain the law, then?

If they choose treason, they must know that we have the police and the army for that eventuality.

You do not give me much of a choice, Mr. Prime Minister. I owe myself the duty to tell you what I think you do not know. I owe you, as head of the government, the duty to let you know aspects of the truth which are kept away from you by your officers. You already have made a public statement saying no commission of inquiry will be appointed. I still wish you could change your mind . . . .

Impossible!

Then, I do not have much of a choice. I have to tell the cruel truth to you, Mr. Prime Minister. I know you didn't know that the new Commissioner of Police, Paul Kritzinger, has a black wife and two sons, who are twins. Fannie and Sampie are their names. They are about fourteen years of age and live with their black mother deep in the bushveld of Swaziland. I have been to the farm; I have statements from Kritzinger's second wife . . . .

His concubine! Not his wife!

The woman by whom he has children, Mr. Prime Minister. You are at liberty to let the Commissioner of Police be privy to what I say and I mention it to you because I want my statements challenged in a court of law, since we cannot get the commission of inquiry.

Chief, do you understand what you are saying?

Yes, Mr. Prime Minister; that is why I am here.

I see.

He might perhaps want to tell you who Fannie and Sampie are.

The prime minister does not respond.

And, if he has the confidence in his prime minister which I believe he has, he will tell you that in an excess of patriotic feeling he killed Sister Anastasia t'Hooft and mutilated her . . . .

Chief! I won't allow these statements to be made to me about a white man! About the Commissioner of Police!

I want you to take action against me in a court of law, Mr. Prime Minister; I want the government to test my allegations in its own court of law and the only person to whom I can talk with any hope of seeing action taken is the prime minister of this country.

What on earth would a decent and responsible officer want to do that thing for? I don't believe you!

First, he's an ambitious man; he wanted to be Commissioner of Police. Second, he is a good Afrikaner patriot; he wanted to create the climate of opinion in which you could reshuffle your cabinet without creating a crisis in the Afrikaans community. Third, he wanted to create an atmosphere in this country and abroad in which the strikers could be shot without the complications which Sharpeville produced. He wanted to strengthen the government's hand in persuading British, American, French, West German, Italian, Swiss and Japanese investors to gang up with the whites against my people.

You talk like a communist . . . .

I love my country. But I do not want to take too much of your time, Mr. Prime Minister. I want to leave you, first, with a question. You mentioned the army and it is a mighty fine army. But don't you see what's happening in this country and all over the world? Industrialisation is moving millions of people from the countryside to the cities where they can't grow their own food; where they have to buy food for themselves and their children. A state is able to maintain its viability as long as it can feed the city masses; that is, as long as it can convert food into the productive potential and then into wealth which must be enough to produce the food.

Whenever a state breaks the cycle and locks up the bulk of its wealth in unproductive armies or burns its accumulated wealth in wars, it reduces its ability to provide for its people and sets itself firmly on the road to final catastrophe. The British empire collapsed that way; so did the French. The Americans have not learned their lesson; they burn billions of their wealth in useless armaments programmes. They are paying for it to-day in the shortages which are becoming increasingly endemic in their economy.

China and Russia do not need to fight any war with America to destroy her power; all they have to do is to play with lightning in remote regions of the world and encourage the Americans to lock up increasing amounts of their wealth in useless arms. I see that the country you and I love is taking the slippery road to final disaster. But the Afrikaner is in a somewhat unique position; he has relative and not absolute power. He needs our labour; he needs the finance-power of the English; he needs trading partners and markets in the world. How is he going to go it alone with these weaknesses?

How do you know about what you call Kritzinger's involvement in the ritual murder?

Bashise Busengi, a black policeman, saw it all happen.

Bashise? Bashise? That's one of our finest police boys?

I wouldn't say he was a boy; not after what he told me. The pity of it all is that he's on leave at the moment.

Where is he spending it?

In Botswana . . . .

The prime minister stares angrily at the African; the latter, too, looks the white man in the eyes. There have been too many flights by black violators of the law into the former High Commission Territories. The prime minister sees the existence of the black states within the geographic area of South Africa as part of the explanation for what he regards as Bulube's cockiness. After a long pause he puts this question to the African:

What you are telling me is that Bashise has fled the country?

I have no evidence, one way or the other. But, speaking strictly for myself, Mr. Prime Minister, I wouldn't blame him if he didn't return. We Zulus say *"impangele enhle ekhala igijima."* The wise guinea fowl keeps running as it raises the alarm.

The African rises from his seat and, standing erect before the prime minister's huge desk, turns his eyes once more to the Afrikaner's.

Mr. Prime Minister, you are, as I said, a very busy man. I do not want to take more of your time. But, I want to leave you with two thoughts. The English oppressed you when they were strong. Now that you have power, you do to us what you found intolerable in the English. We feel as strongly about your rule as your people felt about British rule.

I can understand that; but our goals are different. You want to destroy the present balance of political, economic and racial forces. The white people will not allow this to happen. If you force the white man's hand, there will be a bloodbath in this country. De Haas was savage.

We know the whites won't allow it; they couldn't allow it even if they wanted to. For this reason and with all respect, Mr. Prime Minister, we have taken the white man out of our minds and we are going to create the destiny we want for ourselves as though the whites did not exist.

I warn you, the Prime Minister shouts, the white man is here to stay. I did not want to say this, but you force me to say it. The white man laid down his life for mastery in this land and he will sacrifice his blood again, to hold what he owns. You will have to take the gun out of his hands before you change this position.

You could talk to our ancestors about the gun; we do not need it. You reduced us to the limit of deprivation; we lost everything we had. That freed us from fear, for he who owns something is afraid of losing it. Driven to the bottom, we cannot be pushed farther down; if we move, it can only be toward the top and this is the direction we have taken. You might shoot us; you might have a bloodbath, but each time you kill us, you will also make your name uglier. We can't stop you doing that; the choice is yours. We also have our choice to make; to *xina* the white man. If you throw an insect into a bottle from which you withdraw all air, you *xina* it; it can't survive. You will drown this country in a bloodbath alright, but let me assure you, Mr. Prime Minister, we shall *xina* you.

The prime minister smiles menacingly. His chance has at last come; this is the moment to "put the black man in his place" as they lumberingly say in South Africa, to "teach him a lesson!" The prime minister's manner is coldly sarcastic.

That is why we have the finest police force in Africa to-day, Chief. If the police are too few to cope, well, I don't have to tell you that we have the army behind them; as you know very well, our army is strong enough to smash the combined armies of all Black Africa! All of them! And, if you people give us trouble, why do you think we are friends with Botswana, Lesotho, Malawi, Swaziland and Mozambique ... over your heads? If you withdraw your labour, they'll be glad to send their starving citizens to our factories and farms and, of course, our kitchens. Don't you see what this means, Chief? When we jingle coins in our pockets ... they will come here running ... begging us to give them jobs on our own terms. They'll be glad to accept the wages we offer them. Let me assure you, they won't mind segregation. Make no mistake about it, Chief, those black people in the independent states know power; they know that money is power; they know also that *we* have the money and not *you*. This is what independence means to them . . . .

I know the meaning, Mr. Prime Minister. But when everything has been said, I know also that the Afrikaner is human. This is crucial. There are points of weakness in the human make-up which no number of guns can protect. We know these weaknesses . . . we know where the Afrikaner is vulnerable . . . and it is at these points we are striking.

I must warn you . . . don't play with fire!

Well, as I said, the Afrikaner is human; he does not give us much of a choice; he defines the race problem in terms which cannot be negotiated and forces us to attack the most vital factor in his make-up: his personality. That surrenders to us the initiative to force him to define himself in ugly terms. We need no guns to do this. All we need to do is to help him make himself uglier; he can't stop us doing that now. We shape and mould his personality as we like. If we want him uglier, we go on strike; he panics and shoots us; if we want him to look ridiculous, he offers us freedom and we reject it. See what all this means? He is like plastic clay in our hands. Who wouldn't want us to use this advantage to the fullest?

You are playing with fire, Chief! And you will hurt yourselves.

The British told you that you were playing with fire; that you would hurt yourselves. You did not turn back. You paid the price for holding on to your convictions. We are doing exactly the same, Mr. Prime Minister, and nobody is going to stop us from doing it.

You don't expect the government to give you a licence to do that?

Mr. Prime Minister, you don't expect us to ask for it? Don't you see what is happening everywhere around you or in Mozambique? You have dumped us in the reserves, where we are dying like the Afrikaner in the British concentration camps. But I do not need to tell an Afrikaner that this is the price we have to pay for our freedom. This is the price we have had to pay in order to corrode the Afrikaner's personality. One of these days, Mr. Prime Minister, you will see the internal corrosion; you will see the Afrikaner personality collapse from internal corrosion . . . without a single African raising his arm; without us firing any shot.

Whistling in the dark! That's what you are doing. With so much drunkenness, tuberculosis and syphilis among your people? How can you corrode the white man's personality?

The drunkenness, the tuberculosis and the syphilis are the fire in which the quality of our personality is tested. We know we are being tested; we are passing the test; that is the glory of being an African. We survive tests which no race of men has endured. And we are proud of that. See, Mr. Prime Minister, we are the sort of people who do things first and shout afterwards; we do things . . . *kancane, kancane* . . . inch

290

by inch. I wish there was an Afrikaner somewhere who could grasp the implication of what I say . . . before it is too late. Good morning, Mr. Prime Minister.

De Haas does not return the farewell. The forehead-to-forehead confrontation with the black man has thrown the Prime Minister into a trauma. He is so angry he feels like kicking the African out of his office and saying unprintable things in the process. But the responsibilities of office have done much to tone down the angularities of the phenomenon; he suffers the humiliation silently.

Things begin to clear up when the African has left; at least the prime minister thinks he understands what is happening. The kaffer came on a reconaissance mission, to probe the intellectual defences of the Afrikaner. He tore the white man's system of values to pieces and talked of alternatives, as though he were the superior of the white man. He was arrogant, provocative and threatening . . . as though he had never heard of Afrikaner *kragdadigheid*. He followed in the steps of his ancestors, Dingane and Bongoza. The phenomenon smells blood in the air each time he thinks of Dingane and Bongoza; he sees visions of Weenen, Itala, O'Pate and Mgungundlovu. These evoke terrible memories in the subconsciousness of the Afrikaner. At these places the Afrikaner's gun clashed with the Zulu's spear and the conflicts brought the white man face to face with the prospect of extermination. The Prime Minister's imagination becomes particularly active when he thinks of these same Dingane and Bongoza and of Mgungundlovu, Weenen, Itala and O'Pate from the wrong end of the assegai.

The arrogance of the kaffer! He had the nerve to tell the phenomenon himself that after all, the Afrikaner is human, like everybody, when the Afrikaner had refused to have television in his country in order to make it clear to the whole world that he was a special species of the human race! The prime minister has never been spoken to in these terms by a black man. What have things come to when a kaffer can sit in judgment of the white man's civilisation, his values and achievements? When he can say he has taken the white man out of his mind! Which race on earth can ever do without the white man? Which can survive without him? And, as if all these were not enough, the kaffer even tried to assert leadership initiatives, right inside the prime minister's office, in Pretoria, of all places!

But the black man also said disturbing things about Kritzinger. That sobers the prime minister almost to the point of frightening him, now that he is alone in his office. What if the allegations are founded on fact? What could embolden a kaffer to come and make these charges to the prime minister himself and challenge the head of the government to take action? The thought of the black man travelling all the way from Natal to make such grave allegations against the head of the police force has catastrophic implications. For a moment, de Haas recoils from the examination of the implications.

He tells himself that he knows the kaffers; they are all alike; they are all liars, like their ancestors, Dingane and Bongoza. But the implications disturb his personality too much at the level of fundamentals to be shoved out of his mind. He finds himself asking what would happen if the kaffer told the English press that he had informed the prime minister of the police commissioner's black family and crime. The English journalists would rush to Swaziland with their cameras and South African papers would be full of the scandal; the outside world would send in TV crews. The world would laugh forever and ever at him and his government.

His mind flashes back to the moment when the African boasted that the black people had transformed the Afrikaner's personality into plastic clay in their hands. He had said he did not need the guns to smash the vital things in the Afrikaner's personality. He, Willem Adriaan de Haas, must not only prove the nigger wrong; he must do it in such a way as to teach him once and for all time not to forget his place.

De Haas knows his Afrikaners; they are a tough and disciplined people who travel through life only in one direction. They have never let him down; he knows they never will. That a black man can dare to hint at weakness in the Afrikaner keeps the prime minister's temper flaming for the rest of the day.

That evening the prime minister telephones Kritzinger at his house and orders him to come immediately to the prime minister's residence to explain the kaffer's allegations which he details violently over the telephone.

I am sorry, Mr. Prime Minister, I cannot come over just now, Kritzinger replies. But to-morrow morning, you will know the truth.

After the exchange, Colonel Paul Kritzinger walks quietly to his study, takes his service revolver and blows out his brains.

* * *

XXII. The Continuing Commitment

*U Zulu siquzi esingadli
nselwa zamuntu.*

*(The Zulu thrives on the
essence of his own truth.)*

The Zulu believes there is an ultimate truth behind any fact and this truth reflects the character of a people; he translates it into everything he does, even into the way he works or fights the white man. The moment to translate the truth into action has come.

Most outsiders think the Zulus stupid for setting themselves standards of excellence even when they are exploited and cheated. But to the Zulu, the commitment to excellence goes beyond the present oppression, to the meaning by which he understands reality and his place in the cosmic order. He takes life, as he does himself, seriously; as he says it, he has no time to waste. Whatever he is engaged in doing must be done in the best way he can. The Zulu believes he has an important job to perform in history. Life's purpose for the person is to realise the full promise and the glory of being human; this means that whatever he does must be the best he can produce.

Working to the best of his ability is designed to impress neither the employer nor anybody else; it is a simple act of self-definition and self-fulfilment; it is a stubborn refusal to accept the permanence of defeat. Among themselves, the Zulus tell each other and their children that the commitment to excellence even in adversity is the durable factor in their culture which keeps them sane and alive and which, in the final analysis, is the Zulu's guarantee of ultimate victory. Without it, they swear that they would be destroyed as a people.

There is a cruel, peculiarly South African tragedy in all this. White policy extorts maximum advantage from the Zulu's commitment to excellence; the Zulu does not get value for his labour. The whites are delighted with this. While the Zulus are politically the most trouble-some Africans, they are economically the most co-operative. Most whites and very many non-Zulus in the black community agree that the Zulu is less than intelligent; that if he were not stupid he would not give more value for the little he is paid. Most white liberals are delighted with this; in their writings on the homefront and abroad they tell the world that revolution is a very long way off in South Africa.

One of the arguments they use is that the morale of the white community (the army and the police) is solid; that since the Africans have had no military training, are not familiar with sabotage techniques in an industrial society, and have no political organisations, they are not ready to burn to ashes the power-structure the white man has established. The liberals are not complacent, though; they urge reforms, the abolition of the colour bar, the repeal of segregatory legislation, the abandonment of the Passes, equal pay for equal work and things like that. These privileges, they argue, should be granted without much waste of time; before the African starts thinking of alternatives; before he challenges the basic ideal on which white societies are founded; before he rejects the prospect of being integrated into the white minority's society.

In terms of history, the Afrikaners are nearer the African than the English and the Jews. They fought the African several times on the battlefield, where the African made it clear that he was a determined fighter and a dangerous enemy. On several occasions, the Boers do not hesitate to admit, he brought them face to face with the possibility of extermination. If it had not been for the fact that they did not have the gun, which the white man had, the Africans would have wiped out the Afrikaner or driven him into the sea. And no black nation confronted the Afrikaner with the threat of extermination in the way the Zulus did.

For these reasons the Afrikaner is under no illusions about what is going on in the black mind. The African takes conciliatory positions, talks of non-violence, demands race equality and welcomes a dialogue simply because he is a realist; he realises that he does not as yet have the gun and has not as yet organised decisive political power. The Afrikaner has set himself the goal of preventing the African from procuring the guns and from organising political power-bases. The Passes are an important weapon for controlling African activities at the latter level; so are race discrimination, the differential wage, over-crowding in the reserves and the high infant mortality rate. The Afrikaner regards this control as his only guarantee of survival and does not hesitate to read treason in any attempt to weaken his ability to control. His attitude and behaviour are characterised by all the brutality and shortsightedness seen in wars of survival.

Every five years or so he organises the great treason trials in which the enemies of his rule are accused of conspiring with the communists to subvert order. In South Africa anybody who opposes race discrimination is a communist.

The Afrikaner's attitude has created a relationship between black and white which can be described as a war of minds. Now and then, the war explodes into violence and bloodshed. As has been happening throughout the history of black-white contact, the gun prevails on the physical plane. This leaves the Afrikaner in an impossible position. His reliance on the gun and *kragdadigheid* has transformed his society into a community permanently mobilised for war; as the tide of African nationalism rolls southward, he feels constrained to burden the country's economy with heavier armaments programmes and to tie increasing numbers of his manhood in the armed forces now further engaged in the guerrilla war on the other side of the Limpopo.

The Africans are only too delighted with this position and do everything to encourage him to lock up the country's wealth in arms and the army. They organise strikes, create an atmosphere of uncertainity, and reject the false independence he offers them in the reserves. The Zulu section of the black community argues that it is a condition of its own survival and, ultimately, that of the Africans as a whole, for the Zulus to cling to the commitment to excellence at any price. If the Zulu is punished cruelly for this, the punishment is the price he must pay in order to preserve the values which the African experience translates into action. In a war, whether of minds or of arms, unlimited sacrafice is the price of victory. The African is paying a terrible price every moment of his life; the Zulus argue that the price is worth paying; the more the Afrikaner is pushed to the corner the more violently he will think; the more he will commit himself to arming; the more he will pursue courses and policies which crack the balance based on African labour, Afrikaner political power and English dominance of the economy.

The African offensive operates at two levels: the educated classes and those who do manual labour. A consensus has developed on what to do with the white man which makes nonsense of liberal claims that white power will be around for many more years to come. The educated make it clear that the colour bar, the differential wage, and residential segregation are no longer the issues at stake in the crisis of colour; the point to be settled, they say, is the clash between conflicting evaluations of the person. They say the African refuses to be integrated into the society organised by an alien minority which is committed to a wasteful ideal of fulfilment; he elects to determine his future in the light of his choices, which are different from the white man's.

Stress is laid on the African's responsibility for giving the quality of leadership which will lead Southern Africa along safer routes to a better future. This is the subject of discussion in the trains, the beerhalls, pulpits and, strange as it might sound, the classrooms. The African is seen, no longer as the black community in South Africa; he is the citizen of the Black World, a member of black communities in Africa and the Western Hemishpere. This is the setting in which new attitudes to the Afrikaner in particular and the whites in general are developing.

The white evaluation of the person is regarded as alien, whether it is translated into capitalism or socialism; it determines the person's position in society on the basis of arbitrary criteria like race, power, economic status or class. This categorisation of society has fouled up human relations, fouled up the air, fouled up the land, fouled up the waters and fouled up life itself. To save himself, the African has to opt out of the fouled society; otherwise he would be destroyed by consent.

It had been enough, under colonialism, for the whites to see the African, the Asian or the Indo-American from European or, more specifically, British, Dutch, French, German, Portuguese, Russian, Spanish or white American perspectives. The non-legitimacy of black, brown and yellow perspectives had been taken for granted; African, Asian and Indo-American value-systems had been treated with contempt. The people of colour were expected to define themselves and see fulfilment for themselves largely in terms of the white man's system of values. But the white man's ideals and values together with the patterns of society to which they gave rise had not been evolved for racially or culturally mixed societies. They came under increasing strain or cracked in proportion as the area of white influence widened on the globe. In the resulting conflicts, the peoples of colour developed syncretic cultures to adapt to the demands of survival in the conditions created by white domination. In time the colonial peoples of Africa, the Americas and Asia found themselves divided into the traditionalists and the syncretists. The latter stood between the aboriginal value-systems and the world of the whites. At independence, the international community divided almost automatically into three segments—the demotic states based on tradition-based nationalism; the white nations; and the syncretist black and brown communities of Southern Africa, Asia, and the Americas.

Of immediate interest, the argument continues in this regard, is the Afrikaner's position in the English-speaking world which has been segmented culturally into the black states of Africa and the Caribbean, the white peoples of the Commonwealth and the United States, the English-speaking Asians and the black syncretist communities of Southern Africa and the United States. English is the link which binds this vast conglomerate of races and cultures. It assumes different forms in each racio-cultural milieu and develops different perspectives. The common factor combines with the differences to create the peculiar consensus and identity which distinguish the English-speaking world from the others and to produce the distinctive rhythms which make this world a unity on given planes and the disharmonies which divide it at other levels.

Herbert Dhlomo's poems, Ezekiel Mphahlele's essays, and Chinua Achebe's fiction are read by millions of non-Africans in the English-speaking world, not because Africa is a cultural extension of Britain, which it is not, but because of the syncretic dynamic. The day is coming when the English-speaking whites will go to Africa to study syncretist English because Africa has something vital to give toward the enrichment of the English experience. The ancient Greeks went, after all, to Alexandria to enrich the Hellenic experience.

The Afrikaner is not only a cultural outsider in the English-speaking world, to which he has little to give, he is, as a quick glance at his literature, history, press and political philosophy will show, repulsed by English. He has adopted an attitude to the race question which is as angular as it has become increasingly odious in the English-speaking world where movement is in the direction of progressive identification of the person with his neighbour regardless of race or colour. Paradise is still a very long way off, but movement is in the right direction.

In global terms, the Afrikaner is a negligible and politically expendable minority. His negative racial attitudes create the conditions which destroy his right to a place in the African sun. At the cultural level, the black people insist, he has nothing to give the Africans. His culture is only about three hundred years old, whereas the African's has its roots in the mists of antiquity. The Afrikaner realises his culture's limitations in such a way that he is scared of sharing his cultural achievements with non-Afrikaners, even when they are white. He knows that his culture is as yet so weak it can be wiped out by the African's culture or by that of the English. This awareness of weakness forces the Afrikaner to reject all outsiders in his country precisely at the moment when their goodwill has begun to be one of his guarantees of survival.

In order to continue to dominate politically in the changed power dispositions in the world he has to have a tradition of diplomacy which will enable him to create effective alliances. His ability to establish these depends, on the one hand, on what the Africans finally decide to do with him and, on the other, on the final attitude of foreign investors. The strength of the South African economy, over which he exercises political control, is determined, among other influences, by the availability of Middle East oil which can, at the right time, be used as a political weapon against his racial policies.

This plethora of weaknesses confronts the Afrikaner with a multiple dilemma; it places him in a cleft stick out of which there is no easy way. The Africans argue that it is a condition of their survival and freedom that they should keep him in this position in order to ensure that they settle the race problems on their terms. In the final analysis, this is what the *xina* strategy is all about; this is the justification of the commitment to excellence.

Those Africans who have not gone to school and who constitute the class of manual labourers are gradually dropping their suspicion of the educated. They are encouraged by the strategies of the educated and the latter's use of *umteto wesintu* to hold the Afrikaner in the cleft stick. If they had the equipment, they say, they would take the shortest route to Blood River, instead of moving *kancane, kancane* in the effort to build power-bases between which to *xina* the whites. In the meantime they refuse to be integrated into the white man's economy in ways which destroy their Zulu-ness. They have forced the largest construction companies to yield to their demand for working conditions which preserve Zulu values. These corporations have adopted the policy of employing a chorus-leader for every gang of labourers. The practice is profitable in terms of increased production, the quality of the work and better human relations. The more progressive companies have thus dispensed with the practice of employing white foremen; they engage Zulus who function as *gosas* and foremen.

To the Zulus this is an important shift in the balance of black-white power. In the locations, the *intshumentshu* has combined with other factors to push out the white police. When the Zulus go to war they chant battle-cries. They now regard themselves as being on the march to Blood River. Whenever the white man's sirens wail and call them to work they shout battle-cries in defiance of the white power-structure. Like their educated brothers, the labourers believe that the whites foul up everything they come in contact with; when the sirens wail, these Africans protest that the white man fouls the atmosphere. Defiance is never meant to pay compliments and the cries which the Zulus hurl into space every day, all over South Africa, are not intended to flatter the whites. They are the Zulus' way of rededicating themselves to the Blood River commitment.

The commitment   is not confined to calling the white man names in his hearing every time the siren sound is heard; it is expressed also in the way the Zulu works. The highly disciplined team work is, above all, a declaration of solidarity in a temporary situation of weakness. The *gosa* is the voice of destiny, of the dead ancestors, calling on the men to struggle together. Labour has been transformed by conquest into a continuing struggle with the white authority. Each time the Zulu raises his pick he believes he sets a given quality of vibrations in motion; when he strikes the ground, he plants these in the soil. The more forcefully he strikes, the deeper the vibrations sink. The belief is that vibrations, like thoughts and seed, are living things which will germinate in the soil and one day fill the air with deeds which will make it impossible for the white people to survive in South Africa. When Zulu crews strike the soil hard and do more work for less pay, it is not the money they have in mind, important as that is; they regard themselves as parts of the soil; when they work it, they send messages to it. The white man might build his structures on the soil; but because the soil is the matrix from which the Africans derive their being, it will reject the structures one day. That is the revolution the African has in mind and when it comes it will not be like anything seen or known in white history.

* * *

XXIII. Stand In The Wind And Speak To The Ages

Izinja zoshaba zidla umnikazizo!

(The hounds of ushaba eat their own master!)

Zandile now wishes she had not uttered the terrible words. The dreaded *indlondlo* snake, she had often shouted in moments of anger, lines its grave with the corpses of its hunters. Now, it seems, the moment of lining the grave is either at hand or has arrived. Each hour that goes by deepens her anxiety. It is Tuesday and her husband has not returned home. He left on Saturday afternoon and said he would be back home late that night. He did not tell her where he was going. That did not bother her much; some Zulu men did things that way. She remembers now that he took her leather shopping bag; he did that when he wanted to bring her a pleasant surprise. But then something had puzzled her; almost by accident she had seen him shove something into the bag. That was not the family clock. Saturday night had gone by and the whole of Sunday, and he had not returned. She had risen before dawn on Monday, taken the earliest train to Pretoria to be at the magistrate's court when the trials started, to see if her husband had been arrested.

The African was presumed a criminal every moment of his life in his own country, like the Jews in Nazi Germany; he was required to carry documents to prove that, wherever he was, he was not committing a crime. In the locations, and every white city had its location where the Africans were corralled, the police kept a sharp eye on the movements of the black people. As a rule, police raids were conducted in the locations every week-end; the police searched for pass law violations, vagrants, stolen goods, weapons, liquor brewed illegally and, of course, the dreaded guerrilla fighters trained in China and Russia. The police raided by night, turned houses inside out and arrested whoever did not have the right papers or any whom they did not want in the location. The prisoners would be herded into groups at corners in the streets and were later loaded into huge trucks called *Black Marias* and locked in the stocks on Sunday, loaded into the trucks early on Monday morning and driven to the magistrates' courts in the centre of the white man's cities. The police stations in the cities

299

did not, as a rule, drive their prisoners; they marched them handcuffed in pairs down the streets to the court houses. In the larger towns it was not an unusual thing to see hundreds marched to the nearest court house. Men and boys over 18 were marched and, more often than not, women, too, some with babies on their backs.

The law of the white man required that these raids should be conducted regularly in spite of the fact that they were responsible for some of the bloodiest clashes between the Africans and the police. The black people sometimes fought pitched battles with the arms of the law and killed as readily as they were murdered. The whites insisted on the raids for a number of reasons. First, the locations were security risks; the police had constantly to know what was in the locations and to weed out the "won't-works" who were believed to lead or organise the violence against the police. It was important for the white man's purse that no person was in the location who did not work and who, the law said, was an unproductive parasite. Third, the raids served the useful purpose of creating an atmosphere of danger in the locations in order to immunise the masses of the people against those whom the authorities regarded as the agitators. People had to live in fear of being arrested so that they should not forget who was master in South Africa. The raids were also an instrument of control to create the state of mind in which the African would collaborate in working, first, to entrench his ruin and, second, to produce the wealth which made it possible for the whites to pay handsome dividends to foreign investors.

People were arrested not only in the streets but also in their homes. Every Monday morning almost in every city, friends and relatives flocked to the magistrates' courts to check on their loved ones or to pay their fines or to bring them decent food. White employers had grown accustomed to doing without some of their workers on Mondays. South African whites had come to terms with the sight of scores of Africans in handcuffs on the way to the courts. They were not alone in doing this. Millions of Germans had watched the Nazis beat up the Jews, chase them out of their homes and march them down the streets of German cities to jail. The Germans got used to the sight; they watched while the Nazis fulfilled themselves in one extreme of ugliness after another.

The whites in South Africa watch the CNP hordes march black men and women to jail every week. The wounds this has cut into the psyche of the African are so deep one day there will be no balm to heal them. As the Africans march quietly to jail every week, they work equally quietly for the day when the infamy will go up in flames and its ashes swept into the sea. This was Zandile's prayer as she stood in front of the gate through which the prisoners were marched into the grille to await trial. She spent the whole day around the courts, moving from one corner of the iron cage in which hundreds of Africans were locked to another in the hope that she might catch a glimpse of Pumasilwe.

On the morning of Tuesday she rises early again and walks to Father Maimane. The sun has not risen when she knocks on the front door. A young girl, one of Maimane's daughters opens the door.

Is the father awake?

No. But mother is in the kitchen.

Tell her I am here.

The girl disappears down the passage to the rear of the house. Mother Maimane is a heavy, slow-moving woman in her early sixties. She listens carefully to Zandile's story, and then rises to her feet.

I must wake him up, child. Why do the people call him Father if he cannot be available when they need him most?

She shuffles down the hall and returns a few minutes later behind her husband. The old man listens carefully to Zandile's story and then rises to his feet:

Child, this sounds bad. Puma, of course, was not the type of person whom the police would treat with consideration. Let me dress up. We shall try the various hospitals in the city, to start with and, if we draw blanks, will then go to the police.

Let's start with the police, Father. They'll know if he is in hospital.

Well, child, you don't want them to know you're in trouble when you can help it.

I can't help it, Father.

Let us do that which you consider best, child. But tell me, had you quarrelled?

Not at all, Father.

He did not like your reference to the lining of the grave?

That, I know; but after we'd seen you we never talked about it again.

In the old days a whole regiment would be sent to kill an *indlondlo* on a particular route. Soldiers would die before it was killed. What did you have in mind when you talked about this to your husband?

Well, Father, the passage into law of the Passes For Women Bill killed something in me; it extinguished one flame in my life; it planted defeat in my private personal life as a woman and made humiliation my constant companion. Where I was attacked more directly than I had been in the past, I had to fight back to protect my honour!

I am listening, child.

I had to do something, Father; I wanted to go down with a white man . . . the biggest of them . . . the most powerful . . . to bring him crashing to the ground where he had thrown me!

Kill a white person?

I was ready to kill, to lie, to steal, to do anything to shatter the self-image of the white man; I was ready even to fling myself at a white man to crack his psyche . . . .

Child? Fling yourself at a white man? You are somebody's wife?

Father! Don't you understand? What does it mean to you that any white policeman can rape me in the name of the law? Don't you understand? It is no longer enough for the whites to make it a crime for us to be black; it is now a crime for a person to be a woman!

Zandile buries her face in her shawl and cries bitterly into it. Mother Maimane rises from her chair and embraces Zandile.

Do not cry any more, child. All of us are being tried and all of us feel as you do. We have no choice, child; we have to swallow the stone and survive that which no people have survived. At least for a time we have to.

Mother Maimane turns her eyes to her husband; for a moment their eyes meet and Father Maimane nods his head.

I understand . . . . I understand everything. We have all been provoked painfully, for too long. We put God to shame when we yield further ground. Yes . . . yes . . . just the other day the papers said the prime minister had refused to appoint a commission of inquiry to go into the Boreneng murder . . . because the truth told would hurt the police! Ha! Ha! What do the police have to hide if they are innocent?

Zandile wipes her still hidden face with the shawl. She lifts her head slowly out of the cover and takes a deep breath.

Father, the prime minister's refusal made Puma so angry I feared he would crack. He sat alone into the night in the kitchen. I could not sleep; I dared not sleep. I did not know what he would do. You see, that breastbone of the cat he told you about had been missing for some days; without the prop, he lost his sense of direction. I was afraid, Father . . . .

Puma never really took the white man out of his mind?

I don't know if he ever tried to, for one leg was always in the experience of the mission station and the other in the underground. In a crisis, I never knew where he would stand or what he would do. After midnight he strode from the kitchen to the sitting room and back, talking to himself. I remember every word, for I was awake. He started in a low tone. I heard him say: Then came this evil, from across the oceans; this infamy; this *ushaba*! It came and in the name of Christ, he groaned, it defined us as primitives and savages; the whites showered us with a "love" we had not asked for. They "loved" us so much they stole our land; they reduced us to creatures; we had to sweat, to starve, die and rot to produce wealth for them. Where was their "love" then? How long must we endure it? O, how long?

Don't you think he went out to burn some factory?

For a long while, Zandile does not answer. Mother Maimane,

who has been standing by her moves softly to her own chair. Zandile's voice trembles.

I have never heard him shout like that. He did not do that even when he was angry with me. Father, I don't know . . . . I know nothing. I always told him that to conquer the white man, we had to use our brains; we had to refuse to fight on ground chosen by him, using his own weapons. You leave a bomb here, and kill a woman and blow up a railway line there. You strike at the outer circles of white power; you don't hit at the point of real weakness and the white man . . . .

Up to now, the Maimane homestead has been quiet, as though the old man and his wife were about the only people who lived in it. As the sun rises higher the younger members of the family wake up and make a bee-line for the bathroom. The Maimane house is a sprawling structure which functions very much like a boarding house in some respects. There are three bathrooms, one for the infants, another for the older children and a third for the adults. At this time of the morning there always is war in the bathroom set aside for the toddlers. The arbitrator always is Mother Maimane; it is her task and right to apportion positions in the queue and make peace, and fix the rules for going to the bathroom. This is no mean task in the orthodox Maimane homestead in which three sons live with their wives and children. But the toddlers in the Maimane family include little ones born in the backyards of suburban white Pretoria, who have nowhere to go and no people they can call parents.

According to African tradition, there is no such a creature as an illegitimate child. The principle worked in the old days when space abounded and each family produced its food. In the conditions created by white conquest, the overcrowding and regimentation in the locations strain the principle of legitimacy and its implications. People have less food, less space in which to live and little money with which to buy clothes.

Largely as a result, the orthodox home has begun to be one of the casualties of white civilisation in the locations. *Umteto wesintu* is cited in defence of the African's rejections of the ways of the white man. The rejections are a more complicated stance than the demand for reversion to the ways of pre-industrial societies. For good or for evil, the Africans in the locations acknowledge that they have been caught in the sweep of an industrial civilisation; they insist, however, that they should find their bearings and fix final positions for themselves in it on their terms. This is the basic point of conflict between them and the white man. They have evolved a syncresis of outlooks based largely on African evaluations of the person which have been blended with borrowings from the white man's culture.

Chief Bulube is an outstanding example of the syncresis. He comes from an Orthodox Zulu home. His father was a polygamist and his mother a Christian. His early education followed strict traditional

303

lines. When he grew up he went to white-oriented schools where he studied English and Roman-Dutch Law. Father Maimane himself is another example. While he preaches a rigid exclusivism in which the Africans are enjoined not to defile themselves by adopting white values, he and his followers are christians.

It is true that Christ has next to no place in Maimane's teachings; that emphasis is on the humanism in the christian doctrine. But this humanism is regarded as important because it supports the humanism of the *Buntu Ideal*. The element of selectivity is only one more dimension of the syncresis. The rejection of the "illegitimacy" principle is another. All the children in the Maimane home are taught to regard each other as brothers and sisters. In an orthodox Buntu home, emphasis is on harmony, stability and mutuality. The person lives for all and the group lives for the person. They call this a balanced society; in it, nobody is excessively rich and none desperately poor. What belongs to the person might be shared with all and what belongs to the group is shared with the person. To respond to the demands of the balance to the best of one's ability is to attain *ubuntu* or to realise the promise and the glory of being a person.

Umteto wesintu prescribes five *amabanga okuphila* (phases of becoming) as the stages by which to attain *ubuntu*. These are birth or the introduction into experience, growth or opening up and outward; and the adaptation to the demands of growth, maturity or the highest point of achievement. Then there is the decline, the winding down of experience and death or the conclusion of experience for the person. Each phase is the moment of living out a principle; babyhood expresses the excellence which inheres in the person. During infancy the child grows; opening outward characterises his personality; he needs all the latitude he can have to grow and learn and develop his personality. At the height of his power he identifies himself with his neighbour to project society into the future or to guarantee its survival. Decline is important, too, because it enables the person to reassess his life and to give it meaning; he opens himself to all experience and to all persons; he responds to the call of mutuality. Death ferries him to the world of spirit-forms. Death in the physical world is rebirth into the world of spirit-forms and death in the latter is rebirth into the physical world. The person, like all creation, is always moving between "death" and "birth" and vice versa. The cycle has no beginning and no end; it can neither be caused nor terminated because the person is a cell of the infinite consciousness.

Ubuntu denies that the person owes his existence to any power outside of himself. The consciousness does not create him; he is its constituent organ. Since an infinity is by definition a unity, the consciousness cannot be other than whole; nothing can be taken away from it and nothing can be added to it; it cannot be whole if the person is taken out of it; it needs him as much in order to be a whole as he needs it to survive.

It is this element of mutuality which binds the consciousness and the person and which keeps the cosmic order a unity and gives rise to the mutuality principle by which Maimane sets the greatest store and which he translates into the discipline which regulates the lives of his followers. Maimane preaches that the worship of the person is the only true worship of God for God is the cell of the consciousness infinitised, while the human being is God personalised.

Maimane insists that the person defiles himself when he tries to understand himself by going outside of himself; when he regards himself as a creature. If he is a creature, he is his own creator and if he suffers, it is because of his own ignorance. He radiates self-destructive vibrations or attracts dangerous radiations to himself. The cure for self-destruction is the unending exploration of the self by the self. He recoils with horror from the white practice of regarding individuals, classes, communities and races as expendable. The injunction to his followers to avoid association with the whites is designed to narrow down the possibilities of contamination by the white man's values which divide human beings into categories, and which predicate fulfilment on a creative absolute which is outside of the personal self.

The predication is responsible for the view that some persons or groups or races are expendable. If the white man likes the evils which go with expendability, let him keep his culture to himself and let him not complain when the African refuses to defile himself by being a black carbon copy of the whites. Each person is unique and has something to give which nobody else can. What he needs to develop this potential to the best of his ability is neither the greed for power nor the freedom to become an economic cannibal battening on the weakness or ignorance of his neighbour but to identify himself with his neighbour. He cannot do this in the white man's world, where greed has been elevated to a virtue; he therefore has to move out of the white man's world and create for himself a society in which he will make the best possible use of his life. The first step in this direction is discipline in every department of life.

As Mother Maimane puts it to the toddlers, they have to learn that if they stand in the line, they will all have their chance to go into the bathroom. Teaching these values, living according to them and upholding them has given her a position of tremendous authority in the Maimane home. The teaching is good, but the war at the entrance to the bathroom rages with fierce fury on this particular morning because grandmother is not around. Father Maimane turns to Zandile.

We should not speak of Puma as though he belongs to the past; the mistake was made by me; I started doing that. But, child, you often challenge him to take the white man out of his mind?

Father, I know ... this is the most difficult thing to do. The commitment to the benefits of the white man's culture are very tempting for the fortunate few. I always tell my husband that his leadership will be ineffective as long as his range of thinking is defined by white horizons. The revolution has to succeed in the mind before it can be translated into action. We have to have a very clear idea of our alternative to the white man's way of life and then map our strategy for moving to our goal. I don't think we need bombs, guns and the like to get to our goals . . . .

Of course, Puma would not agree with you there.

He does not, Father. But I'm not an advocate of non-violence; our situation is such that we cannot have the guns we need; we cannot manufacture the bombs we need; we don't even know how to put them together. Such is our education. We don't have much of a choice; we have to use our brains; we have to know our actual points of real strength and weakness and those of the Afrikaner. We have to attack where the Afrikaner is weakest; there are so many vulnerable points in his world; so many brittle points in his make-up . . . we should strike at these and shatter his psyche. We need no guns to do that . . . .

Father Maimane does not comment; he groans like a man whose soul aches, looks at his watch and takes the shortest route to his wardrobe. Mother Maimane turns to Zandile.

You are right, child. Sometimes the men are not the philosophers we think they are. We, black people, have drunk and drained the cup of bitterness. I always ask myself: What sort of human beings are these white people who fulfil themselves in self-defilement? Who regard nothing as sacred? Sometimes I feel sad when I think of the day of reckoning. People will be too angry to think of an eye for an eye then, or a tooth for a tooth. There'll only be the flames to consume the evil ways and the anger which will sweep the ashes of the infamy into the sea. They have asked for it, child, and as things stand, they will get it. We move slowly, *kancane kancane*, and, one day, things will happen.

* * *

The white policeman behind the counter seems amused when Zandile mentions her husband's name. From a drawer he pulls out a file and opens a page with a photograph, and shows it to Zandile.

Do you know this man?

Yes.

He thought he was smart; but he was not smart enough. Come; I'll show you what he's done to himself.

He leads them to the mortuary and hands them over to the constable in charge of the morgue who leads them into a chilly hall with long cement tables. He draws out a tray and points to a pile of frozen human flesh, bones and rags. Zandile does not make a sound;

hot tears trickle down her cheeks. Father Maimane cannot control himself; he cries out:

Shaka! Dingane! Were you asleep? Where were you?

The policeman signals to him to shut his mouth. The only intact portion of Pumasilwe's body is the right hand with the copper ring. Zandile takes it, kisses it, presses it to her bosom and then removes the ring from it. The first policeman waits for them at the door.

Did you recognise anything?

Yes, I did; it was his hand.

Father Maimane moves closer to the policeman.

What happened, O son of a white man?

He tried to blow up an electric pylon and the dynamite blew him to pieces instead. Playing with dynamite is dangerous, you know! Tell this to your people.

* * *

The day has come for Marietjie to be admitted to hospital. She had given Zandile a week off to prepare for the burial of her husband and Zandile has now returned to work. To Marietjie's surprise, Zandile is not in mourning apparel.

Zandile, pardon me for asking this. What do you do when mourning?

We do all sorts of things. Those of us who are christians wear black like the white people. The Pentecostalists tie strips of white cloth around their arms or heads. The traditional way among the Zulus is to shave the head of a married woman when her husband dies.

You don't wear black and you have not shaved your hair?

In my case, custom does not allow me to mourn in public. My husband is a war casualty. If I mourn I shall set up anti-social vibrations; I shall be sending signals to him that I no longer expect him to fight for our cause.

After what has happened, you still felt that you could leave your children alone in the location to come and look after mine?

My mother came up to Pretoria for the funeral and my husband's oldest sister. They are looking after the children . . . .

You are so kind to me, Zandile!

Well, nooi, I have a job to do here.

* * *

Marietjie takes no note of the slightly menacing ring in Zandile's voice. The tradition of "noblemen-farmers"—of country barons— is too old and too entrenched to enable most Afrikaners to have normal human relations with the African. The tradition developed in the Cape under Dutch rule and flourished during the era of slavery and, when the Boers moved into the interior, they took it with them and used it to regulate the relations between themselves and the Africans. The tradition regarded the man of colour as the property of the farmer, regardless of whether or not he was free. In the rural areas to-day, the Afrikaner farmer can still be heard telling his neighbour about an African who works for him in these terms:

Daar gaan my kaffer! (There goes my nigger!)

The black man is free in terms of the law, but the nobleman-farmer approach regards his labour as the private property of the farmer. Since the black man cannot be separated from the white man's possession, the farmer regards him as his property. The reduction to property creates a relationship in which the Afrikaner does not expect the African to behave like a human being. Over the centuries, this has bred an insensitivity which makes it impossible for Marietjie to notice the subtly hostile inflexions of the black woman's voice. The insensitivity characterises almost every situation of African-Afrikaner contact. The man who urinated on the Kruger monument exploited this weakness in his defence. The Africans are presumed to be congenitally stupid, and his profession of ignorance of what a statue is toned down the anger of the magistrate who gave him a light sentence and warned him that next time he is in the white man's city he should not urinate behind any stone.

Maggie and others have long exploited the insensitivity fairly freely. Each time the women in the location want a favour from the Bantu Affairs Commissioner, they go to the white man's office to stress their "loyalty" to the government and proceed from there to create the conditions in the location which eliminate the visits of unwanted white educational officers.

* * *

That afternoon, Piet gets ready to drive his wife to hospital. The rich, red leather seats of his car shine bright in the warm Pretoria afternoon. Piet waits impatiently at the wheel. He starts the engine when he sees Marietjie come out of the kitchen door. She walks with difficulty but puts up a brave face until she settles in her seat. Piet already has his hand on the gears lever when his wife calls out:

Zandile! Zandile!

What are you calling her for, now?

I forgot to tell her something very important.

Marietjie! You had the whole day to remember everything!

Remembering is not m y only problem. Zandile!

The African comes wiping her hands on her apron.

Remind the master about the leading waterpipe if the municipal engineer's people don't come in to-morrow morning. Don't forget, Zandile!

Is that all, Marietjie? Piet's temper has started sparking.

No!

My God!

Keep the children away from the mud, Zandile; otherwise they'll soil my carpets while I'm in hospital.

Have you finished, now? Piet feels like driving the car out.

Yes.

Marietjie wants to say something, but realises that she will be declaring war if she does.

*   *   *

Pretoria is surrounded by vast tablelands which are rimmed by distant mountain ranges. The city itself is laid out in a small valley between hills. That gives it a pleasant climate, not too cold in winter and not as depressingly hot as Durban in summer. There is not an experience more exhilarating than to be in the open air when the sun rises. Hundreds of African nannies pushing expensive perambulators with white babies walk the pavements of the streets in the residential parts of the city at this hour of the day to let South Africa's rulers of to-morrow take in the air. Walking the baby is one of the nanny's most important jobs. The whites value the fresh air so much they want their dogs too to have as much of it as their babies do. In the wealthier suburbs, each household usually has three servants: the cook-housemaid, the nanny, and the garden-boy. The latter is usually an elderly man who can no longer do the rough work on the roads, the railways or the factories. Walking the dog is one of the garden-boy's main duties. Every afternoon, when the weather is fine, he has to take the family dog for a walk. Though the cook-housemaid is the most important and therefore most highly-paid servant, and is also closest to the white family, she has no authority over the other servants. She is also often alone with the Afrikaner.

Like most urban Afrikaners who grew up on farms, Piet rises quite early every day. The habit serves him in good stead. The prime minister is a notoriously early riser and one of the things he likes to do is to get to his office as early as possible these days. The phenomenon does that in situations of crisis. And these are difficult days for the prime minister. His interview with Bulube is given the widest publicity possible. Bokkie, the columnist of *Die Aanslag* has complained that the editorials, feature articles, analyses and commentaries on the interview could be put together into a book as large as the bible.

The English press, contrary to customary practice, praises the prime minister for having met Bulube. Its representatives have already met the African and got the lowdown on what transpired during the conversation with the prime minister which Bulube consistently characterises as having been frank. Asked to elaborate on this remark,

309

he says he looks forward to further interviews with the prime minister to lay the foundations for a meaningful settlement of the problem of Afrikaner security in Africa.

The English do not like the stress Bulube lays on a conversation with the Afrikaner only. The African explains that with the best will in the world, the English and the Jews are in the position of illusory power and that real power is in the Afrikaans community. To talk to the Afrikaner prime minister is to focus on the sources of real power. The South African Unionist Party, which represents English and Jewish economic interests, proposes a Charter of Liberty which is very much like the Bill of Rights drafted by the liberals. The Charter differs from the Bill in that it rejects partition by implication; it commits the Africans to a united South Africa. The Unionists asked the Africans to subscribe to the Charter and promise that when they are returned to power, they will restore the vote to the Cape Africans and extend it to Natal, the Free State and the Transvaal.

Die Aanslag complains that the English are once more at their old game of dividing peoples in order to rule them. It urges that since the English have what Bulube calls illusory power, the prime minister should undercut the English-Jewish campaign designed to create an alliance between black labour and English capital for the purpose of isolating the Afrikaners. It urges the prime minister to give thought to the transference to the Africans of the Transkei of the English-speaking districts of Kokstad, Elliott, Maclear and others. It urges him, also, to consider ceding to the Zulus the Natal province, including the port city of Durban. The independent Transkeian and Zulu states would in turn be asked to enter into a mutual defence treaty with white South Africa. *Die Aanslag* says such statesmanlike action would reduce English opposition inside the predominantly Afrikaner state, rid white South Africa of the recalcitrant English and saddle the Zulus with the Indian problem. At the same time the independent Zulu and Transkeian states, whose shores are washed by the Indian Ocean, could be made into Afrikanerdom's most valuable allies.

The prime minister wants to have nothing to do with the devolutionists in the Afrikaans community. Devolution, he insists, is capitulation to Bulube who, the prime minister argues, has adopted the policy of setting the Afrikaners against the English in the bid to split the white united front. That is what his appeals for an African-Afrikaner treaty are all about. *Die Aanslag* urges the prime minister to meet the black leaders in the effort to open a meaningful dialogue on Bulube's proposal for a black-white treaty on the establishment of a permanent and secure place for the Afrikaner in Africa.

Piet is impressed by the concept of a treaty; the prospect of castrating the English politically and getting rid of the Indians has almost irresistible attractions for him. At the same time he wants to remain loyal to the prime minister who reads capitulation in everything said about a treaty. Largely as a result Piet's temper has been sparking at the slightest provocation since Bulube's interview with the phenomenon.

* * *

Piet sits by the side of his bed, straightening out the conflicts in his head on this particular morning. The air in the house is already charged with the aroma of freshly made coffee. He hears a slight knock on the door. This is the sign for which he has been waiting.

Serving the coffee in bed is a South African ritual. The heavily-creamed stimulant is unlike any other brew of its type anywhere in the world. The Afrikaners made it famous; they do not brew the beverage; they cook it. The freshly ground coffee is first boiled in fresh milk to which a little salt has been added and is then simmered slowly until it is ready for serving.

After waiting for a few seconds outside the door, to enable Piet to clear up embarrassing details, Zandile enters the bedroom with the tray of coffee. She has done this every morning, from the morning after she started working for the van der Merwes. The routine is to lay the tray on the coffee table near the bed and to withdraw quietly. Most of the time when everything is normal, the van der Merwes are still asleep when she brings in the beverage.

Good morning, master.

Goeie môre, Zandile. When will you learn to speak Afrikaans?

It would cost me a lot of money, master.

Bring the cup to me, Zandile.

Piet stretches both his hands and holds the saucer in which the cup stands with his left hand while he strokes Zandile's side with the right.

Somebody's asking for trouble, she smiles.

What trouble?

Baas Kritzinger's trouble.

Don't tell me about that fool; that's what he was, Zandile. Pretoria is better-off without him.

But he was a male.

What's that supposed to mean? That all males are fools?

No. That males love women.

That's right; just as I love you!

Impossible! You can't be serious!

You understand, Zandile .... These stupid laws. But I've always wanted to tell you that you are irresistible; that each time I see you, you do something to me.

Now! Now! You're being naughty; you're playing with fire.

Who will know about it?

Walls often have ears these days.

Not these . . . .

He tries to lay down the saucer and the cup to free his arm for a more powerful grip. The woman swings out of his hold and makes for the door.

Zandile! Where are you going? I want to talk to you.

Not now, baas. What will the children say?

We'll lock the door, of course.

And, in any case, that is not how you tell a Zulu girl you love her.

Understand the position, Zandile! This is our chance of a lifetime!

Are you really serious?

I mean it; every time I see you, you do something to me.

Come to my room to-night when the kids are asleep, Zandile responds.

Why don't you come over here? Near me!

This place belongs to your wife; this is her kingdom and if I come here, I degrade myself. We don't do things that way. My room is my kingdom; there I can do what I like.

What can you do there which you can't do here?

I can be free to test the quality of *your* male power. In any case, if you mean what you say, there's my room, any time when the children are asleep.

He cannot accept defeat at the hands of a black woman or any black person; at the same time to accept the challenge could be a leap to catastrophe. For a moment he cannot make up his mind. Torrid pictures of love-play with the black girls in the barnyard when he was young crowd into his mind. For weeks now, Marietjie has been concerned with her fretful health and did not want even to be touched with a hand. With his coffee still in his hand Piet walks to the window facing the drive and sips it slowly.

The crew from the municipal engineer's department have begun to arrive. Each African has a pick on his shoulder from which a shovel hangs. With the right hand each holds a metal container filled with a gallon of *Mahewu*, a brew made from boiled and fermented mealie or corn meal. This is their breakfast. They drink the fluid for lunch also. Year in and year out, they survive on *Mahewu*. Their wages, rents, taxes, bus or train fares and their other necessities make it impossible for them to buy more nourishing food. The men arrive in singles and groups of two or three and then sit down to drink their first meal of the day. The foreman, a white man, drives in about five minutes before seven o'clock. He supervises the digging out of the fifty yards of corroded waterpiping leading from the street. Apart from supervising and giving instructions, he does no work. He spends most of his time either in his car or under a tree or in chatting with passers-by, explaining the peculiar working habits of the Zulus, who form his crew.

312

When his team has dug the trench and reached the steel pipe, the plumbers will come and the foreman and his crew will move to dig elsewhere.

* * *

The Zulus are great believers in co-ordinated action. This explains the fact that they are eleven in this particular gang. The eleventh man is the most important in the team; more important than the foreman: he is the *gosa* or chorus-leader. He is captain of the crew. He co-ordinates their exertions in a way which gives them the impact and the precision of a digging machine. Without him the Zulus work very poorly; with him they work like a bulldozer.

He never does any digging himself, as a rule. The qualities of a gosa have nothing to do with digging; he must be a poet, a singer and a commander of men; he controls the efforts of his crew with the power and the rhythm of his poetry, music and the quality of his leadership. Without him the Zulus will either refuse to work or complain that the employer lacks the skill to use human resources intelligently! This argument always sounds strange in the ears of non-Zulus. But then, everything the Africans do is strange . . . .

* * *

Piet is still at the window when the seven o'clock siren signals the commencement of a new work-day. The *gosa* jumps to his feet and, shouting as loudly as he can and raising his right fist to the heavens, he cries out:

Nak-o-o-o-o-ke!
Wasuz' umlungu!

(Hear, O World,
The white man farting!)

The Africans break out in uproarious laughter which means nothing to the whites who do not understand the Zulu language. The *gosa* runs in short calculated steps from one end of the row formed by the diggers when the siren wailed, to the other, chanting the praises of a pick. The form of poem composed for action is chanted in a staccato recitative whose rhythm accords with the steps of what the Zulus called the night-march before the collapse of their power. The *gosa* then jumps three yards away from the crew and turning to them he summons the men with this intonation:

313

Walidl' icala we muntu!
Wasindaba ngesilevu seBhunu!
I-i-i-i-i-silevu se Bhunu!

(You know your crime, o man!
You sheared the Boer's beard
And with it wiped your anus!
Yes, indeed, it was the Boer's beard!)

At the commencement of the last line the diggers chant together as they raise their picks:

Se Bhunu!
(Of the Boer!)

at intervals of about two seconds they strike the tarmac with their picks about twenty times at a stretch and then pause for five seconds while the chorus-leader repeats:

I-i-i-i-i-silevu seBhunu!

It goes on like this, hour after hour, wherever Zulu labourers are employed in South Africa. Piet has in the meantime had his bath and is at table with the children, waiting for his breakfast. Hantie is about twelve and sits in her mother's chair.

Zandile, why do those boys recite poetry when they work?
Don't call them boys, Hantie; call them men, Piet tells her.
Why don't the men shut up and work, Zandile?
They work better that way.
Zandile!
Yes, baas.
What are they saying in those chants?
The words are in archaic Zulu and are difficult to translate.
Does the foreman understand the language?
She smiles broadly: I doubt it very much.
You are a Zulu, too. Why do the Zulus chant these things? To keep themselves happy because they don't like work?
The chants are poetry, master; they express thoughts which the crew plant simultaneously in the earth which produced them and in which their umbilical cords are buried. The expectation is that one day the earth will produce persons who will translate these thoughts into action.
That mumbo-jumbo . . . it's too much for me, Zandile.

* * *

Piet has gone to work and the children have, with the exception of Dirkie, who is about five, all gone to school. The telephone rings. The child follows Zandile into the sitting room. She picks up the receiver.

Is that Zandile?

Yes, it is.

We are going out to the party to-night; could we pick you up?

The children sit up until late, say about 8:30. After that I would want to wash up. I'll call you at 10. I would like to return home at about 2 a.m. I can't be out for long—in case the children give trouble.

* * *

That afternoon, Zandile prepares an early supper. Piet strides into the kitchen.

Something smells good in this kitchen. Zandile, Dirkie tells me you are going out?

Friends of mine called and asked if they could take me to a party, to make me forget about what has happened.

But, you know . . . .

Everything is in order, master. I told my friends that the children go to bed at about 8:30 and that I shall call them when free, say about 10 o'clock. That leaves me with one and a half hours to prepare myself.

She bends her head backward slightly and smiles provocatively.

That's alright then; I wouldn't like you to leave before the children go to bed. I'll tell them that you'd like to go out and that they should go to bed early, certainly not later than 8:30.

* * *

The clock strikes a quarter to nine. Piet tiptoes into the bedrooms of the children, switches off the lights, locks the doors and walks stealthily to Zandile's room.

Well, Zandile, this is the greatest moment in my life. I never thought I could be alone with you!

Tell me, Piet, for the night you won't mind if I call you Piet? Not at all.

He flings himself at her and throws her on her bed.

Why fight me, Piet?

I want you, woman!

Steady, now. You don't do it that way with the Zulu woman. See? A Zulu girl is queen when it comes to matters of her heart. Every time you make love to her, you have to woo her until she consents. That's your job as a male. If you can't do that, she remains just a log of wood and dismisses you as a thing; a barbarian not trained in the art of living.

315

Alright, now; how do I woo the Zulu girl?

First, you will let her feast her eyes on your body and she will allow you to feast yours on hers. You know the next step—the kissing and the like. The third is the most important; the *pulula* stage when you show your powers of masculinity by the quality of massaging her body. You do not touch her body; your hand is near enough to her skin until she feels the delicate vibrations radiating from your mind or your heart and passed on to her by your hand. This is a test of masculinity and from there, the doors to heaven are open . . . .

Does every Zulu man know all this?

He better not fool around with a woman if he does not.

Pointing provocatively to her pubic region she whispers something in his ear.

This thing destroys you if you can't play the game according to the rules.

Piet can no longer control himself, much less stand the lecture. He jumps from the bed and grabs Zandile in the middle.

Don't be so rough; you'll have more than your share of me.

What are we waiting for?

We aren't; we are exploring each other; enjoying each other's nakedness; that is one of the beautiful things about sex . . . .

Zandile casts a slow glance around her tiny room and notes that it is fifteen minutes after nine on the clock.

What a man! she says, stroking Piet's legs. You would cause trouble in the location if the girls there knew what you can do to a woman. White women tell me most white men treat them like animals . . . .

Nonsense, Zandile! Where did you get that from?

The university! We went to class with white women.

I'm glad they don't have any more mixed classes; no more white liars to tell all the liberal fibs against their race.

I liked the sessions with the white girls; they gave us the chance to know each other at close range.

She leads him to the bed and switches off the light. Darkness.

Why do you switch off the light? I want to see you! This is my house!

Sorry, baas!

Come off it, Zandile!

You want me to say, "Sorry, meneer"?

Ag, Zandile!

Well, then, "Sorry, Piet"!

That's better.

That was just to make you love me more. But seriously now, Piet, we'll be better off it it's dark. People around know that I usually am asleep at this hour of the night. I want no gossip in the backyards of this neighbourhood. Only the darkness can keep us safe.

The clock has struck 9:30; and heaven itself has just come down to earth for Piet when a powerfully wielded axe smashes the glass and the wooden frame of the single window in Zandile's room, tearing the curtain off the railing. A police torch flashes on the entwined, naked, black and white bodies in bed. Piet grabs the nearest blanket to cover his body.

And so, this is what happens?

The voice has a menacingly familiar ring. The door shakes; the police kick it open. The first to enter the room is Koos Rittner, son-in-law to the late Paul Kritzinger. He is a sergeant in the Pretoria police district. Zandile grins at him and the policeman nods understandingly.

So, this is how the party goes on? the policeman continues. Well, Mr. Secretary to the Prime Minister, it was smart of you to send your wife to the hospital long before the day of delivery; I'm sure she'll have a lot to say about this party. Of course, you'll hear a lot about it from the Prime Minister, too. He's one man who'll be glad to see that we're doing our job!

* * *

Creation has few beauties like a Pretoria morning in summer. The light of the new day lends a tantalising softness to the appearance of the vast tablelands around the capital, long before the sun's rays descend on the city. At this time, at the beginning of dawn, a stillness descends on the countryside to accentuate the beauty of the new day. The noises of the night have vanished and the noises of the new day have not started. The prime minister likes to take advantage of the interlude to walk in his orchard and sort his thoughts for the day. Whenever the weather allows it, he wakes up as early as he can, to the chagrin of the security police who are responsible for his safety.

De Haas is a child of the open spaces and resents intensely the fact that somebody has to watch carefully every step he takes and stand at attention when he turns his head or put his finger on the trigger when the prime minister coughs. While de Haas regards the police as the white community's first line of defence, he does not like the presence of the police around the prime minister's residence. Before his suicide, Kritzinger had ordered the security corps to instruct its men at the prime minister's residence to operate from concealed positions. The compromise makes the prime minister feel a little more comfortable.

These days the prime minister is always accompanied by his wife during his morning walks. The reason for this is not that she has suddenly become his political philosopher and guide (Afrikaner women are too domesticated to meddle in their husbands' politics; even Mrs. Kritzinger who was a terror in the days when she saw a rival in every African woman, never said a word to her closest friends about the black section of the family in Swaziland). No, the prime minister's wife is concerned about his health. Some of the shocks he has been getting of late have revived the pains on his left side. Trouble started during the strikes and got worse when the African women surrounded Union Buildings in a demonstration of female power which puzzled everybody. Nobody knew about it; not even the most trusted spies of the police or their best placed agents. What is more puzzling is that nobody knows precisely what the women hoped to achieve by surrounding the seat of white power, except, perhaps, to demonstrate how brittle the foundations of this power were. When interviewed, their leaders reply with laughter. The English-language press reports the laughter and its readers join in the mirth. The prime minister sees nothing funny in what the African women did. The shock from which he has not recovered and which worries his doctors is Paul Kritzinger's suicide.

What keeps the prime minister awake of nights is not so much the fact that he has lost a personal friend, but that Kritzinger could love a black woman, have children by her and establish a home for her and in every respect treat her as an equal. He never imagined, even in his more imaginative moments, that a respectable Afrikaner could sink so low and maintain an acceptable exterior for so long.

In the years he has been in politics de Haas has resented few insults from the English side more than the charge that the Afrikaner has a split personality; he has always wished he could shoot any kaffer who spoke of something brittle in the Afrikaner make-up. He could defend Afrikaner virtue with the stoutest conviction because he was certain the cream of Afrikanerdom had not been corrupted by the liberalism of the English and the Jews. And who could be placed farther in the forefront of the best Afrikaners than people like Paul Kritzinger? Or Kritzinger's wife? If she knew the scandal, why did she sit on it for so long? The prime minister's answer, forced he realizes, is that she did not know what her husband had in Swaziland. Yes, it was true he rarely visited his black family, if he ever did.

Yet, yet ... there always is a nasty sting in the English laughter. The word *xina* has found its way into the political vocabulary of sections of the English press where it is used as an antonym for Afrikaner *kragdadigheid* (omnipotence). De Haas has never learned the habit of thinking in terms of intangibles or of regarding them as possible determinants of policy. He has always thought in concrete terms and believed he dealt with concrete situations. This does not arise out of any dullness on his part; he would not have become prime minister if he were an idiot; he had always been a man of action who saw the destiny of the Afrikaner from heroic perspectives.

But, still, he goes into a rage when the English press describes this quality as what the Africans call the most brittle point in the Afrikaner make-up. A secret police report given to him after van Warmelo's assassination suggested that the murder was a translation of the *xina* strategy into action, in the bid to shatter the brittle factor in the Afrikaner psyche.

In the years after the assassination he dismissed the suggestion as so much nonsense. Next to God he believed in one supreme power: the inexorable logic of history which moved the Afrikaner to his preordained destiny. History never made mistakes. But, now, things begin to happen which were not good portents for the Afrikaner's destiny. First it was the Zulus in the Valley Of A Thousand Hills making crude guns. Prinsloo, he admits grudgingly, had outsmarted the Africans.

Then van Warmelo had offered the black people balkanised impoverished independence if they wanted it; they had decided to operate the governmental institutions established in the segregated areas to confront South Africa with a dual authority crisis. No less a student of black affairs than Kritzinger himself had explained what this meant to the prime minister.

Next, they organised the strikes after the government had hanged or jailed or banned or thrown into exile all the agitators and proscribed political organisations. Kritzinger, whose understanding of the African the prime minister never questioned, had warned more than once that the Afrikaner should guard against the process of history which determines the course of events among the blacks. But then, viewing everything in retrospect, one could take Kritzinger's conclusions with a grain of salt. Since then, of course, the Africans have been organising strikes successfully in Natal and threatening to extend these to the other provinces. The prime minister is mystified by how they have done this. He remembers vaguely, but does not want to think too much about it, that Kritzinger once told him of what the Zulus called standing in the wind in order to speak to the ages. Well, they might be speaking in the wind, but what they tell the ages arouses de Haas's hatred and fear.

They are using the segregated institutions his government has set up as a stick with which to beat the government; they are using the law to crush government policy. They manipulate the segregated administrations to smash Afrikaner *kragdadigheid*. On top of everything, their lubricious women are now poisoning the very heroes of Afrikanerdom; the finest manhood God ever had the sense to create. History, the prime minister still believes, never makes mistakes; *alles sal reg kom* . . . everything will be alright.

But history, de Haas sometimes notes, is changing. Let a white man kick a nigger or a coolie, the whole world shouts itself hoarse against him. In the good old days, when white men had not been corrupted by liberalism, communism and black women, a Boer farmer could take his gun and shoot a black person walking across his farm

319

without permission. In court he would say he thought he was shooting a baboon and the magistrate would acquit him.

But things have since changed; niggers and coolies now pin their backsides to the seats of power in the world and throw their weight about against the whites of South Africa whose prosperity they envy. History has changed because decadence was allowed to set in, in Western Europe, America and Russia; ideologies were adopted which made the nigger and the coolie the equals of the white man.

But history must under no circumstances be allowed to change against the Afrikaner; if it has to, it then becomes the solemn duty of the Afrikaner to stop it; to reverse its course; to oppose history. As a rule, the phenomenon is always in a rage when he reaches this point. When he cools down he realises that he does not know how to reverse the course of history. It was easy to think he could in the old days, when the white race had sole and exclusive control of the gun. But then the niggers and the coolies and the goons of the world now have the guns and do not hesitate to return white firepower with black or brown or yellow firepower.

The world has become a dangerous place for the Afrikaner to be alive in. How to change this state of affairs in the Afrikaner's favour continues to be the prime minister's headache. Some of his followers try and cheer him up with the statement that the Afrikaner thrives on adversity. De Haas has an ambivalent attitude to the compliment. He wants no comparison of the Afrikaner with the Jew, which is implied in the reference to thriving on adversity. And if people talk too much about thriving on adversity, de Haas often warns, the liberals and the communists and the kafferboeties (nigger-brothers) will soon be shouting that the black man thrives on adversity too.

As the days go by, the prime minister becomes gloomier and gloomier. His worries are complicated by *Die Aanslag's* editorials which have begun to warn that the endorsement of the Africans out of the urban areas and their being dumped in the overcrowded reserves is the time-bomb which history has placed at the foundations of the Afrikaner's destiny. One day, the black administrations in the reserves will refuse to accommodate the Africans expelled from the towns; they will use the very administrations set up by the white government to challenge the authority of the Afrikaner. They will use the laws the Afrikaner has made for them to oppose Afrikanerdom.

In an increasingly hostile world, the Afrikaner could find himself in a very difficult position if he shot the Africans in order to stop them carrying out his own laws. This, the paper says, is the cleft stick in which the CNP might one day be caught.

Die Aanslag, as a loyal party organ, does not urge the government to make fundamental adjustments in its thinking on guarantees of Afrikaner survival; at the same time it gives its warnings in such a way that the thoughtful in the Afrikaans community can draw their own conclusions.

The discovery that events have brought Afrikanerdom to a head-on collision with the inexorable laws of history—laws in which de Haas has believed blindly, and the realisation that in the final analysis he has no solution to this problem, keeps the prime minister awake of nights. The strain is so serious it worsens his health further.

Before his death, Kritzinger had given instructions to the effect that only a threat to the security of the realm was to justify telephone calls to the prime minister between certain hours of the night. There is still chaos in the headquarters of the security police, where the successor to Kritzinger has not as yet been appointed.

The prime minister's youngest son, a student at Stellenbosch University, comes running out of the back door.

Telephone, papa!

Who is calling at this hour?

The Minister of Native Affairs . . . .

Adriaan, his wife cries out in a desperate bid to be helpful, why don't you arrest the governments of the reserves if they refuse to work with you in stopping the strikes? They might paralyse the whole country . . . one day.

The phenomenon does not answer. He trundles toward the door. The rush alarms the wife.

Be careful, Adriaan! Don't strain yourself, she warns. The prime minister is almost out of breath by the time he takes the receiver.

Meneer, says the Minister of Native Affairs, the leaders of the Ndebele, Pedi, Shangane, Sotho, Swazi, Tonga, Tswana, Xhosa and Zulu rural administrations, who are in conference in Pietermaritzburg, have resolved unanimously to call out all the black communities in a national strike . . . .

What did Chief Tomboti do? Your department spent a lot of money on the development of his reserve?

He voted with the rest . . . .

What do they really want?

Independence . . . .

But they refused it when we offered it?

They want it on their terms . . . .

What are those?

The Afrikaners must quit South Africa . . . .

The phenomenon pauses for a while; he feels the tension rise within him. The Afrikaner becomes angry whenever the African confronts him with a situation of challenge. For de Haas, the moment of decision has come sooner than he expected. He explodes:

Nonsense!

He lays down the receiver. He is still turning in his mind the implications of the co-ordinated black revolt when the telephone rings again. He picks up the receiver. The Minister of Justice is on the line.

321

Who? Piet du Toit van der Merwe? Caught in bed . . . . What did you say? . . . With his kaffer maid? . . . Piet?

A man needs to be tough to get to the top in Afrikaner politics and de Haas has been the incarnation of toughness all his life. He has always boasted that sex is not one of his problems; that it is all a question of discipline. There are more important things to live for, he has always said. He has pursued the goal of using the gun to make the Afrikaners the unquestioned masters of South Africa with a singlemindedness and consistency which have given him the dimensions of the phenomenon which now shapes the destiny of the Afrikaners.

The set determination which made de Haas a phenomenon was founded on a fatal weakness. His whole life was built around an illusion; he lived a lie. He presumed the African to be less than human. When the black people tear the illusion to pieces and smash Afrikaner **kragdadigheid** *with their bare hands; when they confront the Afrikaner with reality and strike at the elementally human flaws in his make-up; when they hold the Afrikaner firmly in the cleft stick at last, the phenomenon is hurled headlong into a cruel crisis for which he has never prepared himself. De Haas tells himself that he has been betrayed by those Afrikaners in whom he believed; that he has been betrayed by the Portuguese who did not defend the destiny of the white man with the requisite determination; that all the traitors set him in conflict with the inexorable laws of history. He feels a strange sensation. Something vital cracks within him; something vital drains out of him; he experiences a feeling of internal collapse and loses his sense of direction.*

He is still holding the receiver in his hand, but now speaks to himself:

How could Piet do this to me? . . . How could he?

The momentum of events overwhelms him; he sees visions of black people burning cities, killing white men and raping white women everywhere. Some use weapons manufactured by white nations. Everywhere the blacks are on a wild crusade of vengeance. As the *laagers* and other parapets of race collapse, he sees visions of white men buying diamonds or fleeing the land or surrendering to the African or throwing themselves over cliffs or into the sea. This is the climax he has feared all his life and which made him a phenomenon; when he is face to face with it in his mind's eye, he does not know what to do, for de Haas has never faced the truth in his dealings with the black people. As darkness descends around him he gropes wildly for his gun, which he cannot reach in the deepening darkness.

He hears all sorts of noises; the black hordes shout and scream and threaten. As the world spins chaotically on all sides, he hears the laughter of the English and the Jews. Laughing, also, are the Coloureds and the Indians. Somewhere in the shadows, he hears sounds which

322

chill his blood: the kaffer labourers are also laughing. Their jeers and the insults they hurl into the air when the sirens wail sound like peals of thunder.

When *kragdadigheid* collapses, life loses its meaning for the phenomenon. The prime minister collapses into his chair and when his doctor arrives, Willem Adriaan de Haas is dead.

END